HIDDEN STARS

HIDDEN STARS

A SHASTI RAINHELL NOVEL

EDWARD MCKEOWN

AD ASTRA BOOKS

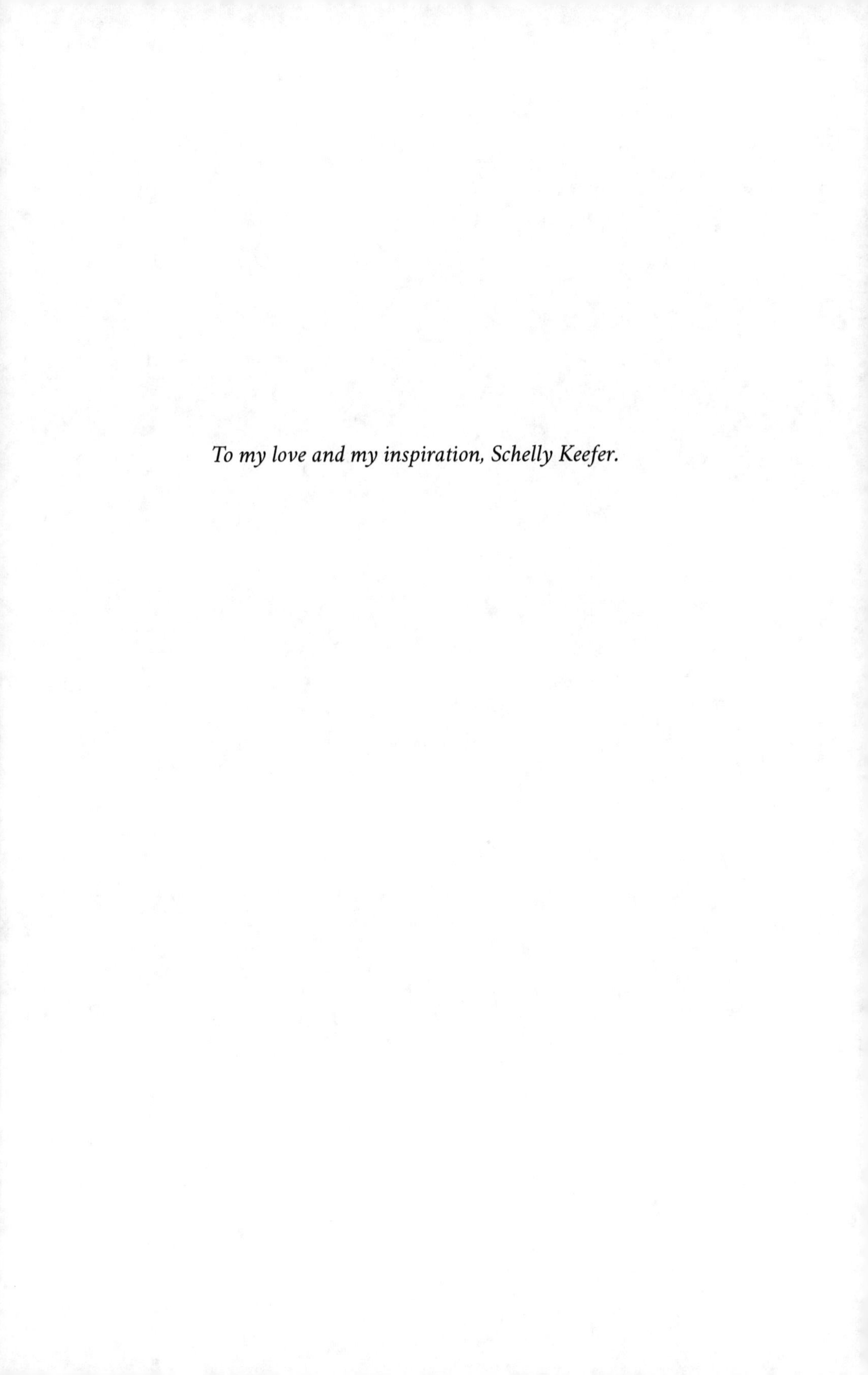

To my love and my inspiration, Schelly Keefer.

1

———————

Wind and rain slapped fitfully against the terminal windows of Lutti Spaceport, main embarkation terminal for the Confederacy world of Morokat. Gray skies muted both the arc lights of the field and the brightly painted hulls of the shuttles and smaller ships dotting it. Thunder growled through the clouds like the warning of some giant angry beast. The city beyond, a vast and chaotic hive, remained hidden from view by curtains of rain.

Shasti Rainhell contemplated the scene from an isolated table in the captain's lounge, three stories above the field. Morokat's sky mirrored her mood, and she greeted any attempt to involve her in conversation with a black glare she was quite capable of backing up. The greatest geneticists of Olympia, unhampered by laws or ethics, had thrown their full art into her creation. She was a creature of beauty: pale ivory skin and jade green eyes, under hair so black it threw back blue highlights. Yet she was stronger than any human male, capable of speed and endurance at inhuman levels. All this came with a price that still scarred her soul.

She'd defied her creators, escaping the Denshi Guild before her training was complete, but a childhood among assassins had marked her heart with a coldness reflected in her jade green eyes, an emptiness like space itself.

"Captain," came a high thin voice.

She turned to see the ship's quartermaster, Dobera, a respectful distance away. The lizard-like Frokossi's scales coruscated in the lounge's blue-tinted lights. His compound eyes fractured the light like a gem's facets.

"Yes?" she snapped.

"Reporting, *Sidhe* is fully provisioned for space," he replied, "your special requirements as well as the standard load." Dobera appeared unaffected by her tone. Either he'd grown used to his captain's occasional tempers, or it simply fell into the gulf between species.

"Well done," she said, meaning it. It was no small job to refit the ship in the few days they were here, especially with anarchic Moroks running the place. Her special requirements included refits for weapons the Confederacy might be less than thrilled about her possessing.

"It would help," Dobera said, "if I had some idea of where we are going."

Shasti looked at him. "What was it Captain Fenaday used to say when he was master?"

Dobera's shoulders shook in Frokossi laughter. "Straight to Hell was his usual answer."

She nodded. "See you at the ship."

Dismissed, he padded out of the lounge. Shasti returned to her contemplation of the field. Her thoughts turned to Robert Fenaday, her friend and former lover. The star frigate *Sidhe* belonged to his Shamrock Line. He'd made a gift of the vessel to her after succeeding in his relentless quest to find his lost wife, Lt. Commander Elizabeth Fenaday.

Of course, Shasti recalled, *I actually found her in the swamps of Thorraken, ended up saving the life of my chief rival. Altruist, that's me.*

A momentary bitterness stole through her. Fenaday was her first love, the first person to treat her with kindness, as anything other than property. She'd loved him with a passion and obsession born from an affection-starved childhood. They'd survived the terrors of doomed Enshar, the battles that overturned Denshi on Olympia and killed her creator, Pard, and finally the journey to rescue Lisa Fenaday. Shasti, made from the genes of a thousand strangers, grew more like a born-human in the process. Even her old tormentor, the half-cyborg, Kyle Mmok, had come to see her as a person and not a biological weapon created by power-mad eugenicists before his death, covering the retreat from Thorraken.

Now Fenaday lived on New Eire with Lisa, and Shasti was master of her own destiny and his old ship. Fenaday had wanted to give her the universe and so he had. *Sidhe* had voyaged under her command for the last two years: exploring, prospecting, performing escort runs during the brief war with the Voit-Veru, even a bit of privateering.

Lightning cracked outside the windows, drawing Shasti back to the present. Thunder rumbled through the structure.

Shasti sipped her drink, hardly noticing the flavor of the tart beverage. At her last port of call, she'd heard from her old flame, just a cryptic recording to put in at Morokat. Robert's letters were usually long and detailed, so the abrupt message was both worrisome and intriguing. She'd landed on Morokat three days ago. An equally terse message awaited her: *"Expect an old acquaintance and be prepared for surprises, some unpleasant."*

A sudden commotion brought her head around. The double brass and wood doors of the lounge had swung open. A man entered the huge waiting room: stout, dark skinned, and otherwise unremarkable. He hadn't come in alone, an HCR accompanied him. The Humanform Combat Robot was one of the Confederacy's newest and deadliest weapons. Smaller than a man, with doll-like eyes set in the pale, rudimentary face, it had long, clear monofilament hair, used for both antenna and cooling. It wore a bright blue sash across its black overalls. She knew both figures, Avery Deveraux, code-name "Mandela," head of Confederate Naval Intelligence and Lisa Fenaday's former boss. The machine was Cobalt, one of Kyle Mmok's quartet.

Cobalt must have been salvaged when the Confederacy swept down on the Voit-Veru base, she thought. *I hope they gave Mmok a decent burial. Wish I'd been told.*

The two made directly for her. Everyone else in the room gave ground quickly, retreating to their booths or tables.

"Shasti Rainhell," Deveraux/Mandela said in his deep pleasant voice, "what a pleasure to see you again."

She looked at him pensively. "Mandela." The use of his old code name served for a warning. He'd dragged her and Fenaday through disaster, death, and terror. She expected no less now.

Mandela smiled broadly. "What? Not surprised to see me all the way out here on Morokat?"

"You're here for a reason, I presume?" she stated, refusing to banter with the spymaster.

"Several," he said easily. "First though, I should reintroduce you to an old friend."

She looked over at the machine. Like most Olympians, she disdained robots, but Cobalt had fought beside her in battles on three worlds. The Humanform Combat Robot was a mere machine, with no personality, still something seemed required. "Hello, Cobalt. I'm glad to see you weren't destroyed."

"Hey, Rainhell," Cobalt said, "long time, no see."

Black fury exploded in Shasti's mind. In a split second she rose, towering over Mandela. Equally quick, the HCR interposed itself between her and the spymaster.

"This is obscene," she hissed, glaring over the HCR's shoulder at Mandela. "That's Mmok's voice. Do you think this is funny? You used him like a machine while he was alive, now you think you can do this?"

"Rainhell," the machine said, "ease up. It's nothing he did."

"Stop using his voice!" she shouted.

"It's my voice," the machine countered, "Kyle Mmok. I'm in here, Rainhell. Leastwise what's left of me is."

Shock spread through her, and she backed away from the machine, staring at it in horror. "What? Mandela, what have you done?"

"As Kyle told you," Mandela said, now somber, "nothing. Kyle, please explain."

"Well," the HCR began slowly, "I was holding the fort while you all bugged-out on Thorraken. The cyber-force and I were doing good work on that Voit-Veru armored cavalry, but it was only a matter of time. Finally, Cobalt and I were the only ones left. She always used to guard me, if you remember."

"I remember," Shasti said, in a small, thin voice. It began to dawn on her that the HCR's claim to be Mmok might be true: the voice, choice of words, even the stance were all Mmok's.

"Yeah. So anyway, a good size high-explosive round went off over us. Shrapnel cut us to pieces. I thought that was the end. I suppose in a way it was. Both Cobalt and I were down. My biological body was shot to hell and the cyber-implant stuff began to go. I started a fast-save to my memory in the hope someone would find it. Find some record of how we were killed. Then it was lights out. Game over.

"I expected Pearly Gates... well, actually fire and brimstone," Mmok continued. The machine looked at her with unblinking doll's eyes and a mouth aperture with a speaker in it, yet somehow a trace of Mmok's sardonic, cold, expression could be divined. "What I got was the repair bay of the *C.S.S. Vestal*. Seems Cobalt here," the machine patted its own chest, "decided to do an upload of my cyber-implant to save as much data as possible. Cobalt linked our neural nets and here I am. Not sure I can tell you that I'm still alive, nothing left of the original human me, but some of the brain-mass the cyber plant kept going. At least, I think I am still me."

Shasti stood dumbfounded.

"It's true," Mandela said. "Originally, we thought it was some artifact or program error caused by the damage and the fact that Mmok had been linked mentally to Cobalt since the invasion of Conchir. For a while we considered reformatting the entire computer, a very difficult job in an HCR, with major data loss. Eventually we realized that something amazing, something impossible had happened. Two supercomputers and a human brain, extreme stress and we have the result here. We don't know if this is just an incredibly complex program caused by the fusion or if..." He hesitated.

"Or if I'm still a person," the Mmok machine finished. "I'm not sure myself. If you'd said something like that while I was still a cyborg, I'd have been pissed off. Now I don't seem to feel anger, or anything else as much. So I am not sure that I am entitled to my old name. If it's easier Rainhell, you can call me Cobalt."

"No," she said, fighting illness. "No, if for nothing else, if only for respect, I will call you Mmok."

"It's not so bad," Mmok said. "There are even some advantages. For example, now, I can kick even your ass."

Shasti gave an abrupt laugh. "Mmok, now I believe it's you in there."

"Shall we talk, Commander Rainhell?" Mandela asked.

"Yes," she said slowly, still staring at the machine Mmok had become.

"Not here," Mandela said. "I've prepared somewhere suitable. It's equipped with a fine selection of Scotch. I dare say we could both do with a drink."

"Gods," she replied, "yes."

"Laid on some super-lube for me?" Mmok asked.

"Quiet, Kyle," Mandela said. They walked out of the spacer's lounge amid a buzz of talk.

"Bit public for you, isn't it?" Shasti asked as they took an escalator down to the car park.

Mandela shrugged. "Since Lisa gave my name away to her husband, and he, rather vindictively, made sure it became known, personal secrecy has been rather less important to me."

"Robert hates and loves with great intensity," she said.

"Alert the media on that one," Mmok said.

"He's the other problem." Mandela gestured at Mmok. "If I treat him as an HCR, as property, I may end up having to give him over to some research lab. God knows what would happen then. So, I managed to keep him classed as personnel. He even gets paid. Since I can't hide him in a closet, I've gotten used to keeping him around. He was always a good bodyguard."

"Didn't do so good guarding my own body," Mmok said, "managed to lose it bit by bit."

"His sense of humor," Mandela sighed, "requires some getting used to."

Shasti shrugged. "It always did."

2

A large black aircar, surrounded by security, waited for them under cover of a building overhang, as the rain continued to bluster. The driver proved to be another familiar face, Rask, a Morok, but born on their Mars Colony. He wore a dark blue Confederate Air Space Assault Team dress-uniform. His red eyes tracked Shasti as she approached, and his blue-skinned, goblin-like countenance split in a toothy grin. "Just like old home week, huh, Commander?" he said in a Terran accent.

Rask turned to the other Moroks and coughed out something in their language. Their apelike shapes faded away into the dark and rain. Shasti followed Mandela into the back of the car. Mmok joined Rask in the front.

Rask looked at the HCR. "You still give me the creeps, you know."

"Boo," Mmok said.

Rask snorted and put the machine into drive. A security divider slid up between the front and rear seats as the aircar sped away.

"Reminds me of when I picked you up in London," Mandela said, "the night I hired you to assassinate your ex-husband."

"Wasn't raining," she replied.

"It's always raining in London. Yes, quite a job. Didn't turn out the way I planned, but it worked out. We both achieved our objectives. You got Pard. I destroyed the Voit-Veru and Olympian Alliance."

"And we lived happily ever afterward," Shasti said.

Mandela snorted. "Would that it were so easy." They traveled on for ten minutes in silence.

The machine dipped toward a well-lit hotel rooftop. They were now well away from the tumbled lights of the barely visible city.

"The Hotel Elshass," Shasti noted, "still traveling first class, I see."

"I have a very forgiving expense account."

They landed and slid into the overhang. As they exited the aircar, rain, driven sidewise by the wind, pelted them, to Mandela's evident annoyance. Security admitted them through the plast-steel doors and again she saw another face from her past.

Shasti was rarely physically affectionate, but she stopped long enough to clasp arms with ASAT Captain Daniel Rigg. Rigg was tall for a standard human, but she still overtopped him by four inches. He'd passed for an Olympian for weeks during their first disastrous infiltration on that world. His powerful but lanky frame measured up to the standards achieved by the Eugenicists before Engineering replaced Mendelian selection. Rigg's long, solemn face creased in a slight smile. "Talk to you later."

She followed Mandela and Mmok into a huge suite, decorated with red wallpaper in a Victorian style. Ornate, dark wood furniture dotted the floor. The paintings in the room complemented the furniture with images of the Orient. Mandela shrugged off his raincoat, handing it to Mmok. Shasti threw her leather bomber jacket onto an expensive green leather sofa, then sank into it. Mandela busied himself at the bar. "Brandy, I think," he said, "to ward off the chill."

Shasti found herself staring at Mmok. "Scotch, neat, and a double."

The spymaster handed her a tumbler, and she drew a long pull, nearly draining the glass. The Scotch released the shudder that had been in her, and she felt better for it. If needed, her Engineered body could shrug off alcohol by an act of will and biochemistry.

"Refill that for you?" Mmok asked.

She nodded and the machine's fingers, capable of bending armor, closed delicately around the glass. An HCR could not have handled such a fragile thing, so it seemed Cobalt had gained something too.

Shasti scanned the room. Something tickled her rudimentary PSI sense. The room had four doors leading into it. Behind the middle one she sensed a presence, male, unfamiliar, but she felt only curiosity, not hostility. In her mind's eye, the door had a shimmering quality from the intensity of his mental activity. Still, she shifted so she could watch the door easily.

"To business?" Mandela asked. He sank into a plush, red-leather chair, then held the snifter of brandy up to his nose and inhaled deeply.

"What business do we have left?" she asked in an idle tone.

"You're a top operative, Rainhell. You're wasting your time with Fenaday."

"Yes," she said, "after all, what has he given me but a life, a home, a few million decacredit star-frigate, and the freedom to go anywhere I want? What a bastard."

Mandela put his head back and laughed. "Oh, excellent, Rainhell, excellent. And to think when I met you, you had no sense of humor at all. You weren't much different from an HCR yourself. Except that you enjoyed killing."

Shasti controlled her temper and drew again on her whisky. Worst of all, Mandela was, as usual, dead-on target. "Someday," she fired back, "I hope to be a real girl, Mr. Geppetto."

Mandela smiled and nodded as if acknowledging a point scored.

"Seriously," he said, "you have done well, and I admire it, from a refugee and criminal, to a mercenary, to captain of a starship. You confound people, Rainhell. From those who created you, to those who think they know you. I like that quality in people. I like that potential. I need that potential."

"I have no need or desire to work for you," she replied. She cast a sidelong glance at the middle door. The shimmering effect on it seemed more intense, as if her statement had an effect on the unseen watcher.

"It need not be a permanent relationship," he said, leaning back to hold the snifter with both hands and regarding her across its rim.

"You forget," she countered, "I work for Fenaday. He would probably blow a seal if he even knew I was talking with you."

"Perhaps not," he replied. "Kyle?"

From the HCR's right eye, a light licked out, projecting a holobeam image of Robert Fenaday onto the carved, cherry coffee table. He looked up at her, a strongly built man in his late thirties, more sturdy than handsome, brown-haired, with thoughtful green eyes. "This is a message for Shasti Rainhell," he began. "Shasti, I am going to use the authentication code we sent up for this situation. Ignore it after this as it will be compromised, 'Queen Maeve.'

"I'm sorry that I couldn't give you a reason before this for coming to Morokat. Security concerns, of course. I spent long nights agonizing over whether I should agree to this, and I don't know that I am doing the right thing. What I do know is that it's up to you. If after you hear what Deveraux has to say, you want out, tell him to go to hell and come back to New Eire as quick as you can.

"There's a threat, Shasti. I've seen enough proof to believe it is real. Enough that I agreed to help Mandela, and you know what that cost me. He'll explain. If afterward you agree to take the mission, you go with my blessing."

Lisa Fenaday walked into the hologram, next to her husband. "If you go, Shasti, it could be terribly dangerous. Be careful and please come back."

Fenaday's voice turned hoarse, choked it seemed with emotion. "Yes, for God's sake be careful and come back. All our love and our best wishes go with you." He smiled that sad, lopsided smile she remembered well. "I'll pray for your safety, each day until we see you again." The hologram flicked off.

Shasti took another sip of Scotch, her eyes bright and full. No one spoke for a minute.

She looked at Mandela. "Tell me."

"Six months ago," Mandela said, "an object fell onto Fenris V, a planet settled by Dua-Denlenn about six hundred years ago. It appears to have been a cross between a device and a ship, and very ancient. Whatever crew, if any, it carried had long ago perished or abandoned it. It followed no known pattern, didn't look like anything seen before.

Despite its age and condition, it made a controlled landing, though it hit hard.

"The Dua-Denlenn governor decided to keep the object secret, doubtless searching for some personal advantage."

"Typical," Shasti said in disgust. "How they could have developed from the same stock that gave rise to the true Denlenn eludes me."

Mandela shrugged and placed his glass on the side table. "I don't find them that different from humans, and of course, your experience of Denlenn is colored by serving with Commander Telisan, who would be a hard act for anyone to follow."

Shasti nodded. "Telisan is a fine being. I never met better. But you need not lecture me on Dua-Denlenn. I've had experience of the devils."

"No matter," Mandela continued. "The governor put his personal scientists and guards on the project. After a few days, they reported that the ship seemed to be repairing itself. Then he received frantic calls. The scientists and guards closest to the ship seemed to be changing—metamorphosing. They began to attack the others. In days, the Dua-Denlenn at the site had mutated, or rather been remade, into something else, something powerful, with an armored body, great strength, and greater intelligence.

"These mutants called themselves The Children of the Makers. They called their ship an Evolver. Evidently the ship-machine had provided them with a new genetic structure and a history. They believed themselves to have been reborn as members of an ancient species from closer in toward the galactic center. Their mission was to sample and collect the best biological genetic material from other species, converting it to their own use and to give the genetic code of the Makers, whether it was wanted or not, to whomever they encountered."

"What happened?" Shasti asked, sipping her drink.

"Fortunately, the Confederate Battlecruiser *Charon* was nearby. Combined with the Dua-Denlenn's own forces, she was able to destroy the Evolver and the infected. In the process we took about thirty-thousand civilian casualties on the planet.

"I had the governor shot, of course," he concluded.

"Of course," Shasti said, chilled by the story despite her long-standing dislike of the Dua-Denlenn.

"There remains an interesting twist to this," Mandela continued. "The Makers spoke to us in Confed standard, hardly surprising considering the people converted were Confed citizens. They retained their identities, though the change completely altered their loyalties and to some degree their memories. So we don't know their language, and their ship went up with a fifty-megaton warhead. We do, however, have the good governor's detailed files. They show the markings and records of the Makers were in an unknown language, yet one that has curious similarities to one we've seen. Almost as if that second language derived in whole or part from the Maker's language."

"Who?" Shasti demanded, putting her empty glass down.

"The Conchirri," he said, surprising her. "Intelligent, insensate, and voracious carnivores, hating and killing everything they encountered. Ever wonder how something like them evolved?"

"No," she said frankly. "Olympia wasn't much involved in the Conchirri War, except for the Selected who fought under General Dominici. The Denshi Order kept Olympia and the Engineered out of combat. Under Robert's command, we picked off some Conchirri fighters and small ships as a privateer escort. I never saw a live Conchirri before the Confederacy exterminated the species."

"Well, I wondered," he said. "I commissioned studies. I came to the conclusion that the Conchirri could not have evolved naturally. They were made. Bio-ordinance, created to kill and destroy."

"I've heard the theory," she said.

"Not a theory," he replied, "though those idiots at the Joint Chiefs still don't believe it. They had all my research from the ruins of Conchir classified and under wraps. No, that was not their home-world. That much is clear. They came from outside our sector, from much farther into the galaxy."

"So," she shrugged, "they were someone's bio-ordinance that got loose and turned on them, as I turned on Pard and the Denshi."

"I don't think they turned on their masters," he said. "I think they were sent, or driven ahead, to break trail and soften up opposition for something else. I suspect that something is the Makers."

"What?" she snapped.

"The Conchirri did tremendous damage to the Old Confederacy," Mandela said. "Our economy has been bad since the war ended. We spent ourselves nearly into bankruptcy. The Okarans, who took the brunt of the Conchirri assault, lost fifty percent of their population. Moroks and humans suffered millions of casualties too. Denlenn and Dua-Denlenn both reproduce slowly. Decades will pass before they make up their war losses. We came together in the war, making something resembling a Federal government. The Enshari and Voit-Veru crises kept that going. Now that momentum has stalled, and the separatists, including Fenaday, are talking about more local control for the member planets. They learned nothing during the war.

"Think of it, Rainhell. No one believed a space war was economically feasible. Our Navy consisted of customs cutters and a few small cruisers. Then we run into a species that existed just for that purpose, to make a space war. Conchirri were all fighters. They didn't have store clerks, insurance salesman, and actors, just a military force, billions strong. Does that make sense? Where did they get their science and industry from?

"No, the Conchirri were sent this way by someone, someone who plans for the long run. I want to find that someone.

"There is my problem," he said. "I believe a storm is brewing. My superiors accuse me of fearmongering. Liberals in the Confederation Congress want money for social programs. Conservatives want tax cuts and less power for the Confederate government. The Navy is a lot smaller than it used to be and still busy policing the Voit-Veru frontier. You may recall that your boyfriend Fenaday touched off the third interstellar war there."

"Ex-boyfriend," she said, letting a warning tone slip into her voice.

"Yes, well," Mandela grimaced, "he also cost me considerable influence in higher circles with his antics. You'll note from the message that Fenaday never misses the chance to use my real name. Now that's turned and bit him in the ass. You see, he believes me, and if there is something he hates more than me, it's the Conchirri and what might exist behind them.

"So, I am hard pressed to find ships and agents that I can commandeer from other, more immediately pressing problems. Harder still to find those I think are up to the task."

"Which is?" she promoted.

"We will take the *Sidhe*," he said, "with the forces and scientists that I will give you, head into uncharted space, back down the direction we think the Conchirri came from. Using records we translated from a dead language, hunt from star to star. Find what's out there and come back and tell the Confederacy."

Shasti looked at Mandela with open astonishment. "You, you are planning to go? Mandela, you never went anywhere with less than a battlecruiser escort. You plan to risk your sacred, irreplaceable ass alongside us mere mortals?"

"I would never describe you as mere," he replied smoothly. "But, yes, I plan to join the expedition."

"Robert did you damage beyond his dreams of revenge," Shasti said. "For you to risk this, you must truly be on the ropes. I still can't believe he agreed to work with you."

Something unpleasant flashed in Mandela's eyes, then he was all bland charm again. "You forget," he said wagging a finger, "I still have considerable influence with Mrs. Fenaday."

She raised her eyebrows. "Engineered live a long time, but a voyage like this might consume more than one lifetime."

"I don't think we will be gone more than a few years," he countered. "If we had to follow normal scout survey protocols, with what little is known beyond the bounds of charted space, we might be gone for decades. No time would pass for us in hyperspace jump, of course, but without favorable currents and proper entry and exit points—yes, it could be that long or longer. I, however, have an ace up my sleeve."

Shasti looked a question at him.

"I have a linguist, an archeologist who reads and understands Conchirri."

"I'm impressed," Shasti said. "I didn't think there was such a person. Conchirri didn't take prisoners and they went insane, or more insane, when captured."

"That's a myth about their not taking prisoners," a new voice said.

"I wondered when you were going to come out from behind that door," Shasti said, turning to face the newcomer. She studied him as he came toward her: a handsome, olive-complected human of about thirty-five, as best she could judge standard humans.

"Captain Rainhell," Mandela gestured, "this is Professor Paolo Romita."

"Professor Romita," Shasti said, rising from the chair.

Romita extended a hand and "Hello—" he began, then stopped as Shasti continued to stand until she hit her full height of six feet, nine inches. Shasti was well aware of the effect her appearance and height had on people, particularly men.

Romita recovered in a second and took her hand. His own palm felt pleasantly hard; the man did work with his hands. "Captain Rainhell," he finished. His voice held a curious accent she was not familiar with. "You're not quite what I expected as the skipper of a rough and ready privateer. You look more like a fashion model, a very tall one."

"She's killed more people than are staying in this wing of the hotel," Mmok said.

Romita kept the pleasant look pasted on his face. "I see. A very lethal fashion model."

"I'm a bit on the muscular side for evening wear," Shasti replied, liking the fact that she had not unsettled him.

"From what colony do you come, Captain?"

"Olympia originally," she said, "and yes, I am genetically engineered."

"Fascinating," he said. "I would like to hear about your world."

"I do not claim Olympia as mine," she said, not quite masking her distaste. "I'm a citizen of New Eire."

"Yes," he said, slipping into the chair opposite her, "so I've heard."

"You said it was a myth about the prisoners," Shasti said, changing the subject back to the Conchirri.

"I was a prisoner of the Xenos for a while," he replied using the slang of the war. "True—it was more an issue of food storage than imprisonment, but I was a philologist on loan to the Naval Intelligence. I was studying Conchirri records in a retaken colony when I was captured. They did take prisoners, to learn our languages, habits, and weaknesses. During those rare occasions they did communicate with us, they used Confed Basic.

"Once they realized I was learning their language, I became a novelty. So I was saved from the stew pot for a while. I lasted two months, until, mercifully, the 27th ASAT Raider Battalion destroyed the Xenos holding me."

"Dan Rigg's old outfit," Mmok added.

"I learned much from my captors," Romita continued. "They called me," he made a hacking–spitting sound, "'food that talks back.' I learned some of their legends about their Makers, about the Great Mission to clean this arm of the galaxy of non-Conchirri. It did seem that they fled these Makers, broke free of their control. They feared being overtaken by them. Of course, I have no evidence of this, and most of the authorities discounted my story. It didn't help that I spent a good year in and out of therapy recovering from the stress of being a prisoner. Mr. Mandela believed me. We both know that the right thing to do is go back up the trail of the Conchirri looking for these Makers."

"We haven't found trouble enough in our own section of space?" Shasti asked, swirling her Scotch slowly.

Romita smiled. "Well, we might find the trouble before it springs on us like the lousy Xenos."

"And you want me to take all of you," Shasti said, intrigued despite her reservations about Mandela.

"You've become something of a legend yourself, for all that I think you tried to avoid it," Romita said. "You're a very hard woman to find a picture of. The few I have seen do not do you even slight justice." He smiled. Even white teeth flashed in his dark face.

Bet that works on most women, she thought. Romita was handsome in a rough sort of fashion, shorter than she was, but so were most non-Olympian men. He was taller than Fenaday, and not so stocky. She shook herself mentally, *back to work.*

"We don't know that we will find anyone out there. This expedition may be chiefly archeological in nature, but in the deep black. Who knows?" Romita concluded.

"We'll bring a robot tender with your ship to increase her range. *Sidhe* is smaller than what I would like to use, but one must make do," Mandela said.

"Tell me, Mandela," she replied, "are you hoping to find nothing? Or do you hope to come back with something hot on our heels? Something to catapult you back into power, to make the Confederacy even stronger over the member planets?"

Mandela smiled. "Papa does need new shoes."

The expression meant nothing to her, but she had learned that when standard humans used such, they were avoiding a direct answer. She stood. "I'll want to see all the raw data, study it myself."

Mmok handed her a computer crystal.

"You'll have my answer in a few days," she said.

"Captain Rigg," Mandela waved, "will return you to your ship. Please be circumspect. Only Mmok and I have this information."

"Agreed."

"Good night, Captain Rainhell," Romita said, rising.

She nodded.

"Mmok," she said. The HCR turned toward her. All easy grace, unlike the clumsy half cyborg he had been in life. "Who else knows about you?"

"No one. I'd prefer it stay that way."

She shook her head. "There are people entitled to know—"

"I heard Fenaday had a bit of breakdown," Mmok interrupted, "during the escape from Thorraken."

Now it was her turn to hesitate. "Yes. He took your…your loss very hard. Leaving you behind like that. I think that if he hadn't found Lisa, he might not have come out of it."

"What do you think this would do to him?" Mmok said, one arm waving toward his HCR body.

After a moment, she nodded, then asked, "What of Leda Jenner?"

"No," Mmok stated, "especially not her. I want her to remember me as I was. This—this, whatever I am now—is a new life for me.

Leda, for the lucky little time I had with her, is part of the old one. She's home on Olympia now and doing well. Let's leave it at that."

"I'll respect your wishes," she said.

"And here I am always telling people what a bitch you are," he replied, in vintage Mmok. "See you at the ship."

She raised an eyebrow. "We'll see."

3

Daniel Rigg and Rask waited by the big aircar to fly Shasti back to the spaceport area.

"Great to see you again, Shasti," Daniel said, as they boarded the black aircar. Rask took the controls.

"Yes," she said, "and both of you. I'd have thought you two would be comfortably secure on some cushy training base, turning out new fools to get shot at."

Rigg laughed. "After supporting Fenaday's raid on Thorraken, we weren't exactly on the high command's hit parade. I think it was a close-run thing as to whether we would be decorated for helping you two rescue the crew of *Blackbird* or be shot as traitors for not killing you both. Fortunately, between Fenaday's popularity and Mandela's influence in the government, we escaped the firing squad, and they had to decorate us. Oddly enough, the promotions were overlooked."

"It helped," Rask said, "that when the Confederacy took Thorraken, it put the Voit-Veru so on the defensive that their military government fell and the replacement civilian government quickly sued for peace. Hell, now they're lobbying for inclusion in the Confederacy."

"Still," Shasti pushed, curious, "haven't you two risked your asses enough on the front lines?"

Rigg shrugged. "We like the work. Feel like we make a difference out here."

"Yep," Rask added in disgust. "Altruists, that's us."

"We were also a bit of a hot potato," Rigg confessed. "Not a lot of commands wanted us. Mandela—"

"You don't call him Deveraux?" she interrupted. "His cover was completely blown after the Voit-Veru affair."

"No, that just reminds him of all the damage Fenaday did him."

"He did a lot of damage to Robert too."

"No criticism of Captain Fenaday intended," Rigg said, raising his hands in a placating gesture. "Everybody had to play the cards they were dealt. Somehow or other the Confederacy always came out ahead—so no gripe by me."

"Good," she said, relaxing.

"Anyway, the boss stuck with us, so we stick with him," Rask finished.

"Do you know what this is all about?" she asked.

"We were on Fenris V," Rigg said in a voice gone grim. "We saw what the Evolver turned people into. They were bad news. Even ASAT teams found them tough to deal with. I wouldn't want to think of millions of the things heading into our space. Make the Conchirri look like school kids."

"Kinda weird," Rask mused. "The Conchirri just wanted you dead and eaten. The Makers want you to be just like them. Have all their benefits, become part of them."

"Assimilation with a vengeance," Rigg snorted. "You don't have to worry about being a second-class citizen—you can come right to the front of the airbus."

The analogy wasn't clear to Shasti, but she got the gist of it. "Everybody wants to be perfect."

"Except for you," Rigg said gallantly, "who are."

Shasti smiled. "You don't have the gift of Blarney that Robert did. Nice try, though."

"Rask," she added, "there's a bar by the field, 'The Magnetic Storm.'"

Rask gave a toothy grin. "I know it. You buying?"

"Yes."

Hours later Shasti left the two ASATS. They'd closed the small hole-in-the-wall bar after making the owner considerably richer. Rigg, who barely showed any effect from the alcohol, offered to drive her back to the ship, but Shasti wanted to think and walk. Dawn wasn't far off, and she found solitude and darkness comforting. They'd been part of her life for so long.

She walked through the old Morok town, past closed shops and darkened homes. A few ground cars sped past. One or two Moroks walked by, giving her a wide berth. Despite the low light, her dark-adapted eyes picked out the wild riot of primary colors the Moroks used on their buildings. Another unintended disadvantage of superior genetics, a normal human couldn't see the eye-hurting colors in the dusk.

The architecture of the Moroks was cluttered and chaotic. Houses jutted out at odd angles and streets seemed laid out at random. Only Shasti's innate sense of direction kept her heading in the proper direction for the port.

Suddenly, her situational awareness twinged. Shasti slid into a doorway and put her hand on the laser riding on her hip. Muggers, she wondered? Powerful as she was, Shasti didn't take foolish chances, but a tension had been building in her since her encounter with Mandela, as if he'd reawakened the younger, desperate, and murderous self she'd left behind. Her Engineered body scavenged the last of the alcohol from her blood stream. A thrill shot through her as she felt the old feelings of hunter and hunted slip into her blood. The whispery dark voice of her unchecked rage, long silent, sounded in her ears again. *Kill*, it said. *Kill. Pay them all back for the pain.* She found herself hoping it was a pack of robbers.

She reached out her still nascent psychic awareness. Colors

around her seemed to dim as she concentrated and saw with something that was not vision.

There, she thought. On the third story of a gabled building, she sensed a single presence. As before with Paolo, she felt interest, not hostility. Still, the presence manifested itself as an image of lazily pulsing blue. No sooner did she touch it than it winked out.

Damn, thought Shasti, her head snapping up as she tried to scan with her vision. All she saw was a fleeting shape skittering over the tiled and spired roof.

Someone or something sensed me. How? Shasti drew her Martini laser and, spotting a small alley, raced into it. As soon as she reached the back of the alley, she sprang up the fire escape. Her opponent was above her, and she didn't want to concede the advantage of height. The close-packed houses made her job easier. Moving silently, she climbed the odd architecture, with its overhanging roofs, gutters, and ornate projections. The local equivalent of cats and dogs reacted to her passing with odd yowls, doubtless waking the Moroks within.

May create more trouble for my pursuer, she thought. She paused on a minaret-like rooftop and peered back. A large, dark shape detached itself from cover three buildings away and raced across an open space before even she could react. She raised the laser and risked activating its illuminated telesight to scan the area. Nothing.

Whoever it is will expect me to head for the port, she thought. *Very well, let them follow me until I find a nice killing ground, then I'll double back.* She holstered the laser to free her hands and ran across the rooftops, leaping a small alley and taking cover in a rooftop garden. She made her way back to the commercial area and the ground. The street lighting in the shopping district was better. As she rounded a corner, her instincts cut in again and she slipped back into cover. This time, her eyes picked out a shape on a first-story roof of a warehouse just behind a streetlight. *Clever,* she thought, pulling her laser again, *and fast to get around me. Whoever it is, they are good and this is getting serious.*

Shasti stared up through narrowed eyes, her plan for an ambush abandoned. *Let's see if they'll break cover,* she thought.

"I know you're there," she called, throwing her voice in an assassin's trick.

The shape stood up and swung off the roof to land facing her, not fooled at all.

"Vaughn," she breathed, recognizing the huge silhouette at last.

With an easy laugh, Mikhail Vaughn, former head of Denshi Special Operations, stepped into the light. His hands hung loose and empty by his side. She didn't relax. Vaughn was a master killer and had served as her creator, Jalgren Pard's, number two. He'd hunted her on Pard's orders through the spaceport of Olympia.

"It would take a Denshi assassin to follow me over those rooftops," she said, scanning behind him with eyes and senses. As near as she could tell, he was alone. She stepped around the corner, keeping the laser pointed in his direction.

"True," he acknowledged, "but I have not always enjoyed the best of luck following you." The deep voice suited his Germanic countenance, matching his black hair and disconcerting blue eyes. Vaughn was handsome in a savage, elemental fashion. A dark tactical jacket devoid of any betraying insignia covered his broad shoulders. She noted the large slug-thrower, belted and holstered over his dark-gray pants. He'd clearly dressed to remain unobtrusive in the dark.

"Oh?" she replied, still looking at the street for possible exits and other opponents.

"When you escaped me by leaping across the gap between those buildings in the offport of Marathon, it put me in some jeopardy with Pard."

"Don't mention that name to me," she growled.

Vaughn raised an eyebrow. "So? Did you not sufficiently revenge yourself on him? You and Fenaday left him dead, smashed in the bottom of a canyon."

"He deserved worse," she replied. Memories she thought locked away flashed into her mind, images of abuse and sexual torture at the hands of her gigantic creator, Pard. He had taken her in her early teens, destroying both her innocence and any trust she'd ever had in the universe, turning her into the killing machine she'd been until she met Fenaday.

"Doubtless." Vaughn sat on a nearby step, stretching booted feet out ahead of him. "So, unquestionably, do I. Perhaps you yourself do as well."

"Come to mete out some justice?" she shot back. Vaughn's posture made it impossible for him to pull the sidearm he wore from his holster before she could fire. If he was alone, the advantage lay with her.

"No. I came to see you. You left before I had a chance to truly meet you. Something I have wanted since I first laid eyes on you. I've come to invite you to return to Olympia, your true home, with me."

Shasti gaped at him. Then put her head back and simply roared with laughter. Vaughn let it run its course.

"Are you mad?" she asked, her weapon still trained on his middle.

He leaned back on the steps. "Not at all. I know your life there was cruel and hard, but the times are changing. Your enemies are gone. I don't approve of all the Confederacy is doing, but we are heading for a civil society, a place of laws—"

"Olympia," she said flatly, "holds nothing for me."

He smiled. "Are you so sure? There are no possibilities?" He leaned back to give her a bold look.

She shook her head, bemused. "You have come a long way looking for a date."

"I have come a long way," he conceded, "to lay a world at your feet. Think of it. With Antebei of the Fourth Generation dead, I am the highest developed of the Engineered, with one exception. You. You are the X factor. No one knows what you are capable of, least of all yourself. With the Engineered overthrown on Olympia and Dominici's Selected Humans in charge, there will be no more generations of Engineered. And yet our kind remains. Who better to lead our people?"

"I hardly know you," she said. "And what I do know does not count in your favor."

"Did I have some choices that you did not have?" he asked, bitterness edging his voice. "No one asked me if I wished to become a master murderer. I was raised in crèche too. I didn't choose Denshi, it chose me."

She had to nod at the fairness of it.

"I will not compare my lot with yours," he said. "I know enough of Pard to know or guess much of what befell you. I've never held your actions against Pard or the Engineered against you. You were tormented and struck back. Who would do otherwise?"

"I just ask you not to be blinded by the past," he said, leaning forward on the steps, his face earnest and open.

"You ask a lot," she said slowly, lowering the pistol to where it pointed at the ground between them. "That past never quite lets its hooks out of me."

"Is that because you face it alone? There might be an answer for that problem."

Shasti studied his face, hunting for truth, for clarity. "Why?"

"Why?" he repeated, resting his arms on his knees. "As if I have not spent many sleepless nights wondering that myself? All I know is that since I first saw you on Olympia when you raced through my men and me like a panther, you have haunted even my waking hours.

"Think of it," Vaughn insisted. "We may be the two most perfect people ever produced. Isn't it our destiny to be together? It may be true that we were literally made for each other."

"Perfect." She laughed bitterly. "You have no idea of what you are talking about. We're not perfect, we are Engineered. We're cripples. Pathetic simulacrums from test tubes."

"We are stronger, better, gifted with abilities beyond Standards," he argued.

"We have no families, no love, no comfort," she countered. "Vaughn, if you only knew some of what I have learned through so much pain…"

He remained quiet for a minute, then sighed, looking away. "There is something to what you say. I saw it in Antebei, before I killed him. He was Pard's protégé and would have replaced me had you not destroyed Pard when you did. Antebei was an Engineered to rival perhaps even you in perfection. Yet he was sick of mind and soul, twisted in some basic way. I've had to do terrible things sometimes. I did not enjoy them. Antebei did. He feasted on the helpless.

"But that is all the more reason that my proposal is reasonable.

Think what one of us could do with a normal life? Not raised as an assassin, not raised in a crèche—"

"A greater good?" she smiled coldly. "Whose, Vaughn? Yours? I was carried off Olympia in a coma, but I learned what followed. You became Dominici's link to the Engineered, but on a short leash that I imagine she jerked a lot. People don't see a lot of future in the Engineered. How much power would flow into your hands if you had the best genes ever produced in your possession?"

He smiled. "Well, there is no question that it would enhance my standing."

"You should take a lesson from my ex-boyfriend," Shasti replied. "Your pillow talk is lousy."

Vaughn stood, annoyance in every line of his body. "We're not children, Shasti. I am offering you a chance to mold the future."

"I'm having enough trouble molding my own present," she replied, bringing up the pistol. "I'll pass."

"Give me a few days to persuade you," he pressed.

"I'll be leaving soon, Vaughn," she said. "We won't be seeing each other again." Slowly, but steadily, she backed away from Vaughn. He didn't move, just stood staring at her. Only when she reached the mouth of the alley did she holster her weapon and walk away, too proud to do the sensible thing and run.

Back in the street, Vaughn struggled with his emotions, unused to being balked, yet exhilarated by finally having a chance to speak to Shasti. Her voice replayed in his ears, as he savored the musical sound of it, even as her words denied his hopes. And yet he still felt the connection between them, as he had ever since she had escaped him on Olympia. She ran through his mind's eye, as she had that night, lithe and powerful, stirring him as no woman had ever done.

His only other sight of her had been the day *Sidhe* carried her and Robert Fenaday, both in medical comas after fighting Pard, away from Olympia to the Voit-Veru frontier. He'd bartered critical information that doubtless led to the death of many Engineered stationed in Voit-

Veru space, merely for the sight of her, even though the mistrustful Telisan had him held by robots ready to tear him to pieces at the first hint of danger. She'd lain silent and wounded, and his heart tore at him with desire to gather her into his arms. Yet all he could do was give Telisan the information and hope she somehow survived.

She did survive, and General Dominici traded intelligence on both Shasti and Mandela's movements to Vaughn, in return for an even more biddable representative among the Engineered humans of Olympia. Vaughn told himself that he was trading present weakness for the hope of a stronger future. With Shasti and her genetics, the Engineered might yet regain a place in Olympian society.

But the truth was that he couldn't get her out of his thoughts. He took ship to follow her. But *Sidhe* left few tracks and followed an irregular path. Vaughn did not dare her one regular port, New Eire. If Fenaday learned of his presence there, he'd kill Vaughn, or Vaughn would be forced to kill him. Either would be the end to his quest for Shasti's affections.

But he had also kept tabs on the Confederate spymaster, Mandela. That trail had been made easier by a vengeful Fenaday's revealing Mandela's true identity. When Deveraux-Mandela suddenly left Earth after the Fenris incident and was sighted on New Eire by Vaughn's agents, he knew the game was afoot. His best guess had narrowed a possible meeting place between Shasti and Mandela to three worlds. Remembering that Mandela had once been stationed on Morokat, Vaughn guessed right, but it seemed now that he was no closer to success.

Why does she have this hold on me, he wondered? *I could have a thousand other women. Why her? It's not merely her beauty that attracts me. I've been surrounded by people created for their beauty since my childhood. No, there is something about her: the way she stands, the fluid quickness of her walk, the clear directness of her gaze.*

I missed her in time and space, first to Pard's selfish perversions and then to Fenaday. But Pard received the hard death he'd earned at both her and Fenaday's hands. Then in a fantastic turn of fate, Fenaday was reunited with his lost wife, leaving the field clear.

It's as if we were created for each other, he thought, *as if she is the missing part of me. With her I can dare anything and achieve everything. Without her I will always be incomplete. And yet when I see her, do I tell her this? No, idiot that I am, I talk to her of power, of molding the future when all I want is a future with her. I propose alliances instead of an affair.*

He fumbled for his com-tab, shaking his head to clear it of frustrations. "Tanaka," he growled.

"Here," came the voice of his aide-de-camp.

"I need information. Shasti's presence must have something to do with Mandela's voyage here. He either wants her, her ship, or both. He didn't come to Morokat for the weather. They must be leaving soon. I need to know where she is going."

"Affirmative. I will see what I can learn. We are far from home, so it will be a matter of placing local bribes."

"Do what you can," he replied. "I will return to the *Paladin*."

His eyes drifted in the direction she'd disappeared. *We are not done yet, Shasti,* he thought. *Our dance is only beginning.*

4

Shasti returned to *Sidhe* and ordered additional guards posted around the ship and her gantry cradle.

As she waited for the guards, Shasti looked up with pride at her ship. The four-hundred and eighty-meter star-frigate had once worn the black and yellow colors of the Conchirri, until her capture. Now, the ten-thousand-ton vessel boasted a brilliant Guard's Red and the green Shamrock of Robert Fenaday's line. Her long aerodynamic hull, with broad wings in amidships under a high tail made her look more like an immense aerospace fighter. *Sidhe* was the largest private warship in Confed space.

Her mind reluctantly drifted back to Vaughn's appearance. His intentions might be as declared, but it did not do to take a Denshi assassin lightly. She debated calling Mandela, but the idea of explaining to the spymaster that the heir apparent of Olympia's Engineered had abandoned his post and taken to space in the hope of wooing her seemed so preposterous that she couldn't bring herself to do it.

Reluctant to leave matters in other hands, Shasti sent for Risky. "Come on, boy," she said after an aide brought the K-9 down. "Let's have a look about."

Risky padded out from behind the crewman, needing no leash or other handling. His mostly black coat was glossy, and his tail wagged with anticipation. Too well-mannered to leap on her, he sat by her feet while she scratched his ears and petted his solid body.

Shasti had rescued the German Shepherd from the ruin of the Confederate embassy on Enshar. Since then the dog had been both a friend and protector. Risky was also the product of genetic engineering, only by the Confederacy, not Olympia. Larger and far smarter than his ancestors, Risky could understand a vastly wider array of commands.

The pair clambered out onto the gantry surrounding the star-frigate. Sensitive to security at all times, Shasti had put *Sidhe* down as far from the main freight and passenger terminals as possible. But the field, as always, buzzed with activity. Carts and workers traveled the spaceport at all hours. She saw a half-dozen Moroks clustered around a maintenance port near the mid-hull of her ship, working on a thruster. Behind them stood one of her landing force troopers, clad in a black and green uniform.

Ships dotted the immense plain of the spacefield. They came in all colors and sizes: globes, aerodynamic pinnacles, and boxy cargo hulls. To the west, the usual line of squalls and gray clouds scudded over and in some cases around the ships. A squarish, bulk-cargo carrier painfully fought its way free of gravity. The ship was only a dark shape in the gloom, blued by distance, so it was difficult to tell its color. The rumble of its AG unit and thrusters reached her a few seconds later.

Shasti scanned the horizon. Wind buffeted her in the exposed position of the scaffolding. She closed her black jacket and drew a deep breath of the distinctive sharp air of the spacefield, feeling a fleeting sense of well-being and contentment. *I have a ship*, she thought, *and I am still free. No man binds me to either a place or his will.*

All her life Shasti had striven to be free. Since the day Pard had drawn her out of a training crèche and made a child bride of her, Shasti had been like the animal that would chew off its trapped leg to escape. She'd fled Pard's net both on Olympia and in the years after. Dead assassins decorated starports all through the Confederacy as the result of Pard's efforts to reclaim or destroy her. Even as a freelance bodyguard, she'd worked and lived alone.

Then she met Fenaday, a gentle and decent man forced into her type of life by the quest for his lost wife. They had become one when he first gave up on his quest. But even then, her need to remain independent had warred with her desire to belong to him. She'd fought making any commitment, terrified of his having a claim on her. That terror made her return to Olympia to deal with her past and her creator. But by the time her demons had been expunged, Lisa Fenaday had returned from the dead. Shasti's arms had opened, but there was no one to embrace.

"Let's go for a walk," she said, wanting to escape the memories at least temporarily. Risky's tail wagged furiously.

Preferring to stretch her legs rather than use the work elevator, Shasti headed down the five stories to the ground, casting a practiced eye on *Sidhe's* red hull as she went. They reached the cracked gray of the permacrete and headed out around the ship. The wind had died down at ground level, but it was still cool and damp. Risky raced about in excitement. Shasti produced a red ball from her pocket. It bounced wildly over the spacefield with the big shepherd racing after it.

After circling the ship with Risky and satisfying herself that no avenue of approach was left unmonitored, she headed under the ship to the area below the main hatchway. Lt. Tivka, the hulking ex-marine who commanded her ground troops, awaited her. In the shadows beyond she saw more of his people walking patrol.

"Captain," he greeted her. "Looks like a nice morning. Finally stopped raining."

"Yes," she said. "Everyone posted?"

"Yep. Everybody's comp has a picture of this Vaughn guy and his known operatives."

"Good, I am going to leave Risky with you. His nose may be one of the best safeguards we have."

The marine grinned. Like everyone else on board, he liked the dog. Risky, sensing the opportunity for some petting before duty called, padded over and sat by Tivka, who began scratching behind the shepherd's ears.

Shasti thought about the fickle loyalties of the male of apparently any species. "I'm heading in."

"See you later, Skipper," Tivka said absently, as he poured water from his canteen for a panting Risky.

As Shasti took the elevator back up to the bridge entranceway, thoughts of Vaughn and his offer raced around in her head. *Children,* she mused. *I never thought that I might have children. Is my body even capable of it? I don't have monthly cycles like human women. I never wondered why before this. Even when we'd had a decent doctor aboard, I never let them do more than the most basic tests.*

Shasti had no feelings about children. Standard humans seemed drawn to them. Was it yet another thing that her makers had left out of her? The familiar frustration built up in her. Shasti shook her long, glossy hair. *No,* she thought. *Not going to do this to myself. I am learning. I am changing. I am becoming.*

Seeking refuge from these unwelcome musings, Shasti thought about Mandela's proposal. She placed his crystal in the reader and spent some time going over the reports. They added convincing detail to the story he'd told her but nothing more.

Still, the voyage offered her a grander purpose than the last year had. Mandela had persuaded Fenaday, difficult as that was to believe, that the mission was critical to Confederate security. There would be money as well. Although Fenaday funded *Sidhe's* operations, it had become a point of pride for Shasti to wean the ship from that funding. She disliked being on charity and beyond that lay her usual desire to retain as much freedom as she could, even from her old lover.

It could also, she thought as she sealed the door to her cabin, *serve to keep Vaughn at a greater distance.*

Decision made, she thought. Shasti walked over and clicked on a desktop communicator. "Bridge-Communications," she said.

"Communications, Fitzgerald here."

"Put me through to the Hotel Elshass on a secure channel," she ordered. "Ask for Mr. Mandela."

"Aye, Captain."

A few seconds later, Mandela's voice came on. "Ms. Rainhell, how nice to hear from you so soon."

"I'll send you a contract," she replied, "with an obscene figure on it. Sign it and file it with the port authority. You'll also be picking up the expenses."

"Of course."

"I am going to assume you have the forces and scientists for the mission nearby."

"I'd like to start as soon as possible. I'm not getting any younger."

"Have Daniel Rigg get in touch with my quartermaster regarding stores and equipment. We'll start getting the ship's complement settled. I'll need a roster of personnel I can draw from you. I may lose some people when they hear about us jumping off the map to a classified destination."

"Agreed."

"One more thing," she said. "I'd like Mmok down here as soon as possible. Have him put a security screen around *Sidhe*."

"Concerned about the appearance of Mr. Vaughn?"

Shasti resisted the urge to swear. How had Mandela found out? Did he already have operatives on her ship? "Yes. I don't believe his intentions are hostile, but I don't trust him."

"Sensible attitude."

"How did he get here and how did he know how to find me?" she asked.

"No doing of mine," Mandela returned. "He arrived yesterday on an Olympian destroyer. I understand he made a deal with General Dominici for the vessel and its crew of Engineereds. He rechristened it the *Paladin* and left. The good General is probably happy to be rid of all three. Has he made contact with you?"

"Yes," Shasti admitted. "But the matter is a personal one."

"So? Well, I trust you will let me know if you feel that it touches on our voyage."

"Yes."

"I'll see you at the ship tomorrow."

The next morning, Shasti called her staff to the boardroom. They filed in, one after another. Few of Fenaday's original privateer crew were left; most had perished in the adventures on Enshar, Olympia, and Thorraken. Of the survivors, many had retired to comfortable lives, compensated generously by Fenaday.

Wardell, a slender man with thinning gray hair, served as the ship's gunner. He loved space and ships and had stayed with *Sidhe* rather than retire. The bottle always deviled the gunner when he was in port, but he was steady as rock on the steel plates of a starship. The lovelorn Carlos Perez, finally divorced from *La Bitch,* still served as engineer. Dobera, the Frokossi princeling Fenaday rescued from a coup d'état, ran the ship as quartermaster. Nye, a short, quiet Asian from a failed colony, had helmed *Sidhe* since she was recommissioned.

Others dated from her own command, particularly her Executive Officer, Alexandra Mollica, a tall, sharp-featured woman with thick, black hair. As they settled around the wardroom table, a steward came in and passed out drinks and coffee.

"I've accepted a commission," Shasti announced. "It means an extended voyage beyond the borders of known space. We don't know how long we'll be gone. Dangers are a foregone conclusion. Pay will be at the triple rate. Destinations are classified, as is the reason for the voyage. If you come—you come blind."

Wardell yawned. "What else is new?"

The others laughed, but nerves lurked just below the humor.

"I will tell you this much—we'll have a very important guest onboard, along with a contingent of government people."

Dobera looked at her. His iridescent eyes blinked independent of each other. "How important a guest?"

She held his eye. "Very."

Wardell and Perez exchanged looks as Perez smoothed on his mustache. Mollica, knowing they'd served with Shasti for years, studied them intently.

"Well, you promised me plenty of adventure, if I signed aboard," Mollica said, running her hand through her shoulder-length black hair. A characteristic gesture Shasti recognized as accompanying a difficult decision for her.

"Actually, I believe I warned you that you had a good chance of being killed," Shasti said without irony. "The chances are increasing dramatically."

"Good thing you didn't go into sales, Skipper," Mollica returned. Another laugh ran round the wardroom.

"Anybody here want off? Or need time to think about it?"

The room remained quiet.

Finally, Dobera spoke up. "*Sidhe* is my home. My only home since the royal family had me declared a traitor. Where it goes, I go."

"The same for me," Wardell said. "I'm a gunner. It's all I know. Without a ship's battery in my hands, I'm not sure what I'd be doing."

Nye, with his usual economy of speech, just nodded, his dark eyes unreadable as usual.

Shasti looked at Perez. The mustached engineer shrugged. "Might as well, I don't fancy the local girls."

Mollica had been pulling her lower lip in concentration. "Triple pay?"

Shasti nodded.

"I'll want the payment in Confed currency and deposited in a trust fund held by Confed bank," she said. "One year's pay down."

"Agreed," Shasti said. "Same for everyone," she added before they could chime in.

"Then that's all," she said. "We'll be leaving in a few days. Fortunately, Mr. Dobera has already completed our basic reloading. Supplemental lists of personnel and equipment will be available tomorrow. Go to your people. Anybody who wants off can be paid off in this port or I'll guarantee return passage to New Eire. Dismissed."

The group filed out quietly. Shasti suspected that they would wait till they were out of earshot to begin the inevitable, "what the hell is going on now?" discussions.

Shasti actually had one of these herself with the few crew left aboard from when Mmok had served on *Sidhe*: Dobera, Perez, Nye, and Wardell and a few others. None had been close to the acerbic HCR controller. Their reactions were muted.

"Not sure it will be much different," Wardell said. "He was three-quarters machine last time."

Mandela himself arrived an hour later, accompanied by Mmok, and a new version of the standard Confederate battle robots. Crab-like, gray and green machines with particle beam weapons and small missiles, these were smaller than the ones she'd seen before, still they were the size of a compact aircar. Mmok stood with twenty of them on the field below the *Sidhe*.

She looked down from the hatchway at the HCR body. So much of her own existence was bound by the question of whether or not she was human—whether she had a soul. Now she looked at a born-human who'd been reduced to some brain matter encapsulated in a computer. Shorn of his original body, the difference between him and a machine existed only in his conception of himself. He believed he was still Mmok—she assumed he must believe that he still had a soul.

But he came into this universe through a mother and father, grew up in a family, however dysfunctional, she thought. *And me? I'm a stew of unrelated genes, tinkered with by scientists, raised in a crèche as a bio-weapon. Yet perhaps, after all, there is hope for me.*

She dismissed further existential considerations from her mind as Mandela walked up the gangway that led from the gantry lift. "Good morning, Ms. Rainhell," he said. His breath steamed in the cool morning air. "Any chance there's hot coffee in some warmer spot?"

"Follow me," she said. They walked to her ready room off the bridge. Shasti ordered hot drinks for them. The spymaster sank into a chair with a sigh and reached for the steaming cup. "I could have stayed in London if I wanted to be cold and damp all the time."

"Getting old?"

Mandela snorted a laugh. "Not ready for a retirement home quite yet. How are you fixed for crew?"

"I've had thirty-three resignations. Twenty from the ground force. The most crucial are on the alterwatch: communications and electronic warfare officers."

"I'll fill those spots for you," he said. "Ground troops won't be a problem. We have Rigg, Rask, and an ASAT team. Mmok will be joining us with a small cybernetic force."

"No other HCRs?" she asked.

"No, they're not that common. Unfortunately, in my reduced circumstances, I cannot commandeer more."

"I assume you have a science team."

"Science and medical: Dr. Mourner you remember, of course. Dr. N'deba and Professor Romita will round it out, along with some techs," he said.

"Ah, so the good professor is joining us."

"Indeed. He's quite taken with the thought of a long space voyage with you."

Shasti shook her head in irritation. "He seems a rather frivolous sort."

Mandela gave her an unreadable look. "He's fond of wine, women, and song, as they used to say. In a pinch, I imagine he'd do without the wine and hum to himself. You do not appear to lack for admirers."

"Meaning?"

"Please, Rainhell. My brain hasn't grown soft. Vaughn didn't come to Morokat for the weather. You are here, bearing the most perfect genes to float to the top of the gene pool, all in a most lovely and intelligent package, a veritable warrior-queen. I'm surprised it took him this long to make a play for you."

"I'm not in the market for a mate just yet."

"Yet, Vaughn is here."

"Let him remain so," she said. "Now, as to the equipment and personnel..."

The next two days passed quickly as *Sidhe* prepared for space. Dan Rigg, Rask, and the ASAT team boarded during the night. The following sunrise saw the science team wander aboard less surreptitiously. Every manner of cargo and store that could be safely brought aboard was packed in the frigate's hull.

Shasti walked onto the bridge, checklist in hand. To her surprise, Mmok was there, hovering over the ship's computer station. Mandela stood behind him.

"Good news," Mmok reported. "Vaughn's ship pulled out of orbit three hours ago."

Shasti was surprised by the faint disappointment she felt. To cover it she turned to Mandela. "One less thing to worry about."

Mandela pulled his lip, deep in thought. "Did he file a flight plan?"

"No," Mmok returned, "and it would probably be bogus if he did."

"True."

"Thought you'd be happy," Shasti said.

"I always prefer to know where people like Vaughn are and what they are doing. It's when I can't see them that I'm unhappy." He turned back to Mmok. "Any other information?"

"He was throwing around an epic amount of money to find out where we are going," Mmok answered. "Other than that, all we know is he's fully refueled and resupplied. He could go anywhere in a *Sword* class destroyer's reach. They're leggy ships."

"Thank you, Kyle." Mandela turned to her. "How are we progressing, Captain?"

"We launch in ten hours."

He smiled broadly. "Excellent. That will give me plenty of time for an elaborate dinner at the Elshass."

"Don't worry," she said. "We won't leave without you."

Sidhe launched in the late evening of the third day after Mandela's arrival. The Morok port officials rolled back the various gantries and supports, freeing the starship of their supporting embrace. She roared up into the atmosphere, flying into space like a plane. Once there, the star-frigate rendezvoused with *Penagat* space station and refueled. The giant fuel and supply sled Mandela had promised awaited them. Nearly as large as *Sidhe* herself, the dark-gray sled obligingly fell in behind the red star-frigate. Shasti had the robot-sled's navigation system slaved to *Sidhe's* own. The blood-red frigate led the sled toward the accelerator.

On her bridge, Shasti watched Morokat and her past fade into a small point of light, then vanish and, as always, she wondered about her choices.

Sidhe lined up for entry to the warp point. Shasti started the jump clock.

"Captain," Wardell called, alarm in his voice. "I'm picking up a vessel."

"Let me guess," Mandela sighed. "A *Sword*-class destroyer. No IFF."

"Half-right," Wardell said. "IFF is operating and identifying her as the Olympian Self-Defense Force, *Paladin*."

"Of course," Mandela said. "He found out our general heading from some bribable Morok, and he's been out here circling, awaiting us."

"Why?" Shasti snapped.

"Why indeed, Ms. Rainhell?"

Shasti shifted uncomfortably, guessing at Mandela's unexpressed thoughts.

"What's his status?" Shasti demanded.

"No active fire control," Wardell said. "No ECM. He's matching course and speed with us, falling astern."

"A vulnerable position should we decide to roll a pattern of proximity mines," Mmok said. "Bad tactics if he's got hostile intentions."

"Incoming message," Communications announced. "Visual and audio."

Shasti nodded. "On screen."

Vaughn's image appeared on the screen, beside him stood an Asian woman, Tanaka, his lead operative. *Paladin's* bridge was larger and more modern then *Sidhe's*, as was the destroyer herself.

"Nice day for a flight," he said with a smile.

"What do you think you are doing?" Shasti replied.

"Indulging my curiosity," he said. "I have great freedom to do so these days. No responsibilities you know."

"What are your intentions?" she said.

"A long space voyage," he replied with a grin. "To parts and places unknown."

"You will find that rather difficult without starcharts," she snapped.

"True. You could remedy that, though," he said, crossing his arms and looking at her.

"I fail to see why I should," Shasti said. "I don't know or care to know what game you're playing, but we hit a warp point soon. You'd better turn back while you can."

"I don't think so. But without your help I guess I will just have to navigate as best I can."

"You're mad," Mollica exclaimed. "You can't just follow us in."

"Very true." Vaughn nodded. If he was discomforted on coming up on the unknown warppoint at two-thirds the speed of light, he didn't show it. "Without the benefit of the exact nav math, I might come out anywhere near our destination. Or I might be shot off in an unknown direction, never to be seen again."

Mmok shrugged. "Not our problem."

Vaughn gave the machine a curious look. *Of course,* Shasti thought. *He doesn't know.*

Scully, the navigator, turned in her chair. "We've just passed point of no return on the warppoint. Transit in forty seconds."

"Vaughn," Shasti demanded, looking into the screen. "Sheer off now."

"Faint heart ne'er won fair lady," Vaughn said, leaning back in his command chair. "Besides, I always did want to see more of the galaxy. Travel broadens the mind, they tell me."

"Thirty seconds," Scully said.

"Transmit the entry coordinates to *Paladin,*" Shasti ordered.

"Captain Rainhell—" Mandela began.

"Do it!"

"Transmitting," Scully said. "I don't know if he has time."

"We have the coordinates," Vaughn rapped, all pretense of nonchalance vanishing. "Altering course."

"Entry point, in five, four, three, two, one…"

Colors and sounds became strange as the Cherr drive ripped at the vulnerable fabric of space. Hyperspace yawned before them, and they seemed to fall forever.

5

The universe reappeared abruptly around Shasti. Sound came back first, blurred and distorted. Then images swam in her eyes, finally settling into the familiar shape of the bridge viewscreens, filled with jeweled stars. The sharp cold air of the bridge held the odd electrical smell that always accompanied jump.

Her bridge crew began to stir. Some lucky souls were unbothered by jump, others looked distinctly green. Shasti began the biofeedback techniques that helped her shrug off the disorientation. Jump troubled Shasti more than most, but she had better control of her body. She knew that Dobera and his department had food, coffee, and anti-nauseants on their way to all stations.

"Emergence," Mollica called, her eyes darting around the screens. "The sled is in formation with us."

"Scan is negative in the short sector," Hafel said. "No radio traffic. Expanding to check on nonstandard frequencies."

"Ahead slow," Shasti ordered. "Mr. Nye, get working on basic system charts. Cartography is a big priority."

"Another emergence flare," Hafel said.

"You seem to attract the most persistent of boyfriends," Mmok said.

"Shut up," Shasti snapped.

"Confirmation," Hafel advised. "*Sword*-class destroyer, *Paladin*, has defolded from hyperspace. She's matching course and speed."

On the screen the lethal, missile-shape of Vaughn's destroyer coasted out of its emergence flare. Almost as large as *Sidhe* and painted light gray, she weighed more than the Conchirri star-frigate, which had large bays for shuttles and smaller ships. *Sidhe* combined the function of an escort vessel and a supply tender. *Paladin* was all hunter-killer, with two mass accelerators, multiple missile tubes, and turreted lasers.

"Well," Mandela said, "you gave him the address and now he's here."

Shasti, still somewhat confused over the impulse that made her save Vaughn, gave him a narrow glare. "You would have preferred I let him and his crew vanish, perhaps forever, into hyperspace?"

"Yes, I would."

"If Vaughn was a danger to us, he could have attacked at any point in Morokat system," Shasti countered. "He doesn't have the Conchirri charts that Mr. Romita translated. It's not simply a matter of jumping back the way you came. He'd need coordinates from us to have anything better than a remote chance of the proper entry."

"Thank you, Ms. Rainhell," Mandela said. "I'm quite aware of the finer points of warp point transition. You might recall that I have controlled fleets at times."

"That's Captain Rainhell."

An ugly tension filled the bridge. People watched Mmok.

Mandela sighed. "Yes, of course, Captain. I hope you will agree that keeping those charts and coordinates from Mr. Vaughn is a priority."

Shasti nodded and leaned back in her seat. "We agree on that."

"I suppose it's not all bad," Mandela mused. "We now have a destroyer full of expendables available to us."

Shasti didn't rise to the bait. "As you say, since they are here, might as well make use of them."

"Indeed," Mandela responded. "Perhaps would be as well if we saw Mr. Vaughn aboard for dinner and consultations."

"Keep your friends close and your enemies closer?" Shasti asked, both disturbed and exhilarated at the thought of seeing Vaughn again. "Dubious philosophy where it concerns a Denshi Assassin."

"Perhaps so," Mandela said. "But I will rest easier with Vaughn aboard *Sidhe* and off the bridge of a *Sword* class destroyer."

"Besides," Mmok added, "I'll keep an eye on him. Two eyes in fact, and I don't even blink these days."

An hour later the small pinnace carrying Vaughn made its way from *Paladin* to *Sidhe*. Shasti didn't allow even this small vessel into her overcrowded shuttle bay but had the rocket-shaped pinnace dock to *Sidhe's* hull. Rask and a heavily armed honor guard brought the Olympians to the wardroom by the main galley.

"Welcome aboard." Mandela smiled, extending a hand to Vaughn as he cleared the hatchway. The huge Engineered, clad in simple black fatigues, shook it briskly. Vaughn looked over Mandela's head at Daniel Rigg. "I know you," he rumbled. "You were on the first team that infiltrated Olympia."

Rigg nodded coolly.

"Watch this one, Misa." Vaughn gestured to the beautiful Asian woman who accompanied him. "He's tough and full of tricks."

"As is your guard," Shasti said. "I remember putting three rounds in her midsection on a rooftop in Marathon."

"I wondered why you didn't go for the headshot," Tanaka said, dryly.

"I'm Engineered, not omnipotent," Shasti returned. "I was running too hard to be accurate and it was more important to put you down than to kill you."

"Wow," Mmok said. "This is getting more like a family reunion all the time."

Vaughn looked surprised at the comment and turned to examine the HCR more closely.

Shasti stepped forward and placed a hand on Mmok's shoulder. "This is Kyle Mmok. His body is that of an HCR, but he's human."

"Hey, watch the insults," Mmok said.

"Quiet, Kyle," she added.

"Yes'm."

Vaughn watched the by-play and raised an eyebrow at Tanaka, who shrugged.

Mandela strolled past them and sat at the head of the long metal table. *King and his court,* Shasti thought. She debated whether to make a point of it and decided not to. Mandela had commissioned the voyage and it was under his authority. Besides, it didn't pay to incur Mandela's enmity needlessly.

The others shuffled around the table, pulling back the plain metal chairs. Shasti took her place at Mandela's right hand. Mmok stood behind them both. Rigg took a seat backed by Rask. Vaughn sat opposite Rigg with Tanaka over his shoulder. A steward came in and served cold drinks.

"Very hospitable," Vaughn said as he reached for a glass. Tanaka stirred as if to object, and he laughed. "We don't need to fear being poisoned, Misa. I'll taste my own drink."

"Force of habit," Tanaka said.

Mandela reached and took a glass as well. "I have prevailed upon Captain Rainhell's excellent chef to prepare a proper dinner in the main galley, but I wanted to attend to some details before enjoying it."

Vaughn rubbed his chin with a hand, his ferocious blue eyes fastened on the spymaster. "Let me guess. I am to agree to your overall command of our little fleet. Your people to be allowed to access my ship and computers at will, and my presence on your ship whenever you require it."

"Excellent." Mandela smiled. "I do so hate to belabor the obvious. It is tedious. We may even get to dinner early."

"You assume I will agree," Vaughn said, spinning his glass idly. It looked impossibly small in his huge hand.

"I assume nothing." Mandela wagged a finger. "I am a senior government official and can commandeer any Confederate registered ship at any time. True, you do have the superior warship, but only we know where the next starjump is. It would be a serious mistake to count on Captain Rainhell saving you again."

Vaughn met Shasti's eyes, and he smiled. "You might be surprised."

Shasti felt her blood stir but couldn't tell if it was with attraction or anger. She flipped her hair away from her eyes, making sure it fell smoothly on her shoulders.

"So," Mandela continued, "your choices are to accept my terms or…you could decide to go home."

Vaughn leaned back in his chair and sipped his drink. "I accept your terms, of course."

"I thought you might," Mandela said, holding up his glass for the steward to refill. "Who knows, we might find the presence of a master assassin and fleet destroyer quite welcome."

"Indeed," Vaughn said. "We are well-armed and provisioned for extended voyaging, though we are somewhat under-crewed. I did not have many takers for a long voyage into the unknown. But between our Denshi and the OSDF people, we are formidable enough.

"Now that we have joined your merry crew, Mr. Mandela, perhaps you will tell me what drags a Confederate official of your caliber to voyage on a privateer beyond the borders of known space?"

"Daniel." Mandela nodded.

Rigg stood up and punched in instructions on a station below a large vidsceen. "Display files on the Evolver incident on Fenris IV."

Pictures of the strange starship flashed on the screen. Smooth, aerodynamic, and colored a brilliant gold, the Evolver ship lay crashed but largely undamaged at the base of a mountain. Quickly, Rigg outlined the details of the deadly encounter with the Evolver. Other images showed corpses from the fighting, the distorted, armored bodies of Dua-Denlenn altered by Evolver. Rigg finished with Mandela's theory about the connection between the Evolver and the Conchirri.

"Fascinating," Vaughn said. "You're engaged in something between an archeological expedition and a reconnaissance. Assuming there's anything out there."

"Oh, there's something out there, all right." Rigg sat back down. "I was on Fenris IV. I saw it. They're out there."

"Yeah," Rask snorted. "DNA raiders from Beyond, here to rustle our chromosomes."

Vaughn leaned back and looked up at the ape-like Morok. "Your friend has quite a colorful turn of phrase."

"Frustrated novelist." Rigg smiled.

The steward caught Shasti's eye. She nodded and gestured to Mandela.

"Dinner is served," Mandela announced.

"Follow me," Shasti said. They accompanied her down the corridor to the main galley.

Shasti had followed Fenaday's custom of a captain's table, both to keep her in touch with her department heads and to help her learn more, however painfully, of human interactions. The heavy oak table with its black leather chairs had come from his estate on New Eire and seated twenty comfortably. Shasti had always felt the table and chairs conveyed something of Fenaday's personality: solid, enduring, and practical. She put her hand on the captain's chair, with its higher back, and stroked the old leather, feeling a shadow of loss steal through her. *You should be here with me,* she thought, then banished the unwelcome musing. Those choices were all long since made.

The science team joined them for dinner. Dr. Shizuyo Mourner trooped in with Dr. Fierman and their assistants, followed by Paolo Romita. Most of Shasti's other officers were on watch and Dobera did not usually dine with humans.

Shasti found herself seated between Vaughn and Paolo. At first, Vaughn seemed interested in Romita's tale of being a Conchirri prisoner and of his work on their records. As the evening wore on, it seemed Paolo's casual and clever banter with Shasti began to annoy Vaughn. At one point, when Paolo interrupted his tale of leaving Olympia with an idle comment on when Vaughn was expected back, Vaughn smiled a chilly smile and locked his wolfish blue eyes with the smaller man's brown ones.

"I am never expected," Vaughn growled. "Like the good assassin I was raised to be, I appear at the time and place of my own choosing."

Paolo reacquired an interest in his drink, affecting an air of disdain. "How dramatic." But he did not return Vaughn's steady gaze.

Shasti found the subtle competition for her attention both tedious and exciting in equal measures. Feeling a need to create a diversion, she signaled the head cook to begin serving. Shortly after Fenaday gave her command of the star-frigate, Shasti hired a few crack chefs with wanderlust. The wonderful scents of baking and cooking began to fill the room to smiles and comments by the guests.

So soon out of port, *Sidhe* was full of fresh fruits and vegetables. Everyone relished the dinner, knowing that in time ahead the fare would be poorer. Salvers of prime rib and Roman chicken accompanied by vegetable tian and French bread circulated. Bottles of fine cabernet and Syrah were opened. Shasti had always paid attention to the commissary, but Mandela raised that to an entirely new level. Morokat might be totally emptied of decent wine, caviar, or fine chocolates and brandies after the assault the spymaster and quartermaster had led.

Shasti triggered a panel at her chair, and a hologram of the rocky coastline of New Eire appeared on one wall of the long room. Ocean sounds accompanied soft Celtic music, creating a relaxing ambience. At Mandela's subtle urging, all difficult subjects were tabled until after the meal had been savored. He had, after all, spent most of his life as a diplomat.

She caught Vaughn looking at a painting on the opposite wall. The image was of a wolf, with smoky-black fur and yellow eyes that seemed to leap off the canvas, running over snow. She'd painted it years ago during the Enshar expedition.

"He runs alone," Vaughn noted.

"She," Shasti replied.

"Ah," he replied. "And you are the artist for all that you did not sign the piece."

"Then how do you know?" she asked.

He smiled. "I know."

"It's beautiful work," Paolo said. "One can practically feel her fur."

The comment froze Shasti momentarily. Fenaday had said the same thing when he first saw it.

"I have never done better," she said. "I started it on the way to Enshar and thought that it might be the only thing I left as a legacy in this life. Our odds of survival seemed so slim then. Maybe it inspired me."

Chocolate mousse, fruit, and coffee interrupted further conversation.

Finally, Mandela tapped his spoon on his glass. "Ladies and gentlemen, it has been a most pleasant beginning to our voyage. Good also to meet our fellow adventurers in person." He smiled at Vaughn, whose ironic expression told what he thought of Mandela's bonhomie. "And to take the necessary steps to integrate our forces, Mr. Mmok will accompany you back to your ship to arrange the little details we discussed earlier.

"We are voyaging to the second world of this system. If Professor Romita's analysis is correct, this is one of the systems that the Conchirri struck as they moved out into our arm of the galaxy. It was neither the last nor the nearest in terms of light years, but it was the most express route through hyperspace."

"How long ago do you think they were here?" Shasti asked Paolo.

He gestured uncertainly with both hands. "I am not sure. The records were fragmentary and our translation sketchier than I could hope. There is also the issue of how the Conchirri viewed time. They seem to pay attention only to major events. Their timekeeping otherwise was odd and haphazard."

"A species without birthdays," Mmok said.

Paolo looked at the cyborg. "You're not far off. They had no civilian economy, indeed no real civilization. They were professional warriors. The old didn't retire; they just died. The only important date for the young was maturity and induction from crèches." If Paolo caught Vaughn and Shasti's uncomfortable looks at the mention of crèches, he was wise enough not to remark on it.

"I am reasonably certain that it was centuries ago," Paolo finished. "We may find nothing but dust and bones."

"If that," Rigg grumbled. "Conchirri liked marrow."

"We'll be in reliable scan range of our initial objective in two days," Shasti said. "This system doesn't have outer gas giants, so the Cherr Drive point was unusually close in. Vaughn, Mmok will update your computer systems with what little data we have on this system."

"Is there a name for the world we are going to?" Vaughn asked.

"One could not say the Conchirri name," Paolo said. "It would just sound like a cat spitting. And anyway it merely means Target 4309. I had," he turned to Shasti, "intended to name it after you, if it were a lovely world."

"Now isn't that sweet," Mmok said.

Shasti picked up a long steak knife and gave the cyborg a meaningful look. Vaughn shot Paolo a sour glance.

"Much as I appreciate the poetry in that," Mandela intervened, "I think till we see if the world can hold a candle to our captain's uncontested beauty that we will refer to it as Lantrim II. If only to prevent confusion."

Shasti played idly with her knife. "I don't see a point in having my name on real estate I don't own."

"May I suggest we call it a night then," Mandela said. "There is much to do and it has been a stressful day."

Everyone rose. Vaughn would clearly have liked to stay, but both Paolo and Daniel Rigg were sticking close to Shasti. She debated the wisdom of walking Vaughn to the pinnace but with Mmok and Tanaka for company it seemed only awkward. Shasti sensed Mandela's amused eyes on her.

She turned to Vaughn. "I hope I won't regret not losing you in space."

He gave a slight smile. "I can be a good man to have around in a pinch."

"As long as he's careful what he is pinching," Paolo whispered.

Shasti's chest constricted. She knew Vaughn had heard him, but his face remained pleasantly neutral, which in itself, she suspected, was a warning sign.

"Good night, Vaughn," Shasti said. Then on impulse, "Sometime you will have to return the favor and give me a tour of the *Paladin*."

"Anytime, Captain. Anytime at all." Vaughn bowed to the assembled crew and headed to the hatch.

Mmok followed him. "Show me the way to go home," the HCR sang to itself. "I'm tired and I want to go to bed."

The others shuffled out. As Paolo passed Shasti, she casually grasped his wrist and jerked it once. "Don't play with Vaughn," she whispered. "Or we will be washing your remains off the walls."

"Some things are worth daring for." Paolo grinned as he raised his imprisoned wrist and kissed the hand holding it. "Goodnight, Captain."

I am beginning to hate men, Shasti thought as the room emptied. *Thank God for my dog. I think he's smarter.*

The next morning Shasti sat in her command chair, watching as *Paladin, Sidhe,* and the robot sled all neatly maneuvered so their thrusters fired along the path, slowing the small fleet.

"Final burn completed," Nye said, as he toggled controls on his board. "We are now down to a safe speed for entry into the inner system and orbit."

Now the rapier shape of her starship led as they pivoted on their singularities and again pointed their noses at Lantrim II. The sled, its blunt prow much less elegant than *Sidhe's* slender nose, followed with less grace. *Paladin*, a wasp-waisted delta shape, also formed up.

"And now back on course," Nye finished with a flair.

"Well done," Shasti said, standing and stretching. She gave a quick glance around the bridge, then nodded at Mollica. "Bring the sled in. I want to top our tanks off and replace the reaction mass we've burned off."

Mollica nodded. "What about the *Paladin*? Or should they have packed their own lunch?"

"For now," Shasti said, "let's keep our groceries to ourselves. It can't hurt for Vaughn to feel more dependent on us."

"Can't say I'm sorry to have them here," Mollica said, sliding into Shasti's command chair. "That fleet DD throws twice the megajoules per second that we do. I like the backup, assuming they don't use it on *us.*"

Shasti gave a grim smile and left the bridge, preferring the gangway to the turbovator. Though she was tired, the exercise felt good. The last three days had been a strain. Vaughn had shuttled back and forth, always shadowed by Tanaka, coordinating with Mandela and with Dobera on supplies. On each trip he found some reason to spend time talking with her, usually over dinner. Shasti, for whom small talk was always a struggle, found it almost as difficult as Vaughn seemed to. Clearly he was frustrated by the presence of so many others, particularly Paolo, who always seemed to be near her when Vaughn was aboard.

Risky had his place in the galley, where he could enjoy his dinner in the company of humans. The genetically enhanced shepherd loved people and was not above begging for treats. Shasti had to watch him so the indulgences didn't fatten Risky, nor make him sick. Curiously, whenever either Vaughn or Paolo was at the table, Risky would not leave Shasti's side.

Well, he did like Fenaday, she thought. Perhaps in Risky's eyes her current suitors did not measure up. She wasn't sure they measured up in her eyes either.

Yet somehow when those ferocious blue eyes of Vaughn's were on her, she felt a link between them, a nearly electric flow. And it terrified her. Vaughn, for all his present urbanity, was of the same strange breed as Pard and the rest of the Engineered. How could she trust an Engineered after the disgusting things that Pard had done to her during their brief and horrible façade of a marriage? She was still engaged in finding out how human she was. Vaughn would seem little use on that quest.

As she neared her cabin, Shasti shook her head to clear thoughts of Vaughn away. She entered to find Risky waiting for her. Roughhousing with the big dog relieved some of her tension. After a bit of fun, he curled up on a sofa with a yawn. Risky had been working out with the landing force troops in anticipation of planetfall.

Shasti contemplated the long evening ahead and decided that there was time enough to do some painting. The thought took her back to the conversation days before, in the galley where Vaughn had admired her painting of the wolf.

Perhaps I will paint something for him, she thought. But when her mind drifted to an image, it was not of the handsome Olympian but of another Engineered, older, even more powerfully built, against whom even Vaughn would have looked like a boy. Pard. Since Vaughn had set foot on her ship, his old master and her ex-husband Pard had lurked in the shadows of her mind. And now his image came unbidden to her thoughts, and the dull fury of her abusive teen years came back to her. She forced the thoughts of Olympia and Olympians away. After a few deep breaths, she was again considering breaking into her paints and brushes when the buzzer to her cabin sounded.

"Yes?"

"It's Paolo. Permission to see the captain?"

Shasti waved a hand over a control and the doors slid open. In came Paolo, pushing a wheeled cart covered in white linen. To Shasti's amazement, the cart held a vase of flowers and, more pressing on her attention, two candles. A number of covered platters sat on the cart along with a chiller filled with two bottles of white wine.

"What's this?" Shasti said, even as she debated shooting Paolo out of hand for having two open flames in the interior of her spaceship.

"Dinner." He flashed a grin at her. "I knew you would be too late for the gallery and I could not stand the thought of you eating scraps alone in your cabin, however luxuriously spacious it is. Besides, I thought it might be fun to have a meal without tall, dark, and scowling looming over everyone." He did a quick and surprisingly good imitation of Vaughn's annoyed look.

Shasti lost the fight she was having with herself and laughed. Paolo took this as an invitation to start setting up the table.

Risky, always interested in food and ever mistrustful of men near his mistress, came over and sat near the table, facing Paolo. His tail was not wagging.

"Umm," Paolo said. "Has your wolf been fed? He seems to have a peculiar fascination with my throat at the moment."

"Risky, come," Shasti said. There was a cushion for him in her studio as well as a water dish. The shepherd left with apparent reluctance, and she closed the door.

Shasti returned to Paolo, who had uncovered the plates and was pouring chilled wine into beautiful fluted glasses. "Smells good."

"Spaghetti Carbonara," he said, "with scallops and shrimp." He served the plates with a deft hand. "Accompanied by a very cold Frascati, which will almost evaporate on your tongue, and followed by a bittersweet chocolate mousse cake and afterward some Sambuca."

The food smelled enticing but what really struck Shasti at that second, was how lonely she was. The feeling had been welling in her unrecognized for days but now it was out and in plain sight. The only people on the ship were subordinates, or in the case of Mandela, uncertain allies. There had been no one she could really talk to since she left New Eire, no one to whom she was Shasti and not "Captain." All her conversations were of the ship and the voyage. Paolo's light and cheerful presence seemed to banish the separateness, the isolation of her nights.

She slid into the chair that he held out for her and watched his face as he smiled and chatted on about some amusing irrelevancy. She found herself laughing and smiling over the food and drinking more of the wine than she suspected was sensible. Paolo cleared the main dishes and produced the promised mousse, which was delicious.

"How," she asked, "did you put this together?"

"Mandela took the most exquisite care to make sure that we were well supplied for voyaging across what he termed the 'barbarous frontier.' And when your quartermaster heard that it was for you, he turned a blind eye to my raiding. The flowers I charmed out of a lady in hydroponics." He poured Shasti a snifter of Sambuca.

Shasti felt a tiny stab of jealousy, wondering what that persuasion had been like. She sipped the drink, liking its licorice flavor.

"Tell me about yourself, La Bella Donna sans Merci?" he said, reaching across the table to take one of her hands with both of his.

"What does that mean?"

"The beautiful lady without mercy," he said. "It's an old poem." Paolo brushed his lips across her hand, gently and carefully. "La Bella Donna sans Merci."

"I've learned mercy," Shasti countered. "Robert taught it to me."

"Ah, the sacred Robert." Paolo sighed. "One hears so much about him on this ship."

Anger flashed in Shasti. She moved her hand away from his face, pressing his to the tabletop ungently. "I call him Robert," she said, green eyes filling with menace. "You refer to him as Captain Fenaday when it is safe for you to use his name at all."

"Shasti," Paolo said. "I meant no disrespect to him, but he's like a shadow hanging over you. He belongs to someone else."

"He belongs to me, too," she said, her temper threatening to slip, her other hand balled into a fist.

"As a friend I'm sure," he said, his brown eyes locked on hers. "There is more to life than friendship, you know."

Shasti forced her hand to open, made herself climb down from the tower of her anger.

"I don't know if I am ready to move on," she whispered, looking away.

"There's only one way to find out, Bella Donna," Paolo said. "Life is short. When I was a prisoner of the Conchirri, facing a stewpot, I swore then and there that if I escaped, I was going to embrace life and hang onto it with both hands."

Shasti finally looked at him. He was not Fenaday, steadfast, resolute, and gentle. Nor was he Vaughn with his elemental power and engineered physique, but there was a quality to Paolo. She tried to grasp it as she studied his face. Paolo seemed more one with the universe than Robert or Mikhail, indulging in its pleasures almost naively. As if the universe offered only sunlight, good wine, and beautiful women. He was so different from the driven men she had always known. For Paolo there was only the now.

Too much confusion right now, she thought, *too much confusion.*

"Come over to the couch," he said. "I think you need something further to relax you. My fingers are very skilled at working out knots. And since you could kill any five men like me, I assure you I will be on my best behavior." He refilled their snifters and they moved to the couch.

Paolo's fingers proved as skilled as promised, and Shasti felt the powerful muscles of her shoulders and back give under his strong hands. She felt light-headed and a bit out of control. His fingers moved up and down with practiced skill.

That's it, she thought, *it's all a practiced skill with him, all physical, no real emotions. He's a sexual technician. Maybe though, maybe that's what I need right now. God, it's been about two years, and I'm not even thirty yet. I sure as hell don't want to start another love affair, haven't recovered from my first one.*

She turned toward Paolo, and he smiled, even white teeth flashing in his olive face. *Handsome,* she thought, *and so very aware of it.*

Paolo read the cue and slowly took her chin in his hand and kissed her. Shasti tensed as she usually did at this stage. A part of her always remembered the humiliation and abuse practiced on her by her creator and husband, Jalgren Pard. Paolo seemed to sense it and slowed, gently stroking her body. Shasti leaned back on the cushions feeling herself relax and enjoying the heat spreading through her.

Paolo kissed her again, on the lips and the neck. She pulled him close, seeming to startle him slightly with her strength. He quickly got over it and began to unbutton her shirt. Shasti obliged by shrugging out of the shirt and the black bra beneath. She enjoyed the lustful admiration in his face.

"Magnificent," he said, touching her breast in a gentle circular motion. "Just magnificent."

Shasti led him to the bedroom of her cabin and pushed him onto his back atop the bed. They kissed and touched playfully, proceeding at a pace she controlled and rose to. They made love twice, Paolo showing fine skill at pleasing both her and himself.

After the second time, Shasti eased onto her back, reveling in the afterglow of the physical act. He lay beside her, breathing heavily from exertion. He smiled. "So my goddess, are you pleased?"

She stretched lazily and ran her hands through his curly dark hair. "Yes," she said with a small laugh. "It's been a very long time."

"Ah, no one could tell. Like Venus, your touch is magical."

Shasti controlled a slight stab of irritation, always the glib words—always on the surface. "Tell me, Paolo. Have you ever been in love?"

"You mean like now?"

Shasti looked at him and his smiled faded. "You don't love me," she said. "Oh it is possible that you like me, but it's more probable that as the biggest, strongest, most exotic, and beautiful woman that you've ever met, I present an irresistible challenge to you."

"Well, you are actually all of those things," he said, stroking her thigh.

"And you are avoiding my question."

"Why do you ask it?" he countered, looking slightly away.

"Because I'm the mixed genes of thousands of people, diced, spliced, and engineered. I have no father or mother, no family, and my sexual life started very, very badly. I've known little of love and what there has been was horrendously complicated."

"Nothing you need fear from me," he returned. "I'm the most uncomplicated of men."

"Or perhaps the most complicated," she replied, "with elaborate defenses against involvement?"

"Ah," he said. "So many deep thoughts, but if you have so much energy, I have better ways to use it."

Well, Shasti thought, *I did tell myself I wanted something physical.*

"Let's try this," he began.

An hour later Paolo stood and reached for his clothing. Shasti looked a question at him.

"Did I thank you for a beautiful evening?" he said, smiling. "Isn't it nice to be with another adult?"

"What do you mean?" she said, leaning back.

"Oh so many women would want to spend the whole night on top of each other in a tangle. Then there is all that morning awkwardness. But you and I are grownups. We know what we want. We both know what we were here for tonight."

Do we? Shasti thought. But maybe Paolo was right. The night had been perfect—could the morning be anything but an anti-climax?

He leaned down and kissed her. "Good night, La Bella Donna sans Merci. Don't get up. I'll show myself out."

Rigg leaned against the corridor wall, partly hidden by a stanchion. He'd long ago mastered the art of standing absolutely still, first hunting with his dad in the woods and later in years of intense infantry training. Most crew passing nearby didn't notice the lean, rangy ASAT.

He didn't stir when the doors to Shasti's cabin slid open in the early morning hours. Paolo pushed a cart out of the cabin, then thoughtlessly abandoned it. The handsome philologist looked well-pleased with himself. His shirt was open, but he'd at least belted his pants.

As he passed Rigg, the ASAT straightened and stepped out. "Hello, Paolo."

Paolo looked a little startled then grinned raffishly. "Hey, Dan. What, did the all-night poker game just break up?"

"Something like that," Rigg said, falling into step with Paolo.

"Ah, my friend, I have had the night of a lifetime," Paolo said.

"Oh? You want to tell me about it?"

"Sure. Shasti had the most magnificent—"

"Shasti?" Rigg said. "You mean the Captain."

"Ah, yes…"

"You see that's what we call her out here in the corridors. We call her the Captain. A select few of us call her the Skipper."

"I see."

"Do you?" Rigg said dryly.

"So you actually don't want to hear about it."

They crossed the side corridor, leading to Paolo's cabin. Standing in the middle of the hallway at easy parade rest, stood Rask, his red eyes expressionless, his fangs occasionally visibly as he methodically chewed a stick of gum.

Paolo came to a stop between the stocky Morok and Rigg. He looked up at the ASAT.

"Not only do I not want to hear about it, but it would be very, very bad if anyone else heard about it. Skipper is very private, doesn't like to be talked about. It makes her unhappy. That would make me unhappy, and I would then come looking for someone to share my unhappiness with."

Paolo swallowed. "There some interest there that I should be aware of?"

Rigg shook his head. "Not like that. I owe the Skipper my life and a few other things. If you're treating her well, and that's what she wants, then that's square with me."

"And if not," Rask said, "it's a small ship."

"Where you seem oddly conversant with my movements," Paolo said.

"On this ship," Rigg said, "I know where everyone is, every minute."

"It's kinda important," Rask said. "Ships are dangerous places, lot of people have died on this one."

Paolo nodded slowly. "Point taken."

"It would not be good if we had to have any part of this discussion again," Rigg said. "Good night, Doc." Rask fell in behind Rigg, leaving a subdued Paolo walking quickly to his cabin.

Shasti woke the next morning and stretched her arm, reaching for… who? Her last lover had been Robert. Her body remembered the mornings after, the warmth of his solid body next to hers. How he would wake and pull her close as if afraid that she'd get out of the bed if he wasn't holding her. When he woke, he'd often rub her back. Sometimes they would fall back asleep. She would wake later to find he'd brought her coffee and was sitting on the bed smiling, just looking at her. Robert was the only person she'd been so comfortable with that he could move around and not wake her.

But she didn't have that this morning. She had the afterglow of fine sex, but it seemed somehow incomplete. More like she'd exercised than made love. And in that she had her answer. She'd had sex and nothing more.

"Isn't that what I wanted?" she murmured to herself. Shasti got out of bed and released Risky from the compartment next door. The German shepherd was intrigued by all the new scents in the room but eventually settled down on the end of her bed in his accustomed spot.

Shasti already doubted her motives and the intelligence of giving in to his advances. Paolo was diverting company, but was that reason enough to share something she had only voluntarily given one man, in a passion that still resonated in her soul?

Or, she thought, *am I making too much of it all, like a schoolgirl in a romance novel? He made me feel good and drove away the aloneness. They can't all slay dragons for you. Each time can't be for a great love. There is such a thing as simple fun.*

She also suspected that she had used Paolo as a way to keep others from her thoughts, one a Jovian figure of old pain and the other a young and vital wolf like herself. With this thought came the realization that she'd done this before. She'd gone on a mission to Earth for Fenaday, shortly after they'd returned to live on New Eire. She'd been caught between her own dark past and the future he'd offered her, a future that she could not imagine for herself back then. She was terrified of his having a claim on her, of owning her in some fashion. She'd thrown herself into bed with a woman she'd met in a bar. An experiment, like Paolo, something to divert her from the real, to break the chains that she feared others might put on her.

And that, she thought, *is my fatal flaw, that I see them as chains. How can I make a life with anyone this way?*

If he hadn't been so willing to be used, Shasti thought ruefully, *I might even be ashamed of myself.* She climbed out of the bed and donned a light robe, then scratched Risky behind the ears. His tail thumped the bed in delight.

"You males," she mock-scolded. "Is that all it takes to make you happy?"

Risky's tail thumped faster.

"Guess so," she said.

Shasti dressed and opened the door, moving around the cart that Paolo had brought dinner on and left just outside. She paused for a moment, enjoying the memory of how he had made her body feel, and the sheer joy of simple, uncomplicated sex.

Or am I kidding myself, she wondered. *Is it ever actually uncomplicated? What do I do about him on the morning after? Or with someone like Paolo, do I even have to worry about it?*

As she stepped out into the corridor, she almost ran into Mollica. Her executive officer glanced over her shoulder at the dinner cart and gave Shasti a broad smile. "Had a good evening, Captain?"

Shasti hit the close switch to her cabin. "Yes," she said, and began walking.

Mollica fell in alongside her. "So, was it good?"

Shasti started to speak then realized no sound was coming out of her mouth.

Mollica shook her head. "You know you might leave some of the boys for me. Seems like all the males on this ship are entranced by you."

"It's less fun than you might think," Shasti finally managed.

"I wouldn't know," Mollica sighed, "never had them competing that hard for me. I saw him pushing the cart with the candles and I suspected he wasn't off for another round of poker with Rigg and Rask. It was pretty obvious. I thought about mentioning the candles but figured I would leave it to you."

Shasti hesitated. Their relationship on board ship was friendly but formal. Off ship, Mollica and she had shared some times together. Shasti longed for someone she could talk to about men, about relationships, about life, but was her XO the right person for a confidante?

"I dealt with him," she said, cutting off the question and the chance to open up.

"Ah," Mollica said, her face closing. She hit the switch to the turbovator to the bridge.

Shasti struggled inside. Something was welling up like a scream, pushing against her chest, against the iron bonds placed on her soul. She half-turned to the other woman who was staring at the indicator for the turbo, her mouth opening to say something, anything about the confusion, the loneliness of her life.

The turbovator opened. Wardell stood inside and nodded to both women. The chance to talk vanished, the old bonds tightened, and she was sealed again in what she had become.

Lantrim II grew steadily in their screens over the next two days as the starships gradually braked down from the high percentage of light speed the Morokat accelerator had given them. Shasti would have preferred air-braking off a gas-giant, but the system had none, so precious fuel had to be spent in thrusting down.

The world in their screens was not a welcoming one. Oceans were shallow and small, unlike the great seas of most Confederate worlds. Thin cloud cover laced over huge areas of burned and slagged soil, visible even from space. The Conchirri had indeed been there, and their handiwork was clear to see. *Sidhe, Paladin,* and the sled closed on the devastated world.

Fierman and Mourner readied their bio-probes. On the bridge, Jasha Tanges, Mandela's planetologist, studied the long scans and, with Hafel's help, drew up maps and made plans for a landing. The slender gray-haired man wore his hair in a ponytail, and looked more like an ascetic than a scientist.

"I'm estimating that there was a big attack here," Tanges reported to Shasti, "a gross of 10-15,000 megatons, maybe 700-1000 years ago. There's still strontium 90 and a larger amount of cesium 137 in the troposphere and stratosphere. In addition, the fusion explosions probably created some tons of long-lived carbon 14. With our anti-rad medicines, it won't be much danger, but no one's going to want a summer home here. Particularly since the nuclear winter must have been severe. This world seems to have had a smaller ocean base than most in this class so it's been persistent longer."

"Where do you suggest we land?" Shasti asked, staring at the corpse of a world.

"Our best choice would be equatorial." Tanges pointed. "The planet isn't icebound, as it must have been for decades after the attack, but the most comfortable zone will be there. If there's anything worth digging for it, will be in the areas that weren't scoured by ice sheets."

"Very well." Shasti looked at Mollica. "Organize a landing force. I'll lead it. I'll want the landing force trouble team, Rigg and his ASATs, Mmok and his machines. I'll leave you one of the *Dakotas* in case you have to send reinforcements."

"Yes, Captain." Mollica looked relieved that she was going to remain on board *Sidhe*. The sharp-faced woman rarely went planet-side, even in the Confederacy.

"I'll want the full science team," Shasti told Tanges. He nodded and left the bridge.

Shasti looked at the long gray hull of the *Paladin*. "Hafel, raise Vaughn."

The gray-haired comtech reached for the controls. "Visual also?"

"No," Shasti said, not quite sure why.

"Vaughn here."

"Rainhell. We will be entering orbit in seven hours. I'll want a team from your ship down with us."

"I'll bring our chief scientist and a full security detail, Denshi and Navy personnel both. Do you plan to stay downworld for an extended time?"

"Depends on what we find, but several days at the least."

"Understood, I will plan accordingly."

"Rainhell out."

Shasti turned to see both Mmok and Mandela behind her. "Is it wise to bring in the *Paladin* people so soon?" Mandela asked.

"You'd rather I took three-quarters of our troops planetside and left him up here with you? I assume that you are staying aboard."

"Oh quite," Mandela replied, giving the scarred brown world a disdainful glance. "Yes, your logic is sound, Captain. Well done."

"Captain," Hafel interrupted. "The first of our probes has located what looks like a city in the equatorial zone."

"Bring it up on the screen," Shasti said.

The main vision screen filled with the image of a series of small towns that gradually merged into a larger metropolis. The sensors displayed half-buried buildings and sections of broad roads that had cracked and broken over the centuries. The rusted and twisted remnant of something that might have been a bridge lay in and about one canyon. There was more vegetation than Shasti would have expected, given their earlier views, but this was the equatorial belt. Still, trees were few and low, and grass and brush more evident.

"Outside of the lack of lights and movement," Mandela observed, "it looks a lot like any other city seen from space. Form follows function, only the details differ."

"Not a large city," Shasti observed. "Less than a million if they live anything like humans."

"It would be too much to hope that a truly significant city would survive a space attack," Mandela said. "If you're landing a large force, you take out the big population centers, eliminates worries about insurgents and prisoners. Even if you're just knocking down their tech so they don't become a threat, you take the big cities and capitals. Still, it is a city. We may learn something."

"We'll let you know," Shasti said.

"Good. Don't get killed, Captain. We have a great deal of work ahead of us." Mandela gave a cheery wave and walked off the bridge.

Shasti turned the bridge over to Mollica and went back to her cabin. There she armed and armored herself. Both she and Risky stopped at sickbay for some anti-rad shots from Dr. Fierman. She trusted the enhanced shepherd's senses and instincts more than sensors and automatics on a new world. Then it was off to the shuttle bay. Shasti chose the *Wolverine* class assault shuttle, *Dagda*, and the smaller *Pooka*, leaving the cumbersome *Globemaster* behind.

The shuttles launched from the small fleet, two from *Sidhe* and one from *Paladin*. They joined up and slipped past the gray bulk of the supply sled, heading for the planet. Each of the shuttles glowed brick red as they cut through Lantrim II's outer atmosphere heading for the equator, coming down slowly over the ruined city.

Whoever lived here, Shasti thought as she looked out of *Dagda's* canopy, *had loved heights from the way they built these dizzying, sharp-edged towers.* To her they looked a little like grounded starships. Glass, or plastic, glinted in many places. But fires and storms had taken a toll on the towers. *Or perhaps,* she thought, *some of the damage was from weapon fire.* More than one tower had collapsed, tearing great rifts in the cityscape.

"I'm still worried," Paolo said from his seat behind her. "Instruments only detect what they are designed to. Any nerve gas or such employed here would have dissipated ages ago. We did not detect anything in the biofilters of the probes to indicate a biological agent. But what if the Conchirri used something unknown here?"

"Doubtful," Rigg said. He'd clambered up from the deck below to look over Paolo's shoulder. "If they had something useful, they'd have used it during the war with us."

"Besides," Mmok said from his standing position by a takehold, "the Conchirri were never much on CBO. That kind of thing takes a lot of research. They were more the run and gun type."

"Still, they used some," Paolo insisted.

"Yeah," Mmok replied. "Some. It wasn't very good stuff. Broad spectrum as opposed to tailored to a specific life form, as our stuff was. I suspect most of what they had was taken from other races they fought."

"Our suits should protect us," Dr. Mourner said. "Frankly, as cold as it is out there, I'd prefer to keep my helmet closed anyway."

"Remnants of nuclear winter." Shasti repeated what the planetologist had told her. "The pasting the surface took threw so much dust and debris into the atmosphere that the temperature plunged. If this world had bigger seas, it might be all glaciated. As it is, this area near the equator didn't freeze or there'd be nothing to see."

"Just like Okara," Mmok said, "but worse. No Confed Task Force 58 showing up at the last minute to drive them off before they could finish the job. Stupid critters, the Conchirri, wasting good real estate like that. Never seemed to bother them. No more than did casualties, bastards bred like lice."

"One wonders if the Conchirri stayed on this world any time," Paolo said. "We didn't see any of their hives from orbit. Perhaps they only stood off and attacked from space."

"Vaughn's shuttle is right behind us," Bernard called, looking somewhat nervously at her instruments and over her shoulder at the other shuttle.

Shasti nodded. As long as Vaughn was here, she would make use of him. She gestured at a circular area of a thousand meters of glassy, green material that might once have been an air/spacefield. A light covering of stunted vegetation blurred the edges of the field and heaps of material that might have been aircraft dotted it.

"Bernard, tell the other shuttles we are landing there," Shasti said. "Have them circle above us and keep watch. No firing unless I call for it."

They landed the shuttle in a cloud of dust. Vaughn's *Wolverine* and the *Pooka* went into hover above them, weapons out and searching. Inside the *Dagda* everyone sealed suits. Since this was not a combat drop, they exited via airlocks. While the air of Lantrim II was breathable, it was damn cold, and Shasti took the precautions Mourner urged on her.

Mmok, Rigg, and Rask exited the other lock. Shasti gave Risky a pat, preferring to leave him in the shuttle for now. The shepherd whined, conveying his intense disapproval about being left behind before sitting obediently by the airlock. When Shasti's turn at the airlock came, she found herself facing Paolo in the confined space.

"Can't think of anyone I'd rather be caught in an airlock with," he said, trying the best smile in his inventory on her.

She returned a cool look. "Not now."

"Aye, Captain," he said with no indication of being discomforted.

The airlock door slid open. Shasti stepped out onto a world no human had ever trod on before. Her foot hit the curious green surface of the spacefield. It was not concrete but rather a fine-grained substance that looked like marble, only not so slick. Windblown sand gritted under her booted feet. She reached down and picked up a spalled piece of the surface, a souvenir. As she walked away from the shuttle, a small thrill stole through her. An alien world, new and unknown, even the ruined towers failed to dim the feeling.

Shasti and the others walked forward, spreading out and taking in the scene. She stopped about a hundred yards from the *Dagda* and turned slowly through 360 degrees.

In the distance, all around Shasti, thin spires of steel and stone speared the sky, standing up from long low buildings around them. It looked as if one could walk from block to block without going outside. Lantrim II had probably been a harsh world even before the attack.

The temptation to breathe fresh air and feel even the weak sunlight of Lantrim on her face was too much for Shasti. She unsealed her helmet and raised the visor. Cold dry air bit at her nose, and she drew the smells of a world into her lungs. *One of life's simple pleasures,* she thought, *after weeks of ship air, the smell of earth and wind.* She breathed slowly to avoid coughing. An onion smell came from somewhere, perhaps the orange lichen that seemed to grow in the cracks of the spacefield's surface.

A particular building caught Shasti's attention. It had been large and broad, but its interior had collapsed. Sunlight streamed through the open center, coming out as multicolored beams of blue and green as it refracted off glass and metal within. It reminded her of the interior of a cathedral.

Wind sighed in her ears, sad and musical as if it had waited a thousand years to sing a lament for her. She shivered. The thrill of discovery retreated under the thought of the people of this world, huddling around failing utilities as nuclear winter gripped their city and radiation sleeted through their bodies, dying one by one.

She flicked on her command mike and her professional persona. "Rainhell to Landing Force. Proceed to land in overwatch formation."

The other shuttles came down. *Pooka* and Vaughn's shuttles landed with their backs to *Dagda* in a defensive triangle. People and equipment spilled out forming a perimeter, the outer edge of which consisted of Mmok's crab robots.

"I don't think we have anything to fear here, beyond the odd ghost or two," Vaughn said.

Distracted by the ruined city, Shasti had not sensed him come up, and she turned to see him next to Dr. Mourner. In his armored suit, Vaughn looked bigger than usual, nearly as large as Pard. The unfortunate comparison made her lips tighten. She fought off an irrational surge of anger. "No point in taking chances. Every new world holds its own terrors and dangers."

"As well," Paolo's voice sounded in her ears, "as its delights and treasures."

"Shouldn't you be off with a shovel somewhere?" Vaughn said.

"Soon enough," Paolo returned. "The world has waited centuries for us. There's time."

Vaughn grunted and ignored the doctor. "Do we set up an encampment here or move into the city?"

Shasti thought about it. "It's midday. Let's set up a camp here and make forays into the local area. By nightfall I want barrier wire up and us dug in. We will see what we can learn about the locals and what happened here.

"You may have less time than you imagine," Shasti said to Paolo.

"Mandela's looking for information on the Conchirri and the Evolvers. Abstract archeology isn't on the agenda."

"True." Paolo frowned, looking about the field. "Odd that there are no major ships on the field. All those piles of rusted metal are way too small to be anything other than lighters, barges and such. Looks like we will have to head to the field's edge to get into any structures."

A mechanical mule pulled up with Rigg standing on it next to a heavy machine gun, Rask sat alongside a driver. A crab robot followed the small vehicle like a dog.

"Doctor," Rigg said. "Captain."

"Joyriding?" she asked, giving Rigg a mock glare. Inaction had been weighing on the big ASAT during the voyage in.

"I left Tivka to set up the defenses." He smiled, dodging the question. "Tanaka's setting up the camp proper. She wants to see Dr. Mourner about the field lab."

"Okay." Mourner nodded and walked toward the shuttles.

Paolo climbed onto the mule. Shasti would like to have taken the ride as well, but she was a captain now and had to see to the security of her command.

"Mr. Vaughn may be right," Paolo said. "Time's wasting. With your permission, Captain, there was what looked like a traffic sign or billboard a few kilometers toward the city. It might yield some information."

Shasti nodded and the mule sped off.

Shasti looked up at Vaughn. "Maybe they'll find something we can use to start translating."

Vaughn raised an eyebrow. "It will probably be an advertisement for beer."

"Well," she shrugged, "even that would be a start." In companionable silence, they walked about the unpacking spacers and the shuttles.

6

Misa Tanaka drew in a deep breath. The sun was still high, and a weather front had moved in and cleared the air since their landing yesterday. The temperature had reached jacket weather and most of the expedition shed bulky spacesuits for more comfortable garb.

A familiar tread sounded behind her. She turned to see Mikhail Vaughn striding up. Huge as he was, he could have moved silently had it been on his mind. His face wore its recent grim expression. Rainhell had become an obsession with him, encouraged by some off again/on again signs from the Engineered woman. Though she could not share it with him, Misa's heart was heavy from watching the two dance their strange dance, a dance where sometimes they were not even conscious of each other. She'd safeguarded Vaughn from his earliest days in Denshi, and knew that buried in the powerful body was the makings of a good man.

At least, she thought, *as good a man as Denshi and the Engineered have ever produced. Poor boy, born among murderers and schemers. It's amazing he's as decent as he is.*

"Afternoon, sir," she said.

"Afternoon," he said. "When will you stop calling me sir?"

She smiled at him. "Sometime soon."

"The day is pleasant," he said, unzipping his jacket.

"Yes," she said. "Maybe things are looking up."

"Not for me." He sighed, a strange sound coming from so powerful a man. "She remains fascinated with the Terran, Romita. He seems to possess an ability with women that bypassed me."

"It's not an ability." he waved a hand. "It's skill. One I think he has practiced since his teens. It's all for show."

Vaughn shrugged. "Yet he has all that I want. How it galls me to see her with him." His big fists knotted unconsciously.

A small cart passed a hundred meters away. "Speak of the devil," Misa growled. "Looks like your rival is sneaking off in a mule."

Vaughn's hawk-like eyes fixed on the cart. "Alone, I see. Where could he be going?"

"There was something like posters and signs on one of the buildings near what we think was a gatepost. They discovered it last night, and he didn't have time to examine it before curfew. Rainhell wouldn't let anyone beyond the barrier wire after dark."

"Sensible," he said. "For all that we have seen no sign of life."

"Yeah," she said. "There's no survey scheduled for this afternoon. My guess is he's snuck off early on his own to take a look. He thinks all our security measures are mere paranoia."

"Then," Vaughn said slowly, "no one knows where he has gone off to. And he is alone."

Oh no, Misa thought. "Sir, that's not a good—"

He raised a hand. "Silence," he said. The look that slid over his face was one she had rarely seen and knew better than to argue with. "Go back to the camp. You did not see me. Mr. Romita and I are going to have a heart to heart. Perhaps I will even pull his out of his chest." Vaughn took off at what appeared to be an easy jog, but his big stride ate up ground.

"Mikhail, no," she whispered. "This won't work."

But he was already speeding off, running not much slower than the mule. Even had she chased him down, how could she restrain him? Vaughn, unlike most Engineered, had a sense of fair play and would normally consider Romita beneath his notice. But not now.

Frustrated and jealous, Vaughn could kill most men with a single blow. And with that blow he would end any chance he ever had with Rainhell. In an expedition under martial law, Romita's death might bring others, including Vaughn's.

There was only one thing to do and only one person who could avert disaster.

"Tanaka, to base." She hit her command mike. "Put me on discreet to Rainhell, ASAP."

A few seconds passed.

"Rainhell."

"Tanaka. Get in a mule by yourself and get over to the southwest corner of the perimeter as fast as you can. And for god's sake, hurry."

"What the hell—"

"Not on the air, not even on discreet. Guess, Rainhell. Employ all those Engineered smarts and goddamn well guess."

There was a brief pause. "On my way."

A minute later, Rainhell zipped up in a mule. She was the picture of controlled fury.

"Vaughn's gone after Romita. Down at the gatepost three klicks that way." Tanaka pointed. "He said talk, but it could get out of hand. You're the only one who could stop him if he decides on killing."

Rainhell floored the mule and pulled away. Tanaka waited a few seconds until the mule had peeled away around the rubble of a building, then sped off at her best pace, planning to keep out of Rainhell's sight. She hopped on a two-wheeled *Interceptor* and stood on the accelerator.

Rainhell was in no danger from Vaughn, she knew, but the reverse might not be true. *If Rainhell reaches for a gun while she's near Vaughn,* Tanaka thought, *I'll make sure it's the last bad choice she makes in this life.*

Shasti coaxed the mule to its best speed, cursing under her breath. "Another Pard," she muttered. "Just another damn killer." In minutes she reached the relatively intact structure that Paolo had called the gatehouse. She slammed the mule into park and leapt from the car. A few strides took her around a collapsed wall to where she heard the sounds of a struggle.

"Freeze," she yelled as she slipped around the wall coming upon the two men.

Vaughn was holding Paolo by the throat, his feet well clear of the ground. Blood ran from Paolo's mouth and his face was pale. Red marks showed where Vaughn's hand had cracked across his face. The big Engineered had been so intent on Romita that for once in his life he'd been taken by surprise. Guilt flashed into Vaughn's dark grim face. He started to speak, then stopped.

She looked at Vaughn. What emanated from her should have cloaked him in ice. "You won't touch him again."

Vaughn stared back at her. With a savage growl, he shoved Paolo away from him, spun on his heel, and stalked away. Within seconds, he disappeared amidst the ruins.

Shasti turned to Paolo. He had climbed to his feet, coughing, pale and literally shaken. He wiped blood from a split lip.

"Ciao, Bella," he rasped, "your timing was impeccable."

Shasti pulled a small hand-held regenerator from her medkit as she walked toward him.

"It's all right," he managed.

"Quiet," she responded, holding his chin in one hand as she played the device over his lower lip. The bleeding stopped in a few seconds and the swelling began to subside.

"What was that about?" she demanded.

"You," Paolo said, looking into her eyes. "We both want you. He figures to take me out of the running by roughing me up."

"Your strategy was to stand there and get slapped around?" said a bemused Shasti.

"No point in fighting that monster." Paolo shrugged. "He could kill five men like me without breaking a sweat. I'm a philologist; he's an assassin. Oh, if I thought he was seriously trying to hurt me, I'd do my best. He just wanted to scare me with what a powerful brute he is." Paolo smiled. "He doesn't know a damn thing about women."

"What do you mean?" Shasti asked, exasperated but curious.

"Who are you standing here with?" he said.

"So I am supposed to be impressed with this?" she said, replacing the regenerator in her pack. "Come on. Let's get back to the ship. I'll send someone to pick up your mule."

Misa watched the tableau end from behind a pile of rubble and some scraggly bushes. She let her breath out in a whoosh as Vaughn spun on his heel and stalked off. As she stood, she said softly, "You can come out now, Mr. Rigg."

Daniel Rigg materialized from inside a roofless ruin. "You have good ears."

"You were unlucky," Misa said. "Your boot scraped on something; otherwise I wouldn't have known you were there." She turned and gave him a frank look. "Not easy for a big man to move so quietly. I didn't hear a vehicle either."

"I was raised hunting with my dad, in Wyoming," Rigg said, walking forward casually. "And I was already out this way on a scout. Mmok spotted you leaving. He has standing orders to keep me posted on your movements."

"Damn Tinman," she said. "He must have hacked my discreet channel."

"It's all over?" Rigg whispered, gesturing to the where Shasti ministered to a flustered Paolo.

"For now," she said. "Thank God it wasn't worse."

"Why did you call for Rainhell?" he asked, looking down at her.

Misa shrugged. "She was the only one who could break them up without someone dying. Maybe. I wasn't sure."

"So you figured you would tag along in case Shasti threw down on your guy."

"I've raised that boy from a puppy. Be damned if I was going to let him get shot over some boy toy by a woman with no goddamn sense."

"Can't have you perforating my skipper," Rigg said. "Looks bad on my performance review."

"Humph," Misa said. "She was in no danger from Vaughn. He loves her, or thinks he does."

"Skipper's not fond of Olympian men," Rigg said, "particularly other Engineereds. Come on. Let's do a fade. They're heading for the mule."

"Not my fault if she's too dense to see the quality in Vaughn," Misa said as they walked back through the building Rigg had laired in. "If you ask me, that earthman is more of a threat to your skipper than Vaughn is. Honestly, what can she see in him?"

"You, a woman, are asking me, a man, why women make lousy choices about men? Besides, Paolo's not so bad."

Misa stepped around some debris and looked up at Rigg. "And if he was dating your sister?"

Rigg smiled. "I'd break his arm in two places, for starters."

A brief laugh escaped Misa. "Yeah, I thought so."

"Paolo's an okay guy around the guys," Rigg said. "Can't hold it against him that he likes the girls."

"Yeah," she scorned, "all girls, between sixteen and eighty, blind, crippled, and crazy."

"Well," Rigg said, ducking under an archway, "you'd better watch out then. He might set his cap for you next."

"Only if he wants it jammed up his ass," she said. "I'm not at an impressionable age. Boys don't do it for me."

"Pity about that," Rigg said as they walked down a ruined street of one-story buildings, heading for where she'd ditched the *Interceptor*. "I've heard a lot about the virtues of older women."

Misa laughed again but not unkindly. "Are you flirting with me, Mr. Rigg?"

"Am I so bad at it that you need confirmation?" He rubbed a hand over his solemn-looking face. Misa thought she detected a spark of mischief in the big man.

"A while ago you were willing to shoot me."

"Yeah," he said, "but I'd have felt bad about it."

"So," she raised an eyebrow, "do you always keep tabs on my movements?"

"Yep," Rigg said. He pointed to where she had ditched her bike. "You and all the other bad and dangerous on this expedition. I just enjoy it more when it's you."

Misa pulled up the *Interceptor*. She didn't start it but began pushing. On its frictionless wheels, it glided forward easily. "No need to race back. Plus I think it might be a good idea if we gave all the lovebirds some time. You never can tell what the Engineered will pick up on their special senses."

"Okay. Let me take it for you." Rigg walked the bike for her. They made their way up on a section of elevated roadway that headed in the direction of the camp. Once up there they walked on until they were in sight of the glimmering barrier wire of the camp. Tanaka sat on some concrete block; she patted a space beside her. Rigg dropped the kickstand on the bike and sat with her. Both looked toward the westering sun.

"Here we are," Misa said, putting her chin in her hands. "Sitting on the wreck of superhighway, on a nuked world, watching a red sun go down over a dead city. You sure know how to show a girl a good time."

Rigg unscrewed the top from his canteen and passed it to her. "Hey, in our trade this counts as quality time."

Misa sipped from the canteen, ignoring the plastic taste the water held.

"It's not just a job between you and Vaughn," Rigg said.

Misa looked at him for a few seconds. "No, it's not."

"Did you actually raise him?"

"Mostly I kept him from being murdered by other Engineered. But," she paused, "I saw something in him that wasn't in the others, an essential decency. He always wanted to be the knight, the hero from the stories. He wanted to be good even though there was scarcely any example of it on Olympia and especially under Pard. Jalgren Pard put that boy to killing at age thirteen. What the hell chance did he have?"

"He had you," Rigg said, sipping from the canteen. "You seem to have taught him some of what matters."

Misa shrugged. "One woman and not even related. No mother, father, brothers, or sisters, so little of humanity," and then, staring at the broken pavement under her feet, "and Dan, I'm no proper teacher. I'm as much of a murderer as any Denshi. God, the things I did serving in Pard's forces…"

They sat in silence for a while. Finally, Rigg said. "Your way of fighting wars was to have the powerful slug it out among themselves with assassins. I've seen humans blast whole cities full of other humans or other Confed species. Is that better?"

She shrugged. "Maybe each way holds its own special sin. Maybe we are just bound for different rings of Hell."

"Maybe," Rigg said. "Well, if that's the case, and it may well be, you'll just have to visit me and Rask over in our ring. There will be beer and a card party."

Misa laughed. "I might prefer champagne and a romantic sunset walk," she teased.

"Well," he said, standing, "there's no champagne, but we have a sunset."

Misa grinned up at the big man. "You're on."

Shasti and Paolo drove back in silence, looking at the odd, stunted growth of the planet, with its drifting red and brown sands. Over their heads the red-tinged sky was darkening to purple. *Storm clouds of all sorts are gathering,* Shasti thought. *How am I going to manage all this?*

They crested a hilltop overlooking the campsite. Shasti stopped the mule. "I have to think," she said in response to his questioning glance. She leaned back in her chair and shivered a little in the dropping temperature, studying the base.

Tivka had them well dug in. The delicate tracery of barrier wire glimmered in the gathering dusk. The safety element was on; otherwise the wires would be invisible. Paolo reached out and touched her arm. She drew it back, offended, and looked at him.

"Disappointed in me?" he asked.

"What are you talking about now?" she said.

"I guess I don't measure up against your Robert Fenaday," he said, looking up at her. "I imagine he'd have swung on the bastard."

"Then he'd have lost," Shasti said. "Robert is gifted from a lifetime of training, but he would stand little chance against Vaughn. Even I would have trouble with Vaughn, and pound-for-pound, I'm probably stronger and faster. Vaughn is *big*."

"Still," Paolo grimaced, "he'd have done it, and you think less of me for not."

She cocked her head at him, puzzled. "I've known Robert to back away from a fight, even run if he felt it wasn't worth it. True, if he was protecting someone, he'd attack anything. But for ego? No, he's too much of an adult for that. He used to tell me that to be worth fighting over, a thing needed to be worth killing over, and damn few things were worth killing over. Stop thinking of Robert as some sort of Three-D star, he's just a man."

"Good to know," said Paolo. "Maybe then I have some chance against him."

Shasti sighed in irritation. "Let's get back to camp."

"I'm enjoying our moonlit drive," he protested.

"There is no moon," she replied.

"Only the one that shines from your lovely face."

"This is just a form of insanity with you, isn't it?" she wondered.

"Love always is." Paolo smiled.

Inside her chest something felt funny, and she found her lips stretching into a small smile in response. She shook her head to hide it. "Let's go."

They drove down the ridgeline in the deepening purple twilight and a different type of quiet. Guards dropped the barrier wire for them. Shasti parked the mule and with a glare that discouraged questioners, escorted Paolo back to the camp. Since he shared a tent with a half-dozen others, she left him resting in her own.

"I need some time to myself," she said when he protested her leaving. "I've got to figure out what to do about Vaughn."

"Don't tangle with that monster over me," Paolo said, worry creasing his forehead. "I'll stay out of his way and I don't think he'll try anything with witnesses around."

Shasti felt momentary warmth at his concern for her. "It's not as simple as that." She walked out and headed back to the mules. Her situational awareness twinged as she drew near the collection of small vehicles and crab robots. She reached out mentally and touched a familiar metallic tang.

"I know you're there," she said.

"Not bad, Engineered," Mmok said. He came out of the shadows by the vehicle park. "I was just spending some down time with my steel brothers."

Shasti looked at the non-computerized mules, simple and sturdy. "Right now I might prefer their company myself."

"I picked up Tanaka's broadcast despite the discreet," he said. "It wasn't too hard to figure out what was going on. In case you were curious, Tanaka had you covered from a building nearby. Of course I had her and Vaughn covered as well.

"So, the boys are getting a little frisky competing over you?"

"Am I some prize," she wondered, "to be won in a game?"

The HCR that held Mmok's "soul" rocked gently with a rhythm. She stared at it, then realized it was laughing. The sight raised the hair on the back of her neck.

"Sorry," Mmok said. "Creeped you out again, did I?"

"Yes."

"Remember, I was once people and had a sense of humor."

"You're still people," she replied, even as she wondered about the metaphysics of it.

"Nice of you to say," Mmok returned. The HCR walked over to her, its monofilament hair lifting in the breeze. Mmok looked star-ward, and Shasti joined him in contemplating the heavens.

"It's hard for me to feel that way," he continued.

"Why?" Shasti asked. Questions on what made one human were central to her own struggles.

Mmok's HCR shoulders shrugged, but he kept his eyes on the night sky. "Oh, this stuff about the boys chest-butting over you. When I was a cyborg, I would have understood it, maybe even been a little jealous, wanting to be in on it. As a full man, I would have been.

"Now I don't have an endocrine system and beyond some little brain matter, no flesh at all. It just seems foolish and childish behavior."

"It is foolish and childish behavior," she snapped.

"I wouldn't have agreed back when I had a penis."

Shasti snorted a laugh. "Men, you really are your penis, aren't you? It's not the end all and be all."

"Says someone who never had one," he returned. Then after a moment, "Hey that's true, isn't it? I mean, I know they monkeyed with your genes—"

"Mmok!" she yelled, turning.

But the HCR was already meters away and accelerating, leaving behind only a trail of mocking laughter.

Shasti fumed for a few seconds. "Just because I'm bigger than average doesn't make me less feminine," she growled. As usual, Mmok managed to finger a sore spot. Her temper passed after a few moments and she found herself oddly relieved that Mmok wasn't entirely changed. She did not want to think of his acerbic personality entirely disappearing into the cool remoteness of machine logic. If it did—he would no longer be Mmok. *Of course,* she thought, *if he makes another crack about my having a penis, I'll kick his shiny metal ass into a low orbit.*

Misa finally found Vaughn far from the camp sitting on a pile of rubble that looked like a huge chair. She'd left Rigg back at the camp. The younger man would have liked to stay in her company, but she thought Vaughn might want to talk to her alone.

In his brooding posture he looked like some ancient king. *'Look on my works ye mighty and despair.'* But it was Vaughn who was in despair.

She waited in his view for nearly ten minutes before he spoke. "I should have listened to you, born woman. I should have listened. My grip on my temper slipped and I was going to kill him. Then there she was. I could see in her face what she thought. It was as if I could hear the words. Pard. You're just like Pard. Brute and killer. Just like Pard. And the worst of it is that she is right. I am just like him."

"No," she said.

He waved a hand. "Yes. I am the better man than Romita and I know it. Did I seek to prove it or let it reveal itself? No. I did the one thing that she could not forgive. I used force on the helpless. I would have killed him out of jealousy. She will never trust me again. Just like Pard."

She strode over, drawing almost face to face. "Damn it. You are not Pard. And don't tell *me* otherwise. I knew Pard as well as you. Do you think for a second that he'd have felt any remorse over a mistake? Never. He'd have killed Paolo and taken Rainhell."

A small smile lightened Vaughn's grim face. "Poor Misa, you never give up hoping that I will turn into a man you can be proud of."

"I am proud of you, Mikhail," she said, "and never more than now."

He stood slowly. "God alone knows why. In any event, my reason for being here is ended. I will return to the *Paladin* on the next launch window. I am sure we can trade something to Mandela for the return coordinates. We will head back to the Confederacy."

"Mikhail, I don't think it is as bad as that."

He shook his head. "You did not see her face. It is over."

***

Sharon Hafel studied the microwave emitter on *Sidhe's* main weapons board. From it she coordinated the ship's electronic warfare suite. "Ian," she called. The ship's gunner turned in his seat. "Come over and take a look at this."

Wardell leaned over her screen. "What's up?"

"Don't know. I've been running the usual scans. There's a shadow on the microwave recorder at irregular intervals. It could be anything: a little solar activity, irregular power fluctuation, anything. I don't like the fact that it's repeated, though."

"Can you pull up the scan?" he asked. She brought up a holo. "Hmmm," he said. "It barely registers."

"Yes, it's so low a regular ship's scanner wouldn't even pick it up. The only reason we do is because of the special scanners installed from when we had the experimental holo-camouflage from the Voit-Veru expedition. They left those on."

"Exec," Wardell called.

Mollica joined them at the scanner. "Yes?"

"Maybe nothing, maybe something, a few microwave emissions from the planet. Might be natural."

"Any source?"

"Not enough signal," Hafel said.

"What about interposing the sled between us and the planet?" Wardell said. "If someone's tracking us, they might up their signal."

Mollica nodded. "Mr. Nye. Move the sled Z minus 10,000 meters."

"Aye, ma'am." The short stout Asian manipulated his controls with a surprisingly delicate touch.

They watched the gray ingot shape of the sled slowly dip its nose as reaction jets fired.

All hell broke loose.

"Firing lock," Hafel yelled as all her boards lit up, "massive electronic scanning."

A sword of light leapt up from the planet's northern latitudes and slashed into the sled. The powerful beam penetrated instantly. Fluids and gas vaporized into space and bits of hull tumbled free as the 9,000-ton sled shuddered.

"Alarm!" Mollica ordered, leaping back to her chair. "Nye, full power ascent. Hafel, max power on ECM. Wardell, weapons online. Communications, warn the *Paladin*, then get me the captain."

Sidhe bucked as her engines awoke to desperate life. Below her, the sled vented stored fuel as the laser ripped compartments. A second beam reached out, but it visibly sputtered, as if its power source was intermittent and fading.

"Missiles coming up from the planet," Hafel said, "hundreds of them. ECM in full effect."

"All chain guns and secondaries up and locking. Preparing to commence fire as soon as they're in range," Wardell snapped. "My board shows the *Paladin* locking on as well.

"I've tracked it all back," he continued. "There's a buried starfort below us. A big one."

The flash of a giant laser lit up screens and portholes alike. Death whiffed by *Sidhe,* missing by mere meters. Then as abruptly, it sputtered out.

"Launch the ready-reaction fighter," Mollica said. "Then get *Space-fire Two* out there as fast as you can.

She turned. "Wardell, counter battery fire?"

"No, ma'am," he said. "No angle for the main gun. We can climb or use the main gun, not both. It's not likely to be effective on a hardened site like this anyway.

"Missiles in range of secondaries," he added. "Firing."

Mollica turned to Nye. "Put her in the red. We need altitude. Prepare to break orbit."

A flash appeared on the *Paladin*.

"A hit," Wardell said. "A slug from a mass accelerator I bet. Doesn't look like it penetrated her armor. She's firing."

"I can't raise the captain," Fitzgerald called from the communication station.

"There goes the sled," Wardell called.

Mollica watched the sled, without ECM or other defenses, draw an inordinate amount of the flock of missiles. Some detonated on the sled. Others were taken out by the fratricide of explosions.

On the main board, Wardell locked on the first of a larger, slower group of missiles and fired his forward 10cm laser. He was hoping that the larger missiles did not contain the payload he feared.

They did. On screen the perfect globe of a spaceborne nuclear blast filled the screen with harsh white light.

Shasti had gathered Mmok and Dan Rigg before summoning Vaughn to a quiet spot. The big Engineered walked up, trailed by a grim-looking Tanaka. To Shasti's surprise, Vaughn showed up unarmed. His face was closed and foreboding, but his hands hung loose and in plain sight. Tanaka was similarly weaponless. Shasti was suspicious of hidden weapons but decided to take it as the peace offering that it clearly was. They stood facing each other in a loose circle.

As Shasti opened her mouth to speak, a flash above them lit the night sky. She spun to face the source. Above them hung a glowing ball of gas, like the malign eye of such ancient god.

The others stared skyward, shading their eyes.

"Airburst," Mmok said. "five megatons or better. Pretty high up."

"Orbital?" Shasti demanded.

"Can't tell for sure. But it's high."

"*Sidhe*, come in," Shasti said, hitting her com and refusing to admit even to the possibility that her ship was gone.

Mmok shook his head, the monofilament hair rising in the breeze. "Everything is going to be ionized and screwed for hours. Even if they are still there, we won't be able to hear them."

"Telemetry?" Vaughn asked.

"Risky," Shasti said, not looking at him. "A tight beam might draw an anti-radiation missile from whoever attacked us."

She turned to Mmok. "Hook into the shuttle's automatic link. It'll show us what they saw before the blast."

He nodded and raced for the shuttle.

She finally turned to Rigg and Vaughn. "Get everyone ready to pull out. If the ships still exist, we need to make it possible for them to pick us up. I don't plan on homesteading on this rock."

Both big men nodded and raced off with Tanaka trailing Vaughn.

Overhead, another hellish globe burned into life.

Troopers and scientists raced about frantically loading supplies and equipment. Shasti stood with her senior officers on the flight deck of the *Pooka* trying to figure out what to do next. Though it had pained her, she included Vaughn in the group. She needed the Engineered and his people. He and Paolo stood on opposite sides of the shuttle's small flight deck, ignoring each other.

"This is what came down on the auto-feed before the atom blast cut off communications," Mmok said, from where he was jacked into the shuttle's communications system. "It's a fortress, a big one. I'm reading weapons fire from 75 kilometers of dispersed hardened sites. From the look of this thing, I'd say this was meant to stand off a starship-mounted airborne assault."

A data screen lit up in a front of Shasti, displaying multiple views of the landscape below *Sidhe* and *Paladin*. Computer artifacts popped up showing the hardened sites and possible weapon emplacements.

"It's mostly underground," Mmok added. "The large squares seem to be silos for missiles. Each one is surrounded by pillboxes and hardened bunkers set into the earth. They'd hold artillery, anti-tank, and anti-personnel weapons in case someone landed on the silos. They really poured the concrete and metal into this baby. I wouldn't want to assault this fucker, God."

"We may have to," Shasti said. "We don't have the fuel to fly to the other side of the planet and climb out to the ships. If the ships are still alive, they'll have to come over to our position. We and they would be sitting ducks."

"And what do you think you would be attacking on this base?" Mmok said.

"I'm betting there's no one there," Shasti said. "That plateau may not have been covered by the northern glaciers, but why would anyone be living there? From all the evidence we have seen, this world's been dead for a thousand years. We haven't seen anything more than lichens and some small bird-like creatures and rodents."

"So," Vaughn said, "you think we are attacked by automatics?" The big Engineered was all professional.

"Good automatics," Mmok said, "to wait a thousand years."

"But possible," Shasti replied. "Think of it. These people did not have interstellar flight, from what we can tell. But they knew of enemies that were dangerous enough for them to build such forts. There is probably another one on the other hemisphere. But there's a problem with forts, isn't there, Mr. Mmok?"

"Well, yeah. If you don't have any ships, then the bad guys always have the initiative. No ship can lift the power plant you can use for fort lasers, but all you have to do is lie out of range and motor down some asteroids or nukes. Won't do much to the fort. But it can do this." He gestured at the devastation outside their canopy. "You can keep the bad guys from landing, but they can still wreck the place."

"A thousand years ago," Shasti said, "some dying commander must have set automatics, hoping that Conchirri would eventually come into range for a landing and that revenge would come then, even if he would not live to see it. Maybe that's why there are no Conchirri hives on world. Perhaps they weren't able to force a landing."

"The volume of fire the fort put out is only a fraction of what I would expect." Vaughn rubbed his chin with a big hand. "Much of it must have failed in the interim. Otherwise, our ships would have been vaporized in the first salvo. Assuming," he concluded, "that they weren't. We still have had no word."

"We don't know if that's EMP or jamming," Rigg said. "Or…"

"There's nothing to plan for if the ships are gone," Shasti said. "So we will assume one at least survives to rescue us.

"Mmok, what's your estimate of the fort's firepower?"

Mmok looked at her. "Back when I was people, I would be complaining about your unrealistic expectations. Fortunately, I am beyond that now."

"Right," she said. "Estimate."

"Based on what's we've seen and if their designs are anything like ours, not much, ten to twenty percent maybe. There are holes in that analysis you could push a starship through sideways."

"It's all we got." Rigg shrugged.

"If we can get into the fort," Mmok said, "we should be able to find the main computer and knock it out. That's going to be a lot safer than trying to knock out every surface sensor and weapon."

"Where would we force an entrance?" she demanded.

"More unreasonable expectations?" he said.

"You're the only supercomputer I've got. Supercompute, that's an order."

"Yes'm. My best wild ass guess would be this area here." Mmok gestured at a flattened area overgrown by scrub. "A penetrating microwave pulse showed that to be a sally port for AFVs."

"Huh?" Paolo said.

"Tanks," Rigg answered.

"Reinforced permacrete under the dirt," Mmok continued. "It's not directly above where the base HQ should be if they use standard logic in the design. But it's less covered by interlocking fields of fire. Also, it's near that range of low, rounded mountains." He gestured at the holo. "We can approach from that angle and be safe from direct fire from the fort, pop over the hills, and do a combat drop on sally port. Nothing to it."

"Lovely," Rigg said. "Just f-ing lovely."

"Glad I don't have an ass to get shot off anymore." Mmok crossed his arms with a smug attitude.

"See any nuclear battery stores open around here, Tinman?" Rigg asked.

"Good point," Mmok said.

"Let's go," Shasti said. "It won't get any easier with time."

7

The shuttles climbed out from the ruined city and turned north. Knowing there were at least some active mechanisms on Lantrim II, the pilots kept to treetop height with ECM ready and turrets manned.

Vaughn had asked to take the lead. "My *Wolverine Mk IV* shuttle is superior to both your *Dakota* and your *Mk I*. I have additional weapons and better ECM."

Shasti had looked at him coolly. "Very well," she'd said. "You first, then I'll land. Rigg will bring up the rear with *Dagda*. You will lay down suppressing fire, while we land Mmok and his robots to secure an LZ."

"As you wish," he said. For a second, he had hesitated and then turned his back and headed to his ship. Minutes later, they had taken to the air.

That was hours ago with no word from the starships since. The fort ahead of them had ceased fire, though Shasti had no way of telling if the base was exhausted, if the ships were destroyed, or merely fled.

"Coming up on the mountain range before the starfort," the pilot told her.

Shasti hit the intercom. "Combat drop in sixty seconds. Everyone stand ready."

The small fleet popped up over the range of low, rounded hills and plunged toward the earth, spitting flares, chaff pods, and small emitters.

They needed them all. From the featureless plain of the starfort, tracer rounds rose lazily toward them. Smoke trails spiraled as missiles lifted off. It seemed the fort was not dead yet.

"Crap," the pilot yelled as *Pooka* slewed around. "My goddamn watch won't work two years out of warranty and here I am dodging thousand-year-old weapons."

The hull rang as something bounced off. *Pooka* dropped with sickening speed. Above them Shasti could see Vaughn's shuttle firing furiously. With a savage burst of deceleration, *Pooka* was down and the hatches popped open. Soldiers and robots raced out. The civilian scientists huddled aboard except for the medical officers, who, armored like the soldiers, plunged through the hatches.

Shasti ran for thirty meters and hit the ground. It was as cold and unyielding as the bitter wind blowing over them. She could hear explosions and see flashes above them.

Mmok joined her. He held a 10mm triple-auto, the same weapon Shasti preferred.

"Sitrep," she demanded. Overhead, *Dagda* was coming down, and Vaughn's *Duelist* was still firing and dropping flares. A heat-seeker turned from the big, battle-gray shuttle and exploded on a flare. Shrapnel fell around them.

Shasti saw dirt clods fly as crab robots raced to form a perimeter around the humans who lay in such cover as they could find on the plain. Some huddled behind the large, aptly named crabs.

"Not much ground fire." Mmok crouched alongside her. "There's a lot of emplacements with nothing coming out of them. If there are mines, they ain't working." Something stuttered in the distance. A second later, a dull boom sounded. "Scratch one bunker," Mmok said. "Got a damaged crab-robot though."

A missile corkscrewed up from nearby; it didn't seem to be

tracking anything. Mmok hit it with his tri-auto, and it broke up without exploding.

"The robots report that fire is slackening all over," Mmok added.

"I had hoped for this," she said. "No matter how good their machinery is, it's been unmaintained for a millennium."

Duelist ceased firing for lack of targets and settled in to land. The last of the ancient installation's working guns seemed to have failed. More troops spilled out from Vaughn's shuttle.

"Let's get on to that sally port," Shasti said. Mmok nodded and relayed her order. Shasti waved to the landing force troops nearest her. They began making rushes from cover to cover. Mmok kept the crab robots well ahead. The company of soldiers from the three shuttles formed an arc behind them, with Shasti in the center, Vaughn to the right, and Rigg on the left.

They reached the sally port without incident. Shasti's sharp eyes picked out the artificial outlines of the entrance, even under a millennium of debris and overgrowth. Mmok confirmed it.

Dan Rigg and Vaughn joined them in the fold of earth a hundred meters from the underground entranceway.

Rigg studied it. "Not used to seeing them so buried, but that should be an entrance capable of taking two main battle tanks at once. There would be smaller sally ports around the main one for infantry or small vehicles. Guys, it has got to be covered by live installations. They would have been concentrated here. We go up there, we get shot at."

"We could have the shuttles high angle some fire, guide it in with laser designators, then rush with the robots," Vaughn said.

"Not bad," Mmok said.

"Agreed." Rigg nodded. "Never send a man where you can send a bullet."

"Do it," Shasti said.

"I'll designate," Mmok said. "I've got a built-in laser designator in my right eye."

They relayed orders to the troops and shuttles.

Mmok popped his head up and triggered his laser. The weak beam was invisible but served to guide a volley of missiles and high-angle chain-gun fire onto the site. Dirt and rock erupted. The crab robots raced forward.

At first it seemed that Rigg had been too pessimistic. Then Mmok's head snapped back, a metal slug bouncing off it. "Motherfucker," Mmok yelled, tumbling back among them.

Shasti and the others fired at the flashes from one side of the sally port. "Mmok, are you all right?"

The HCR body had sprung up almost instantly. "Other than being royally pissed off, I'm fine." He picked up his weapon and joined them in firing on the emplacements.

A crab robot stopped moving and began to smoke as an AP round found a vulnerable spot.

"Medic," a voice called on the net. "Man down."

Mmok popped his head up again. "Redirecting fire."

A blast shook the ground.

"Ah." Mmok waved a fist in glee. "Secondaries, I love it."

"Cease fire," Shasti ordered.

"Let the robbies do it," Mmok warned as she peered over the rock she'd taken cover behind. "Something might still be active." The crab robots swarmed over the sally port and began digging with their manipulators.

"Casualties?" Shasti asked.

"Two," Rigg reported. "Both shrapnel wounds. Doc says she can handle them."

After ten minutes of digging, rooting and firing, the crab robots secured the entranceway and the company moved into the darkness of the tunnels. Pincers, lasers and a few shaped-charges made short work of the heavy alloy doors. Scouts shone red torches in to keep their low light vision intact and followed the robots in.

"Look." Rigg pointed. Just inside the armored hatchways lay two fearsome tracked vehicles. Thirty meters long and camouflaged in gray and green from when the planet's biosphere had supported more vegetation, they looked as formidable as Confederate *Dragon* tanks.

"No indication of chemical or biological agents. No electronic activity," Mmok confirmed. "These vehicles were meant to be manned. I'm glad of that. We don't have the firepower to deal with these."

Behind the two behemoths were lesser vehicles, hovercraft, and small weapons-carriers. They checked the machines for bones, but found only whirling dust motes kicked up by their passage that reflected their lights and quiet. Air stirred about them, and a breeze created by the blasted opening behind them brought up air from the depths, cold and tinged with dankness.

An ASAT sneezed the sound made everyone but Shasti and Vaughn jump. Embarrassed laughter followed.

They stalked forward, spreading out as far as they could in the broad hallway behind the tanks. Crab robots moved first, followed by a mix of Rigg's ranger-trained ASATs and a half-dozen of Vaughn's special security people, all easily identifiable by how much they bulked over the rest of the landing force. Behind this first screen, Shasti, Mmok, and Rigg pressed on. Vaughn and Tanaka joined them.

The interior of the giant fortress proved to be a maze of tunnels and levels. From the city they had learned the natives of Lantrim II had been bipedal and about the size of humans, so the levels were not hard to navigate. Indeed it had a familiar utilitarian look common to such places. Only on the stairs, with their long, narrow run and rise, was the alienness more obvious. Ladders too betrayed a strangeness. From the interval between the rungs, the denizens of Lantrim II must have been limber.

Overall lay a sense of stillness, as if there had never been life in this place of whirling dust motes and red lights. They trudged on, changing levels.

"Remember the Enshari underground cities," Mmok said to Shasti.

"All too well," she replied. "All too bloody well."

"They were prettier than this," Rigg said. "People lived and worked there. This is a hole to kill from."

"Now who's the frustrated novelist?" Rask added. The apish Morok appeared in front of them. "Rangers report the tunnels ahead seem to be converging on a single point. They think it's the command center."

"Excellent," Shasti said. "Let's go."

They reached a wide spiraling ramp, large enough to allow a company of men to walk side by side down its pebbled, green surface.

"Captain," Rigg said. "I'm thinking that we are right above the command center. I'd recommend against taking our whole force into a confined space. These walls aren't like regular buildings. Our armor-piercing ammo is likely to generate a lot of ricochets. My thinking is to take the rangers, the Denshi specials, and a half-dozen of the robots only. Have the rest hold up here in reserve."

"Makes sense," Shasti said, standing.

"No need for you to go," Rigg added.

She grinned. "Thanks, Daniel. I'm not the lead from the rear type." *And,* she thought, *the sad truth also is that I was made for this sort of thing. Literally made to enjoy it.* Adrenaline sang in her ears, and much as she loved her ship and the freedom it represented, Shasti found the old routine of stalking and hunting…exhilarating.

Rask shook his head sadly. "You'll never see retirement that way."

"Mmok," Shasti said, "have the crabs go over just to pincers and mask any fire with their bodies. We can't afford 30mm ricochets unless they are firing into middle or long distance."

"Check and set. I've got them in close-in, anti-personnel mode."

They moved out onto the ramp. Somewhat to Shasti's surprise, she saw Vaughn himself leading his group of six. *At least in that respect he's not like Pard,* she thought. Taking point was never Pard's style. Vaughn noted her regard and gave her an enigmatic look. She turned away.

Four of the crab robots led. Their articulated legs were covered in soundproofing material, but they still made an unpleasant skittering noise as their six legs tapped on the green surface of the ramp. The dark-gray robots would have been invisible save for the red battle torches that projected from their armored hulls. Their long guns were retracted, and each held out a formidable set of pincers on articulated arms. Behind them came Mmok holding his long, 10mm tri-auto. Shasti was flanked on the right by rangers and on the left by Denshi. Two more crabs brought up the rear.

Down they spiraled, five levels until they came to a flat area before a large door set on massive hinges, hanging half-open. Passages to the left and right of them were choked with boxes, crates and debris and they could not see far down them. Mmok and his machines closed in on the entranceway. Rigg and Rask moved out to the right.

As they passed a paused crab robot, a long, pantherish form leapt from behind the wall of crates and rubbish with an explosive snarl. It lunged over the unmoving crab and crashed into Dan and Rask before anyone could fire. Both went down in a shouting tangle of clawed limbs and fury.

Shasti didn't have time to wonder why the crab robot hadn't protected them. Knowing she couldn't fire for fear of hitting her men, she instantly dropped her carbine and snatched out her long-bladed knife, leaping headlong in the same move. She landed on the creature, which looked something like a cross between a black jaguar and lizard, as it seized Rask's armored forearm in its jaws. The Morok yelled and clawed for his own knife. Shasti plunged her blade in to the hilt. The creature bucked under her, emitting an ear-blasting shriek and dropping Rask. Shasti's knife bound in the twisting body and she could not pull it free. She wrapped her right arm around one clawed forearm and braced her other arm against the lizard's neck so it could not arch and bite her.

They rolled and tumbled. The creature's other paw drew back to strike at her face and was seized by Vaughn's powerful arm. With a roar, he slammed his fist against the narrow head, then duplicated her position. They braced on each side of it, each tying up a foreleg and its neck.

It tumbled again, trying to shake them free. Powerful though its frenzied efforts were, the Engineered humans clung stubbornly.

"Pull it upright," Shasti yelled. Both strained every muscle and brought the two-meter long, panther-lizard upright. Mmok raced in, leaping straight onto the lizard's chest. He wrapped his legs around it and grabbed its snout in both hands. A powerful twist was rewarded with a crack, and the monster went lifeless in their grip. They all leaped off as it dropped to the ground.

Even Shasti was panting from the effort. "Dan, Rask—" she managed.

"Okay," Rigg said. A thin rill of blood trickled down his face from where he'd been thrown to the rough flooring.

"Yeah," Rask said, holding his forearm. "May have a busted forearm bone."

Shasti looked at Vaughn.

"I'm uninjured," he said, reaching down and pulling her knife free of the limp body with an effort. He passed it to her.

Tanaka ran up to him. "Mikhail, are you all right?"

He grinned at her and stretched powerful arms. "Much better. Less tension."

"God damn son-of-a-bitch, bastard," Mmok cursed monotonously, kicking the fallen creature.

"Mmok," she demanded. "Why didn't the crab robot stop it?"

Mmok was silent for a few seconds. Shasti almost restated the question then realized there was no way the machine hadn't heard her.

"Fire me, Skipper," Mmok said, his voice gone toneless and mechanical. "Replace me with a toaster or something useful."

She walked up to him and stood by his side, looking down at the creature. Her shoulder touched the machine man's. "Talk to me."

"I'm a stupid tin can."

"I'm still listening."

"You said set the crabs to anti-personnel. I got machine literal on you, too much thinking like a computer. I set them only to react to bipedal weapon-bearing threats. Stupid."

"A mistake," she said. "How reassuringly human."

The machine man turned to look up at her. She couldn't read anything in its voice. "No excuse, ma'am. I fucked it up good and proper and almost lost us two of the best men I know."

"Okay," she said. "Don't do it again. If you feel that you are losing perspective, ask questions."

"I deserve a bigger chewing out than that, ma'am."

"I'll schedule some time for it when we get back to the ship."

Rigg and Rask walked up.

"Forget it, man," Rigg said.

Mmok looked at Rask.

"You've saved my ass a bunch," Rask said. "You're still in the plus column with me. How about we drive over it to the next thing?"

"Won't happen again," Mmok said.

"Wasn't worried," Rask replied.

Dr. Mourner and an ASAT medic joined them. Mourner, pushing past Shasti and Vaughn, quickly gave Rigg and Rask a professional work-over and first aid.

"How are the casualties topside?" Shasti asked, surprised to see Mourner.

"Patched and resting comfortably," Mourner returned in a tone that suggested Shasti was foolish for having asked.

"When you are done," Shasti said, gesturing at the dead lizard "tell me what you make of our friend here?"

"Splint and numb this," Mourner said to the medic after running a scanner over Rask's forearm. She stood up and walked over, looking at the creature from a respectful distance for a few seconds. "I'm not a xenobiologist," she said, "but there's some obvious stuff: no opposable digits, small braincase. This isn't people and never was if that is what you are worried about. It's an animal."

"One of a thousand things I'm worried about," Shasti replied, rubbing her upper arm where the muscle was somewhat strained after wrestling with the lizard. "What else?"

Mourner pulled out her instruments but hesitated.

Mmok put a steel foot on the animal. "When I kill 'em, they stay dead."

Mourner ran a sensor and poked and prodded for a few minutes. "It resembles a Terran lizard. I think it's cold-blooded. That would match up with the rest of what it tells me."

"Which is?" Vaughn prompted.

"Something this big needs to eat big," Mourner said, standing and wiping her hands. "If it was warm-blooded, it would have to eat a lot more often. So it's cold-blooded and probably not that active. It didn't hesitate before attacking all of you, right?"

"Damn, right," Rask chimed from where the medic was splinting his forearm.

"That tells me that it's probably an apex predator, top of, or near the top of, the food chain. It can't afford to pass up a meal and it didn't think there was anything down here that could outfight it. A smart animal, however, would have bided its time rather than attack so many big creatures it didn't recognize. It's just teeth and a belly."

"Any thoughts on how common?" Shasti asked.

"Hard to say. This fort's been abandoned long enough to develop its own ecology and who knows what has bored or crawled in. I doubt that there are many, even a low volume predator is going to need a fairly large hunting territory to maintain itself. Not common is my guess."

"Good," Rigg said. "One was plenty."

Mmok turned to Shasti. "Permission to take point, ma'am."

She nodded.

Mmok and the other machines cautiously approached the door. Then after a quick peer-in by Mmok, they rushed through with a clatter of mechanical limbs. Shasti and the others waited, staring at the dark hallways, ears and eyes straining for unknown dangers.

"All clear," Mmok called from within.

They entered a huge amphitheater space of what seemed to be the main control center. It was nearly an acre of consoles and tall slender chairs. Over it hung screens of one sort or another, most were dark and quiet. On the largest one, a small section was lit with blocky orange script in an unknown language. The screen itself looked like a long-range targeting scanner. It was so dim and covered with dust they couldn't make out anything useful on it. In the distance toward the center, more consoles glowed with weak telltales.

"Combat Information Center," Rigg confirmed. "Looks like the big one under Cheyenne Mountain on Earth."

Mmok gestured. "That center section there would be where the command staff sat. I can see from here that there's a ton of extra equipment piled around. It has the look of something added later."

"The fail-safe trigger," Vaughn growled. He started forward, but Shasti put a hand on his arm.

"Mmok. Check it out."

The robots faded into the distance, raising so much dust that Shasti and the others closed their facemasks.

A gleam of silvery reflection caught Shasti's attention. She walked over to a side tunnel, her carbine ready. She heard Vaughn's familiar tread behind her along with his shadow, Tanaka. Their torches played on a thick trail of reflective slime. It started above their heads as if something had hung there and then slid down the wall to the floor. The red light reflected off the trail, turning it the color of fresh blood, as it bent out of sight with the turning of the corridor. Shasti looked at the thick ropy slime and knew better than to touch it. It looked both unclean and unhealthy.

Next to her, Vaughn raised his hand to his facemask, working his visor. He suddenly cursed and snapped the small port in the mask closed. "Nothing," he coughed, "should smell that bad and be alive."

"What else haunts these tunnels, I wonder?" Shasti said. "Is this connected with our friend outside? Somehow, I feel no. Predator? Prey?"

"Something would have to have an iron stomach and no sense of smell to eat whatever left that trail," Vaughn added.

Shasti refused to turn her back on the foul trail. "Vaughn, place two of your men here, with a flame-thrower. I want this flank covered. Warn everyone that there is something else down here too."

He nodded. "Tanaka."

The Asian woman silently slipped away.

Rigg appeared. "Mmok says it's clear to the command dais. No traps."

The three made their way to the center dais. Shasti looked for bodies, bones, any sign of the previous occupants. But they did not seem to have died there. Or if they had, something had removed the bodies. She thought of the creature that might have left the slime trail and shuddered.

Mmok stood amid a maze of boxes and cables. On a few, lights still glowed. She heard a sound that might be fans, some still-functioning computer trying to shed heat.

"This is it," Mmok said, "the automatic firing point for the attack on our ships. From the dust level I would say it was done hundreds of years ago." He pointed at the apex of a horseshoe-shaped console ten meters across.

"What do you want?" Rigg asked. "Ten pounds of C-8A ought to blow everything to hell."

"Tsk-tsk," Mmok replied. "No need to be unsubtle. Me and the robbies will snip and clip, physically and electronically. Might be stuff here we want to study later." He turned to Shasti. "With your permission?"

She nodded.

Mmok and the crab robots moved among the ancient machinery, and for all his talk of subtlety, it was smash and cut. Lights flickered and once a voice sounded over their heads, a few words in a booming, rolling tongue. They froze but the message was not repeated and nothing threatened.

Mmok cut a last cable and the few lights operating in the room faded as did the sound of the lone fan. "Done," he said.

"Good," Shasti said. "We can head for the surface and see if we can contact the ships."

"Wait one," Mmok said. "Maybe not done. I am picking up some small emanation of a power source on my own sensors."

"Where?" Rigg demanded.

"Let me link up with some of the crabs and triangulate." Mmok went silent and still for a while. "My best guess is about one-thousand meters on seventy-three degrees and about another fifty meters deeper."

"Form up and let's move," Shasti said. "Mmok, leave a crab robot with the men watching that corridor back there."

"Trouble?"

"Maybe. Something icky that way went."

"Got it."

A sound of tapping feet drew her attention. Dr. Mourner showed up, trailed by Rask, now wearing a sling. The Morok had given his carbine to someone and carried a heavy auto-pistol. To Shasti's surprise, Paolo was with him. He too, carried a carbine and greeted her with a grin and wink.

"Let's take everyone else and go," Shasti said. "Our friends might have created a backup in case this installation was taken out. Rask, you guard the good doctors here."

They moved out across the acre-wide room, guns covering the dark spots beyond the reach of their lanterns. Shasti was glad that Mmok did not lead them to the noisome corridor with its trail of evil-looking slime. No ropy trails disgraced this hallway. Ten minutes brought them to another huge, valved door, only this one was tightly shut.

"I'm picking up an EM radiation source on the other side of this door," Mmok announced. The HCR moved closer to the massive portal.

"Interesting," Shasti said, flicking back a strand of night-black hair. Behind her Dan Rigg's arm snapped up in a series of abrupt gestures that sent ASATs scattering to positions of cover. Half covered the portal, and the others scanned the maze of empty dark hallways and rooms. Rask moved up behind Rigg; his pistol and red eyes never left the portal. Vaughn disdained cover and Tanaka perforce stood near him, but the dozen Denshi followed the ASATs.

Paolo started toward the door but checked at a quick gesture from Shasti. "Leave it to Mmok. It could be dangerous." Paolo looked like he might argue, but a glance at her set expression dissuaded him.

Mmok stood before the massive greenish metal entranceway, outlined in the lights of the dozens of battle-lanterns scanning the mechanism.

"Can you open it?" she asked.

"Can try," Mmok said, moving closer to the door and extending a hand. The HCR's metal forefinger split and monofilaments waved out of it, playing over what seemed to be the lock mechanism. Meanwhile Mmok's metal body rocked back and forth, and an odd sound came from him. Shasti realized that he was humming; it made her skin crawl. "Binary, binary," Mmok sing-songed, "one-oh, one-oh, oh-one, one-oh, and so on and so forth. Talk to Poppa, little lock."

"Hey," Rask said, "he isn't having sex with that thing? Is he?"

"Rask," Rigg growled.

Mmok ignored the comment and continued to work. "I used to bring a can opener," he sang, "and now I are one."

Suddenly there was clunking, crunching sound of long-unused machinery. Air hissed around the door seal.

"It's opening," Mmok said, backing quickly. "Hope this was a good idea."

The bronze valve slid open. A few electronic telltales broke the darkness beyond it. These disappeared as their battle lanterns cast a ghastly red light about. Even the lanterns didn't penetrate the far areas.

"That's a medical center," Mourner said. She darted forward past Shasti, heading for the room. Shasti grabbed the incautious doctor by the shoulder, jerking her to a halt.

"Mmok," Shasti ordered, "check for booby-traps."

Mourner glared up at Shasti but said nothing.

The HCR moved up to the doorway and scanned the area.

"It's clearly a medical center," Mourner said.

"Could be," Rigg said. "It does look a lot like the sickbay on the *Sidhe*, but this is all alien stuff, Doc."

"Form follows function," Mourner insisted. "Those are beds, auto-claves, med-scanners. It looks like a ward to me."

"Yep," Mmok said, the tone of his voice changing. "It's a ward alright. Looks like these guys never paid their medical bills. Some of those beds are occupied. It's safe to enter, Doc, but I'd say we are a few hundred years too late to help."

"Any reaction from that power source?" Shasti asked.

"No," Mmok said.

"Okay, wedge that door with some of those metal pieces there." She gestured toward a pile of steel just outside the immense valve. "Drs. Mourner, Romita, Mr. Vaughn, come with me. Mmok, you lead. Everyone else keep an eye out on your own front."

Mmok quickly wedged the door and preceded them into the cavernous space. They shone their lanterns over the nearest shrouded bed: other nondescript piles of bones and skulls lay about the floor. These they carefully avoided. Mourner reached the bed and put a hand out for the sheet, then glanced back at Shasti, who nodded. Slowly she pulled the dust-covered cloth back. It seemed to stick a little, then pulled free, swirling up motes into the red of their lanterns.

The corpse revealed was mummified, a parchment of skin stretched over slender bones.

"Looks human," Vaughn said.

"Not very," Mourner said absently, her eyes devouring the evidence of the new species. "The skeletal structure looks more Denleni with the extra joints. Skull is similar but certainly not Homo sapiens. No big incisors like Moroks or Okarans and certainly not anything as unusual as Voit-Veru. These people had two arms, two legs, no tail, and one head. The spine," she said, rummaging through the bones with disquieting enthusiasm, "looks more like a cat's, for all they seem to have been bipedal."

"Mmok," Shasti said, "find that power source." The HCR nodded, walking confidently into the darkness beyond their lights.

Shasti looked at the disarranged corpse that Mourner was studying. *I have spent too much of my life among sights like this*, she thought, *too much. God knows what I would be if I had some other life than this.*

"Captain," Mmok's mechanical voice called from the darkness. She leveled her weapon in a practiced move and walked forward, other thoughts shelved. Rigg and Vaughn and Rask followed her.

They found Mmok standing over a large sealed container of some clear material, yet thick enough to distort the contents. Piles of machinery with an ad hoc look to them surrounded it and a half dozen large cables led to it. Inside, she could see a body, not gone to bone as had the others, but slender and with variegated gray skin and pale silver hair. From what she could see there was a feminine delicacy to the features, though any clues as to gender, if it had any, lay concealed under a light silver cloth.

"A well-preserved corpse?" Rigg asked.

"This is the source of the power," Mmok said.

"We cannot be this lucky," Vaughn said.

"Get Mourner," Shasti said. Vaughn nodded. In seconds, he returned with the doctor.

"Oh my sweet God," Mourner said, "a cold sleep chamber." She peered in. "It's either the best-preserved corpse I have ever seen, or we have a sleeper. God," she said, almost hopping up and down in excitement. "I need a ton of equipment from the ship. No, wait. Mr. Mmok, you're a supercomputer."

"And a hell of a good one," he said, striking a modest pose.

"Spectral analysis," she said. Mourner began rapping out one technical detail after another, all of which Mmok seemed able to handle with his built-in equipment. Finally Mourner turned to Shasti.

"Whatever it is, it's alive," Mourner said.

"The tenth species," Rigg murmured, staring at the spindly alien.

"Galaxy is getting kind of crowded," Rask replied, "but on the other hand, the odds of your getting a date may have improved. I think it's female."

Rigg snorted in a mixture of amusement and irritation.

"Suspended animation," Shasti mused. "I've never heard of it going for so long."

"It used to," Mourner said, "in the early pre-hyperdrive days. Even after hyperdrive there were some trips that required cold sleep. Ships were small, people went stir-crazy. I studied it during my residency."

Shasti looked at her. "Do you think you could revive her?"

Mourner remained quiet for a few moments. "Normally I would say no. Researchers might spend a decade before altering a setting. She, if it is a she, is the last of her kind.

"But the circumstances aren't normal. We are way beyond our own borders and we don't know when, or even if, we'll ever get back to Confed space. It will be years before a properly prepared research expedition could get back here.

"This installation was jury-rigged to some degree and could fail any second. If we do leave her here, we might return to find only bones."

"There's another concern," Mmok said. "The reason for the expedition is to gather intelligence on the Makers and the Conchirri. This is a prime intelligence source."

"It's also a person," Shasti said.

"It's taking a big risk either way," Mourner added. "I don't know which is more hazardous—revival or waiting years for the proper equipment."

"Maybe I can answer that," Mmok said, advancing on the machinery, finger probes out. Before anyone could speak, he inserted the filament probes into the alien mechanism. "Give me a few hours," Mmok said. "I'm running a kind of diagnostic—I learned some of the language talking to the lock. It will take me some time to learn this more complicated stuff."

They occupied themselves with careful inspection of the medical center, as Mmok stood motionless over the cold sleep chamber, communing with it. Dr. Mourner did some forensic work on the corpses in the center.

"It's impossible to say for sure," she told Shasti, "but I think some of these people died from malnutrition. Some show indications of a CBO attack in what's left of the lung tissue. I'm guessing that our friend there was a doctor or tech attending the wounded. When the Conchirri or Makers hit this complex with penetrating missiles and CBO warheads, it wiped out most of the base, but there would be lots of hardened secure enclaves for weapons and medical.

"At some point the survivor back there must have given everyone a 'one way' needle shot to put them out of their misery. She finished rigging the cold sleep chamber in the hope of a ride to a better tomorrow."

"Practical," Shasti said. "There was only the one chamber."

Mourner shuddered. Shasti noted it, but did not comment. "Why was there a cold-sleep chamber in a med-center anyway?"

Mourner looked around. "This is a pretty good layout here, but it's an infirmary not a hospital. You might need to stabilize a badly injured patient for later transport. Before we had cell regenerators, we used to do similar things. Cold sleep has its perils too. After we developed regenerators, the risks of cold sleep as a temporary measure were too great.

"We might wake our friend there and have a babbling idiot on our hands. Not that we'll be able to understand what she has to say anyway."

"I wish we had Arpen at hand," Shasti said. "With her Denlenn empathy, she could be a great help."

"Something wrong with my bedside manner?" Mourner asked archly.

Shasti frowned at the tiny woman, unsure how to respond. "You are an excellent human doctor, but Arpen was an empath."

Mourner gave Shasti an exasperated look, which dissolved into a small laugh. "I was kidding, Shasti."

"Oh," Shasti replied, now more confused. A slight depression settled on her—something that had come to follow all the human interaction errors she made. *I'm never going to get this right,* she thought.

"I'm afraid I don't have much of a sense of humor," she said aloud.

Mourner laid a hand on Shasti's arm. Surprised, Shasti looked down at her.

"Yes, I know," Mourner said. "I shouldn't do that to you."

"It's all right, Doctor."

"You know," Mourner added, "after all this time you can call me by my first name. You can even shorten it to Sue if you like. Most people do."

Shasti looked down at her, a rare feeling of affection stealing through her. "Thanks, Sue."

Mmok straightened up. "I'm back."

"What's the situation?" Shasti asked.

"I'm amazed this stuff is still functioning," Mmok said. "Most of the main subsystems have failed. She's on her last set of backups and one or two of those look shaky. Her main power system is a trickle generator running off the solar regenerators on the surface, but their efficiency is down to only barely above the minimum power require-ments. My guess is at this low level the system might run for another few years, but if any main system fails now, she's out of backups. I think that the odds are we'd find bones here if we got back in a few years."

"That's it," Mourner said. "On those facts I'd have to say the patient's best chance is a revival here and now. I'd want to do as much research as we can here before we try anything though. I'll need every resource of the ship to make this work if it can."

"You'll have it," Shasti promised, "assuming the ships survived."

"I'll also need Paolo."

"I think," Shasti said, "I'd have to shoot him to keep him out of here."

Vaughn shifted as if he'd thought of saying something. Wisely, he kept his mouth shut.

"Let's get back to the surface," Shasti said, "and see if we have any ships to return to."

8

"I've got them!" the comtech called. "I've got both the ships."

"Thank God," Paolo said. He sagged back in the navigator's chair of the *Pooka*.

"Yes," Shasti said, trying not to show her relief. "I didn't fancy moving into the starfort permanently."

"I have Mr. Mandela, for you," the comtech said.

"On speaker," Shasti said.

"Captain Rainhell," Mandela's rich brown voice sounded. "Please report on your situation."

"We have eliminated the command post for the starfort with only minor casualties and damage. No fatalities. Our situation is stable and secure at the moment. Most of our personnel are below ground in the fort, safe from radiation. The big news is that we have discovered a cold sleep chamber with one of the natives still alive in it."

"How remarkable. Truly. I trust you have not disturbed the occupant."

Shasti suppressed a flash of annoyance. "Not as yet, but our investigations show that she, if it is a she, will not last much longer, certainly not long enough for an expedition to come from the

Confederacy. Now would you be so kind as to inform me of the status of my ship?"

"My apologies, Captain, of course you are concerned for your vessel. *Sidhe* is undamaged, though the sled was destroyed. *Paladin* took a glancing blow, no significant damage, but they were unlucky. A burst pipe caused one fatality and an injury."

She turned to Paolo, then thought better of it and waved to the comtech. "Get Vaughn. He will want to know."

"Aye, ma'am." The slender young man squeezed past her and down the shuttle ramp.

Paolo raised an eyebrow. "Perhaps I should get back to the chamber. There is a vast amount of work to be done."

"That might be best," she said.

Paolo left. Shasti turned back to the mike. "Please bring the ships into geo synchronous orbit over our position. Dr. Mourner has a long list of supplies she needs. Is she required up there to deal with casualties?"

"Dr. Fierman is coping with the situation."

"Then we will proceed with the recovery of the native. Here's what I want to do..."

They established a base on world. Characteristically, Mandela remained aboard the *Sidhe*. Vaughn returned from *Paladin* with an additional troop of Engineered security, after the funeral for his crewwoman. Rigg billeted the soldiers in the area around the entrance to the underground fort. They secured the side entrances to the tunnels with barrier wire. Guards scanned the passages, nervously watching for lizard-panthers and whatever had left the slime trail. Other scientists from Mandela's contingent started a tech survey of the base, always accompanied by fire teams of troopers.

Shasti noticed that Rigg seemed to find working with Vaughn's bodyguard, Misa Tanaka, enjoyable, inventing excuses to spend time with the attractive Asian woman. Tanaka returned the attention occasionally, clearly preferring to deal with him rather than with Shasti.

Shasti imagined that the Olympian had not forgotten how Shasti shot her three times in the sternum while fleeing Vaughn in the chase over Marathon's rooftops. Body armor had saved Tanaka, but one of her teammates had been less fortunate.

Carlos Perez and most of *Sidhe's* engineers shuttled down from the starship and spent the next three days assisting Mmok in tracking the circuitry of the ancient machinery, making sure there were no additional booby traps.

"The builders of the starfort were master engineers," Perez said, as he sat next to an open panel in the Command Center of the old fort, "though their technology was inferior to Confed. But what they built, they made well with amazing redundancies and strength. I'd like to have met these people."

"You may get that chance," Shasti told him.

"So I've heard." The engineer shook his head. "Incredible."

"I'm off to the med lab," Shasti said. "Keep me posted."

"Yes, Captain."

Shasti walked out through the huge, valved door to find Risky waiting for her. She enjoyed the dog's company in the silent halls of the fort. Those halls were now lined with work lights. It seemed to her, as she passed the pools of yellow light, that they constituted a tiny defiance of death, but the darkness and silence were only temporarily banished, biding their time in the assurance of their eventual victory.

Damn you, Robert, she thought. *It's all the time I spent with you that gives me these maudlin thoughts. I was made to be unafraid of the dark, of death and of loss, and I learned all of that from you. Engineered could never have produced an Edgar Allen Poe.*

She reached down and petted the animal, glad to feel his sturdy body. Risky whuffed, as if sensing her desire for reassurance. Shasti picked up the pace, and they entered the medical center, passing both Denshi and ASAT guards.

Dr. Mourner greeted her with a bare wave. The tiny surgeon looked tired, but she stooped down to pet Risky. The genetically enhanced shepherd wagged his tail slowly and carefully. He knew that the lab was no place for boisterous behavior.

"What's the situation?" Shasti said, looking over Mourner's shoulder at the glassed chamber beyond.

"My staff," Mourner said, rubbing her face with a hand, "is working with samples from the stasis chamber's occupant and studying the various medicines and fluids in the chamber itself. We've learned a great deal about the native's biology. The medicines in the chamber were clearly made for the task of inducing and ending the life-preserving cold sleep. As best I can tell, they're still stable and effective, having been stored in non-reactive gas. I don't dare experiment on the native, and analysis is a far cry from having any clinical expertise with the species."

Shasti looked up at a sound to see Paolo in the back of the stasis chamber, pouring over the wealth of written material found within.

"Has he even left the chamber?" Shasti asked.

Mourner smiled. "No. Mmok managed the machine language, but even with his supercomputer brain, the language of the natives is a harder challenge. The idea that a member of that native race might be only days from resurrection has been driving Paolo into a frenzy. With Mmok's help he's located what he called 'Rosettas' allowing him to leap from binary code to language. He hopes to be able to communicate with the sleeper."

"When will you be ready?" Shasti asked.

Mourner blew out a breath. "Fifteen years, if we had it."

"Which we don't," Shasti said.

"Then fifteen hours," she said, her tone grim. "I'm going to knock out for some hours of hard sleep. I want to be fresh when I try to save this patient."

"I'll want to be there," Shasti said.

Mourner nodded and headed back toward the lab her team had set up.

Shasti slipped into the chamber, Risky, moving quietly at her heels, to again give the cold, delicate features of the gray-skinned alien a hard look. The slender gray occupant lay immobile, and to all appearances quite dead. Then she turned to Paolo, perched at a makeshift desk staring at a number of computer screens, surrounded by piles of disarrayed paper.

"How goes it?" she asked.

Paolo started, apparently so deep in concentration that he hadn't heard her come in.

"Fascinating," he said. "Fascinating. A whole new universe to explore. It's wonderful."

"Yes," she said, smiling quizzically at his enthusiasm, "but can you read anything?"

"Oh yes," he said, leaping to his feet. Paolo grabbed a stack of papers, sending some flying. "Look at these!"

Risky gave a low growl, disapproving of the sudden movement near his mistress. She patted the dog to calm him.

"These symbols," he said, waving his hands and the papers, "mean 'medical center.'" These others must be the name of this fortress, though I grant that I have no idea how it would be pronounced. I've deciphered a thirty-letter alphabet and about five thousand words with Mmok's help."

He cast an excited glance toward the chamber where Mmok, the medical staff, and engineers labored over the cold-sleep chamber. "If only she will awaken."

Shasti felt a surprising twinge of jealousy; it seemed Paolo had returned to his first love. "They're doing their best," she said, hoping her face had betrayed nothing.

"Yes," Paolo fretted, "of course. It is just so hard to wait. Think of it, in just a few hours I might see a dead language burst into life before my very eyes."

"If she awakens," Shasti cautioned, "it will likely be in a confused and agitated state. There may even be brain damage."

Paolo looked suddenly crestfallen. Moved by some feeling, she added, "Let's hope for the best. Do you have a plan for communicating with her?"

"Yes," he said, nodding at the encouragement. "I have the most common symbols on flash cards. They won't make a grammar, certainly not a sentence, but it will show we are attempting to communicate. Then we will turn to the computers for phonetics, until we have a grammar, from there it will be a small step to a translator program."

He smiled broadly. "It's a philologist's dream, an undiscovered country."

Shasti, whose education included the classics of human literature, felt a moment's unease at the reference.

Fifteen hours later, they gathered around the stasis chamber and its frail occupant. Shasti had evacuated most of the engineer crew into the hallway on Mourner's recommendation. The doctor wanted to limit the strangeness the alien would awaken to. Mourner, Yamata, three med-techs, Paolo, and Shasti stood near the stasis chamber. Mmok and his robots were banished to the chamber door. Mourner judged them too frightening for her patient. Shasti made an exception for Vaughn. He stood farthest from the chamber, cloaked in shadows.

She had a reason for Vaughn's presence. She remembered another awakening. True, the slender alien had nothing in common with the immense pile of bone buried in the bowels of Barjan Deep on Enshar. The Prekak that Shasti and Fenaday had fought had looked the part of a monster, being both dead and alive and nearly thirty meters tall. The malevolent spirit that haunted those bones nearly wiped out an entire species. She wanted to take no chances, and so the master assassin stood ready in the shadows. He would strike only at her signal.

Everyone in the room was clad in isolation suits. "In evolutionary terms you're a million times closer to Risky," Mourner told Shasti, "than to our friend in the chamber. No Confederate species has ever transmitted a disease to another.

"Of course," Mourner gave an evil smile. "If is ever does happen, you're talking about a bug that would probably be 100% lethal and unstoppable by any medicine we know."

"Wonderful," Shasti said. "I'll happily stay sealed in my environment suit."

Mourner nodded at Yamata and the med team. The Asian doctor, spare of speech as usual, only nodded. She looked at Shasti.

"Proceed, Doctor," Shasti said.

The two physicians bent to their work. Machines hummed;

computer screens began displaying data as they interfaced with the alien mechanism. Perez had felt the alien machinery was too old to risk using for the resurrection and installed new components, using the originals only where he could not work around them. The med-techs began spouting figures and medical arcana. Shasti quickly lost track of what was going on.

Mourner took a deep breath, then she and Yamata slid back the lid on the stasis chamber, frosty air tumbling out of it. They quickly began giving a series of injections and then hooked up medical devices.

"Heat induction proceeding on both hearts," Yamata said, his voice flat and professional. "Up to twenty-seven."

"Good," Mourner replied. "See if you can raise it to thirty-six bilaterally. I think that's a right combo for initial blood pressure."

"Regenerator?" he asked.

"Too risky," said Mourner. "The tissue's been frozen for a long time, and there may be some variances from what we are used to. Later."

"Getting dual sinus rhythms," said one of the techs.

"And respiration," added another.

The nude, pallid body began to jerk and twitch.

Shasti glanced back at Vaughn. The assassin stood immobile at the edge of the light. Only his eyes moved, glimmering in a reflection of the surgical lamps. She turned back toward the chamber.

"Back the electrical stimulation down twenty percent," Mourner ordered. "I wish I knew what sort of anti-seizure meds I could use. I feel like a damn witchdoctor."

"Got a brain wave!" the third tech called. "It looks kind of primitive, I'd say hind brain if it was one of us."

"Good," Yamata said. "That's how most Confed species come out of cold-sleep according to the old texts."

The alien's large eyes fluttered open. Large blue pupils on gray sclera flitted about the room without seeming to focus on anything. A low moan escaped her lips. Then her eyes rolled up and closed.

Mourner checked her instruments. "As best as I can tell, she seems stable at a low level. I think she just lost consciousness. I am going to raise the temperature of the mattress—let's see if this helps."

Fifteen minutes later, the native's eyes opened again. This time Paolo was ready with a placard containing what he hoped was the base's name. Her eyes opened again, and again they seemed to focus on nothing for a while. Gradually a spark of something like reason seemed to glimmer in the depths of them.

The creature opened its mouth and screamed.

"Readings fluctuating," a med tech called.

Mourner reached over and touched the alien, which seemed to be struggling and twitching with its thousand-year-dormant muscles. "That's all right. It's all right," she said in a soft, soothing voice while gently stroking the alien's arm.

Whether it was Mourner's soothing voice or hand, or fatigue, the alien stopped screaming. Her eyes focused on the doctor. Then on Paolo's placards. Slowly he replaced one with the other. Her eyes tracked on the cards but dripped tears, whether from grief or just the effort of using them after a millennium, Shasti could not tell.

Mourner kept a hand on the alien's arm. She smiled but without showing teeth. No other species they had met, bared its teeth in friendship.

The native started speaking, much to Paolo's evident delight. But it was repetitious, Shasti realized after a few seconds.

Then the native's head dropped back and her eyes closed again.

"Readings steady," the tech said. "Best guess, asleep."

"So what do you think she said?" Shasti asked, looking at a frustrated Paolo.

To her surprise, Vaughn spoke. "My guess would be name, rank, species, and serial number. She's a military officer, awakening after an unknown period. When she was last aware, her base was under attack by aliens. Now she is in the hands of aliens—we don't know that she ever saw the Conchirri or the Makers before entering cold sleep. For all she knows, we may be Conchirri."

"Yes, yes," Paolo said, "excellent reasoning. I can work with that." He grabbed up a headset and began listening to the alien's speech.

They left the sleeper with Paolo and the doctors. Shasti brought

Daniel Rigg in to keep an eye on the alien, lest it turn out to be more dangerous than previously expected. She would have preferred to leave Vaughn but did not completely trust the Engineered either with the new find, or with Paolo in the deserted fort.

No threat emerged in the following hours. After her first burst of unreasoned terror, the alien settled into a stupor, rousing only for food and water the next day.

"It's typical of cold sleep reactions," Mourner told Shasti by com. "The body doesn't quickly snap out of a thousand-year sleep."

"How do you feel about the risk of infection?"

"So far so good. I had a nice test subject. Paolo got excited and forgot to seal his suit properly. Neither he nor the lab animals are showing any effect. I think we can drop the contamination protocol."

Shasti swore under her breath.

"She's done some basic work with Paolo in the last hour," Mourner continued. "I think she's realized I'm another female doctor. It seemed to reassure her. Can you send a field latrine and shower down here? She may feel better after some basic maintenance."

"I'll put Dobera on it," Shasti said.

Shasti returned to see the alien after she woke again. The alien had just finished a shower and appeared wearing an ill-fitting Confed jumpsuit. She stopped as soon as she saw Shasti and they traded measuring looks. The alien was humanoid, slender and willowy. No humans had ever had such large eyes or had them slant so extremely. The arms possessed extra joints like a Denlenn. The skin, where it showed, had a silver undertone with a darker gray on top. The alien's face was small and oval on a neck too long for a human. To Shasti she looked a little like a frightened deer.

"One of these days," Rask spoke from the corner where he sat on guard, "we'll run into some good-looking aliens."

Shasti suppressed a laugh. For all she knew, the red-eyed, goblin-like alien might be serious.

Paolo appeared. "Ah, I see you have met Eris."

Shasti turned to him. "Eris? You're able to communicate with...her?"

"Her indeed," Paolo said. "As I make it, Eris is her last name. As with the Denlenn, she seems to have a taboo about giving her first name. Vaughn was right. She gave us her name, rank, and species. I've translated her rank, Toraku, as Doctor-Colonel of the Vikadia species. Vikadia, like all such words, just means 'the people' or 'the humans.' She's a medical doctor and since she appears to have been in charge of the complex, we've used the equivalent Confed rank."

"She seems young," Shasti said, "though that is just an impression."

"We don't know," Paolo said, "but Dr. Mourner had the same feeling."

"That happened a lot with both us and the Okarans," Rask said. "During the war we both took a lot of casualties and the ranks filled up with younger people. It's only during peacetime that the high ranks are fossils."

Eris watched them through the interchange, her large, liquid eyes following each speaker in turn.

"Toraku Eris," Paolo said into a small throat mike. "This is one of the leaders of our expedition, Captain Rainhell." From a small speaker on his chest a translated voice spoke in trills and notes.

"We have a small vocabulary," Paolo said. "Only a few hundred words and mostly guesses on those."

Eris faced Shasti and made a clenched fist to open hand salute.

"She's only able to speak a few words and fatigues very easily," Paolo said.

Even as he spoke, Eris wavered and suddenly Paolo took her elbow, leading her to a chair. The small, slender, gray woman focused on Shasti after she was seated.

"Captain Rainhell," the words were mangled, only barely recognizable. Eris's voice was breathy with an accent vaguely similar to Yamata's.

"Yes." Shasti nodded, a little surprised at being addressed by the Vikadian. "Does she know how long she's been—"

"Shasti," Mourner interrupted. The diminutive surgeon appeared in the doorway. She gave a quick shake of her head. Shasti took the cue and followed the doctor into the hallway.

"Sorry," Mourner said. "We haven't told her much yet. Paolo's doing amazing things with the translation program, but I'd like it to be much more advanced before we tell her what has happened. If she's anything like a human psychologically, it could make her suicidal. While there doesn't seem to be anything medically wrong, her systems are very weak. Any shock might kill her."

"Do you think she suspects?" Shasti asked.

"Yes. She's clearly highly intelligent. She used some of her own equipment to check herself out. I think she was taken aback by how thick the dust in the medical center was. She knows we must have removed the bodies and she may have figured out that she's been gone for a long time.

"Also this is a top military base. We're wandering all over it. It tells her that her service, at least, is gone, or we wouldn't be here. I imagine that when we tell her, she'll be expecting it, but I want her to be stronger."

"Do what you can," Shasti said. "She's the only being that can tell us anything about this sector of space. We've already taken damage and casualties from things we don't know. Debriefing her could save lives."

Mourner nodded, her lips pursed.

Shasti busied herself with the continuing tech survey and the other details of running the camp while waiting for Mourner and Paolo to advance matters to where they could start questioning Eris. The base was vast, and portions of it had collapsed in a thousand years. Over a thousand years of decay had turned the immense starfort into its own ecology and not all of it was friendly. The expedition's medical staff were kept busy with scrapes, bumps, and other minor injuries from working in the decrepit warren.

Overhead, *Sidhe* and *Paladin* conducted salvage operations on what was left of the sled. Little useful remained and the sled was left to a slow orbital decay into the world below. They decided to keep the starships over the defunct fort rather than risk other orbits, though the fighters and probes continued to survey. Only silent ruins, empty ice fields, and windswept deserts greeted their cameras and sensors.

On the evening of the third day, Paolo called up to her that they were ready for the next step with Eris.

"I believe we need to tell her what is going on," Paolo said. "The translation program is at that point, and she clearly understands some of what's happened. She's becoming agitated and we risk losing her trust if we delay."

"Very well," Shasti said. "I will need you and Dr. Mourner to help with her emotional reactions. I'm a trained interrogator but with prisoners, not victims. Hysterics aren't my specialty."

Shasti made her way to the med center and the quiet guarded room in the back where Eris recovered. She remembered to knock before entering. No point in unsettling Eris by treating her like a prisoner.

Mourner opened the door. Eris and Paolo sat on one side of a table. Paolo had a camp chair, and Eris sat in one made for her people, which would have caused considerable back pain to a human. There was, Shasti noted, a distinctively proprietary, even protective air about Paolo's body language toward Eris. She controlled a stab of annoyance.

"Do you remember me?" Shasti asked.

Eris spoke softly in her own language, and the voder on her chest emitted perfect Confed Standard with a feminine accent. Clearly a Paolo touch. "I recognize you, from when I first awakened. They told me that you lead this expedition."

"I am one of the leaders," Shasti acknowledged. "I command one of two ships in orbit, and I carry a high government official who commands the expedition."

"Please tell me what has happened," Eris said, leaning forward. "I already suspect the worst. Please."

"You must prepare yourself mentally," Shasti said, "for the news is as bad as you fear."

Eris gripped the table tightly.

"You are the only member of your species that we have found alive," Shasti said, best to get it done fast. "Our information is that you entered cold sleep one-thousand-forty-three years ago. Your world has experienced nuclear winter since then. While we have seen some life onworld, we have seen no evidence of intelligent lifeforms."

Eris gave a soft cry and collapsed against the table. Paolo and Mourner both leapt to her aid. In a few minutes and after a glass of water, Eris recovered enough to speak with them again, and Shasti learned that Eris's species shared tears in common with humans.

"I felt this in my *****." The translator cut out as it hit the unfamiliar word. "The enemy had attacked furiously with nuclear and biological weapons. We had no communication with the outside."

"Eris," Paolo began gently, "tell us what happened here."

"The aliens came from deep space. We ourselves did not have stardrive vessels but we had met and traded with a people called the Nekoans. It was from them that we learned of the ****," the voder cut in with a male voice, *"90% probability the word means Conchirri"* before returning to Eris's soft accent. "The Conchirri had attacked the Nekoans in all their systems. There seemed no limit to their numbers. The Nekoans withdrew and our government went into an emergency weapons and fortification program. Three years later, the skies filled with black and yellow ships, and they attacked immediately. There was no parley, no negotiation, offers of treaty, tribute, even outright surrender were ignored. Our fleet was destroyed and our planetary assets could only reach the enemy if they came close to our world."

Eris put her head in her hands, looking weary. Mourner looked as if she might stop the interview, but Shasti quelled her with a gesture.

"The Conchirri did not come close, but bombarded us from long range. Oh, how many billions of my poor people perished? We waited and waited for Conchirri to close in, but they did not. At the end, the monsters fired tunneling missiles at our underground bases, with chemical and biological weapons in them. Our filters and defenses worked at first but were overwhelmed by the volume.

"The base commander ordered us to put the wounded out of their misery. He announced that the staff was setting all weapons on automatic, a huge salvo for when they finally came to celebrate in our ruins. Then they committed suicide.

"I was the coward. I eased the wounded from this life. Then helped my staff do the same for themselves, but I could not give up hope. I prepped the cold sleep chamber and sealed the medical lab. Fool and coward, I hoped there might be a future. How I wish I had died with my world and my people."

"I do not know," Shasti said softly, "how much it will ease your pain. But the Conchirri attacked our Confederacy fourteen years ago. We exterminated them, male and female, young and old, every single one."

"Oh, this is glad news," Eris said, bringing her hands up to her face. "Glad news indeed. Maybe tonight the ghosts of Fortress Xetrok will sleep well. We are murdered but avenged. Thank you."

"We have many questions about this area of space," Shasti said. "About these Nekoans or any other races you knew of—"

"I will answer all your questions," Eris said. "But I have a condition first. Take me to the surface of my world. Let me see the sun. I have been buried alive for over a thousand years. I must see the sky and the sun again. After that you may have all you wish."

"Fair enough," Shasti said.

"I don't think she can walk that far," Mourner said.

"We don't have wheelchairs or anything like that. I'll send for one of our robots so you may ride it to the surface," Shasti said.

"Now, please," Eris said, entreaty clear in the large, blue eyes. "Now."

Shasti hit her throat mike. "Mmok, have one of the crab robots rigged with a litter and sent to the med center. We are taking Eris up to the surface."

"Affirmative," he responded.

Minutes later a crab arrived. Medics had rigged a litter on its side and Mourner and Paolo strapped the frail alien in. The base, outside of the sections heated by the spacer's portable generators, remained cold and damp. The humans all wore cold weather clothes over armor. Eris seemed less affected by the cold, but Mourner insisted on the heavy jacket and a short stay. There was more radiation above the base than was healthful, and they had no anti-radiation medicines for Eris.

The trip was considerably eased by the crab, which sped along indifferent to Eris's litter and Mourner and Paolo riding on its back and other side. Shasti simply jogged beside it, keeping the pace without effort.

They made their way carefully around the armored vehicles that clogged the space where they had blasted their way into the fort. Eris dismounted slowly and, flanked by Paolo and Mourner, stepped out onto the surface of her world for the first time in a thousand years.

Three shuttles, two of *Sidhe's* in red, and Vaughn's gunmetal gray *Duelist*, sat on the plateau in front of them, along with a black-painted *Wildcat* fighter. A delicate tracery of barrier wire glimmered about the ships and shelters set up nearby. The barrier was thinner than Shasti would have liked, but she had a lot of area to cover. Because of the radiation, most of the spacers remained in the fort's deeper levels or in the shuttles themselves, though a few crew were unloading a mule into the *Globemaster* shuttle, more booty on its way to Mandela.

Eris stood, the cold wind ruffling her heavy coat and her blue-gray cap of hair. She looked up at the sun, then away at the mountains as if searching for anything familiar.

"This was all a forest when I was last here," she said finally. "Those bare mountains were covered in trees."

She turned to Shasti. "Is it winter?"

Shasti shook her head. "No."

"God," Eris shouted, her natural voice competing with the voder translator. "How could you let this happen?"

"Some of us," Paolo said, putting a hand on her arm, "asked such questions on our worlds when we were struck. How? Why? I wish I could tell you that we were ever answered."

"I have seen enough," Eris said. Her face had become a lifeless alien mask. The blue gray skin tone gave her a corpse-like appearance. "Please, I wish to rest now."

They returned the alien to the medical center. Whether it was emotional exhaustion or the lingering effects of cold sleep, she could not be awakened. Shasti carefully lifted her from the litter and placed her in the bed inside her room.

"I'm going to keep a suicide watch on her," Mourner said. "Poor thing: even after all I have seen, even after Enshar, I cannot imagine what she must be feeling. To be alone, to be the last."

Shasti nodded. "We'll start again in the morning."

9

Shasti woke to the faint sound of distant gunfire. She sprang to her feet, racing out of the medical center, carbine in hand. Risky loped along beside her. In a few seconds Shasti caught up to a mixed reaction team of ASATs and Denshi security running up the rampway. The Engineered Denshi in their black uniforms outpaced the ASATs in their gray and green. At the head of the group, she saw Vaughn's broad back and black hair as he passed under a work light. She put on a burst of speed and raced through the others to pull even with him.

"Post Number Seven called in," he snapped in answer to her questioning look. "The call was cut off. I've alerted all posts."

A minute later, they reached a spot below the circular ramp, with Vaughn and Shasti in the lead. Sandy, a young woman from Dan's command, stood there, pale and shaken. Her triple auto wavered in her hands, pointing down the side corridor.

"What happened?" Shasti demanded.

"Broza went down the hall," she said, her voice shrill. "He said he wanted to take a leak, maybe look around. He turned off the barrier wire. I told him not to go. Damn it, I told him not to go—"

"Focus," Shasti snapped as Vaughn shone a battle torch down the hall. "What happened to Broza?" Shasti remembered Broza, an Engineered from Vaughn's team, almost as big as Vaughn, a scarred and dangerous man.

Risky stood in front of the side corridor. He was snarling, fangs in evidence.

"Something leapt on him. Something huge. I couldn't see it well. There aren't any lights down there and his flashlight beamed right into my eyes. I fired. But he was gone. I called for backup. I went down the hallway, but all I could see was some sort of slime trail and a stink. I followed for a hundred meters...then I decided to wait for backup."

"Look," Vaughn said. "And smell."

Shasti followed his pointed finger and saw the slime trail in the distance. She drew a foulness into her lungs and coughed. Risky continued to growl.

Tanaka and more troops joined them. "Let's go," Vaughn said impatiently. "I have a man missing."

"You, me, Tanaka," Shasti said. "Everyone else, hold here. Come if you hear firing." She turned to the young trooper. "Call for Mmok."

"You should wait for him," the soldier said.

Shasti shook her head and took a firm hold on Risky's battle harness. She didn't want the angry shepherd dashing off into the dark hallways. The underground starfort ran for dozens of kilometers in all directions. Once lost, he might never be found.

When they reached the slime trail, their weapon-mounted lights showed scorch marks and blasts indicated where the ASAT had fired high, trying not to hit Broza. A dented and twisted weapon lay on the green pebbled flooring. Its barrel-mounted flashlight beamed back toward the entrance at low power, lighting dust motes from the disturbed ground. Vaughn picked it up, then quickly dropped the weapon with a hiss of pain.

"It burns," he said.

"Acid," Tanaka snapped. She grabbed her canteen, grounded her weapon, and poured the whole container on Vaughn's outstretched hand, then did the same with his and Shasti's canteens. Shasti handed him her jacket, and Vaughn scrubbed at the reddened flesh.

"It's okay," he said finally.

"That weapon was hit with tremendous force," Shasti said, shining her light around.

"Damn it," Tanaka said, as she wrapped a field dressing with burn cream around Vaughn's hand. "I told everyone to stay inside the barrier wire."

Vaughn grunted. "You know Broza, arrogant, too proud of his strength by half. He believed he could best anything."

"If he's alive, I am going to shove my foot so far up his ass—"

Risky's continuous growling stopped. He raised his head and sniffed. The genetically enhanced shepherd's demeanor changed. He gave a soft woof, and his tail dropped. Both sound and gesture held meaning for his handler.

"Follow me." She let the line out on Risky's battle harness and hefted her triple auto. They moved out, their lanterns lighting the dark halls of the fort. This section was intact, but they passed side corridors that were partly collapsed. One even held the hull of a Conchirri boring missile. The tunnel it had cut coming down from space had collapsed behind it, though a small steady stream of water splashed down the tube. Shasti didn't like it. The splashing could cover the sound of an approaching menace. But Risky's tugs did not beckon them down that partly collapsed corridor. The shepherd drew them forward down a slope into another corridor. There was no slime trail now, but Risky was not in doubt of his path.

Sixty meters down a side corridor, they reached a passage they might have missed in the darkness had the dog not guided them around the odd, sharp angle. Shasti drew up short as her searching light fastened on a pile of something on the floor. Ahead of them lay the lower half of a man, only recognizable by the boots at the end of the legs.

Tanaka cursed.

"Ah, Broza," Vaughn said, his voice heavy and sad. "You would never stop taking chances. Would you?"

They spun at the sound of tapping behind them, lights frantically flicking. But the beams showed a reassuring figure. Mmok ran up to them, his HCR feet making rapping sounds on the dark-green permacrete. They straightened up from their gunfighter crouches.

"I got briefed on the way in," he said. Mmok's HCR body produced a number of glowing red panels. It filled the hall with a steady, reddish light. They cut back the brightness on their own lights to help their low-light vision, making it easier to look at what remained of Broza.

"One of your boys," Mmok said. "Or what's left of him?"

"A good man," Vaughn intoned, "but he was always reckless."

"Sometimes I wonder if engineering the fear out of humans is that good an idea," Mmok said. "You wouldn't catch a standard human walking off into the dark alone."

"Hubris, Mmok?" Vaughn said with an edge in his voice. "Pride goeth before the fall?"

They were all silent for a few seconds.

"Sorry," Mmok said to Vaughn. "Lousy timing and my big mouth."

Vaughn nodded after a bit.

"Look," Mmok said. "I'll gather him up. We can take him back for burial."

"No," Vaughn said. "But thank you. Do you have a white phosphorus grenade on you?"

"You sure?" Mmok asked. "Wouldn't his folks…"

Vaughn looked at the suddenly silent HCR. "No, Kyle. We Engineered have no 'folks' and we have no god. We have only ourselves."

Mmok took out the grenade. "I'll do it if you like."

Vaughn gave a grim little smile. "That I think I will take you up on."

They retreated to the end of the hallway. Mmok joined them and they heard the whump of the WP grenade.

"I used two," Mmok said. "Ain't nothing left behind."

They made their way back to the barrier-wired entrance. Mmok recovered Broza's weapon. Tanaka warned him about the acid and insisted that he use the remnants of Shasti's jacket to carry the weapon.

They met Rigg and Rask at the entranceway. Shasti quickly relayed what had happened.

The young ASAT looked at Rigg. "Sir," Sandy said, her eyes bright. "I screwed up. I should have gone farther in. I shouldn't have stopped. My fault."

Tanaka beat Rigg to it. "My man disobeyed orders. If you'd left this hallway undefended and got killed, God knows what might have been in among us before we knew what was happening. If Engineered have one failing, it's too much confidence in themselves."

She glared at her own troops. "And this is what comes of it, a man down and gone."

Vaughn looked down at the diminutive ASAT, so tiny compared to his hulking troopers. "Broza's weapon wasn't fired, was it, Mmok?"

"No."

"Then he was dead as soon as it struck him. I knew Broza. He was a first-class killer. He would have gotten a shot off with that or his sidearm. I imagine from the damage to his weapon he was crushed instantly."

"Yes, sir," the ASAT said. "Sir, I want in on the team that's going after it. Nobody gets into me for a teammate and lives."

Growls of agreement from the soldiers filled the hall.

Shasti was struck silent. She'd heard similar words once before in the skies over Thorraken. They'd been carried through, but at a heavy price.

"No," Vaughn said. "The base is immense, and we have no need to hunt through the darkness and risk more lives."

He held Shasti's eye. "People should read the classics. There is no revenge to be had on an animal, no gain in it, whether you hunt with a harpoon or a laser."

Shasti nodded, then turned to Dan and Tanaka. "Double the guard. All entrances are already under either barrier wire or mines. I want a crew-served weapon on each, or a crab robot set to fire at anything that moves. Move all nonessential personnel who aren't in the tech survey or the medical team above ground to the shuttles. Make preparations for launching back to the ships.

"Meanwhile, no one goes anywhere except in teams of two or

more. Five-minute check in with team leaders. Anybody violating any rule gets a week in the brig on bread and water."

"Aye, Skipper," Rigg said.

A crab robot scuttled over to them as the small ASAT rehung and flicked on the barrier wire. The cold illuminated lines had never been so comforting to Shasti.

"A full fire team here," Rigg said. "Rask, you take it."

"Sandy," Rigg addressed the female ASAT, "I'm going to check every post. You come with me and watch my back."

"Yes, sir." Her voice was subdued and lifeless, her head hung down.

Vaughn put a huge hand on her shoulder, which sank under the weight of it. "Not your fault," he said in his deep growl. Then he looked over her at the other Engineereds in the hallway. "And no one is to say otherwise."

Heads nodded.

"Thank you, sir," Sandy said.

"Go with Rigg," he said.

Vaughn turned to face Shasti.

Shasti gave him a long, measuring look. "Are you okay?"

"I have lost two lives on this trip," he said. "A venture I started for ambitions of my own. One wonders sometimes. One just wonders."

"Let's talk to Mourner," she said, making the invitation to accompany her as neutral as possible. She cast a cool glance over at Tanaka.

"Rigg," Tanaka called, shouldering her carbine. "Wait up."

Vaughn and Shasti walked off toward the medical complex, accompanied only by Risky. Shasti hesitated a few seconds, waiting until they had passed out of earshot of the others. "Paolo will be there."

"Bah." Vaughn waved his injured hand. "I have already committed all the stupidities with him that I can and paid dearly for it. You need not fear for his safety. I will do him no harm. It would be best, however, if he kept his sly sense of humor to himself. I have lost a man today. Maybe not a good man as many would judge such things, but he was brave and loyal to me."

"Paolo says anything smart to you," Shasti promised, "and you won't have to hit him. I will."

"So?" he said, with that sad half-smile Shasti had come to like. "Then I will rely on your protection." Hours later, Shasti found herself back at the base infirmary. She'd seen to the removal of most of the expedition and the few treasures that they had uncovered. The section of the base that her forces secured was now much smaller. Shasti wasn't sure she wanted to keep the toehold that the spacers still held. The most important treasure that the expedition had found was Eris, and she was unsure that anything else worth the risks would be found. She also hoped the slender, gray-skinned alien would have some information on the underground menaces.

She found Mourner in the office the tiny woman had picked out for herself. She quickly briefed Mourner on the morning's bad news.

"I want to move her to the surface," Mourner said. "Being in this tomb can't be any better for her than for the rest of us. I think she's healthy enough. We also don't know if there are any more of those creatures down here."

"Fortunate for her that she sealed the great doors before beginning her long sleep," Vaughn said. "Otherwise that thing that haunts the tunnels might have visited her while she dreamt."

Mourner shuddered.

"Let's go see her," Shasti said.

"This way." Mourner pointed. They waited as she knocked at the door of a room in the back of the medical center. Paolo opened it. He saw Vaughn and took a step back.

"I want to talk to Eris," Shasti said. "Is she up for it?"

"Yes, I think so," Paolo said, stepping aside. "She's doing remarkably well considering the shocks she's had."

They walked into the room. It was full of medical equipment and tables, painted an antiseptic white and green. At the far end were doors to storerooms that they had converted into bedrooms.

"I'll get her," Mourner said, knocking and disappearing behind the middle door.

Paolo looked at Vaughn. "I heard you lost a man. I'm sorry."

"Thank you," Vaughn said, leaning against the door. "At least we believe it was quick."

"Quick or slow, there's no good."

"Yes, it is so."

Shasti simply wondered at the mystery of how men's minds work.

Eris came out from behind the door space, followed by Dr. Mourner. Her large dark eyes fastened on them. "I heard alarms earlier."

"Yes," Shasti said. She walked over to a table and put down her carbine then dropped her long body into a chair. Vaughn did likewise while Paolo moved next to Eris, giving her an encouraging smile. "It seems that we are not alone down here. We lost a man."

Shasti described what little they knew of the creature that had slain Broza and the lizard panther than had attacked them earlier.

Eris's face twisted in concentration, an expression surprisingly similar to a human's. "I know of the creature you call a lizard-panther, though the one you found—"

"Actually, it found us." Vaughn grimaced.

"Yes," Eris said hesitantly, "well it is common to this part of the world. Though as I was about to say, it seems the one you encountered was uncommonly large. We called them Shakatilins. They are great tunnelers and eat anything they can catch. Not very bright, though. We used to have problems with them digging into the power tunnels and chewing through the power cable insulation. They seemed to like the taste. Every once in a while, one would get in the underground water caverns and security would have to shoot it. We never could figure if they swam in through underground rivers or what, but it's why everyone carried sidearms in the lower levels."

"The base is huge and parts of it have been flooded," Paolo added. "It's not too surprising that creatures that like to den or dig would start to move in over a thousand years."

"But of this other creature," Eris continued, "I know nothing. While you do not give me much to go on, it does not sound like anything that was native to this area. Or for that matter, anywhere else on my world."

"Where did it come from then?" Mourner wondered.

"A mutation perhaps?" Eris said. "Maybe it was something that came down in the Conchirri missiles as part of their chemical-biological attack? Maybe something they sent into the tunnels? It seems most unlikely that this creature would date from the time of the attack. Probably they have lived here for a thousand years. But who knows? After all, I date from that time."

Her slender body shook. "When I think that I have lain here helpless for a thousand years while such things haunted the shadows…"

Shasti shrugged. "We don't know of any species that lives that long naturally, but who can say? There are examples of hibernating creatures, and this may not be anything natural. We suspect that the Conchirri themselves were someone's biological ordinance that got loose. Maybe what made them made this."

"Indeed," Eris said. "If indeed some race made these horrors, may God pass the most severe of judgments on them. They deserve," her translation program cut out and the voder voice said, "probability, hell or damnation."

"That they do," Paolo said, his lips pressed thin.

"Dr. Mourner," Shasti asked, "is there much to be gained by staying here?"

Mourner shook her head. "Not with a live Vikadian to study. We have uploaded what little remains intact in the computer databases. There were some medical texts that we have here. Equipment wise, there's nothing particular to be learned here."

"We'll head for the surface," Shasti decided, "and reseal the fort for some future expedition. There's no purpose to our hunting monsters in here. We haven't come to stay, and the science team's found no tech here that we do not have the equal of."

Relief spread across Mourner's face. It abruptly occurred to Shasti that if the place had bothered her at all, it must have been far worse on the standard humans. *Got to remember that sort of thing.*

"Let's get packing," she said aloud.

The alacrity with which everyone readied to evacuate confirmed her suspicions. Fearing another attack, they withdrew by bounds. First went the remaining scientists and their equipment. Eris and her entourage of medicos followed. Then came most of the troops, after rolling up worklights and the deadly barrier wire that had sealed the side tunnels. Shasti's team, Mmok, and two of the crab robots served as rearguard.

As the lights were removed and the spacers fell back toward the surface, night and silence moved in to reclaim the fort. The dead base felt darker and angrier for their intrusion. Shasti, Rigg, Rask, and Vaughn came up the main ramp, trailed by Mmok and the scuttling crab robots. Risky began to growl. Shasti held his harness close and felt the ruff on his back standup.

"Yeah," Rigg said. "Do you get the feeling that something is following? Just beyond the light?"

"Yep," Rask said, unlimbering his pistol.

Vaughn grunted and pulled his weapon. "Could be your imagination."

"Mmok," Shasti called.

"Nothing close, boss," he said. "But his nose is better than my sensors."

As they backed away, unease grew in each of the humans. The darkness grew closer, heavier, and the air became foul. Shasti recognized the scent from the corridor where they had lost their man. They quickened their pace. The smell grew no worse, but the sense of malevolence grew in Shasti's mind. She felt something, a cold and somehow filthy presence. She throttled down her PSI sense and glared into the darkness beyond their lights.

"Mmok, do you feel anything?" Rigg called, as they started up one of the main hallways.

"Getting nervous in the service, Big Dan?" Mmok returned. "If you mean like the Prekak on Enshar, no, I ain't getting a brainwave. But then neither did Cobalt or the other machines. I may not be able to pick up PSI waves."

They climbed a seeming endless series of ramps and stairs. The way to the surface had never felt longer, and the uneasy feeling of pursuit never left them.

Shasti, Vaughn, Rigg, and Rask walked backward now, going up the last ramps to the surface level. Mmok had only two of the crab robots with him. Shasti had to resist the urge to order the crab robots to charge back into the choking darkness, guns blazing.

"We could run," Rask suggested. "Pretty close to the surface."

"We could do that," Rigg said, maintaining his steady pace, eyes sweeping the corridor.

"Could," Vaughn said idly.

"Hardly dignified," Shasti added.

They continued to walk backward, stiff-legged and tense, past the armored vehicles blocking the entrance, reaching the terminator of sunlight that streamed in through the ruined doors. They did jog the last few meters out into the cold sunlight. Weak as the afternoon sun was, it seemed brilliant after the gloom of the starfort. They stared about like people waking from a bad dream.

Suddenly Risky barked furiously, dropping his chest to the ground. They spun back toward the entrance. In the distance, beyond the tanks and armored vehicles something large and shapeless bulked. With their day-blinded eyes, they had only a fleeting impression of something leprous, filthy, part of some other primeval reality.

Their weapons chattered in their hands almost without conscious volition, sending a stream of lasers, bullets, and mini frags blasting to the far end of the chamber. An undulating howling attacked their ears until it abruptly cut off.

"Mmok," Shasti shouted, "the crabs. Have them collapse the entrance."

The spacers fell back as the crabs fired their main guns. A few well-placed HE rounds from the machines brought down the entranceway. Then, without Shasti's ordering it, they proceeded to bury the damaged entrance with rock and steel from its blasted exterior bunker.

"What the fuck was that?" Rigg said.

"Did you get a look?" Vaughn asked Mmok. "I couldn't see well."

"Count your blessings," Mmok said. "You don't want to know."

Shasti looked at the crabs, then turned to Mmok. "Do a thorough job."

"Will do," he said. "You all go ahead and catch up with the others. Get back to the shuttles."

"We'll wait," she said.

"Boss," he said. "I leap tall buildings in a single bound, and I can bend steel with my bare hands. And I have the equivalent of two light tanks with me."

"Yeah," she said. "Okay."

"Boss."

Shasti turned back.

"I appreciate the thought."

She nodded. "Don't linger."

10

Once on the surface and free of the fort's oppression, Shasti concentrated their efforts on Eris. Paolo tinkered constantly with the translation program, and Mourner worked on physical therapy with the revived alien. The others set up camp among the shuttles. Their few radiation-resistant tents were reserved for the scientists and Eris's medical team.

Each day Eris walked across the barren surface of the plateau covering the ancient fortress, accompanied by Engineered guards. The small, gray-skinned alien's strength returned gradually, particularly when it came to running. She quickly achieved a fleetness of foot that made it impossible for any but Shasti or another Engineered to keep up with her.

Shasti felt an almost hysterical quality in Eris's running. She wondered if at some point Eris would flee the unpleasant future that she had awoken to, either physically running away till death claimed her, or fleeing to some fantasy in her mind that offered more solace then the present. She arranged for a tracking device to be planted in Eris's clothing to guard against the former.

In between Eris's bouts of depression, Rigg and Shasti, both trained interrogators, debriefed her. Eris seemed desperate to fill their tape banks with the information on her species' history, as if to prove they had existed. She resisted their attempts to drag the conversation onto more useful matters until she had relayed as much of the history of her world as she easily could.

"I may die any second," Eris told Shasti. "Although I was young when I went into cold sleep and appear young still, there is no telling what effect time has had on me. There may be diseases of your kind, or even of my own, latent in my body. If I die, then my people are truly gone, as if we never were. Record and bear with me for a few days. After that I will have no other purpose than to aid you."

Knowing that Mourner and Paolo would resist any pressure applied to Eris and feeling some sympathy for the lonely alien, Shasti let her be, despite Mandela's needling.

"For the same reason," he'd said when she called up to the *Sidhe* to report, "that we do not know how long she will live. We need answers soon."

Shasti shrugged. "Any intel she has is a thousand years out of date. Would you be that interested in a debriefing on the battle of Waterloo? It would be as relevant."

"Your point is well taken, Captain. But remember both the Evolvers and how far we have come in both space and time. The machine that landed on Fenris was more ancient than this conflict."

"Very well," she said. "On to another point, I think that we have accomplished as much as we can onworld. I am thinking of a withdrawal to the ships. We could stay longer, but the anti-radiation protocols are wearisome and I don't want to cut into our supplies of meds. Nor do I want to return to the starfort."

"I leave those matters in your hands, Captain. I'm satisfied that there is no useful tech to be found here and nothing about the Evolvers. The rest I'm content to leave to xenoarcheologists and scholars."

Paolo had left word with Shasti that Eris was moving into areas that she might be interested in, and Shasti decided to debrief her personally. She brought a long, flat case with her to the next session. The small slender alien was staring at the walls of her tent with its cot and few bits of field furniture when she walked in. Eris hardly looked up at Shasti's entrance.

"Hello," Shasti said.

Eris finally noticed her. "Hello," she replied. The voder that Paolo had created for her now sounded more like her own soft and sibilant voice. While Eris was learning Confed standard with commendable speed, it would be a long time before she could communicate more than the basics of language without the translator's help.

"I brought some of my art supplies," Shasti said. "I wanted to see if we could come up with a sketch of the Nekoans you mentioned yesterday. Do you have any skill with drawing?"

"No," Eris said, "I regret that I do not. I've always wanted to but have no talent in that direction. Medical school consumed all my time."

"Perhaps between the two of us we can accomplish something," Shasti said. "Let's sit outside. The light in here is terrible."

They walked outside and sat under a canvas flap of one of the bigger shelters overlooking the plateau. Its austere, wind-blown beauty stretched before them in the afternoon sun. It was hard to believe the high desert countryside concealed both a deadly fortress and a monstrous, nameless horror that had taken one of their crew. Shasti pushed aside the dark thoughts.

"Tell me about the Nekoans," Shasti said, laying out her pencils and paper then starting a recorder. There were computer programs for this sort of work, but Shasti enjoyed the opportunity to use her skills. Art had been the first talent that Shasti learned that was unrelated to her life as an assassin, the first doorway into normalcy, even beauty. The tactile sensations of manipulating paper and pencil both pleased and relaxed her. "What were your impressions of them?"

"I was fortunate enough to be at the Capitol Hospital when the first delegations arrived," Eris said. "I was helping with the medical protocols." She leaned forward and zipped her jacket. The sun was bright but weak and it didn't throw much heat. "They were a tall people. Most were near your size."

"Two genders?" Shasti asked.

"Of course," Eris said, with what Shasti recognized as amusement, then, "Are there other species that are different?"

"Yes." Shasti nodded. "The Denleni are a Confed species with three genders."

"Fascinating," Eris exclaimed, with more enthusiasm than Shasti had ever seen her display. "I must see the medical texts on that."

"I'm sure Dr. Mourner can arrange it," Shasti said, pleased. "But back to the Nekoans."

"Yes, of course. The Nekoan males were only slightly larger than the females but much less numerous. Males once dominated their society, a hangover from their prehistory when the males had harems of females. Later, the females asserted the economic power of their numbers and the males lost status. A triumvirate of two females and a male led the expedition that landed in our capital.

"Their technology was marginally superior except in one area, stardrive. They had lucked onto the principles for entering hyperspace. Naturally we tried to buy the stardrive, but the Nekoans were quite content with things as they were, with them controlling the trade. They were fair traders beyond that, and we both benefited from the relationship."

Eris stood and stretched, then continued. "The Nekoans were always tight-lipped about the other species. We did learn that there were three major species living in our sector of space: Nekoans, Ribisi, and Skurlock, with a trading empire that centered on a mysterious world called Kandalor. But they were careful to keep information on the others to a bare minimum.

"Then came the Conchirri," Eris said, using the Confed term for the carnivorous aliens. "They apparently struck all three species at about the same time. The Nekoans had few warships, and these were driven off quickly. That's all I know of them."

"Tell me more of what they looked like," Shasti said, selecting a pencil.

"The females did not differ in build from you," Eris said, "two eyes, large and forward, as with anything that evolves from a hunting animal, a nose similar to yours and mine, but a little broader with more flared nostrils. They appeared taller because of the rough mane of hair atop their heads."

Shasti envisioned something like a lion's mane and sketched it in to Eris's approval.

"The ears are atop the head and toward the back." Eris pointed. "No, the ears are far larger. Nekoans are not furred."

Shasti penciled away on two images, one of a face and the other of the full figure. She shaded in the details.

"Legs were perhaps longer and the waist smaller," Eris critiqued from over Shasti's shoulder. "They have long tails, slender and slightly furred on top."

After a few minutes Shasti had a result that Eris approved of.

"Your talent is remarkable," Eris said, "and seems to extend to so many areas. Are you typical of your people?"

Shasti froze at the unexpected question.

"Have I offended you?" Eris asked, leaning back.

"No," Shasti said. "My history is an odd one. It wouldn't teach you much about humans or even Olympians. I am essentially one of a kind."

"I am also one of a kind," Eris said, "and must learn to live in your time. Perhaps it would help me to know some of your story."

Shasti's jaw knotted, and she fought an irrational surge of anger.

"I have answered all your questions," Eris added.

"Fair enough," Shasti said, putting down her pencils. "I am an artificial person. On my homeworld we had humans who mated according to a selection process for genetic improvement. Tanaka is one of these, called the Selected.

"But that was not enough for Olympia's leaders, so they moved into genetically engineering humans carefully moving the species forward a step at a time in artificial wombs. Vaughn and his soldiers are of that kind. But even there I am an exception. I was created by power-crazed eugenicists in a clandestine lab, from the genetic material of thousands of humans. All the safeties were thrown out, monsters were produced in the thousands and then...me."

"This is your government?" Eris said, aghast.

"No," Shasti said. "My homeworld's government was destroyed by the Confederacy. I am pleased to say that I had a hand in it too."

Eris stared at her. "Were you created this size?" She gestured.

"No, I was decanted as a baby and raised in a guild of assassins on my homeworld. I did not know that even among Engineered I was something unusual until a few years ago."

"Thank you," Eris said after a few seconds. "It is strangely comforting to know that others struggle with being alone."

"We have a saying," Shasti said with a bitter smile. "Misery loves company."

Hours later, Shasti stretched booted feet on a case of camp equipment. The sun was westering, and the usual campfires were being lit around the encampment. She was digesting what Eris had said about the Nekoans when Paolo rounded the corner of the shuttle and waved. She nodded, keeping her face neutral but secretly glad to see him. Talking with Eris had put in her in a pensive mood, and she thought some time in Paolo's light and easy company might cheer her.

"I think we have something," he said, face flush both with excitement and the cold, "in the download from the command computer. It's the last communication from the Nekoans during their battle with the Conchirri. They were hoping to lure the main Conchirri battle-fleet to a place called Kandalor, an ancient world that served as a trading concourse for a number of civilizations."

"Kandalor," Shasti said, sitting up in her chair. "Eris mentioned it earlier, probably annihilated by the Conchirri."

"Perhaps not," Paolo said. "According to the records we translated, Kandalor has been inhabited for over 50,000 years and has never fallen to attack. The legends are confused, as no race seems to call Kandalor home, though many used it. It had some unknown type of defense and entire fleets had perished trying to take it. The Nekoans hoped to lure the Conchirri into attacking Kandalor and provoking those defenses."

"Now that," Shasti said, "sounds like the sort of thing Mr. Mandela would be very interested in. Have you spoken to Eris? Does she know where this Kandalor lies?"

"No. She's a medical officer and strategic information wasn't shared with her. But there is a reference to it in some partially burnt plastic records. With that and what we know about the star type, Mmok and I may be able to refine my Conchirri map to where we can come up with a substantial probability."

"Excellent." She switched on her throat mike. "Vaughn."

"Here," came his deep voice. Paolo didn't bother to disguise the look of dislike that slid over his face.

"Join me on the command deck of *Pooka*. Bring Rigg, Rask, Mmok, and Tanaka. I think I know where we are going next."

"Sounds interesting. I'm on my way."

She looked at Paolo. "Get Eris and Dr. Mourner. Vaughn and I will have some more questions."

"You can control the brute?" Paolo asked. "I won't have him frightening Eris."

"I have a way with brutes," she said, standing. "And watch your tongue or you may get a taste of it yourself."

Paolo's eyebrows shot up but he wisely kept silent.

<hr>

Shasti gathered the essentials of her command staff on *Pooka's* deck. They were, she admitted, a grim-looking crew: Vaughn, Rigg, Tanaka, Mmok, and herself. On Eris's "side" hovered Paolo and Dr. Mourner as if bodily protecting their treasure from the past.

I wonder if they think I'm going to order her served up as dinner, Shasti thought.

"Eris," Shasti began, trying for what she hoped was a gentle tone. "You told me something of Kandalor before. Tell the others and if there is anything else you can recall—"

"If you are up for it," Paolo said.

I swear, Shasti thought, *I'm going to stuff him up his own asshole if he doesn't knock it off.*

"Thank you, Dr. Romita," Eris said. "I am all right." She drew a deep breath and retold the story of the Nekoans and the mysterious trade world. "I do recall that one of the Nekoans let slip that it was a far larger world than either theirs or ours. Evidently it is very low density as the gravity was similar."

"With some of Paolo's records," Mmok said, "and what we found in the base, we should be able to locate the star. It's a K-class, but there's an M-class red dwarf only two lights out from it. If their hyperdrive is anything like ours, that combination would have to be within fifty lights of here, even with favorable currents, for Nekoan traders to have made as many runs as they did during the five years of contact."

"Finding hyperdrive entry points will be more difficult, but the Nekoans clearly had some good entry points here for the trade," Shasti mused. "With two ships, running opposite-angle Hawking search patterns, we have a decent chance of finding one."

"I'll need all the navigators and cartographers from both ships," Mmok said

"Oh, I think you can count on Mr. Mandela's support there," Vaughn said. "He could no more resist Kandalor than a cat can resist a plate of cream."

True enough, Shasti thought. A trace of excitement stole through her. *It sounds pretty good to me too.*

"There may be nothing there," she said aloud. "The Conchirri may have scoured the world clean. We know they weren't exterminated at Kandalor because they attacked us centuries later."

"Perhaps they were driven off," Rigg suggested. "Maybe something survives there."

"So we're off on the road to Kandalor?" Tanaka said.

"As Vaughn said," Shasti noted, "we will have to talk to Mandela, but I cannot imagine that even with the loss of the sled he will want to turn back."

She turned to Vaughn. "But he does not command you in that. You have lost two people already. What do you say?"

Vaughn looked a little surprised at being consulted. "I had given some thought to returning," he said slowly. "Mandela could legally order me to stay, but I do not believe he would do so against my will. The adventure sounds very intriguing, but I came uninvited on this expedition. I am also perhaps a little older and wiser now. So I will ask you. Would you have my help and company on this voyage? Or would you prefer to journey on alone? I'll abide by your decision."

Now it was Shasti's turn for surprise. It took her a few seconds to collect her thoughts. "We are doing something very important here. And very dangerous. Two guns can handle more trouble than one. We will have a greater chance of success and survival with your help." Shasti felt a slight tremor in her soul. "Stay."

"Then *Paladin* sails with you." Vaughn smiled.

Shasti nodded, glancing away to conceal the emotion that smile stirred. Her glance fell on Paolo, who cast a dark look at Vaughn's back. She noted that Tanaka had slipped behind Paolo and was watching him intently.

No need there, Shasti thought with a touch of amusement. *Paolo was no match for Vaughn, save perhaps in a bedroom, and far too smart to fight the Engineered in any other arena.* She turned back to Eris.

"Will you take me with you?" Eris said to Shasti.

"We can't leave her here," Mourner said.

"Of course not," Shasti snapped. *Why does everyone still feel that they have to teach me even the basics of being human?* "You are welcome to voyage with us and return to our space."

Eris looked out of the clear canopy at the sere and windswept plateau of the fort. Her facial expressions meant little to the humans at the table, but there was no mistaking the grief and sorrow in the slender alien as she rocked back and forth in her seat, arms about herself.

Shasti wondered what she would decide if she had awoken as the sole remaining human. Would she have chosen to live on?

Finally, Eris spoke. "All here is ended. All time, all possibility, and all potential. No more poems, no more music, never again to touch or fill my lungs with the scent of my kind. Perhaps it would be better to die now, to return to the fortress and let the darkness of this place reclaim me. How I wish I had never awakened." Her body shook in grief, and Paolo placed a hand on her shoulder.

"The darkness," Shasti said, "awaits all of us, someday. There is no need to rush to it. You're alive, and you will have companions, maybe friends, if you come with us. There will always be other times and places to die."

After a few moments, Eris said, "I will come with you, but you must promise that if ever the day comes when I tell you that I must die, that I can endure it no longer, swear that you will let me go."

"Done," Shasti said, "though in this I can speak only for your life aboard my ship."

"It is enough," she said.

"Then the sooner we go," Shasti said, "perhaps the better. Gather anything you wish to take with you."

"Dan," she looked at the big ASAT, "you stay with her."

Rigg nodded, though Paolo gave him a dark look, apparently unhappy at anyone else being involved with his self-imposed charge.

Rigg would keep Eris from harming herself, Shasti thought. He would also carefully search for any hidden dangers in her personal effects. It did not do to trust too much to the psychology of a creature they barely knew.

Later that evening, the shuttles, escorted by *Sidhe's* fighters, kicked free of Lantrim II's surface. Shasti invited Eris to the flight deck of *Pooka,* and she was able to watch her world drop away from her. Shasti was unsure if it had been a kindness or not. Eris stared silently down at the ruined world as they drew away from it.

"I did want to warn you about my ship," Shasti said.

Eris turned to face her, her posture tense.

"It was once a Conchirri vessel, taken as a prize of war."

"Black and yellow?" Eris whispered.

"No," Shasti said. "It's been repainted."

"How did you acquire the vessel?" Eris asked. "Paolo tells me that you are not military, but rather a privateer. Are you wealthy?"

Shasti raised an eyebrow. The crewmen around her carefully kept their eyes on their instruments. "The vessel was a gift."

"A star-faring vessel as a gift," Eris marveled. "From whom?"

"It's a long tale and for another time," Shasti said. "We are having a dinner with our leader tonight. He wants to meet you. It gives him the opportunity to throw another fancy dinner."

As promised, Mandela held court on *Sidhe* with Eris as guest of honor for dinner in main galley. They entered the room en masse to find Mandela and Zandra Mollica there, awaiting them. The oak table was set with a festive tablecloth as if Eris were a visiting head of state.

Eris gave a stifled scream that brought everyone to a halt. Shasti spun about to find Eris staring at Dobera. The-lizard-like alien backed away from Eris, his hand claws raised as if to ward off the frightened Vikadian. "Captain?" he said.

"How foolish of me." Mandela strode forward and put a protective arm around Eris. "We should have told you about the new species you'd meet. This fine gentleman is not a Conchirri, I assure you, but rather a Frokossi prince. Isn't that right, Mr. Dobera?"

"Yes," Dobera said. "Ex-prince since my brother had me outlawed. On the *Sidhe* I am the quartermaster."

"Forgive me," Eris said. "I was startled."

"The Frokossi," Paolo assured Eris, "are Confederate members in good standing, though Dobera is the only representative of his species onboard. Conchirri were much larger and tailed."

"The differences between Frokossi and Conchirri will take all night to list," Dobera said frostily.

"Of course," Mandela said, steering Eris to the table. "Dr. Mourner, I believe you've cleared our newest crew member for all human foods except for shellfish and caffeinated beverages?"

Mourner raised her eyebrow, seemingly amused at Mandela's solicitude. "Correct, not that the caffeine will harm her. It seems to affect her as alcohol does humans."

"Well then, perhaps a small cup will be good for her nerves," he said with his usual broad smile. "Captain, would you have the stewards begin serving?"

Shasti nodded to the lead steward, and everyone was seated. Eris sat between Paolo and Mourner. Her depression and listlessness seemed to have been left on the surface of her world. Whether she was adjusting to the idea of a new life, or merely overwhelmed by all the strangeness, was difficult to say. She studied everything and everyone in the room with intense interest.

Vaughn leaned in and spoke softly in Shasti's ear. "It is perhaps as well that she was rescued by humans."

"True." Shasti nodded over her glass. "Eris looks more like a human than like any other known species. It would have been harder for her had a Frokossi, Morok, or Okaran ship recovered her."

Eris peppered Mandela with questions about the Confederacy during dinner. To Shasti's surprise, Mandela was open and forthcoming about the recent history of their government. She was rapt in regard to any details of the annihilation of the Conchirri. Paolo's stock, already high with Eris, rose further when she learned that he had survived captivity with the carnivorous enemy. It was a harrowing tale, and he told it well. Even Vaughn looked at him with grudging respect afterwards.

Shasti had hoped that in all the excitement Eris would forget her interest in Shasti's past, but she was not so lucky.

"You promised to tell me how you came to receive this ship," Eris finally asked. "Is this not a good time?" Vaughn and some of the others also turned toward her, signaling their interest.

Shasti sighed, but the tale of her life was too well known. If Eris did not hear it from her, she would only get a distorted version from others. "After I fled my homeworld of Olympia as a hunted criminal, I did a variety of jobs. Most involved guns. On one I was captured." Her mouth drew into a hard line at the memory. "I was a prisoner on a ship of Dua-Denlenn pirates when the *Sidhe* under Robert Fenaday ran them down.

"I gave Captain Fenaday an impromptu demonstration of my talents by overcoming his security, disarming him, and executing my former captors."

"One of a long series of things I had to give her legal pardon for," Mandela said. "I used to keep a list." Brief laughter followed the comment.

"Captain Fenaday was looking for his wife's starship, lost in the Conchirri War," Shasti continued, swirling the cabernet in her glass as she spoke. "He wisely decided to hire me to prevent the usual cutthroats and screwballs he employed from either selling him out or wrecking the ship.

"Robert was a very different kind of man from what I had met up to that time. Kind, generous, not the sort you would expect to find privateering, save that he was looking for the woman he loved. We served together for a number of years, through some adventures, the telling of which we do not have time for tonight.

"Then fate and a series of my own bad decisions took me back to Olympia. I went to kill the man who had created and abused me. Robert came to rescue me when it went bad." She smiled at Dan Rigg, who nodded his head. "We brought down the government."

"And everything else," Vaughn said, raising his glass.

"And in the wreckage we found a clue to Robert's wife's whereabouts. There was no holding Robert back then." She shook her head.

"Or anytime," Mandela rolled his eyes.

"She was a prisoner of a new alien power, the Voit-Veru. We attacked the outpost where they held her."

"Touching off a short but victorious interstellar war," Rask added.

"Also pardoned for that," Mandela said, raising a finger.

"I was the one who found his wife, Lisa. I rescued her from the compound and reunited them. Robert gifted me with this starship."

"How remarkable," Eris said. "How utterly remarkable."

Shasti sipped the full-bodied cabernet. "Enough about my past," she stated. "Do we go on from here? We've lost two crew, with ten more injured, the sled is destroyed, there's minor damage to *Paladin*, and we've certainly gone through stores and ordnance at a greater rate than expected. We are no closer to finding the source of the Conchirri and the Evolvers."

"What do you think, Mr. Vaughn?" Mandela said.

Vaughn gave his wolfish grin. "This moment comes to every expedition. The way ahead is unclear and dangerous. The expedition is largely intact but beginning to show cracks. Prudence would dictate a return and replenishment. But," he said, picking up his glass, "no one remembers the expeditions that turn back."

"Whereas the other ones make for fine tragic tales of hubris and overconfidence," Rigg added to an appreciative chuckle.

"Dr. Eris," Mandela said, "what reaction do you think we can expect if we approach the Kandalor?"

The alien looked back at him. "I know so little. Kandalor has been an open world for all of its long history. But your vessel is a Conchirri ship for all that its color is unusual. I am unsure of how the defenses will react to you."

A small smile quirked Shasti's lips. "Robert's doing," she replied. "He had money troubles at the time, and red was the cheapest color the dockyard possessed."

"More likely a mid-life crisis," Mmok said. "You know what they say about men and red spaceships."

Shasti wagged a finger at Mmok. "No speaking ill of my ex."

Eris watched the interplay between the two with a confused expression. It matched the bemusement on the faces of the others, some of whom had served from the days of the Enshar Expedition when Shasti and Mmok had been the bitterest of enemies.

Vaughn shifted impatiently. "The question is, will we be blown from the skies or not?"

Paolo turned to him. "No way to know. There's no information on the defenses or how they worked. The tales of their last operation were legends in the Nekoan's time. I don't even know if they were real."

"The answer is simple then," Vaughn said. "We go. I will take the *Paladin* and approach the planet. If it proves safe—you follow."

"The *Paladin* is a fleet destroyer," Shasti said. "She practically bristles with weapons. *Sidhe*, with our large storage bays and hangers, may seem less threatening."

"If it wasn't painted blood-red," Mmok added.

"There are some other factors involved," Mandela mused. He sat back in his chair. Fortunately for Shasti's sensitive nose, he had not proceeded to the cigar stage of the evening. "I think it would be sensible for us to conceal our point of origin initially. Not for long, that won't be practical. It would be prudent to establish some contacts before the powers on Kandalor have to consider what we represent. We have a native Vikadian with us, and I am sure Dr. Mourner can work up something to dye a few of us in a matching gray."

"Why would we need to disguise ourselves as Eris's people?" Mourner asked, putting her chin in her hand and leaning on the sturdy table.

"Do you recall what happened last time we met an alien species?" Mandela said. He picked up his snifter and drew in the scent of the brandy.

"A bit of a special circumstance," Mourner answered, with a sidelong glance at Shasti.

Mandela caught the look. "Oh, tempting as it would be for me to blame the outbreak of hostilities with the Voit-Veru on Robert Fenaday, he was just the particular catalyst in that matter. No, fleets had been stacked. Governments and their economies had already come into alignment for conflict. If he had not set it off, something else would have. First contact is a time of peril, unparalleled in a society's history. Everything is called into question.

"The Nekoans who traded with Eris's people were a deep-space culture. And this mysterious Kandalor evidently has fantastic weaponry. If we traipse into their space, representing a power made up of seven species, winners of a conflict in which we exterminated the Conchirri, we could destabilize worlds and possibly bring on a war. No, it must be carefully managed."

"By spying?" Shasti said, shifting back in her leather seat with a creak.

"Intelligence gathering, Captain," Mandela said with a wounded air. "We will control our exposure, revealing ourselves slowly to those in power in a safe manner. Trust me in this. I know politics. There is nothing worse or more disruptive to a government than the unknown. People sometimes react with their fear instead of intelligence."

"So we pretend to be Vikadians?" Rigg mused.

"What do you think, Rask?" Shasti asked. "Would an alien see the differences between us and Eris?"

The Morok looked at Eris and shrugged. "Remember, Captain, I grew up on Mars. I've been among humans my whole life. Eris doesn't look human to me, but to a Morok from homeworld, hard to say."

"Dobera?" Shasti asked, turning to the Frokossi quartermaster.

Dobera looked at Eris with his usual impassive gaze. "I'd be hard-pressed to tell her from a human. The differences are subtle to the eye, like those between the Denlenn and Dua-Denlenn. I think she could pass for one of your kind."

"Skin tone is wrong," Mourner noted.

Dobera shrugged his thin shoulders. "Humans come in more skin tones than any other species. Most others are monochromatic."

"Consider it a blessing," Rigg said. "It's caused enough trouble among us."

Rask laughed, canines in evidence. "Doesn't matter. On my home-world, we are all blue-skinned. We fought about the shades. I," he said, admiring himself in a darkened monitor screen, "am the handsomest shade of Royal Blue."

After dinner broke up, Shasti made her way back to her cabin. To her surprise she found Paolo waiting for her outside her door. She walked up to him and raised an eyebrow.

"I wanted to see you," Paolo said. "With everything that went on back on Lantrim II, it seemed that we had little time for each other. Our various duties kept us busy. I thought now that we have some peace, at least till we hit Kandalor space, we might pick up where we left off."

"No, Paolo," she said. "I don't think so."

"Ah," he said, his face closed and distant. "I had sensed that we were drifting apart. Now I know."

"We were never that much together," she said, then, relenting, "listen, we had exactly what you and I both wanted, some fun together."

"No denying that," he said with a sensuous smile. "We could have more."

She shook her head. "I may not know what I want out of life. Indeed, for the most part I'm not even sure I know what the questions are, much less the answers. But though I enjoyed what I had with you, I feel I have to move on. What we did was a side trip for both of us."

"Side trip," he said, leaning against a bulkhead. "I guess so. My life just seems to be that way. Even before I ended up in a Conchirri holding pen, it was always about now. About grabbing every last fine and beautiful sensation life has before it all runs out. And it runs out so fast, even when mischance or some devilish thing like the Conchirri doesn't cut us down.

"Sometimes I wish it wasn't and I could want some of what others want. Settling down and being with one woman. It just isn't me. I can't seem to force myself into that mode. I don't think I could change if I wanted to." There seemed to be a note of sad longing in his voice.

"You might be surprised about the changes that can come over a person," Shasti said. "Though I will be the first to admit they come in their own good time."

"I will dream of your magnificent body." He grinned, retreating to the shallows.

But not of me, she thought, *and therein lies the problem.* "You'll find others."

"And so will you," Paolo said. "Tall, dark, and menacing. You will make quite the couple."

"Perhaps."

"*Ciao,* Bella."

"I'll be seeing you, . It's a small ship."

"You'll be looking at me," he said over his shoulder. "But you won't be seeing me."

It didn't take long for the cartographers to find the star that Kandalor circled. Only one combination of K- and M-class stars at the requisite distance existed. Hyperspace entry points and currents would be another thing entirely. Shasti ordered Mollica to take the reduced fleet out toward deep space, in the direction of Kandalor, theorizing that the hyperspace point would have been between the two stars. It would take time to find the points, even with two ships working the Hawking pattern. The sooner they started the better.

Days of effort finally paid off with the parameters for hyperspace entry. Between the two ships and their navigators, the parallax and course for the jump point were plotted. Using the system's outer planet for a booster, they dove into its gravity well and were slung for the system's edge at high speed. They lined the two Confederation vessels up for a run at what they hoped was the old entry point for returning Nekoan traders a thousand years ago.

On *Sidhe's* bridge, Shasti watched the countdown clock tick down as they readied for the star jump. A familiar sense of unreality gripped her as hyperspace yawned wide to take her in. *I wonder if I will ever get used to this*, Shasti thought, and gave herself up to the fall.

11

"Collision Alert, collision alert," an automatic voice shouted in Shasti's ears as a klaxon beat her into consciousness. Her vision swam as the lingering effects of jump gripped her. "Nye," she ordered, "evasive turn to port, max delta-vee thrust."

"Affirmative," he called back, terror helping him shrug off the effects of jump.

Pressure gripped them as *Sidhe's* AG field strained to keep them from being flung into the bulkheads with lethal force. Shasti knew that at *Sidhe's* emergence speed, a degree or two of alteration was all she could hope for before they were upon whatever had triggered the ship's automatics.

"Scan is still disturbed, but I am picking up a small asteroid dead ahead," Sharon Hafel called. "Estimating three-hundred meters length and 45,000 metric tons. No other targets."

"Are we clear?" Shasti demanded as *Sidhe* shuddered around them.

"No confirmation," the navigator called. "It's still in our probability cone. Scan is still too whacked to tell."

"I can salvo all forward weapons in a spread—" Wardell began.

"No!" Mollica snapped. "It will just spread debris in front of us, then we're sure to hit something."

"Hold weapon fire," Shasti said, fighting the increasing G-force that wanted to tip her over in her seat.

Mollica's knuckles had gone white from holding onto a bulkhead takehold. "If the AG field fluctuates…" Mollica said.

"We won't even know it," Shasti said.

"*Paladin* has appeared from jump," the com officer shouted. "I'm relaying a warning."

"He's maneuvering," Hafel confirmed.

"Scan," Shasti turned with effort, "best fix?"

Hafel's eyes met Shasti's. "It's going to be close."

A rock grew suddenly in the main screen. A misshapen lump of utter insignificance left over from the making of the system or drifting out of the deep dark. The screen constantly adjusted the image so they could watch the distance close.

In all the mind-numbing emptiness of space, Shasti thought with a fierce hate. *You had to be here today in front of my ship.*

"We're going to make it," Nye shouted, his dusky face glowing with animation. "We'll clear by two kilo—"

Sidhe's hull rang like a giant bell. Light flared on the main screen before it could cut out. Their blinded eyes were plunged into a darkness lit only by a shower of sparks and then by the dreary red glow of emergency lights. A pitifully few panels glowed with lights and telltales.

Shasti drew a painful breath. The straps of her chair had tightened painfully over her abdomen. She could hear someone in the dark, moaning.

"Status," she said in a loud but calm voice, as if they were safely in a parking orbit. "Are we airtight?"

A murmur and more groans sounded around her.

"Status! Now, damn it."

Hafel, her voice weak and shaky, spoke first. "No damage control reports yet. Main power is off. The remote hull systems board is working and it's not showing a hull breach."

"Get me Perez. Send a runner if you can't raise him. Who's hurt?" Shasti unbuckled from her seat. Her Engineered eyes quickly adjusted to the low light, and she spotted a body on the deck. Mollica. She quickly went to her XO, noting that the ship's AG field had settled again.

We'd be a fine, red mist if it hadn't, she thought.

Mollica lay unconscious on the deck, a nasty gash on her forehead. *The webbing on her takehold must have failed,* Shasti thought.

Wardell knelt beside her, opening an aid kit. "Weapons are offline," he said. "May as well be of some use. I've got her."

Shasti nodded, leaving him to it. She could see Hafel opening the panel with the hardwired phone to engineering. Even with the intercoms down it should still work.

"I have Perez, Captain."

Shasti took the handset. "Status."

"Main drive is offline. We've had a system cascade failure, but I think it was mostly safeties cutting out due to overload. Emergency power is on except forward of Frame 22, below D deck. We have no maneuvering control. Damage control reports no major atmosphere leaks."

"You're getting more there than I am here," Shasti said, looking about. "Bridge is still down."

"Com is coming back ma'am," the communications officer said. "I don't have voice, but I have keyboard. *Paladin* is matching course speed and rotation. They should dock at our main shuttlebay portside. They are already alongside."

"I'm going down there," Shasti said. "Get a team up here from sickbay to collect the XO. Nye, hold the bridge. Hafel, make sure system info is passed to me every five minutes."

Shasti made her way down the companionway to the shuttle deck, five down and amidships. With the intercom up, Hafel kept broadcasting information to Shasti. She found wandering crew and sent them to the bridge, engineering, or with the injured to sickbay with able-bodied help.

Power, she thought, *is the big issue. It's already getting cold on the ship.*

"Shasti," a deep and unmistakable voice called out in the darkness ahead of her. Torches shone and bounced off the corridor.

"Here," she called.

Vaughn was beside her in an instant. "Are you hurt?" He placed a hand on her shoulder and looked into her face.

"No," she said very conscious of the weight and warmth of his hand on her, "but my ship is. What did you see as you closed in on us?"

"There is a scar running half the length of *Sidhe's* starboard side," he said, dropping his hand. Behind him the corridor filled with more crew from *Paladin.* "Our instruments did not detect penetration or atmosphere leak. You must have been tagged by a micro-fragment off that asteroid."

She grimaced. "Bad luck. Something must have hit the main asteroid, God knows how long ago, and thrown up some fragments into orbit. Our luck to hit a piece of gravel at two-thirds the speed of light."

"The perils of being a first-in jumper," he said.

"Can you run power cables—" she began.

The lights in the corridor went on along with the blowers, and the myriad noises of a living ship came with them.

Vaughn smiled down at her. "My engineers were already so instructed. *Paladin* was designed for this sort of battle damage aid. We have power load to spare. I ordered cables run into the docking apertures for planetside maintenance. I told you that I would be a useful man to have around."

Shasti gave him a sidelong glance. "Then I was right not to let you disappear into the depths of space."

"Careful," he said. "That was very nearly encouraging."

Shasti shook her head with the tiniest of smiles. "Send your medics to my sickbay and half your team to engineering. As for you and the rest, we are off to Frame 22. Follow me."

"It does seem to be my fate," he said.

With *Paladin's* power available to restore *Sidhe*, the immediate repairs went quickly. Casualties proved light, mostly bruising and some fractures, Mollica being among the worst. Shasti worked the next forty-eight hours without a break, helping in repairs, directing damage and engineering teams, even managing the paperwork details of revised watches to account for the casualties. Mollica regained consciousness and tried to return to duty, but Mourner confined her to bed for two more days.

On the third day after the collision, Shasti called her officers together in the wardroom for some badly needed food and to see where everything stood. Mandela was there with Eris, though Mourner and the med staff were too busy to attend.

Vaughn walked in, and she waved him over. Since the collision, he had spent all his time on *Sidhe*, filling in for Mollica and serving as Shasti's powerful right hand. Shasti remembered how the two of them had placed their shoulders under a bent stanchion to lift it off a trapped crewman. The man would have bled to death before Mmok or a powerjack could be found. Both Engineered had thrown their full power into lifting it, while Tanaka pulled the man free. She remembered with a thrill the admiring look he had given her.

"You are as strong as I," he'd said, "and with so much less mass. I would love to know how that was achieved."

But the reference to her past had reinvoked the distance between them, and for the rest of the day, they spoke only of the ship's needs and yet did not stray from each other's company.

Shasti dropped into a seat gratefully as the steward brought her a pasta dish. She could have banished fatigue by altering her body chemistry, but that only delayed payment with interest. She ran her hand through her long black hair. *Probably looks like a cat's bed,* she thought.

"Are you all right, Captain?" Mandela asked.

A little surprised at the solicitude, she looked over at him. "Now that I know my casualties are attended to and my ship is nearly space-worthy, much better, thank you."

"You are to be congratulated," he said. "You too, Mr. Vaughn. I haven't seen better in the regular Navy."

Vaughn nodded. His big hand engulfed a bottle of water. "Credit belongs to our crews."

Shasti paused in devouring the pasta. "We no longer need worry about how fearsome we look to Kandalor as we close in. With the main drive damage that we have, we'll be linked to *Paladin* on the voyage in. We'll look like what we are, a cripple being shepherded in."

"So we are committed," Vaughn said, sipping his water. "Your engineers cannot repair the stardrive?"

"Not hanging here in space. We need a dockyard. Or at the very least we'd need to land and set up our own factory and shipwright yard."

"I would prefer to have all our powers intact, but we were only two small warships." Mandela shrugged. "We came neither to conquer nor to overawe. As we have no choice but to forge ahead, we will do so."

Shasti fingered the desk comm. "All members of the approach team report to sickbay for 'Operation Grayscale.'"

Mandela smiled at her. "I'll be in my cabin, watching the show. Be diplomatic, Captain. Be very diplomatic. We are further away from home than any humans have ever been."

An hour later found everyone from the approach team lining up for the improvised spraybooth Mourner had set up. Those who were to be on the bridge crew during the approach had to submit to the indignity of being spray-painted gray and have their hair dyed silver. Laughter and horsing around slowed the process.

Nye, the helmsman, grimaced in distaste as his dusky, yellow-tinged skin disappeared under the light-blue gray of the Vikadians. The process amused Wardell until it came his turn.

"At least what little hair I have is the right color," he grumbled.

"Hey, doc," Rigg said, looking down dubiously at his now gray torso. "This stuff will come off? Won't it?"

Mourner shook her head. "The tough guys are always the biggest pain in the ass in a sickbay." She turned to face Shasti, who'd been sitting on a diagnostic bed, legs crossed and in apparent concentration. "Your turn, Captain."

Shasti's skin suddenly turned the exact shade of gray that Mourner had been painting the others.

"Hey, that's cheating," Mourner said, after a second's open-mouthed astonishment.

"I remember that trick," Rigg said. "You did that just before we dropped on Olympia. The rest of us were getting into camo and zap, there you were, black as night."

Shasti gave them a smug look. "Yes. I have refined the technique. Having my own built-in melanin camouflage was very useful. It actually takes a little more effort than just going as dark as possible, but it seems less strain to maintain it."

"Remarkable," Vaughn breathed. "Truly."

"Can you do anything for your hair?" Mourner said.

"My hair," Shasti said, with a distinct tone of menace, "will remain as is."

Mourner started to say something, then thought better of it. "Dying three feet of hair would be a pain. I don't suppose you would consider a haircut?"

Glare.

"Nope," Mourner said, "didn't think so. Well, Eris did say that dark colors occasionally occurred in her species."

"Good," Shasti said. "I'll be on the bridge." She hopped off the bed and strode out of the sickbay.

Vaughn looked a question at Rigg.

"She has a thing about her hair," Rigg said. "Whenever she gets like that, it has something to do with her past. I wouldn't ask. If she wants to tell you, she will. Never push her when she's in that mood."

"Sounds like good advice," Vaughn said.

The approach team caught up to Shasti on the bridge, relieving the normal watch, who shook their heads in rueful regard on seeing Team Gray.

"Man," Rask said, shaking his head, "I wonder what Eris is going to make of this? I think Mandela's gone off his nut."

The converted crew took their station around Shasti.

"Anything yet?" Shasti asked.

"No," Mollica returned. "No patrols, no buoys, space stations, or traffic. No one seems to have noticed or challenged our advance. Hardly what one expects of a major trading world.

"Either," she continued, "we are not observed because there is no one left to observe, or care, or they are so sophisticated they use instrumentation we are not aware of."

Shasti debated a moment longer. "Hafel, start sending our hails in Vikadian. Let's see if there is anyone to talk to. We are getting close to the inner system. I don't want to be shot for sneaking in. If their instruments are anything like ours, they'll be seeing us shortly, even with just planet-based sensors."

Hafel nodded and began broadcasting a greeting that Eris and Paolo had labored many hours over.

"Shall we deploy probes?" Mollica asked.

"No," she said. "The planet's defenses or the orbiting ships might confuse them for missiles or fighters. We'll have to go in with nothing more than the ship's sensors."

Kandalor filled their screens with wild colors. The planet was roughly three times the diameter of Earth with vast orange deserts, immense polar icecaps, and shallow green seas that dwarfed the Pacific. The tropical belt girdled the planet in green.

"It reminds me of an old-fashioned Christmas ornament," Rigg said.

Shasti, whose childhood had not included such pleasantries, could only nod. "It's a beautiful world. So immense, and still only slightly over one standard gravity. I've never heard of such a world before."

"Three times the size of Earth and only slightly more gravity," Mollica said. "It must be made out of custard."

"Any reaction to our approach?" Shasti asked. "Any response to our communications?"

"Nothing yet," Hafel said.

"Wait one," Wardell said. "Detecting two vessels in orbit over the northern hemisphere."

"Type?" Shasti asked.

The gunner shrugged. "I'm not getting any IFF or anything as to types. They are both unfamiliar. Looking at size and energy readings, I have low to medium probabilities that they are merchants, armed merchants, or auxiliary warships. I don't see anything that looks like a purpose-designed warship."

"Surely they see us?" Vaughn said.

"No reaction yet," Wardell said. "Their sensors may not be as good as ours, which would also tend to indicate they're not warships."

"Watch them for when they react. It will tell us their max range," Shasti said.

Behind Shasti, the turbo doors whooshed open. Eris and Dr. Mourner entered. Eris did a double-take on all the gray-painted humans on the bridge.

"Doctors," Shasti acknowledged. "We have arrived. That's Kandalor's capital, Bizi, on screen."

Eris nodded in a queer diagonal gesture, her eyes on the screen.

Shasti turned back to it. "Well, Eris? Does it look familiar?"

"Hard to say," Eris's whispery voice was turned into basic by the translator. "Only one small party of my people has been here before. They came in a Nekoan vessel as trade and contact delegation. They ignored the Nekoans advice about trying to find a central government and barely got out alive. Bizi was a lawless pile of species and structures back then. There's no form of central government, just tribes, mobs, and gangs. Bizi hides almost anything and is inhabited by almost anything."

"It doesn't make much sense," Mollica added. "There's no traffic control, no port officials. Even a frontier world has more control of space than this. I can't believe that anyone with space-based defenses would tolerate this."

"Captain," Wardell said. "Those two ships are moving, and I am now detecting a third. They are giving us a wide berth. I am not getting any hails or other expressions of interest, but they are changing orbit away."

"Analyze the range they move to when they reach stable orbit," Shasti said. "If we can figure at what range they start feeling safer, we may get a sense of what armaments are in use out here."

Wardell's reply was cut off when Hafel spoke. "Incoming message, Captain. Running it through the translation program. I am getting voice and video."

"Put it up," Shasti ordered. "Only incoming for now. Let's see if we want to reply first."

The image on the screen stabilized, and a remarkable face looked back at Shasti.

Eris was dead on in her descriptions, Shasti thought. The face on the screen was an attractive cross between human and feline. The eyes were similar to a human's though larger, under the pile of a rough, lion-like mane through which large cat ears protruded. One ear twitched as Shasti looked at the creature. If the shape of its upper body meant anything, it appeared to be female. A voice spilled out of the speakers, smooth and nearly singsong.

"We'll see how good Romita's translation program is now," Vaughn said. He gave her a smile and headed for the turbo. "Good luck. I'll be on *Paladin's* bridge."

"Yes," Shasti said, watching him leave with an unsettled feeling. She shook her head to focus. "All right, clear the bridge of anyone not in gray."

The other unpainted fell in behind Vaughn to go wait in the antechamber to the bridge. A clearly nervous Eris walked over to stand with Shasti.

"Translation in progress and coming through," Hafel said.

From the speakers the translated message sounded in neutral Confed standard. "Greetings to unknown starships approaching the planet Kandalor. This is the Nekoan trade delegation calling. I am Teleera D'abo, charge' d'affaires of the trade delegation. Please acknowledge and advise on your intentions."

The message cycled again. Shasti took a deep breath and looked at Eris, who nodded with only a slight hesitation.

"Greetings to Kandalor," Eris began. "I am Toraku Eris of the planet Vikadia calling from the starships' *Sidhe* and *Paladin*. We approach with peaceful intentions seeking to establish trade and diplomatic relations with the Kandalorian authorities and with Nekoa."

There was a pause as their message, limited to light speed, winged its way to the planet. They could tell when it arrived as the Nekoan started suddenly, then its image froze, though of course the image lagged reality by nearly a minute.

The image unfroze briefly. "Starships, we acknowledge receipt of your peaceful intentions. Please wait."

After a minute, the image unfroze again. "Teleera D'abo to Toraku Eris. Request visual communications. My staff is resurrecting our records on your species. We have not had contact with your kind since the plague of carnivores swept through our space a thousand years ago. Indeed, we believed your kind had succumbed to their attacks."

Eris started to speak, then stopped, overcome by emotion.

Here goes nothing, Shasti thought "Hafel, put us through on visual."

"This is Captain Shasti Rainhell of the *Sidhe.* We see you, Charge' d'affaires D'abo. Can you see us?" She knew the ship's computer would wash her voice through the translation program. Any difference between how her mouth moved and the sounds coming from it would hopefully be chalked up to light-speed delay and alienness.

The alien's eyes swept over the bridge a few seconds later as the link became two-way.

"Your records were very nearly right," Eris said, the translator program changing her words to Nekoan at the far end. "Our world was severely damaged by the attacks. It has taken us this long to reestablish ourselves. We hope to be greeted in friendship by you, as was our custom before."

The alien's eye fastened on Shasti. Even the light-speed delay did not account for all the silence that followed, and Shasti cursed herself for being talked into the deception by Mandela. Her eyes shifted to Eris, as if pondering the differences between Shasti and Eris, despite the melanin change.

Maybe I should have been less of a bitch and let Mourner change my hair, Shasti thought.

The alien looked off to its side and apparently muted its speaker as they lost sound. Then it turned back to them. "My staff tells me that a hospital ship from our forces visited your world after the attacks by the Conchirri ceased and no life was seen."

"The only survivors," Eris began, "were in the starfort deep under the Keliglace plateau. We did not detect your ships as all of our surface equipment was obliterated and you did not detect us. Would that it had been otherwise. Still, it is good to know that you sent help."

"Our dealings in the past," D'abo said, "have always been mutually beneficial and we rejoice that your kind has survived the dark time. Things went ill for the three species of the Trade Guild after the beasts attacked. Had our stratagem of luring the bulk of their fleet to attack Kandalor not been successful, we would have been annihilated. As it was, the Skurlock disappeared from the star lanes, and the Ribisi and we suffered terrible losses."

Someone interrupted D'abo again. When she turned back this time, her eyes had gone narrow. "I am advised that you are flying a ship of Conchirri design though the color is different. You seem to be flying very close to another vessel whose design we do not recognize."

"This ship is a prize, found in orbit of our world. The other is of our own design," Shasti said. "As for our proximity, we struck a small rock coming into your system at high speed. This vessel is space-worthy but has significant damages. We are hoping to land on your world to effect repairs. Perhaps you could put us in touch with the Kandalorian authorities so that we may make arrangements for an eventual landing and to open relations."

Shasti drew the distinct impression that the alien was amused. She looked at Shasti, her eyes more open and friendly.

"You are indeed strangers here," D'abo said. "There are no Kandalorian officials, at least when it comes to matters off their world, in which we have never known them to take interest. There is no planetary authority as such. An interlocking web of kingdoms and priesthoods governs the planet in a somewhat chaotic fashion. The spaceport is administered jointly by ourselves and the Ribisi, but our influence does not even extend to the city beyond."

"Surely there is a Navy or Military—" Shasti began.

"No," D'abo said. "We and the Ribisi administer the port directly. We Nekoans have conducted most of the contacts. The Ribisi are a reclusive group."

"We would like to land and conduct repairs. We did not detect a space station to dock at," Shasti probed.

"We have none," D'abo confirmed. "Our attempts at creating a stable orbiting platform have always been defeated."

Shasti noted the use of the word defeat. Translation defect?

"So we have no orbital facilities to offer you. You may proceed to land at the port. We will provide you with the coordinates to make a powered landing, if your ships are capable of dry surface landing."

"An upload of maps is in the buffer," Hafel said.

"Finally, Captain Rainhell and Toraku Eris, a friendly word of warning, safe your weapons before you come into orbit. You seem friendly enough, for all it appears that both your vessels are formidable warships. It might seem inordinately trusting of us to offers such free access to…to aliens we have not seen in a thousand years. You will see no defenses as you approach and certainly none of ours. But this world is protected, never doubt it. It is the only reason my people still live. So heed my warning."

Eris looked at Shasti, who nodded. "Our intentions are peaceful. We will follow your instructions."

"You will be met after you land." Charge' D'abo made a curious head and hand gesture, then her image disappeared.

12

Their orbit brought them over what Eris's records indicated was Bizi, the capital city of Kandalor. Lights dotted the night side of the world below them, in what seemed an utterly random fashion. To the east of the capital stood a titanic mountain, star-shaped when viewed from above and dominating the river valley that held Bizi. Curiously, it did not seem to be part of a range.

"Weird-looking place," Mmok complained, staring down at an infra-red view of Bizi. "Doesn't make a damn bit of sense the way it's laid out. It sprawls for dozens of kilometers in all directions."

"Yes," Hafel said, "energy readings are all over the place on sensors. It looks like parts of it are high-tech, but most of it looks like it's made from stone and mud with very few power traces in those areas. I think some of that lighting may be wood fires or natural gas.

"We can't use probes, but the spectrographs and other remote sensors show the nitrogen-oxygen atmosphere that we expected. Everything checks out with the old Vikadian records."

"What are you picking up on general broadcasts?" Mandela asked.

"I haven't seen any images of us on any planet-based channels, nor any other reports that we've been sighted. Mr. Romita seems to think most of what I am seeing is entertainment stuff. He and the staff are working on it, but it's like standing in front of a firehose with a teacup. There's so much coming in and we think it's in multiple languages."

"The Nekoans," Eris responded, "said the natives of this world were not technic and had not been for as far back as they could tell. Whoever built the mythic weaponry may have been from somewhere else, and this place was merely an outpost of theirs."

"So the knuckle-draggers are running the shop into the ground," Mmok said. "It would explain the look of the place, barely developed. I could probably smell it from here if I still had a nose."

Mandela shook his head and sighed. "Please take us in, Captain."

Shasti put *Sidhe* into hover over an immense area of flattened dirt toward the edge of what passed for a spaceport. The field bore the signs of many a ship landing, with charred vegetation and flattened areas of burned earth. *Paladin* hovered alongside her, no longer tethered, but protecting her damaged side

"Back 10% on power," Shasti ordered. "Sink rate of one meter per second."

"*Paladin* is in position, nose to stern alongside us," Mollica reported. "She's one hundred meters off our port side."

"Have him land thirty seconds after we do," Shasti answered.

"Surface contact," Nye said. "Ground is as solid as radar said."

"Cut engines," Shasti said. "Secure from flight but standby." The rumbling of the engines died as *Sidhe* settled and balanced on her jacks. On the main screen, Shasti watched *Paladin* start down for its landing. Each ship's forward weapons covered the blind spots created by the other ship's engines. The Confed vessels were nearly five-hundred meters long, but Vaughn's *Paladin* was heavier than Shasti's frigate and sank deeper into the crushed dirt.

Shasti and the others walked to the hatchway behind the main bridge. The hatch doors slid open, giving access to a broad flattened area of hull. Railings snapped up into place as they stepped out, and people hitched on lifelines. A sensible move, as a stiff breeze was blowing. Dirt and vegetation and a hundred less identifiable things tickled their noses, causing a few sneezes.

Shasti looked about. The vast horizon captured the eye first. None of them had ever been a world so large, but with normal gravity. The world seemed to stretch away forever in all directions. Above them, the sky was a deep blue, with yellowish clouds scudding along the western horizon. The earth, where it wasn't covered with scrawny green-brown vegetation, was a mix of ochres, reds, and browns.

"Make for nice pottery," Mollica called over the breeze. She looked reluctant to step out of the shelter of the ship.

"Interesting ships," Mmok said. He pointed at two vessels that occupied the field proper with gantries and tarmac below their engines.

Shasti turned to find Rigg holding out a spare set of field glasses. She put them to her eyes. Between her engineered vision and the optics, the vessels leapt into view.

"All hatches closed on both of them," Mmok said. Shasti knew he was scanning with instruments built into his HCR body. "No crew in sight."

"Neither looks military," Rigg added, looking through his own glasses. "No turrets anywhere. Break-bulk freighters is my guess."

"Yes," Mandela said. He'd brought an ornate walking stick with him, disdaining a lifeline, and looked about the spaceport as if he were the new owner. "Civilian indeed and no obvious ground defenses."

"Notice something else?" Shasti asked.

"Yeah," Rigg said, "different design philosophies and aesthetics. I doubt the same people made these ships."

The farther vessel, a tall ship, sat vertically on fins and was painted white with orange swirls over her hull. The closer vessel couldn't have been more different. It squatted on four immense jacks and looked like a collection of children's blocks. Its dark-green metal hull appeared to be unpainted, and no decoration was visible on its chunky shape. It gave an impression of tremendous strength and of having been over-designed for its function. Shasti, who had run cargo and preyed on cargo ships, could not understand the massive design.

"That ship's designed like a safe," Rigg said. "Could it be made for

Jovian atmospheres? It looks like some of the gas miners that I've seen around Jupiter."

"You're right," Mandela said. "It has that look, only more so. Perhaps we've finally met a gas giant species?"

"I don't know," Eris said. She hadn't ventured far from the hatch and seemed uncomfortable at the sight of the vast world beyond. "The Nekoans never gave us any detail on the other species."

"I think you're right," Mmok chimed in. "The blockship is sealed spacetight, unlike the dreamsicle over there," he pointed at the orange and white ship, "which is exchanging atmosphere inside and out. I can see heat coming out of vents. Why breathe expensive canned air when you can get the real thing for free? Only reason I can think of is that the blockship boys ain't breathing the same stuff as us."

"Makes sense," Rigg said.

Hafel walked out behind them with a portable and handed it to Shasti.

"Vaughn here," came his deep rumbly voice. "One notices that we are not met."

"Which," Shasti returned, "makes one wonder if the other powers here are less than happy with the Nekoan's effusive welcome of us? Thoughts?"

"Press the advantage of surprise," he said. "Make the events rather than be moved by them. In short, let's go looking for catpeople."

Shasti smiled to herself. Vaughn was aggressive as always, but this time their instincts ran the same way. She looked at Mandela, who had brokered more treaties with aliens than any other living being, and raised her eyebrows. He nodded.

"Agreed," Shasti continued. "A small contingent though. Your best people, one mule, fifteen minutes. Over and out."

She looked at Rigg. "Same thing. Eris, Paolo, and Mourner as well. Two mules. And yes you can take Rask and Mmok. Get them both in travel cloaks. It risks the deception, but I don't think that will last long anyway."

He flashed her a grin. "Yes, ma'am!"

"And I am sure he'll be bringing Tanaka," Shasti added slyly.

"Course," Rigg said. "You asked for his best."

She turned to Mollica. "I'm off to town, Zandra. Keep buttoned up. Make preparations for an emergency take-off. If you have to abandon ship and flee aboard the *Paladin*, do it. Park the *Sidhe* somewhere secret in the system so she can be recovered later if it comes to that."

Mollica grimaced. "Be careful and bring me back a souvenir."

"Wish me luck," Shasti said to Mandela.

"You've always made your own luck, Captain, and have done quite well. Just continue to look below the surface. Reverse everything and see what it looks like."

Teleera D'abo, head of legation and lead huntress of the Legation's Secret Service detail, watched the two warships settle on the field. Both vessels were the size of Nekoan cruisers and had lean, predatory lines. She and her team laired in the ruins of an old, Skurlock custom office, unused since the Skurlocks disappeared from space millennia ago. They'd reached a third story tower, despite the aged and sagging flooring. The customhouse sat on a hill and gave a good view of the field.

Her second hunter looked at her in dismay. "Warships, Huntress. What does this mean?"

"They say they come in peace," she replied, her tail swishing.

"Well, that is something," Second said. "The Conchirri and the Evolvers never said anything. They just killed."

The vessels were of similar size, though different in outline. One, the scarlet vessel, showed the clear evidence of a micrometeorite strike, with a long scar running down the side. As soon as both vessels settled, ramps came down and figures scurried out under the ships, avoiding the areas superheated by the ship's jets.

"Those are quality ground troops," Second observed, tail lashing. "Nice job of securing a perimeter. Look, they are already beginning cover and concealment."

"Now are they merely prudent?" D'abo muttered to herself. "Or are they planning an attack?"

"Look atop the red vessel," Second said, handing her field glasses.

D'abo sighted in on a flat, railed area behind what she thought was the bridge of the scarlet vessel. It filled with Vikadians. D'abo studied them intently, dialing up max magnification. Gray-skinned and tailless aliens wandered about, seeming intent on the nearby Nekoan and Ribisi ships and the city beyond. They looked like Vikadians, though larger than usual for that species, according to her field glasses. One seemed older or at least he appeared to be leaning on a stick, and his coloring appeared a bit off, though at this distance it was hard to say.

"Neither Conchirri nor Evolver," D'abo said, "that much for sure. Vikadians perhaps, at least the one, but my instincts tell me no."

"Why?" Second asked.

She shrugged. "The same instinct that told my ancestors that a relak was in the tree over the path. They are more than they seem, and the universe is about to change."

"I hate change," Second sighed. "I wonder if Minister Kadesh has settled the Ribisi back down."

"Thank the Great Hunter that Kadesh was onworld," D'abo said. "I'm not as much of a diplomat as the part calls for."

Second smiled without showing teeth. "I think you have done well, pretending to be a glorified shopkeeper."

"That's charge' d'affaires to you, ignorant lout," she said, "a respectable head of legation, interested in trade and relations."

Second laughed softly. "Do we attempt to get closer to observe them?"

"No. They are very alert. You won't get to any better vantage than here without being observed. This will have to do. Let's hope they stay… Damn."

"What?" Second said, his ears snapping forward.

"Small vehicles and a cluster of people. Some of whom were on the bridge platform before. I do not think they are going to wait on us. The damn Ribisi should not have kept us from meeting them. These are bold people, and they are going to come to us."

She slid back from the window. "Keep the others here. Do nothing provocative. Withdraw if seen. I'd better get back to the legation and get into dress uniform. Civilizations are about to collide."

"Good luck," Second said.

"To all of us," D'abo said. "We must be due for some by now."

D'abo got down to the street, racing through the decrepit building then hopped aboard her portable flyer and set off at rooftop height and top speed.

Shasti went back to her cabin and picked up weapons and armor, along with the various secret gadgets she'd acquired in a lifetime of desperate fights in the off corners of space. She took Risky with her and walked down to the ramps built into *Sidhe's* landing jacks. Tivka and his landing force troops were busily digging in, along with Vaughn and Rigg's forces. The crab robots remained aboard but ready to deploy in a moment's notice. The entrenchment might look warlike to a watcher, but their welcome had not been effusive so far and the ships were most vulnerable on the ground.

"Risky," she said in her "handler" voice. The genetically enhanced shepherd's ears pricked up. "Patrol. One watch. No kill." The shepherd whuffed his understanding, and she turned the K-9 over to Tivka, knowing that his nose and eyes would serve them well.

Overhead, an elevator opened and lowered two scarlet mules and the rest of the contact team. The mules were small, sturdy six-wheeled vehicles. Rigg had left the covers off, along with the heavier weapons that usually sat in the traversable rings. As soon as the platform touched down, Rigg drove the first vehicle off. Mmok stood in the ring, his HCR body muffled in a coverall and a travel cloak. Rigg was covering his bet by keeping the combat robot's nature less obvious. Mourner and Eris sat squeezed in the back. Rask had the wheel of the second with Paolo and two other ASATs.

Rigg stopped to pick up Shasti. At the same time, Vaughn drove up with a similar vehicle, in the more prosaic gray of Olympia's Navy. As predicted, Tanaka rode shotgun. Two Denshi troopers in black uniforms filled the back seat.

"Woo-hoo," Tanaka said. "We're off to town."

"Adventure and excitement on foreign worlds," Rigg said. "Just like the recruiting posters said."

Shasti raised an eyebrow at Vaughn, who simply smiled.

"It's good to be on a planet again," he said, stretching in his seat. "The ship was beginning to feel small."

"I'll lead," Shasti said. "I'd feel safer with you covering our tail."

"Done," he said.

"Let's go," she said to Rigg.

They drove out from the protected space between the ships, passing under *Sidhe's* shadow into the bright sun. Shasti wore a light jacket over her armor, as did the others. The breeze from their passage cooled them, but she began to wish they'd rigged up the fabric tops. Shasti pulled a band from her pocket and tied back her long glossy hair before the wind could tangle it more. "Looks like many of the native structures are made from this clay."

"Yes," Mmok said. "Those tall buildings in the distance seem of a more modern design. I see orange and white on them. Maybe they're the dreamsicle people."

"We'll head out that way then," Shasti said. They drove in that direction, giving the grounded and secured ships a wide berth.

"This is bizarre," Mourner said. "No quarantine. No medical surveys. They just let us drop out of the sky. The Okarans spoke to us by radio for six months before we could even dock at a space station. This is the Wild, Wild West, folks."

"Let's hope the usual disease immunities across species continue to apply," Eris said. "Remember though, they think that you are Vikadians. They went through all the biological protocols with us a thousand years ago."

Shasti looked sidelong at Rigg. "I'm not persuaded that they've bought the impersonation."

Rigg shrugged. "Well, they're playing along for now."

"Are they?" she countered. "We'll see."

As they ground over the rough tarmac of the field, Mmok pointed out something new. A line of animals and bipeds stalked across the field, roughly parallel and ahead of them. As they drew nearer, the group bunched up. Shasti waved Vaughn and Rask's vehicles away and approached more slowly.

"A caravan," Mourner said. "These must be the pretechnic natives we've heard about."

"We should avoid getting too close," Eris warned. "They are unpredictable."

"And ugly as hell," Mmok added.

"No closer," Shasti said. The mule slowed to a stop, and Shasti stepped out. About twenty meters away, the nearest of the Kandalorians stood facing her, with a dozen more behind him and a circle of twenty beasts. The creature's shape was difficult to tell through the loose beige clothing. The Kandalorians' heads were swathed in a brighter yellow cloth. The leader facing Shasti had a large, bare-bladed knife stuck through its belt. Shasti realized that what she'd taken for a mask was the creature's face, rubbery dark skin, with large dark eyes over a trunk-like nose that extended in her direction. The beasts behind it were equally unlovely, six-legged animals that seemed to be a combination of lizard and horse. The beasts were piled high with boxes and fabrics. Even from this distance, the smell of the collection was enough to make Shasti's eyes tear a little.

Shasti raised both hands, palms out.

But the leader gave back an ambiguous signal, raising one dark-skinned hand palm out, but the other went to the white handle of his large knife.

"Okay," Shasti said. "Not curious and not friendly. Back away slowly. Mmok, you've got an auto pistol."

"Yep. If it pulls something, I'll nail him."

"Bet he wouldn't smell any worse dead," Rigg said.

They pulled away as the caravan began to sort itself out behind them.

Rigg steered for the tall, modern buildings, avoiding the native sections, which seemed to be full of people who were equally incurious about the aliens.

"From this distance," Shasti said, "they probably aren't noticing us as being very different from the other spacers. Let's hope it stays that way."

As they drew closer, they saw two other styles of buildings, dark, windowless cylinders that reminded Shasti of the sturdy ship at the port. A third section featured odd buildings of an organic-looking base, with metallic towers linked at various levels by slender bridges. They sparkled in the sunlight in shades of green from emerald to aquamarine. Shasti wondered at their apparent fragility.

"I don't think anyone is home in Spiderville over there," Mmok said.

Shasti raised her field glasses, but the jostling of the vehicle made it difficult to see. "What are you seeing?"

"Disrepair," Mmok said. "Windows out, crumbling masonry, rusted metal, and not a sign of power. Nobody is home, not even the trailer trash."

Vaughn pulled up. "Is it worrying anyone else that the streets are completely empty?"

"Yes," Shasti said.

They pulled onto a broad street of pale concrete lined by large gray warehouses and port facilities. A few vehicles sat parked on it, wheeled types that wouldn't have been out of place on any Confed world. At the far end of the street stood a formidable building with flags snapping in the breeze over it. Shasti noted three flagpoles. One was bare. Another bore a strange sigil with eye-hurting combinations of purple and dark green on a black background. The third flapped with colors of orange, white, and gold.

They could see figures running into the building.

"Nekoans," Mmok called. "They looked like armed troops."

"Must be the legation. That's our destination," Shasti said. "Let's drive up slow."

Kadesh was still arguing with the Ribisi legate when D'abo returned. The dark-maned minister was seated at her desk when she burst in, buttoning up her dress tunic after having slid out of her field coveralls.

He raised a hand to still her out of view of the camera pickup, but she could see the Ribisan ambassador on the screen. It wore an environment suit, for all that it was still in its legation, a sign of urgency and fear. The barrelish creature was hard to see in the murky light, and Teleera was just as glad. The hydrogen-breathers were masters of engineering and chemistry, but ugly as carrion. Legate Ilken had nothing like a proper face; its head resembled a cluster of grapes above the arm tentacles. All communication from or to the Ribisi was electronic, as neither Nekoan nor Ribisan could survive the other's environment unprotected for even a second.

"We must proceed with utmost care and caution," Ilken said. "You should not have invited these aliens to land. There must be detailed conferences with 'those from below.'"

D'abo frowned. She knew the expression meant the homeworld court of the Ribisi, deep in their gas-giant, months or weeks of travel away.

Kadesh made a gesture of hand and tail, indicating polite negation.

"The Vikadians," Kadesh said. "If this be them, could be powerful allies and were once trading partners of ours. We enjoyed peaceful relations before the Conchirri plague. Legate, the ovoid vessels of the Evolvers haunt your space as much as they do ours."

"We avoid them," Ilken countered. "And it is rare that they pursue us."

"Not so for us," Kadesh said. "Or would you invite us to hide in your gas giant worlds?"

The rhetorical question seemed to sting the Ribisi. "Our alliance remains intact."

"Your alliance is sometimes carried more in your words than in actions," Kadesh snapped. Then, recovering, he added more diplomatically, "We are hard-pressed by these golden ships, Legate. A few more years like the last and you will have no one with whom to trade."

"All the more reason to fear these new arrivals!" Light flashed on the screen, an indication of emotion with the Ribisi.

"They are a fact, Legate Ilken. In our skies and able to land here with, or without, our assistance. They will not wait months for us to deal with them. They are here now."

"In a ship, Minster Kadesh, in a ship the like of which has not been seen in these skies since the Terror. We fear this. We fear this. The Gods taunt us with this."

"Legate, I cannot speak to your religious concerns. But we both know this planet has a way of dealing with those who initiate hostilities on it. We must trust to that ancient protection."

"Your rash actions have left us no other choice. We will have no direct dealing with these returned aliens. I will pray that your actions do not bring disaster to us." Though the electronic voice could not convey anger, the words contained enough.

The picture snapped off abruptly.

Kadesh stood, retractile claws flexing in and out in agitation.

"Not only are they ugly," D'abo said, "but they had to be afraid of their own shadows too?"

Kadesh gave a snort of amusement. "If you cast such a shadow, you'd be scared too." He stood, stretching to release tension. An older, small male, Kadesh had made a career of being underestimated by his opponents. He was not directly in her chain of command, but she knew him to be an ally of her Section head back on the homeworld. "Report."

D'abo filled him in.

Kadesh grimaced when she told him the aliens were moving out.

"They'll come in here," she said. "These are smart people. Our legation doesn't look like the fortress that the Ribisi one resembles. We're in the high-tech area of town. It will be obvious."

A screen chimed musically on her desk. Kadesh triggered it. "You appear to be right as usual. Your personal guard spotted them turning onto our street."

"Bid the guard to withdraw into the embassy," she said, quickly adjusting her half-cape. "I think it best that I meet the aliens outside. I'll take two guards with me. But minister, no matter what happens, we must befriend these people. I am expendable. Aid to our people is not."

"Just so," Kadesh agreed. "Keep your ears up. Look friendly."

D'abo headed for the doors, adjusting her half-cape. *Bastard,* she thought, *you could have disagreed with me.*

The Confederates pulled to the curb before the building and idled their engines, looking about. The building towered over them, throwing back the afternoon sun from its white stone and metal. Shasti noted the orange highlights in the building and in the flag fluttering over it. A set of large, chocolate-brown doors fronted the building.

"Do we knock?" Mmok asked.

The large doors swung open and three Nekoans stepped into the light. They paused as if to regard the Confederate spacers, then came on at a relaxed pace.

Shasti, Rigg, Vaughn, and Tanaka dismounted, along with Paolo and Eris. "Everyone else stay seated and quiet," Shasti ordered. "Mmok and Rask, keep those travel cloaks over you."

Shasti studied the three Nekoans coming toward her. The two trailing were obviously guards, in bright blue uniforms with contrasting white sashes and belts. They wore boots and holstered sidearms. Unlike humans, who would have worn helmets or hats, they had only manes and large ears atop their heads.

She turned her attention to the female in the lead, recognizing Teleera D'abo. The Nekoan stood as tall as the males, though slimmer. Muscles rippled on her thighs, which were easily viewed as she wore something like a bronze one-piece bathing suit with a matching half-cape. The sun sparkled off her golden mane and the tiara-like headgear in her pile of rough hair. As with the males, a furred tail stood out behind her. All three advanced with a sinuous, feline grace.

"Wow," Rigg said. "Legs right up to her neck. Nice ones too."

"Indeed," Vaughn added, a note of admiration clear in his voice.

D'abo stopped well out of reach and raised both hands, palm out. She was, Shasti thought, a pretty creature to human eyes, with small delicate features under large violet eyes. Beyond the mane and ears, she was very human in appearance. Her face gave such a feline impression that Shasti was almost surprised by the absence of whiskers or any fur beyond a downiness that covered the sides of her neck. Faint bands of a tigerish striping ran over her cheeks, heightening her resemblance to a Terran feline. *Makeup?* Shasti wondered.

"Greetings in the name of the Nekoan people," D'abo said, looking from Shasti to Eris, her throaty voice coming out of her voder in Vikadian and being translated in their earpieces as Confederate.

Eris answered for them. "Greetings we return. We come in peace, hoping to be met in peace."

"You are so welcomed," D'abo returned, her ears twitching. "I apologize that you were not met as promised. There have been some complications."

"Complications?" Vaughn rumbled. The guard's ears flattened at the sound of his deep voice, and Shasti shot him a warning look. Vaughn overtopped both of the guards by a head. They relaxed some as the translator rendered his question in to Nekoan.

D'abo lowered her hands but gave him a frank and friendly look. "Yes, but let us not discuss these matters under the heat of the sun. We invite you into the legation, but first, please understand that those of your party who enter must do so unarmed. The others who retain their weapons may rest in the glade there." She gestured to a section of trees near a fountain. "We'd provide you with refreshments, if we knew what of our food or drink would be safe or palatable to you."

"Doctors Romita, Mourner and Eris and Mr. Vaughn and I will accompany you," Shasti said. "The rest will remain where you indicated." She handed her weapons over to Rigg. The others followed suit.

"I'd love to take you with us," she whispered to Mmok, "but I don't think we dare."

"Agreed," Mmok said, his voice muffled by the overhanging hood of the travel cloak. "I'll be listening on your translating circuit. They can't jam that unless they simply don't want to talk to you. If there's trouble, you say, 'Oh Canada' and I'll come running."

"Good."

Another alien came out of the building. This one appeared male and gave the impression of being older. He wore bronze colors of a less eye-catching cut than D'abo.

"This is my assistant, Careel," D'abo said. "He will remain with your people and see to their comfort until you return to them. He is, of course, unarmed."

D'abo walked up to the three vehicles, displaying a confidence that she did not feel and that she hoped came across the gap of species without seeming arrogant. Her two guards flanked her. They were for show. She'd instructed them not to draw their weapons for any provocation. Neither of them was happy about it.

As she approached, five of the Vikadians dismounted. The others sat, alert but not tense. The wind brought their scent to her, and she controlled her reaction. Vikadians, hell, there was one. The others smelled entirely unfamiliar. She recognized the leader, a female taller even than D'abo, who was unusually big for a Nekoan. The female had been named Rainhell. She was striking, with long glossy smooth hair that caught the sun. Her eyes were like gemstones. The scent of her was pleasant, almost spicy-sweet, unlike the duller, nuttier scent of the actual Vikadian. But for the absence of ears atop her head, she looked like a Nekoan. D'abo wondered if the other woman was cold. She seemed to be wearing a great deal of clothing. Maybe they came from a very warm world?

The male next to her stood, and he took D'abo's breath away. Huge in every dimension, he massed twice what either of her guards did and looked capable of simply flinging the small vehicle at them. Brilliant eyes sat in his dark face, but they were lit with intelligence and drive. Another sniff brought her the scent of the dye that the big alien male had used to color his skin.

These two, she thought scanning the group, *are damned dangerous.* But the combination of males and females reassured her. Females were not marginalized in whatever culture she was facing. *And they have sufficient tolerance that a true alien*, D'abo thought, *is among them. No, there were more*, she realized, as her delicate nose continued to sort information. *There's another alien type in the vehicle, under a travel cloak and hidden behind a visor. The other cloaked figure standing so utterly still in the weapon ring gives off machine smells. Some form of robot.*

The deceptions frightened her. *They like aliens*, she thought, *remember that. They are made up of multiple species. That's hopeful.*

She gave her prepared speech. Rainhell replied. D'abo found herself liking the musical voice of the alien woman. When the huge male, Vaughn, spoke, both her guards twitched.

Ears up, claws in, D'abo reminded herself. *Look friendly.*

D'abo arranged for them to enter the legation, noting that Rainhell left behind six of her fighters and took three who appeared to be scholars or scientists. On the other hand, she did bring the huge Vaughn. D'abo turned off her translator long enough to brief Kadesh on what to expect.

Careel and the two guards led the others and the mules away. Shasti's group followed D'abo into the legation. Once inside, the chill of air-conditioning struck them. Glassed hallways and exotic plants and artwork greeted the eye. They continued to follow D'abo down the unoccupied halls past desks and the paraphernalia of a modern office. Shasti noted with a secret amusement that the men in her party had a hard time keeping their eyes off their host's elegantly swishing tail and round, athletic hips. Shasti wondered about her outfit that, in human terms, seemed quite revealing. Still, cultures varied and the ursine Okarans wore no clothes beyond vests. Enshari and Voit-Veru used clothing mostly for the pockets.

D'abo brought them into a spacious room with a large, marble-like central table, decorated by beautifully sculpted hunks of crystal and a jade-like stone. The walls were covered in some exotic wood that gave a faint scent of vanilla and hung with portraits of Nekoans. Some freestanding tapestries of brilliant colors and abstract shapes hung about the room, rippling in the breeze from silent fans set below them. Overhead, glowing silvery bars moved slowly, like a cloud of languidly schooling fish. It all combined to make the room feel open, airy, and light.

On one wall rested the image of a different alien, or perhaps machine. To Shasti, it looked like a barrel with four jointed tentacles. Atop the barrel was a smaller transparent hemisphere through which could be seen a dark mass of gas or fluid and something that looked like a bunch of grapes. *Eyes?* she wondered.

Vaughn noted her gaze. "A suited alien? Perhaps from the blockship?"

She nodded.

Rigg was looking around. "A legation for sure. Almost enough to make one homesick for when I was a guard at the Terran Embassy."

An older male rose from his seat at the head of the table. His ruff of hair was almost black, and he lacked the sinuous grace of the Nekoans they had seen so far. D'abo moved to stand next to him. Overhead, several small silver bars broke free of the cloud and took station over them. Shasti looked up to find she had her own attendant light, but that she rated only one glowing bar.

"Our legation here," D'abo said, "is small, and as we have so little to do with the natives, we do not staff a full ambassador here. I am charge' d'affaires, and this," she gestured at the smaller male, "is Howal Kadesh, undersecretary for trade. Your arrival coincided with his visit to my humble station."

Kadesh made an elaborate looping gesture with his arms. "Please be seated and make yourselves comfortable."

Shasti and the others pulled out the wooden chairs, noting with interest the holes in the base of them for tails. Vaughn settled in as if he expected the chair to fail under his weight.

As D'abo introduced the Confederates, Shasti noticed that D'abo had committed their names and exact pronunciation to memory on just one hearing.

"We will be most interested," Kadesh said after they all sat, "in the miraculous survival of your species, Dr. Eris, and even more interested in how you came to Kandalor abroad a ship of Conchirri design in the company of these new aliens." He gestured to Shasti and the others. "Are they of two species or one?"

Eris gave Shasti a helpless look. Mourner's facial expression said, "I told you so."

Shasti and the others sat very still. But no guards barged in and D'abo's stance remained as relaxed as before, her ears up and her tail gently swishing. *Girl's got good control,* Shasti thought. *She can't be as relaxed as all that.*

"The gray coloring was a nice effort," D'abo said, "and might have worked with a species that did not evolve from a plains-hunting cat with an excellent sense of smell. Unlike the other species we have met,

Nekoans use scent for communication. Our libraries contain scents as well as pictures and words. You clearly do not all smell Vikadian."

So much for Mandela's stealthy approach, Shasti thought. She sensed Vaughn gathering his powerful legs under him and made a small quelling gesture.

"The minister from my government aboard my ship," Shasti said, "feared that our sudden appearance would cause disruption and worse. He was concerned about your reaction."

"He sounds very sensible," the undersecretary said. "Indeed, the meeting we planned with you at the spaceport was derailed by near panic from our trading partners, the Ribisans." He gestured to the barrel-shaped alien image on the wall.

"They objected strenuously to our opening contact with you even though they believe you are Vikadians. Fortunately, we did not share our suspicion with them that you were more than that. They are xenophobic in the extreme as a result of the Conchirri attacks and very frightened by the military nature of your vessels. While I applaud your minister's caution and may even choose to abet you in this deception, full disclosure is now requested."

"I would like to summon our political leader then," Shasti said.

"I would prefer to learn a little more about you before you communicate with the formidable ships at the port," Kadesh said. "Forgive my caution, but as your initial moves contained elements of deception, however prudent, I think it falls to you to earn our trust."

"Very well," Shasti said, knowing Mmok and hence Mandela would be listening in. "We represent an alliance of seven species of intelligent life from over ninety parsecs from here. My ship, which is in fact a Conchirri prize, contains members from five of those species. As you both noted, our vessels are warships, though the one I command is privately owned.

"We are on a peaceful journey of exploration, contacting new species. In our journey we stopped at Vikadia, which was destroyed by the Conchirri about a thousand years ago. There we discovered Eris in cold sleep, the only survivor of her kind and added her to our crew."

"Why have you come all the way to Kandalor?" D'abo asked.

"The Conchirri who swept through your space millennia ago attacked our Confederacy. We annihilated them."

"Ah," Kadesh said. D'abo straightened, and the two Nekoans traded looks. "This is great news that you bring us. Great news. We suffered terribly at their hands. I doubt that we would have survived at all had we been in their direct line of march to wherever they were going. We have always feared their return."

"You must represent a very powerful military," D'abo said, "to have destroyed the Conchirri. We had guessed as much from the size and apparent power of your warships."

"Our ships," Vaughn said, leaning back and very much at ease, "are of the escort class. We judged it impolitic to travel in one of our capital ships, though with the end of the war we had those to spare. They are expensive to run."

Even across the gulf of species, Shasti saw the chilling effect of Vaughn's casual announcement on the Nekoans.

"We learned of Kandalor from Eris," Shasti continued, "and heard of its mythical defenses. We assumed that those defenses are real, both from what you said and from the mere fact that this world survived the Conchirri. It seemed to us that peaceful relations with such a formidable power could be useful to both our sides."

"A thought we too had when we returned to this world," D'abo said.

"We assume that you had some contact with the power here," Shasti probed.

"When the Conchirri swept through the Concord," Kadesh said, "which is our name for the trading association of the Nekoan, Ribisans, and Skurlocks, they drove us all from space. We were forced to fall back on our homeworld and single colony. The Ribisans are hydrogen breathers, silicate lifeforms from gas giant worlds. The Conchirri could neither eat them, nor use their gas giant worlds, nor their resources. Unlike our small, rocky worlds, gas giants are hard to bombard. The Ribisans suffered less than we, hiding out on the gas giant worlds.

"As for the Skurlock, so far as we know, they perished. We can find no sign of them on the worlds we once shared. Of the Vikadians you know more than do we.

"We know that the Conchirri struck here," Kadesh continued, "following one of our retreating fleets. But none of our vessels survived to tell the tale. As for what the Conchirri met when they assaulted Kandalor, we cannot say. There are no defenses that we have ever been able to see. We found the tiny fragments of ships—very many ships—adrift in orbit. Even now an occasional piece reenters the sky, lighting up the night.

"When we finally rebuilt our civilization and emerged from behind our defenses, we found Kandalor as it had always been and the Conchirri gone for many hundreds of years."

"Surely the natives have some idea of what happened?" Vaughn asked.

"The Kandalorians," D'abo answered, "for all that we believe they did not evolve on this planet, are remarkably incurious about doings beyond their world. Their religion reverses the usual pattern where heaven is above and the land of the dead below. So the sky above is something taboo to them. We have learned that there was a period of remarkable activity in the sky, coinciding with the arrival of the Conchirri."

"Remarkable," Shasti said. "Part of our mission was to travel up the path of destruction that the Conchirri blazed and see if there was some power behind them."

The Nekoans exchanged glances. Shasti found herself wishing Mandela was with them.

"Have you suffered attacks from any other force since the Conchirri?" D'abo asked.

"At this point," Shasti said firmly, "I wish to summon the minister from my government. His expertise in these matters exceeds my own, and he can speak for our government."

"Very well," the undersecretary said, though if the rapid swishing of his tail indicated anything he seemed nervous at the idea. "We are most anxious to receive him and open relations with your formidable Confederacy. We will try to involve the Ribisi Legator, but I am not optimistic that they will respond immediately. If you wish to return to your vessel, we will not impede your coming or going. If you prefer, I can send a car to pick up your minister and his entourage."

"I'll check." Shasti stood and walked away from the table, reaching for her throat mike. For show she said, "Put me through to Mr. Mandela."

"Here," he answered.

"We've met the Nekoan authorities, and they are aware that we are not Vikadians. However, they seem to appreciate your thinking in that regard. They would like to meet you in person."

"Excellent," Mandela said. "They do not seem too put out by our little camouflage?"

"No, though it did add a few moments of excitement to the meeting. Not as much as if I had suddenly sung, 'Oh Canada.' Shall I send a mule for you?"

"Please advise the Nekoans that I will be coming with a full security detail and request that they send an escort to the *Sidhe* to accompany us in and guard against incidents. Advise them that I carry the rank of Ambassador Plenipotentiary of the Confederacy of Seven and will require the honors appropriate and customary to such a rank. In essence, how their own ambassador would expect to be received."

"Let's hope that doesn't include some ritual like hacking off a limb or dancing naked atop the embassy," Shasti said.

"Such are the perils of a diplomatic career," Mandela returned. "I shall see you shortly. Please let them in on the matter of Mr. Mmok. I will want his assistance."

"Because diplomacy is my thing," Mmok cut in.

13

Fortunately, Mandela was not required to dance naked on the embassy roof. Rather, he was closeted along with Paolo and the Nekoan undersecretary, Kadesh. The Nekoans, who had met several alien races, were experienced enough to go slowly and courteously through the initial protocols.

Shasti often found herself in the company of D'abo, who had arranged for quarters for the group and a regular shuttle of people and material to and from the ships. She knew that in due course Mandela would bring up the subject of repairs to her ship's outer hull. Meanwhile, Perez would be using all the resources of both vessels to do what he could. So she relaxed on a divan of exotically carved wood, upholstered with a simulated animal skin and looked out of the guest quarters of the legation. D'abo had showed them how to use the plumbing facilities and other amenities, all the while keeping up a bright conversation through the translators that Mmok had synchronized between Nekoan and Confed standard. The Charge' disguised a thorough grilling as a combination of curiosity and pleasantry. Shasti recognized the interrogation technique though it was one she herself rarely used. She contented herself with honest answers, only demurring on military matters. She kept the others back and handled D'abo on her own.

D'abo, Shasti mused, seemed to have a fair grasp of the sort of questions a military planner would want answers to. Speculating on aliens that they had just met was a dangerous business, but something about the way the athletic, young alien's mind and body worked told Shasti that she was more than a trade bureaucrat. *I'll be watching this one*, Shasti thought.

As if divining Shasti's thought, the Nekoan female dropped into a broad chair opposite her, carefully tucking her long elegant tail under her, and switched subjects to Nekoan diplomatic history.

"Our worst difficulty in diplomacy," D'abo said, "comes from the fact that we derive so much information from scent. When we first met Ribisi, we could not scent them, or for that matter, even meet in person. One of us always needed the protection of the strongest of environmental suits. So the initial meetings were very confused. Mercifully, as we were not after the same real estate or resources, there was no reason for conflict in the short term. Otherwise, things might not have been so peaceful."

"It matters so much?" Shasti asked.

"The closest analogy I can give you would be if you and I had to communicate, but you were deprived of your hearing. Worst still came when we met the Skurlock, who smelled actively bad to us. A considerable amount of a diplomat's training is to disregard alien scents as a form of communication."

"And how do we smell to you?" Shasti asked.

"Good enough to eat," D'abo said.

Shasti gave her a curious look, which D'abo interpreted correctly.

"Humor, honored visitor," D'abo hastened to add, flicking an ear, "merely humor. Like you, we are omnivores."

"Mostly omnivores," Shasti replied, feeling a liking for the cat-like alien. "We do have some people who are vegetarians." She then had to explain about vegetarianism. Shasti got the impression from D'abo's flicking ears and twitching tail that she found the concept of voluntarily forgoing meat to be highly amusing and perhaps slightly scandalous.

"Tell me about yourself," Shasti countered, "if such a request is not impolite in your culture."

"It is not," D'abo said. She ruffed up her mane of hair and settled back. The gesture stretched the smooth muscles of her legs. Shasti again wondered about the brevity of the Nekoan's clothes. The males had been bare-armed with light clothing but it covered more than D'abo's gold shorts and cape.

Perhaps it's just as well that I sent Vaughn back to the ships, she thought. From the reaction he and Rigg had to D'abo, it appeared the Nekoan females were a hit. The males had been good looking too, but the females had a more human appearance, if D'abo was anything to go on. Perhaps it was the smaller and more delicate features.

"I'm the youngest of five," D'abo continued. "We are all from an old trading family. Merchants from as long ago as there are records. My family felt that we needed more influence in government and so I was groomed for the service from when I was a kit. I was to worm my way into the bowels of the bureaucracy. A simple-trader girl given to the night-feeders in the hope that taxes and regulations would get better.

"I have a knack and a liking for aliens and ended up here. With the Skurlock and Vikadians gone, there were only the Ribisi and the Kandalorians, till you arrived, and I made a study of both. I've been working on expanding our trade with both groups. Ribisi are fantastic engineers in metals and liquids. Kandalorians trade handicrafts and natural products along with the occasional mysterious objects dug up from this planet's past. We have identified traces of eleven other species on this world at one time or another. It's a fascinating place." She shifted forward, ears up and muscles rippling.

Shasti switched her gaze from the Nekoan's dynamic physique to the world beyond their glass walls. In the distance, Shasti saw the mountain that she'd first spotted on descent. It dominated the north-eastern sky.

D'abo noticed the direction of her gaze. "The Natives call it Sorokol, the Mountain of Destiny. It's the center of their religious worship. The area around it holds some of the oldest structures on the planet."

"Do they allow you near it?" Shasti asked, a faint excitement touching her.

D'abo nodded, a gesture she shared with the human species. "They are pretty casual about visitors or having their ceremonies observed, but they do not allow scientific studies. As is usual with priests, or at least as is usual around our space, religious orders are jealous of their privileges. We quickly lost interest."

Shasti wondered about the Nekoan's cavalier dismissal of the planet's central religious center. It seemed out of character with their brisk efficiency and tremendous curiosity about every aspect of the Confederacy. *Religious taboo?* she wondered.

"I've never been around religious people much," Shasti said cautiously, "but it doesn't sound different than our own experience of religions."

"Hmm, interesting. After dropping some remote sensors and a few probes in the area, all of which failed almost immediately, we decided to leave well enough alone."

Shasti gazed at the immense tower of stone. It seemed to rise to the few clouds. Something about the sight made her shiver.

D'abo excused herself not long after their discussion of the mountain. Shasti, Mandela, and most of the others remained in the legation. While the Nekoans did not allow them weapons, they relented in regard to Mmok. With the HCR standing silent sentry in the antechamber of the suite, Mandela felt there was little to be worried about.

Shasti spent a restless night. The circular bed on which she slept was comfortable enough, but visions of the strange mountain troubled her dreams. That in itself was unusual. Shasti rarely dreamed, or at least remembered dreaming. But it seemed that whenever she dropped into a deep sleep, she found herself wandering in dimly lit tunnels under the fantastic mass of granite.

The morning came and with it a breakfast that Dr. Mourner pronounced safe for consumption, though Dan Rigg had a close encounter with a pepper-like substance that resulted in his draining several glasses of water. That particular omelet was put to one side.

Shasti stuck to Confed coffee and something bread-like. The

coffee cleared away last night's cobwebs, and she found herself following Mandela, Mmok, and Rigg down to the conference room. The other Confed personnel were being given tours of the legation and some basic lessons in the history of the Nekoan trade confederation.

The four entered the same conference room they'd been in yesterday to be greeted by D'abo and Kadesh. Shasti sat back and watched with interest and growing respect as Mandela and Kadesh sparred verbally, each trying to extract the most information while revealing the least. Mandela seemed to relish the intellectual challenge, and after a while, it was clear that Kadesh was overmatched.

"I'm curious," Mandela said. "There are only you and the Ribisans left in space in this region and yet this huge planet with its indigenous, if pretechnic, society is clearly underdeveloped both in trade and military potential. Is there some treaty?"

Kadesh and D'abo exchanged glances. It seemed as if she was asking to reveal something. Whatever the non-verbal cues were, D'abo seemed to be satisfied as it was she who stood and walked to the large bay window facing the native section of the city.

"The planet," she said, "does not allow it."

"Really?" Mandela said, leaning back in the awkward Nekoan chair. "How does this world express its disapproval?"

"Establish a colony outside of this region," she waved her clawed hand at the scene outside, "and it will fail to thrive. Rainy seasons will go from six weeks to six months. Crops will fail. Vermin will multiply. Sinkholes will open under buildings. Nothing major, nothing grandiose, but you will find that any such installation soon becomes a burden rather than an asset. Pour in more people and material and the troubles multiply exponentially."

Shasti and Mandela exchanged looks.

"Trust us in this," D'abo said. "We have observed it from our own experience and our records from the first legation here a thousand years ago. The Ribisans, who have been here over a century now, share this experience. We have no idea of the how or the why. But it is an uncontestable fact, at least for our two species."

"Have there been conflicts between you and the natives?" Shasti asked. "Does this world take sides in those?" She stood, still a little restless from her dreams, and walked over to a wall near the window, leaning on it.

"There have been such incidents," D'abo said, regarding her from across the window. "The natives are tribal and hence war-like. They fight each other and occasionally us. There were even attacks on the Ribisi legation once. So long as we confine ourselves to defense, there are no 'supernatural' manifestations. Yet when a Ribisan punitive expedition landed and moved beyond the capital, it began to suffer catastrophic life-support failures. Their weapons began to explode."

"I imagine," Shasti said, "that there have been occasions when you also suffered from these effects? Perhaps conflict between you and the Ribisi?"

Mandela looked at her from the side of his eyes but signaled nothing further.

Kadesh gave an impression of disapproval as D'abo answered. "We have learned not to proceed in a large force beyond the capital zone. However, small expeditions have been unmolested. As for locally, we have rarely faced the Ribisi over weapons; neither side dares bring in major forces. Occasional incidents have not brought down the wrath of this governing power."

"So it remains a place where all parties can meet and trade," Mandela said. "Yet none can dominate. Very useful."

"You have been very frank," Mandela continued, "but I must ask you to be even more open with me. Openness now will get relations between the Confederacy of Seven and your trade association off to an excellent start. You are both clearly intelligent enough to know that it is vastly more difficult to retrieve a situation than to get it going in the right direction initially."

Both Nekoans studied him without comment.

"You have enemies," Mandela said. "It is a thousand years since the Conchirri swept through this area of space on their way to extinction at our hands. Yet the Ribisi have reacted with near panic to our arrival. I am advised their blockship lifted from the field and is now in orbit. The vessels orbiting Kandalor instantly altered course away from us when we were detected. The caution in your stationing a small, special forces team near our ships, while understandable and we are not offended by it, bespeaks a caution born of hard experience."

"Ambassador Mandela," Kadesh began smoothly, "perhaps it is too soon to venture into these areas."

Shasti studied D'abo, reading tension in the body and felt that the Charge' disagreed.

Mandela sensed it too. "Have you been plagued by large golden ships?"

Kadesh exchanged a long glance with D'abo. Shasti sensed that for some reason power in the room was shifting between Kadesh and D'abo. It was as if in some psychic hourglass, that Kadesh's control of the encounter was draining before their eyes. Kadesh scratched his ear, a gesture of indecision Shasti felt. "It seems we venture on military intelligence matters, Charge'. Shall we await instruction from homeworld?"

"I think," D'abo said carefully, "that delay risks events overtaking us from many sides. And who is better positioned to deal with these matters?"

"It will be your responsibility," Kadesh said.

D'abo studied Mandela for a minute. "We have faced such ships and with disastrous results. At first they were a few, striking minor colonies. Of late they have multiplied. Our fleets have fought them with mixed results. Only when we mass most of our warfleet have we had success, and even then at a cost."

"Do the Ribisi suffer as well?" Mandela asked.

"The golden ships do not seek their worlds out. As I suspect you already know, when these golden ships land, they do something to our people, converting them into slave soldiers in their service. The golden vessels destroy the Ribisi when they encounter the hydrogen breathers, but they do not seem to wish to convert them or their worlds. We fear our alliance with the hydrogen-breathers will avail us little. Once before, they hid in their giant hydrogen worlds and survived. They are apt to do so again."

"And now it is your turn," D'abo said. "I have extended to you the frankness you demanded. What do you know of these vessels?"

"We destroyed one of these ships after it fell on a colony world of ours. We call these unmanned AI vessels, Evolvers. It appears that its mission is to analyze and confiscate the DNA characteristics of races it encounters, wedding the strong points of any species they encounter with their creator's matrix. Then the Evolvers somehow processed living members of our species into willing, even fanatical 'Children of the Makers.' We encountered only the one, but it was my belief that whatever force sent it was linked to the Conchirri and that its assault presaged more to come."

"Your people," Kadesh said, "seem very effective in matters of war. You destroyed the Conchirri, and it seems that you are capable of handling the Evolvers, as you call them."

Mandela smiled grimly. "If we have a talent for war, it was forced on us by the Conchirri. Before they attacked, it was a widely held belief that wars in space were too difficult and expensive to be practical. They evidently studied other textbooks. As for the Evolvers, we have not taken their measure. The one we destroyed was badly damaged even before it fell on our colony. It still created terrible damage.

"But as you say, we are seven races. There is an eighth who will likely join us before long. If there is a threat, we have resources."

D'abo's disturbing cat-eyes focused on Mandela. "One wonders if there might be room at that table for still another race." Kadesh stirred, as if alarmed by how quickly matters were proceeding, but said nothing.

Mandela studied the young alien standing so casually before him. "Ah," he said finally. "You are no trade bureaucrat."

"Forgive me," D'abo said, dropping her large ears to half-mast, "if I gave you an overstated impression of my powers."

Mandela wagged a finger at the Nekoan. "Now, now, the game is already up. I recognize a kindred spirit when I see one. Your people are fighting a delaying action against a deadly enemy. You cannot find the Skurlock, the Vikadians are gone, and as I suspected, your hydrogen-breathing allies are not reliable. Only on Kandalor is their hope of a defense in the mysterious powers that cloak and protect this world. Yet the world will not tolerate a mass influx of Nekoan operatives and scientists. So, a small legation, run by a very young member of an ancient trading family. Yes, an excellent cover, I would have been hard-pressed to devise better myself."

"I don't understand your point," D'abo said. Her voice was calm and carefully modulated, but she watched Mandela intently. Shasti shifted slightly enough for D'abo to regard her and the implied warning in the move.

Mandela smiled and shrugged. "Play it out to the end if you like, but you are no more a shop-keeper or bureaucrat than I am. You're either the head of Nekoan intelligence, doubtful on account of your evident youth, though one should never make assumptions across species, or you are the number two."

D'abo considered them both for a few more seconds, then stretched and stood, all attitude of the lazy indolence she'd feigned before vanished. Even across species she seems to bristle with intelligence and energy.

"Number Two," D'abo said. "My superior is getting on in years and prefers the comforts of his luxurious headquarters. He keeps me around for the work that requires getting one's claws dirty. I am a little older than I appear, and I still like the field work."

She looked at Mandela. "And you?"

"I am rather more like your boss," he said. "Hard times put me back in the field, obviously, or you wouldn't be meeting me. But I have already discovered enough to have my old office upholstered and get some plush new carpet on my return."

D'abo gave what they'd come to realize was a laugh, shaking her shoulders with a noise that sounded more like a sneeze. "You do sound like him."

D'abo walked over to stand in front of Shasti, not quite nose to nose but close. "And you of shining black hair? Are you my opposite number, Captain Rainhell?"

"Not quite," Shasti said. "Let's say that for now we are hunting on the same trail."

"Someday perhaps," Mandela said.

Shasti threw him a warning glance.

"Well then, it may be that we shall all be comrades on that same trail," D'abo said.

"Maybe," Mandela said. "I will send for all the information that we have on the Evolvers. We may at least start by sharing that with you."

He stood. "You have given us a great deal to consider in a short while. I take it that the Ribisans still refuse to have any contact with us?"

"They do," Kadesh said, seeming more comfortable now that the discussion was back on more diplomatic matters. "They defer to us on the pretext that we initiated the contact."

Mandela pulled his lower lip. "Undersecretary Kadesh, as Minister Plenipotentiary of the Confederacy of Seven, I would like to use your good offices to arrange for the rental of suitable property, preferably close to this legation, for a temporary consulate. Once open, I will present my letters of authority and introduction to you and the Ribisi legate. Please inform him that while there are no present consequences, the Confederacy is now a fact of life and will take a dim view of being continually dismissed."

"I believe we can accommodate you in that regard," Kadesh said.

"Excellent." Mandela smiled. "There has been great progress made, indeed in diplomatic terms we are proceeding at break-neck speeds. There is much to consider, not the least of which is Charge' D'abo's question about alliance and treaties." He nodded toward D'abo. "But as I am sure you can both perceive, there is much to do to bring those stars into alignment."

"Of course," Kadesh said.

"Meanwhile, while we turn to issues of the new consulate, my captains would doubtless like to discuss matters of repair and reprovisioning with you. We have traveled long and hard and repairs are necessary. We will have various methods of payment available, specie, credit and, perhaps more valuable to you, information."

"Yes," D'abo said. "Information is most valuable. But there will be no charges for repair or reprovisioning. It will be merely a small investment in our warm, future relations. If you will come with me, I will introduce you to our chief shipwright and we can begin work on your vessels."

Shasti spent the rest of the day with D'abo and a crew of engineers and shipwrights coordinating trades and supplies going out to the starships. The Nekoans understood Shasti's security arrangements around the ships; for all that Shasti was sure there were a number of agents and spy devices among the contractors. If the circumstances were reversed, the Confederacy would do the same, so it was more or less an understood professional necessity. They worked late into the night, making multiple trips to the ships and legation. Shasti finally dropped into bed sometime around local midnight.

The next day began with another series of ministerial meetings. Shasti's eyes began to glaze over at the thought of the diplomatic minutiae that would have to be filled in before anything substantive could be done.

She looked up at a knock at the door. "Yes?"

Rigg opened the door. "Charge' D'abo, to see you, ma'am."

The Nekoan entered on Rigg's heels. She wore an eye-catching outfit of black leather, as usual it seemed to show a good bit of leg, though the jacket, which sparkled with silver metal, was of a more modest cut. Shasti noted that Rigg was keeping his eyes front and center today. She spotted Tanaka through the open door and smiled at Daniel's newfound discretion.

"Good morning," D'abo said. Her face, with its large violet eyes, radiated an infectious cheerfulness. Shasti noted that the faint tiger stripes on her cheeks and neck were more prominent and again wondered if the tinting came from some form of make-up.

"I have come to enlist you in an irresponsible enterprise," D'abo said.

Shasti's eyebrows shot up.

"If you are at all like me," D'abo said, "and I think you are, then the mere thought of working on leases and diplomatic details has filled you with a desire to run screaming into the wilderness. Our staffs can deal with the ships. The diplomats can blitz each other with words. Come, escape with me to the Old City. We'll tell everyone it's a cultural exchange."

Shasti could not help smiling in return at the Nekoan. "What?

Evade our responsibilities? Confound our leaders and generally misbehave?"

"Exactly," D'abo cried. "You have it."

"Excellent," Shasti said, snatching up her jacket. Like D'abo's it was simple black leather but possessed nothing that would raise a reflection.

"Uh," Rigg said. "How about I round up an escort—"

"An escort?" D'abo said archly. "Are we not powerful and dangerous females?"

"Uh," Rigg repeated, "yes, ma'am."

"And," Shasti said, slipping around a befuddled Rigg while taking D'abo's arm, "I did manage to stay alive for a whole twenty-five years before you were hired to babysit me."

Before Rigg or Tanaka could slow them, Shasti and D'abo slipped out of the suite. With a feeling of a child playing hooky, Shasti sped down the back stairwell to where D'abo had an orange and cream two-seat aircar. "Where are we going?"

D'abo leaped easily into the open aircar. "The Old City trade plaza. Let me show you some of the oddities of this world. I can also check in with my contact and see how the locals are reacting to your arrival. Plus we can get a breakfast of fresh crelick. You'll love it."

A few Nekoans waved from the embassy, and Shasti thought she spotted Vaughn. "Gun it," she said. "Or our responsibilities will overtake us."

"I see you are like me," D'abo said. With a whine of engines, they sped off.

14

Shasti looked over the hood of D'abo's orange and cream-colored aircar. The huge mountain lay to the east. She frowned up at it. The peak seemed incongruous, erupting from the planet's crust by itself and yet showing no sign of being volcanic in origin. It bulked far up into the sky. Its white crowned peak made an odd contrast to the desert growth cloaking its lower arms. Shasti noticed that D'abo scarcely gave it a glance. *Guess the view has paled on her*, Shasti thought.

At first, they cruised over a rise of modern structures used by D'abo's people and the Ribisans. Then their aircar slipped over the nondescript beige buildings that made up most of the Kandalorian city. But Shasti ignored all this as a city within the city came into view. The Old City was just that, walled and turreted, an ancient fortress of white stone incongruously spotted with solar light panels and antenna. It seemed that not all the local Kandalorians were as hostile to technology as the caravan drivers.

"The local name is Quezat," D'abo said. "It's rumored to be the original habitation of the Kandalorians, but it is full of structures built by the Predecessors. Aliens who have disappeared from our space before we or the Ribisi arrived. That's why it looks so different from what the Kandalorians build. There are ruins from these Predecessors all around this huge world. Some are dangerous to explore, even though they have decayed little, as if some effect from an ancient weapon haunts them.

"As for these here, many are still habitable." She gestured. "Look there."

Shasti's keen eyes picked out the differing buildings that D'abo pointed to. Bizi itself had been a queer mix of modern permacrete and metal structures, liberally interspersed with older buildings of native material. But these below the aircar's windows were like nothing she had seen. Quezat had a fairytale look to it. Beyond the white walls and turrets stood one building in particular that caught Shasti's eyes. The main building was circular, like a layered honey cake. Atop it stood a tower crowned with a mass of topaz crystal. Sunshine refracted from it in deep, buttery tones. Another tower ended in a globe of green. Around the globe slowly spun immense hoops of silver, supported by nothing Shasti could see. One ring was broken, with a cut and fused end made ragged by some disaster. Yet it still spun easily around the green globe.

Fountains dotted the broad plazas, though the streets themselves were narrow and close, as if to offer shade from the fierce desert sun. Shasti saw another of spidery buildings, similar to the one near the port, with its multiple shades of green and the slender black bridges joining different levels.

A coliseum of the same white stone as the walls could be seen to their left. Curious pillars of brass, whose purpose she could not guess, stood sentinel around it. They shimmered in a heat haze not generated by the winter sun.

The Old City extended for kilometers behind its walls, with a mass of three and four-story buildings of differing shapes and sizes. Vastly different minds had been at work here, yet somehow the disparate architecture was bound together, if only by the hundreds of fabric awnings and pennons that decorated the structures. Shasti was sure the colors and patterns stood for groups and trades, providing a map for those who knew the designs.

They dropped down to treetop level, heading for a plaza of fountains, tents, and carts. D'abo set the aircar down in a roped section with a flourish of piloting. Evidently the aircar was still sufficiently unusual that they attracted stares, pointed arms, and what looked like warding gestures from some in the busy crowd.

"Kandalorians are a superstitious lot," D'abo explained as she cut the engine. "They are never too happy about us 'star-demons' as they call us. Unless, of course, they are making money off us. The yellow turbans are dwellers of the deep desert. Avoid them. They're as often raiders as traders. We've had more incidents with them over the years than with all the other tribes. Two years ago, they murdered one of our traders. I personally dealt with the leader of that band." She flexed a clawed hand. "Occasionally I need to make it clear that we are not easy prey."

D'abo triggered a plastic shield that covered the aircar's interior as they climbed out. It polarized to keep the interior from heating up. *Not that,* Shasti thought, *it was all that warm.* They had landed in winter and the nights and early morning hours were still brisk, for all that the sun was a brilliant ball.

They walked out into the plaza. Shasti's booted feet found easy purchase on the textured stone of the original surface. She spotted areas where cobblestone or native concrete patched the original, more refined surface. The new work was clearly inferior.

Several of the ugly pack-beasts grumbled from their positions near hitching posts and water troughs. Shasti stepped carefully around the droppings left by some of the beasts, wondering anew at the cheek by jowl arrangement of ancient and new technology on Kandalor. D'abo, who wore only light shoes, was even more careful.

"Ah," D'abo said, gesturing, "Mookesh's food stand. He always has the best."

The two walked over the cracked stone of the Old City, heading for the courtyard's entrance, where a large, shaded cart with a red canopy stood. Smoke wafted up from braziers and pots. A heavy and unlovely Kandalorian, swathed in the usual shapeless clothing that natives favored, tended the pots and pans. This one wore a head covering of black, which seemed to be the most common color.

"Male or female?" Shasti asked. "And how do you tell?"

"Male," D'abo said. "The female's clothing includes a sash that corresponds to the headscarf. They are about a third shorter than the males. They lack the longer proboscis of the males. They are equally ugly, however."

Shasti smiled. "That observation was made by several of my staff."

D'abo greeted Mookesh with a clapping gesture and a face turned down to the ground. The alien turned its large dark eyes and prominent nose downward, and Shasti remembered the Kandalorian version of heaven was underground. The translator in her ear fed her conversation, though she noted that D'abo spoke to the native in its own language.

"May the earth protect you, Mookesh," D'abo said. "How's business?"

Mookesh looked beyond D'abo at Shasti. Though she could read nothing of his expression, she sensed curiosity. "And protect you too, D'abo Star-Demon. Business is, as usual, poor and poverty haunts my steps and will continue to do so at the rates you pay me. Is this another of your people?"

"Yes, Mookesh, she just forgot her ears and tail." D'abo said tartly. "No, she is of a new race of aliens called Humans, as you well know from the broadcasts. Whip us up some fresh crelick with a pint of drel for me and some mild formish for my new friend."

"More star demons?" Mookesh said. Then with a curiously lackadaisical response to the clash of cultures, he began pulling out bottles and laying out flatbread to fill with sizzling meats. "Are there no end to the creatures from space?"

"Not so far. In fact, the universe is about to get much more crowded," D'abo said. "Not that your people ever seem to care about that."

"The doings of star demons in the outer dark are no concern of ours," Mookesh said. "Did you want ice in your drel?"

"Not if it's cool."

"It is," Mookesh said.

"Will these new aliens be coming here?" He looked up at Shasti and handed her a mug of formish, which seemed to be a spicy nut beer, and the wrapped bread sandwich of grilled crelick meat and peppers.

"Undecided as yet," D'abo answered.

Shasti looked at the food dubiously.

"Your doctor pronounced them safe," D'abo said, catching her glance. "Drel is an acquired taste, however. Fortunately," she said, taking a swig from the flat green bottle, "I have acquired it."

They applied themselves to the savory bread rolls and drinks. Shasti bit into the rolled bread and waited a few minutes after her first cautious bite. But the mouth-watering smell overcame her caution. Fresh crelick proved as delicious as D'abo had promised. Fortunately, the smell of the Kandalorian himself was far less powerful than the malodorous caravanner they'd encountered on the landing field and didn't interfere with Shasti's enjoyment of her meal.

D'abo peppered Mookesh with questions about the comings and goings of various Kandalorian officials, tribes, and factions. Mookesh, who Shasti began to suspect, served as a go-between for various parties, asked a lot of questions about the new ships for a race that was unconcerned with the "outer dark." Still, she reflected, there was no alarm or agitation in the alien. He had the underlying confidence of a person whose world was never under threat. The new aliens could not mean a radical change for Kandalor. Something was protecting it, something that gave a stall merchant confidence to talk to a new form of alien as if it was nothing more than an oddity.

"I assume that there will be some statement from your legation to the Council of Elders," Mookesh said.

"There will. It will announce that they are friendly. You will pass the word through the bazaar."

"I will. Still, the arrival of even friendly aliens will add to the tensions."

"Tensions?" Shasti asked.

The alien turned to regard her. If he was disconcerted by the mix of mechanical translator voice and Shasti's own, he did not show it.

"We have conflicts of our own, New Star-Demon. There have always been battles between the cities and the desert dwellers, not to mention various sects of the true believers and the heretics. Matters have gone ill, lately. The Ribisans have not made things easier by backing of this new desert priest, for all that he promises to give them a new base in the volcanic flats. It will never come to pass, and the

Ribisans are fools to believe it will. Star Demons have been given only the one place on our world."

Shasti finished her meal, enjoying the formish. D'abo finished her drel and handed back the flat green bottle, then placed an abundance of coins on the wooden cart's stone top. These vanished immediately without comment by Mookesh.

"I shall spread the word through unofficial channels of these new aliens," Mookesh said. "The official channels you can deal with on your own."

"Thank you. The Ribisans will not be pursuing matters with the desert folk for a while," D'abo said. "They have been badly frightened by the arrival of my pretty friend here and her ships."

"Pretty?" Mookesh said. "Well, to each pot its own lid. Stay in touch, Star Demon, D'abo."

Shasti and D'abo wandered away from the food cart. They passed statues that lined the plaza. Shasti had no idea if they were of ancient gods, or aliens long since vanished into the Great Dark, but they looked nothing like Kandalorians or any other of the species she'd seen so far.

"Is he a local source?" Shasti asked, nodding her head back toward Mookesh's stall.

"Yes," D'abo said. "One of the more obvious ones. You might think of him as an unofficial ambassador of sorts. I have much more secret sources, but none so easily contacted and none so effective at getting word out. Everyone uses Mookesh. And he does actually have the best crelick."

The two tall females wandered about the courtyard and the market beyond. Kandalorians continued to give both aliens a wide berth, though occasionally one would wave or call out a greeting to D'abo. Shasti found herself the subject of dark and nervous looks.

They went over to one stall, fronting an old, beige-stone building, where a wide variety of knives hung from rafters or sat on folding tables. Shasti, who enjoyed a good knife both for practical and aesthetic reasons, looked over the offerings. The shopkeeper, a female in white robes and red headgear, hesitantly approached until greeted by D'abo. She hung well back and watched Shasti with evident misgiving.

Shasti eyed a short, broad, curved blade with a handle of animal horn. Threads of silver, gold, and copper had been woven through the handle in pleasing circular patterns. A beautiful, wooden scabbard with intricate inlay sat next to the blade.

"A nomad knife," D'abo said, "in pattern anyway. No nomad smelted so fine a steel as that."

"I'll have to come back here after we get some of the local money," Shasti said.

"No need for that," D'abo said. "Your Mr. Mandela has arranged for considerable credit from my government. I will buy it for you."

Before Shasti could demur, D'abo launched into a spate of bargaining with the Kandalorian female, whose hesitancy about Shasti vanished under avarice. A few minutes hard bargaining led to a deal, with a special condition. The Kandalorian knife merchant wanted some item from Shasti. She reached slowly into her jacket, opening a sealed pocket, and pulled out a small folding knife. Plain and practical, it was none-the-less sturdy and well machined. The merchant made a cooing sound and nodded vigorously to D'abo.

"Throw that in and you have a deal," D'abo said.

Shasti handed the small knife over. The merchant gestured to the ornate weapon. Shasti picked it up and slid it onto her belt then drew the thick curved blade, admiring the heft and feel of it. The blade was something like old Damascus steel, and when Shasti tested it on piece of paper from her pocket, she found the weapon held a razor edge.

"I can see," Shasti said, looking about the bazaar at stalls of fine woodwork and fabrics, "why their handicrafts hold such trade interest for you."

"Yes," D'abo said. "Only the unique can justify the price to freight through space."

They walked on, admiring the old towers and walls of the Old City. Kandalorians preferred bright colors in the awnings and fine lacquered screens in doors and windows, livening up the beige and gray of the stone and mortar walls. They passed a wooden corral where Shasti saw six-legged animals that looked like a cross between a horse and a deer. They were a beautiful rust color, save for a black one that bulked over the others. The animals were far more graceful than any other Kandalorian life she'd seen. Shasti walked over to the wood and metal corral with a feeling of excitement that she had not felt since Robert had taken her riding on New Eire. She remembered that day vividly. Robert and she had ridden out to the cliffs over the sea and made love in a hollow above the booming surf.

"Luracils," D'abo said, joining her at the fence, her shoulder touching Shasti's, but her bright eyes on the animal's well-muscled bodies. "Beautiful, aren't they? You give them the look of one who has ridden."

"Yes," Shasti said. "Something similar though with four legs, not six. We used to ride them on my adopted homeworld."

"We?" D'abo asked. "You and the big man?"

Shasti froze.

"I am sorry," D'abo said quickly. "I have upset you."

"No," Shasti said, trying to physically relax and wondering if D'abo had leaned against her only to sense her emotional state, or if the Nekoans had a different sense of personal space.

"It's all right," Shasti continued, surprised to find that she did want to talk. Something about the open-faced catgirl inspired confidence. "Vaughn is not mine. He wishes to be so, but my past love life is very complicated. No, it was another man I referred to, a kind and gentle man. He offered me a life, and I turned it down. I was after something else, retribution on someone who had wronged me. In pursuing my revenge, I lost him. Not because he abandoned me, no, he followed me almost to his death. But during that journey he found his first-mate, who had disappeared during the Conchirri war."

"And he went back to her?" D'abo asked.

"Yes."

"And you let him?" the cat-like alien said.

Shasti controlled a flash of anger. "There was no question of that. Perhaps I could have kept him by me, but he would not have been the man that I thought he was. Could I keep him and destroy him at the same time?"

"Yet you keep your heart for him while Vaughn wishes for you?"

"For now," Shasti said. "I am content to belong only to myself. And now," Shasti said, turning the tables on the curious cat. "It's your turn."

D'abo gave a short laugh. "Fairly returned. Like you, I belong only to myself. I have had my share of males, and they account themselves lucky. I sense that our mating arrangements are more flexible and short term than your own. We tend to contract for children who belong to the wider family. Some people have a life-mate as opposed to a term mate—but it is rare. I've not had such fortune. Oh, there's a young officer or two I have taken a fancy to, but with my life it's hard to envision a domestic existence.

"Perhaps someday I will sit by the stream surrounded by kits, but not now. The universe is too big and exciting for me to give it up."

Shasti gave the shorter alien a sidelong look. "We are surprisingly alike."

"You're taller and you call those ears?" D'abo shot back with a grin.

They exchanged looks and both began laughing.

"You can call me Teleera, if you wish," D'abo said. "It is a custom of ours that friends use the first name."

"We do the same, Teleera, and you can call me Shasti." It occurred to Shasti that she couldn't recall the last time she had given anyone leave to use her first name. Paolo, of course, but that had been different, assumed in an intimacy, now regretted, during the heat of sexual passion.

"Very well, Shasti it is then."

"And, Teleera."

"Yes?"

"Vaughn's mine till I say otherwise."

D'abo smiled. "Fine but I can't help wondering if he's built all on the same scale."

"If I ever decide to find out," Shasti said, "we'll continue this conversation."

Shasti and D'abo strolled about in companionable silence for a while, examining stalls of merchandise and crafts. Shasti had the strangest feeling that D'abo had somehow always been at her side. The odd feeling of déjà vu and companionship gave the whole day an unreal air, as if she wandered through a dream. Eventually they found themselves atop a portion of the old city wall that looked out over a bending and meandering river. Toward the westering sun they could see ships of various sorts. Some with lateen sails, some paddle wheelers, other machines that were obviously modern skimmers and hovercraft also plied the river. The banks were covered with nodding trees more like willows than the palm trees she expected.

"Beautiful in its own way," Shasti said. "The horizon is so immense. I've never been on a world as large as this that didn't have more oppressive gravity."

"Alien and mysterious," D'abo added, "a vast unknown."

"You love it," Shasti said.

"You're perceptive."

"I imagine that we should be getting back. We've spent most of the day away."

D'abo shrugged. "We both have coms; they could call for us if we were needed."

"You're an irresponsible sort, aren't you?" Shasti said.

"Say rather that I am infinitely curious," D'abo returned. "But your point is not without merit. The undersecretary has doubtless not called me as he assumes I am drawing critical secrets from you with my wily ways. Doubtless, your Mr. Mandela hopes the same, and as a result, we have been given rare hours as tourists. Still, no doubt they wish to hear what we have both learned from each other."

"You'll leave my love life out of your report," Shasti said, raising an eyebrow.

"Of course," D'abo said. "While it was fascinating to find out that you, for all you have no decent tail or ears, are a proper female. And I trust my own romantic past will be safe with you."

"Deal," Shasti said.

They climbed down from the old turret, passing black-turbaned city-dwellers apparently going up to enjoy the coming sunset. Shadows had begun to fill the close streets, and Shasti was glad to be heading back. She had spent most of her teens and early life on the run and the old habits of caution died slowly.

"There seems to be quite a variety of people in your crews," D'abo said.

"Yes," Shasti said, stepping around a handcart of beads. "Less now than in the past. Presently we have four species aboard."

"Even among the ones you call human there seems a wide variety. You and Vaughn's people seem dramatically larger than the others."

"We have two types of people," Shasti said, her lips thinning. "Homo sapiens, which would be all of *Sidhe's* human crew, then there are the Selected. They're simply Homo sapiens from a program of selected breeding. Finally, there are those like Vaughn and myself, the Engineered."

"Created people," D'abo said, stopping.

"Yes," Shasti said, "created people, a mix of the genes of thousands of so-called superior specimens. Some of us were tinkered with even on the genetic level. We were born as infants but raised in crèches. Fodder for the ambitious. As they bred more of us, they bred more ambition still. It caused a brief civil war, and I am happy to say the technology is now outlawed for use on sentient beings."

"And you were something special, even among them, I sense."

"Yes," Shasti said, a touch of a growl in her voice, "but I will speak no further of that."

To Shasti's surprise, D'abo linked her arm in Shasti's, and they started forward. "As you wish," D'abo said. "I will ask no more about it and we will talk on trivial things. As you insist Vaughn is yours for the taking, tell me about this Daniel Rigg. He is handsome in a strong, silent way."

"Is that all you think about?" Shasti said, with a faintly scandalized air.

"We are a very sensual people," D'abo protested, "intrigued by sight, sense, sound, and particularly touch. I have noticed that your kind seem to rarely touch each other. Is this some form of taboo?"

"No," Shasti said. "Touch tends to be much more restrained among us. We reserve it more for intimacy among friends and lovers, though we Engineered are even more restrained in this regard for cultural reasons. We grow up without families, so touch is much less common. It's something of a complaint among the females of the human species that touch is only used by males when they want to initiate sex."

"Must make for a lot of bad sex," D'abo mused. "We touch for many reasons other than sex, to judge truthfulness or tension, or even for sheer tactile delight. Indeed, it has been a struggle for me to keep my paws off your shiny silky hair."

"If you are so curious," Shasti said in a teasing tone, "you might want to discuss these matters with Dr. Romita. He seems to have made touching females his secondary career."

"Hmmm," D'abo said, her ears flicking about. "Intriguing, but I cannot abide overly talkative males, and I prefer the bigger ones. Like Rigg, who you avoided my question about."

Shasti found herself laughing again and struggling with an almost giddy feeling. She throttled it down, telling herself that she needed to remain on guard with the infectiously disarming D'abo and wondering if she had unintentionally given up any critical information. She suspected the other's openness was at least in part a tactic and resolved to keep her feelings more closely guarded.

Sounds of a distant clamor reached Shasti. "What is that?"

D'abo looked at her strangely. "Your small ears are very effective. I just now heard it myself. Voices. Angry ones."

"And," Shasti added grimly, "they are between us and the aircar."

"Well, it seems my ears are superior in one respect," D'abo said, taking her arm out of Shasti's. "The noise is all around us. It begins to sound like a riot. I smell smoke too."

Kandalorians nearby began slamming doors and shuttering windows. A few running figures pounded past. D'abo snagged one by the arm and demanded an explanation in its own tongue.

"The desert madman," the rubber-faced Kandalorian said as he pulled free. "His followers are in the bazaar. There's been a fight between them and the City Guard. It's spreading everywhere. You must leave, Star Demon. The madman's followers hate Nekoans." He wasted no more time and raced down a side alley.

"Damn," D'abo said. "The desert folk never come into the city. Why now?"

"These streets," Shasti said, "are too small and narrow. Let's get some height. The roofs are low in this section."

"Agreed," D'abo said.

Shasti put her back to a wall and cradled her hands. "I'll boost you up."

D'abo sprang forward putting a foot in Shasti's hands, who thrust upward. D'abo gave a squalling sound. Between her own agile leap and Shasti's powerful boost, she sailed well over the second story of the building, shooting up another three meters before coming down to land on the roof.

Shasti turned and leapt. She found purchase on a window and pulled herself swinging up and over onto the roof.

D'abo faced her with a wide-eyed look. "You are powerful," she breathed. "You threw me up here like I was a newborn kit."

"That way." Shasti pointed, knowing her inborn sense of direction was unerring. With her other limited PSI sense, she picked up feelings of rage and hate till it seemed as if the very air around them was red-tinged. "We have to hurry."

The pair sped over the rooftops of the old city, negotiating the roofs of clay tiles, wood, and metal. Heat from the metal roofs beat at Shasti's face and hands.

They were not alone in seeking the safety of the heights. Other Kandalorians with black or green headcloths used them for refuge as well. They kept their distance from the pair. The off-world females leapt from building to building, climbing various levels, while in the distance, smoke roiled into the sky and shouts grew louder accompanied with the clangor of weapons.

"Ah," D'abo said, after they leapt the last full street before the plaza, "we're near the aircar."

Cries sounded from the street below them. For a second, Shasti thought they had been discovered, but D'abo grabbed her arm and pointed. At the far end of the street below, a half-dozen figures rounded the corner, running hard, city-dwellers from their black headscarves. One figure staggered and reeled as he came down the alley. Exhaustion or wounds, Shasti couldn't tell, but he was near collapse. Behind him came a mob of Kandalorians wearing the yellow headscarves of the desert tribes, but striped in red. Wicked-looking long knives glittered in their hands.

"Mookesh," D'abo said, recognizing the flagging Kandalorian.

Before Shasti could say anything, the Nekoan raced off, heading for a spot over Mookesh. After the briefest of hesitation, Shasti was hot on her heels. But she didn't catch the cat-girl before D'abo reached the roof's edge and dove off into the swarm of desert nomads just as they reached Mookesh. She sent several sprawling as she hit, rolled, and launched herself on another startled nomad.

Shasti also dove off but somersaulted in mid-air. She came down, crushing a nomad under her boots, landing upright and plunging into the hedge of knives.

The nomads might never have seen star demons in the flesh before, but it gave Shasti and D'abo only a few seconds of reprieve. In that time, D'abo clawed one Kandalorian's arm, causing it to drop its knife. A big male stepped in to take a swing at Shasti. She blurred toward him, leaping inside of the weapon and hitting him three times with such speed and power that he simply dropped to the ground, unconscious or dead. Fists and feet flashed and three more fell. For the first time in years, Shasti gave full rein to the rage that lay bottled under her calm exterior. She seized a nomad and lifted him over her head, flinging him into the group of his fellows.

Shasti became a maelstrom of fury in their midst, smashing and striking at will. With her accelerated perception and reflexes, the Kandalorians seemed to be moving almost in slow motion. She ripped free a pole holding up an awning. It collapsed on two struggling tribesmen. Stepping around knife thrusts and swings with a dancer's lithe grace, she laid waste to all in reach with the six-inch-wide pole. Kandalorians fell screaming around her or fled the alley.

A sword blow snapped the staff, but Shasti immediately bound the swordsman's weapon with one half and felled the tribesman with a blow of the other, hitting so hard that the wood snapped over his headcloth. *Helmet underneath,* a distant cold part of her mind thought, while noting with satisfaction that the force of her blow had dropped him anyway.

She parried with the remaining piece and whipped out the desert knife she'd purchased. As she spun about, she saw D'abo, bruised and cut on her face, standing over a fallen tribesman. Another bore down on her. Shasti leapt over D'abo. With a murderous shriek, she struck with both weapons, downing the Kandalorian. She reached down, grabbing him by the throat and raising the broad-bladed dagger to finish the job.

Something grabbed her hand. She released the Kandalorian and spun, her iron fingers bunched.

D'abo. Shasti barely stopped the strike in time.

They stood facing each other over an alley floored in moaning and writhing bodies.

"Enough," D'abo said. "Well done, but enough."

Shasti's lips were peeled back from her teeth, her eyes glazed and glaring. "Mercy for these?" she managed thickly. "How much would they have shown your friend?" She gestured to Mookesh, who leaned against a wall, his huge dark eyes fastened in terror as much on Shasti as on the nomad tribesman.

"None at all," D'abo said gently. "But I prefer only to kill as much as I need to. Mookesh," she threw over her shoulder, "are you all right?"

"I will be," he gasped, his nose trunk waving. "Refuge awaits me at the door of the sanctuary of Gordesh at the end of this street. They will not dare break in there."

He looked at Shasti, standing shakily. "I thank you both, Star Demons. I thank you for my life."

"I'll be in touch when things quiet down," D'abo said, still hanging on to Shasti's arm.

Mookesh fled.

D'abo looked up at Shasti, whose rage was cooling, leaving behind it the usual emotional deadness. "Thank you, my friend, Shasti. I would likely have been killed had you not followed me into battle. Your strength is quite terrifying."

"Sometimes," Shasti said, "it terrifies me too."

"I believe it, tall one. Come, let us flee while we can. We have had quite enough adventure for now."

15

Shasti and D'abo returned to the legation, landing the aircar on the roof. D'abo disappeared to brief Kadesh on the trouble in town. Shasti did the same for Mandela, returning to their private quarters on the third floor of the Nekoan building. The Confed chief watched her with pursed lips, clearly aware he was getting an edited version of their mishap in town.

"It might be as well," he said, leaning back in the comfortable leather chair he'd had brought from *Sidhe*, "for us to return to the ships for now. The legation seems quite safe, but a native uprising is hardly the thing to test that supposition with. In addition, these tensions between the Ribisi and the Nekoans call for more consideration. Our Nekoan hosts have been very friendly, almost desperately so. Charge' D'abo seems intent on seducing you."

Shasti waved his suggestion away. "I don't believe she has a sexual interest in me."

"Who said that she did?" Mandela returned. "There are many types of seduction. D'abo is alarmingly clever and has a flexible mind. You two seem to have a natural bond. Just be sure she doesn't control it to your detriment."

Shasti nodded reluctantly.

"Are you planning to make direct contact with the Ribisans?" Shasti asked. "You think you will do better with them?"

"No," Mandela said. "We would find them no better allies than the Nekoans do. Their interests and biology are too dissimilar to our own for that to be feasible. I like the Nekoans. I like our prospects with them. But it doesn't do to let one's feelings overwhelm one's common sense. We'll proceed as before, just a bit more cautiously. For now, though, it is back to the ships until these tensions with the desert nomads can be managed."

Shasti stood and looked out the window at the Mt. Sorokol. Its white-capped height dominated the eastern horizon and drew the eye. "Somehow, I feel that caution is not going to work here."

"Captain Rainhell, emergency call. Captain Rainhell, emergency..."

Shasti slipped out of her cabin bed, passing from deep sleep to instant wakefulness in a flash. Risky hopped off the bed, alarmed by the sudden movement. Shasti strode over to the panel, wiping sleep from her eyes, and punched up the audio. At the last instant, she remembered she was naked and cut the visual. "Rainhell."

"Captain, I have an emergency call from Charge' D'abo."

"Put her through."

"Captain Rainhell," came D'abo's voice, "is there something wrong with your visual? I cannot see you."

"One minute," Shasti said. She spotted her robe on a chair and threw it on. "What's wrong?" she demanded, snapping on the screen.

D'abo's catlike face filled the screen. Her violet eyes glittered, and her mouth was taut. "Shasti, one of our freighters has discovered an Evolver in our system."

"Interesting," Shasti said. "Perhaps we will now see the fabled weaponry of Kandalor in action."

"Would it were so, but the machine is not heading toward Kandalor. Our best guess is that it has entered this system from an unknown warp point, but it is headed for the warp point to Selena, a recently established colony. We have over a million people there with only basic defenses, no match for an Evolver."

"Unfortunate," Shasti said. She surreptitiously pushed a button on her panel. It fired a pre-programmed signal to Mandela and Mmok.

"Captain," D'abo said, leaning forward, "we are desperate. We have only one real warship in this system. Fortunately, the cruiser *Fearless* will be able to engage, but we have only had success in massed attacks on these machines. A lone cruiser will simply be destroyed. They are prepared for it, but they can only die uselessly unless we have help."

"The freighter?" Shasti asked, buying time to think.

"It trails the Evolver—which may turn and destroy it at any moment. Its armament is minimal." D'abo drew a deep breath. "The Evolvers are your enemies as well as ours. Already they have attacked your worlds."

"We did not come here to fight," Shasti said.

"I know," D'abo said, "and we are not your people, but if there is any way I can obtain the help of your two mighty warships, then I must try it. Your vessels are each as large as our cruiser. From what you have shared with us and I have learned, I know that your ships are more powerful than anything other than one of our battle-cruisers."

"I hear you, Charge'," Shasti said. "Please stand by." She switched channels then reached over and hit the alarm on the panel. Lights flashed and a klaxon sounded.

"Rainhell to bridge."

"Mollica."

"Send to *Paladin* on a discreet channel: Action stations. Make immediate preparations for launch and standby."

"Aye, ma'am."

Shasti switched again. "Mandela," she said, assuming he was on the line by now.

"Yes, Captain," his rich brown voice came back. "I was listening."

"This is politics, your bailiwick. What do we do?"

"You seem to have taken the first steps without waiting for me."

"Simply preserving our options. If we are to launch, it will have to be soon. D'abo wouldn't have called if there wasn't an intercept vector, but I can't imagine that time is on our side."

"Sound logic."

"Do we help?" she asked.

"I'm curious, Captain," Mandela said with maddening slowness, "what do you want to do? What do your instincts tell you?"

Shasti considered. "I say help. They've repaired and reprovisioned us, but beyond that our choices are stark. The Evolvers have no better side to appeal to. We want the Nekoans' help, their resources, and bodies in place of our own. If we want the front lines here, then we fight today."

"Very good, Captain. I may vote for you myself."

"Thanks. I'll need you to evacuate your staff, Eris, and all noncombatants as well as the ground forces. No point in taking them into a deep space battle and you'll need them for security. I want Paolo and Mmok. I've got an idea that I'll need both of them for."

"Very thoughtful of you, Captain, but we will fare into danger with you."

"No, you won't. You are vastly too important to risk, much though it pains me to admit it. If there's to be an alliance, you're the person for the job. Get your stuff together, Ambassador. It's planetside for you."

"Your logic," he said, "is faultless, though I must say it pains me to think of my supplies of brandy, caviar, and cigars going into battle without me. So much for my plans of a slow and cautious approach to the Nekoans."

"I'll be careful of your sundries," Shasti said, "and I told you that caution was as likely to be blown to the winds. We'll clear the ship for action as soon as possible. I'll talk to Vaughn and see if he will help."

"Oh, please, Captain. He would no more sit here while you dashed off to battle than he would dance on the bridge in a tutu. Your difficulty will be keeping him from racing into danger ahead of you, especially when he hears you're taking Paolo."

"Mmok," Shasti called. "I assume you are on here too."

"Enchante, my queen."

"The rest of the landing force goes with Mandela. You stay with me. You've got a better brain than the *Sidhe* does. I want you at my elbow."

"I always get killed on suicide missions."

"Too bad. Meet me on the bridge." She switched channels. "Charge' D'abo?"

"Yes, Captain, I was becoming most anxious," D'abo said, her ears threatening to lie flat on her head.

"Please make arrangements for all my non-essential crew and Ambassador Mandela to be taken care of at your embassy."

"Excellent, though I will delegate the latter. If you have room for one more, I would accompany you on this battle. You fight for us, after all."

"Hurry," Shasti said.

Shasti dressed in a minute and headed toward the bridge. She ran into her XO in the hallway. The women headed down the ship's Broadway as crewman scurried about them. Shasti quickly filled Mollica in.

"What!" Mollica said, jerking to a stop.

Shasti turned to face her in surprise.

Mollica looked at Shasti, her face a mixture of anger and fear. "You're taking a frigate and a destroyer into battle with an Evolver," she whispered. "For God's sake, it took a Confederate battlecruiser to finish off a downed one."

Shasti looked at her narrowly. Ever since the asteroid strike, Mollica had been a changed woman, cautious and even less willing than usual to leave the security of the ship.

"We are going," she said evenly but in a tone that brooked no argument. "That is policy from Mandela and orders from me."

Mollica's mouth drew into a hard line. "It's never enough for you people. We didn't have enough war in our own space you have to come looking for one here."

Shasti's eyes narrowed. "The war that is here is looking for us already. Just as the Conchirri were. This time we found it first. And that's enough. You get your mind on the job and your head into this fight or get off my ship."

Mollica struggled with herself for a second then gave an abrupt nod. "Yes, Captain," she said, in a forced tone.

"Get a report on available thrust and launch status," Shasti said.

Mollica spun on her heel and stalked off toward Engineering. Shasti headed for the bridge, badly disturbed and disappointed by her First Officer. A wild idea began to crystallize in her head. *Later,* she told herself. *When there is time.*

Mandela's prediction was accurate. There was no holding Vaughn back, and he was insulted that she'd phrased it as a request. In record time, both ships shook free of the ground and thundered skyward, cleared for battle.

As the ships recklessly burned fuel and headed out for the battle zone, Shasti pulled her command staff and D'abo together on the bridge. Mollica was tight-lipped and professional, but Shasti knew the woman retained her objections to the plan. It made her wonder how many others held reservations. She put these thoughts aside as Vaughn checked in by screen from the bridge of *Paladin*.

"I have an idea," Shasti said. "The holo-generators Mandela installed on *Sidhe* during our venture to Enshar have never been removed."

"Yes," Mollica returned, "but so what? The supercomputers used for all but the basic functions were. They were what was special about the rig. The rest of it is just variants on standard sensors and imaging equipment."

"We've got a supercomputer right here." Shasti gestured at Mmok.

"Uh, boss," Mmok said, "you're not considering busting me up for parts?"

"Don't be an ass," Shasti said. "But you can interface with *Sidhe's* systems. You've done it before."

"Yes," he said, "much as it pains me to admit it though, my HCR brain isn't up to the sheer volume and processing power of those units. They filled the forward compartments."

"What I have in mind," Shasti said, "is a great deal simpler than the deceptions we used in Voit-Veru space. Using the ship's systems and your own, could you generate *Sidhe's* original colors over the red hull? I want her to look like she did when she was Conchirri."

"Wow," he said. "Let me plug in and see."

"Do it," Shasti ordered. "You'll find tons of images of her from the dockyard inspections when Robert bought the ship."

"What is the purpose of this?" D'abo's tail lashed in evident agitation.

"We know that there was some relationship between the Evolvers and the Conchirri, some linkage in their language. This was a Conchirri ship, and we have the only living expert on the Conchirri language on board." She gestured at Paolo, who sat hands pressed tightly together, on the edge of his seat.

"If we'd had a week's warning, we could have simply painted *Sidhe* back to her original colors. Maybe Mmok can do it for us with optical camouflage. With that and some work from Paolo, we can pretend to be a Conchirri vessel fleeing from both your cruiser and the *Paladin*. The Evolver might come to our aid, getting us closer to our target."

"Getting us close enough for an 'alpha strike' salvo of all your ship's weapons," D'abo finished, her violet eyes aglow at the thought.

"Desperate," Vaughn said, "but perhaps our only chance given the disparity in power. In a straight slugfest we stand little chance."

Mmok, who had used the time to hook into the main computer, waved a hand. "We can do it from here. It's so much simpler than what we've done before. No changes in shape or radar signature, just color patterns. I'll get to work. It would help if we could use *Paladin*'s spare computer capacity by the tight-beam connection."

Shasti looked at Vaughn's face on the screen. "Done," he said.

She turned to Paolo. "Start preparing a message that we are a Conchirri ship. Find the original name in the computer or make one up. We are being pursued. Demand help."

He looked at her with wide eyes. "And if it replies?"

"Pretend it's a beautiful woman you're trying to seduce and use some of your best bullshit on it."

Choked laughter ran about the bridge, fracturing the tension.

Shasti enjoyed the smile of pure enjoyment that cut across Vaughn's dark face.

"Transmission coming in from the cruiser, *Fearless*."

"On screen," Shasti ordered. "Make sure to route our return signal through the *Paladin* so the Evolver doesn't detect us communicating with *Fearless*."

A Nekoan face appeared on the main screen. By now Shasti could recognize it was a male and young in appearance. He had a thick orange mane, streaked with black.

"This is Rokas Shen of the *Fearless*," the image said. Then, "Hello, Teleera."

"Hello, Rokas," D'abo replied her ears flicking this way and that. "How I wish our meeting was under different circumstances."

"As do I," Shen said, "though I am glad to see you with such help."

"This is Captain Rainhell of the *Sidhe*." D'abo gestured.

"What's the situation?" Shasti asked, cutting through any pleasantries.

"The news is grim," Shen replied, lips drawn back over his teeth. "The Evolver decelerated suddenly and got the *Murakil* into weapons range. The freighter is destroyed."

D'abo cursed.

"The machine ship changes speed faster than a crewed ship's AG field can compensate for the Gs. It has resumed course for the warpoint to our colony. Unless you can increase your speed by twenty percent, you will not arrive in time."

D'abo looked at Shasti, who shook her head.

"We're at max acceleration to reach the battle area."

"Then I must attack alone," Shen said.

"No," D'abo ordered. "It would be useless."

"I cannot let it pass," he snapped, ears flattening. "A million lives are at stake."

"Listen," Shasti said. "We have a stratagem that may work. Open long-range fire on the Evolver. Engage it only to make it pursue you and then shape a course to meet us. Be prepared to attack with all force when we do."

"Understood," Shen said. He turned and growled out orders to his crew. "Missiles away. I'll close to max range and open fire with guns to provoke its pursuit. Shen out."

A few minutes later, Shen signaled again. "I have provoked it. The machine follows me." Shasti notice the flickering of the lights behind Shen and a few wisps of smoke in the air.

Shen noticed her regard. "We have taken a few hits. I rolled a pattern of mines as we fled. It had to go around the mines, allowing me to open up to a safe range. Still, it accelerates more quickly than *Fearless* and the range closes."

"Intercept course," Shasti ordered the helmsman, Nye. "Give me an ETA."

Nye sweated over his instruments, changing the course. "Time to intercept is between twelve and thirteen minutes. I can't call it better. We should be in range of the Evolver's long-range sensors in a minute."

"Mmok," Shasti said, "initiate optical camouflage."

"Wardell, open fire on *Paladin* with the minimum power setting on bearing weapons. Save the mains for the Evolver."

She looked at Vaughn's image on the secondary screen. "Return fire, Vaughn. Be sure not to hit my pretty ship."

He grinned as his image faded, replaced by the silhouette of *Paladin*. Light rippled on its flanks as it fired at the *Sidhe*. The weapons fire would carry across space to the alien's sensors.

Shasti turned to Paolo. "You're up. Make it good."

Paolo turned to the console they had rigged up for him. He bent over the pickup intense and focused, and began coughing and spitting in Conchirri. Above his head a translation scrolled across another screen. *Conchirri Frigate-leader Stonesha, under attack by Nekoan vessels. We are badly damaged and demand all assistance.* The message cycled.

Shasti switched to an exterior view of *Sidhe's* hull. Her Guards Red hull was replaced with the black and yellow bands of her original colors, complete with the squadron insignia and other markings she had worn in the service of the reptiles. Inspiration struck Shasti. "Mmok, can you alter the optical camo to look like we've been hit a couple of times?"

"The most I'll dare is some fuzzing of the yellow stripes. It will look like lasers have charred the paint. More than that and I risk losing the image."

Did she detect a faint note of strain in Mmok's voice? "It will do."

"Signal from *Fearless*, Captain," Hafel said. "The Evolver is splitting its course between chasing them and our position."

"Any signals from the Evolver to us?" she asked.

"None detected."

"I'm sputtering the beam on our return fire at *Paladin*," Wardell said. "It will look we have power damage."

Shasti nodded. She turned to Paolo. "Keep up the Conchirri chatter. Demand help. Demand repairs. Order it to attack the *Paladin*."

"Signal from the Evolver," Hafel interrupted. Her hands flew over controls as she routed it to Paolo.

Paolo donned his headphones to help him catch the nuances of speech as the screen in front of him lit with the text of a "best guess" translation. "Yes, yes," he said to himself. "Like Conchirri...only strange. Odd. Demand for a ship's name, a clan, no, a sept and clan." His voice cracked with the uncouth and bestial language of the Conchirri, as he shot back some information to hold the Evolver's interest.

On the screen Shasti again saw the results of his efforts scroll by in Confed standard. *Conchirri Frigate Leader Stonesha, Sept Ukol, Clan Fiuni demands aid*. She saw a glitter of coordinates from a burnt-out black dwarf system in Voit-Veru space and nodded her approval. If they were destroyed, the information would give the Evolver nothing useful. Paolo followed with reports of damage to their weapons and com systems.

"It's asking me for tactical information on *Paladin*," Paolo said, his voice jumping in excitement. "But it's also demanding IFF and codes we don't have." He turned to Shasti, alarm on his face.

"Tell the Evolver that its codes and IFF are a thousand years out of date. Argue with it, keep it talking. Send it tactical info on an escort-class vessel. We'll make *Paladin* look weaker than it is. Keep it up, Paolo; you're doing well for us."

"Enemy vessel is ranging on us and *Paladin* with active fire control," Hafel said. "Should I try to jam?"

"No," Shasti said. "We are supposed to be friendly. Wardell, get a passive fire control lock on the Evolver."

"No need," the gunner said. "I've got *Paladin*'s active fire control lock through the tight-beam."

Shasti cursed herself for missing the trick.

As if sensing it, the white-haired gunner cast a glance at her. "Pays to have an old hound in the pack sometimes."

Mollica stood next to Shasti, who noticed a rill of sweat on the other woman's brow. "We're about to find out how smart an AI we are dealing with," Shasti said, studying her.

"What?" Mollica said. D'abo also turned to Shasti.

"A dumb machine," Shasti said, "is just going to fire at us. Our IFF doesn't match its records and it shoots. That's it. A really smart AI may be curious and want to know more. It will consider the implications of recontacting the Conchirri."

"Range closing," Wardell said.

"All weapons prime and lock for alpha strike," Shasti said. "Hold fighter launch. We don't want to leave them behind."

"Captain," Wardell and Hafel yelled simultaneously. "Target massively accelerating, at least twenty Gs. He's bearing on *Paladin*. He's firing."

On screen *Paladin*'s prow flared as the Evolvers weapons scored a glancing blow on the desperately maneuvering destroyer.

Vaughn, Shasti thought.

"Target lock reacquired," Wardell called. "We are on top of him."

"Fire, alpha strike," Shasti shouted, rage in her heart. If Vaughn was dead...

Sidhe's optical camouflage snapped off and the frigate's blood-red hull reflected the fury of her weapons battery. Lasers licked out as the main mass-accelerator spat its lethal load. An anti-shipping missile surged from the missile bay. Even the chain guns spat depleted uranium slugs at the massive Evolver. The Evolver's surging rush had brought it close enough to be seen visually.

The Evolver's golden surface erupted and shattered under *Sidhe*'s weapons. Most of the damage was from the mass accelerator shot, which crumpled the forward quarter of the golden ovoid. An energy weapon whiffed *Sidhe*'s large anti-ship missile out of existence and her lasers only cut into the armored outer hull. The wounds were deep and unexpected, but not mortal.

Sidhe flashed past the Evolver, which had braked brutally hard to stay in weapons range of *Paladin*. Nye managed to spin the nimble frigate on her axis, as tight a turn as could be managed at tactical speed. Only a few degrees could be added with vectored thrust, but any change decreased the probability of a hit. Mindful of the recent damage to her vessel, Shasti fought the urge to take *Sidhe* into an even tighter turn. As the frigate spun, it unmasked rear batteries. They added their fire into the Evolver's hull.

Sidhe belled and lurched. Power flickered.

"Hit aft," Hafel said, "Damage—" What she said next was lost as *Sidhe* was struck again. It was as if an enormous foot shoved the ship to the right. "Hit on the port wing."

"How bad?" Shasti demanded, knowing from the force of the blow that her ship was hurt.

"Captain," Wardell answered, "half the port wing is gone."

"Get me Vaughn," Shasti said. "Is *Paladin* still firing?"

"Negative," Wardell said. "*Paladin* is ballistic. No ECM, no weapons fire."

"And no return to our call," Hafel added.

"She's dead," Mollica said, eyes wide. "And we're next."

"Main gun up," Wardell said. "No firing lock."

"*Fearless* is closing on the Evolver and firing," Hafel said. "He's sending us a warning; he's firing nuclear missiles."

"Fire our conventional ones," Shasti ordered. "Maybe it will use up its anti-missile capacity on us. At least it will be firing at missiles and not ships. Keep trying to raise Vaughn. Get me a damage estimate on the Evolver."

Wardell looked at his assistant, who manipulated more controls. "His fire is down 80%," Wardell reported. "Most of his outgoing fire is on the missiles but he's doing damn well on those. He's not...damn... he is maneuvering. He's bearing on *Fearless*.

"Captain, can you give me three more degrees deflection? It will put him in firing arc."

"Nye," Shasti ordered. The AG system strained as *Sidhe* again tried to turn. The mass drive ran the length of the ship; the only way to point it was to aim *Sidhe* herself.

On a split screen, Shasti and the others could see the small Nekoan cruiser and the Evolver closing, firing furiously. Suddenly *Fearless* was flayed open.

"No!" D'abo cried.

"I've got lock," Wardell said. "Firing all bearing weapons."

Sidhe's mass drive again blasted out its lethal load of metal, accelerated to almost light speed. Lasers lanced ahead of it and missiles followed. The Evolver flared as the mass drive connected, and this time its fire did not stop *Sidhe's* trailing anti-shipping missiles. The huge machine began to tumble, its insides opening to space.

"Keep firing cyclically," Shasti said, cold and focused on the kill. "Open the range. I don't want to risk being rammed."

Sidhe altered course, still spitting death at the Evolver.

"Launch the *Wildcats*. Have the fighters missile the bastard," Shasti said.

"*Wildcat 1* launching," Mollica said. "Number 2's linkage is damaged. No launch."

"Main gun recycled," Wardell said. "Record time, Captain."

"Kill him!" Shasti said, eyes blazing.

The sabot round from the mass accelerator knifed and hit something deep in the bowels of the Evolver that made the marred, golden ship flower into a new star.

Cheers and shouts rang through the bridge. Wardell and his assistant slapped each other on the back.

"*Sidhe*, come in *Sidhe*," Vaughn's unmistakable voice sounded over the speakers.

Shasti felt her heart skip a beat. She wanted to dash to the speaker.

I am not a schoolgirl, she said to herself, forcing calmness on her heart and voice. "*Sidhe* here," she said, then relenting a little. "Are you all right?"

"Nothing major," he said. Suddenly a screen lit. An image fuzzed, derezzed then stabilized. She could see his face. It was bruised, smoke-stained, and Shasti's grip bent the arm of her command chair.

"You are unharmed." He smiled. Then he was all business. "We are blind here and most forward weapons are gone. I have full engine power again and stern weapons only. What of our enemy?"

"Stripped atoms and melted metal," she said.

They shared wolfish grins at the victory.

"Excellent, a good day's work."

"It appears," Shasti said, "that I will have the chance to return a favor. We'll rendezvous with you and linkup. This time you can lean on me."

"With gratitude," he said.

"Nye, plot an intercept course. Best time to a soft docking."

"Mollica," Shasti continued, "send *Wildcat 1* to check *Fearless'* location. *Wildcat 2* as soon as they can clear the mech-link. If they can't clear the link send a *Wolverine*. I want an SAR sweep of the area."

Mollica, her face pale and staring, took a second to react to the orders. "Yes," she said slowly. "Yes. Search and rescue, aye."

D'abo turned to face her. Grief marred her delicate face. Her eyes were bright, and it occurred to Shasti that she didn't know if Nekoans cried. "Thank you. I fear it is hopeless, but thank you."

Shasti nodded. "I'm sorry about your friend."

"He was more than that," she said and turned away.

D'abo's prediction proved true, and no survivors were found from either Nekoan vessel. It took thirty-six hours to nurse *Paladin* back to orbit Kandalor, and it was not the only nursing that needed to be done. Vaughn had been more injured than he let on, having been hit by a falling stanchion on the bridge of his destroyer. He refused bed rest and divided his time between Shasti and the casualties of his own more-wounded vessel. Four had died on his ship compared with two on the *Sidhe*.

Shasti found herself grateful for the time together but still a bit wary of Vaughn. Sometimes the wall between them, made from her own fears and remembered pains, filled her with frustration, but she could only remove the bricks so fast.

She also found that Tanaka, contrary to orders, had remained aboard the *Paladin* when she launched. Shasti began to understand the nature of her relationship with Vaughn, when she observed the older woman watching over Vaughn during the brief period he lay sleeping under a regenerator in *Sidhe's* sickbay. There was no mistaking the almost parental worry on her face. Tanaka was never overly friendly to Shasti, but they shared the time watching over Vaughn and parted with an easier feeling between them

Pieces fell into place in Shasti's mind. *Of course,* she thought. Tanaka hadn't been worried about Vaughn killing Paolo on Vikadia; she'd been concerned about what would happen to Vaughn after, both with the expedition and with Shasti. It all made sense now.

I suppose, Shasti thought wryly, *I should be grateful she hasn't taken a shot at me. He's lucky to have had someone who cares so much for him. People have cared for me, but sometimes it's hard to tell if it was only because of what I could do for them. Even with Robert I was a strong right hand and a protection for his back. Of course, for a long time I've just been a gun with feet. I am more now, but who sees me just as a person and not as a means to some end?*

On reaching orbit safely, D'abo left on a Nekoan cutter, with time for only a brief goodbye to Shasti. The Nekoan's thanks were heartfelt but shadowed by the loss of so many of her people aboard both the freighter and the cruiser. "Kadesh is demanding my quick return for consultations. We have won a great victory together," she said, as Shasti walked her to the shuttle. "I only wish I could enjoy it."

"I know," Shasti said. "Will I see you at the embassy?" Shasti wanted the young Nekoan to stay, but between her ship's demands and Vaughn's presence, she was run ragged and distracted, with little time for her new friend.

"In a few days," D'abo said, exhaustion haunting her voice. Shasti knew that the Nekoan had hardly slept since the battle. "Be well until then, my friend." They clasped arms, and D'abo disappeared into the cutter.

Neither of the Confederate vessels could handle atmospheric reentry, so Shasti and her company shuttled down to the planet later that day, after the initial repairs were made. *Sidhe's* high tail had taken a glancing blow, and she had lost much of one wing. It had become a standing joke on the star-frigate about her getting shot in the ass all the time. The high tail made for a better target lock than the main hull, and an inordinate number of the hits suffered by the ship in her voyages landed there. Fortunately, there was little in the tail beyond liquid storage and electronics.

As no better medicine was available on the surface than in the ships, the wounded stayed aboard. The dead lay in *Paladin's* cold storage. On *Sidhe*, where the bodies had been vaporized with the wing, there were only small packets of personal effects. Shasti had no idea what to do for a ceremony, and it evidently had not even occurred to Vaughn. With Mollica distanced and drugged, Shasti had no one to seek advice of aboard ship.

Mandela will know what to do, she told herself.

With the situation on both ships stabilized, it was time to return to the planet. *Pooka* was greeted with wild enthusiasm as she settled at the spaceport, both by those they had left behind and by the Nekoans. As the ramp went down, Rigg and Rask ran up. Both seemed hard pressed to control their relief on seeing Shasti and Mmok. Rigg was shaking Shasti by the shoulder and slapping her on the back, something no one else would have dared. "Glad to see you, Skipper. Damn glad to see you."

"Yep," Rask added. "You took names and kicked ass." He looked at Mmok. "Hey, you came back with all your pieces this time."

"Everything all right here?" Shasti asked.

"Yeah." Rigg grinned. "Mandela kept pretending he wasn't worried, but when word came back that you'd survived, it was brandy and cigars all around."

"Sure," she said, "now that he knows his supply is safe."

"He's a practical kind of guy." Rigg nodded. "He's waiting for you at the Nekoan embassy. There's a party in your honor tonight."

"Oh, crap," Shasti said.

Rigg looked at Rask. "You owe me a fiver. I told you she'd say that."

"I don't feel that much like celebrating," Shasti said. "We lost two on *Sidhe* and four on *Paladin*. Orel and Finnegan were in the damage control party in the wing. Nothing left. Scholl, Furtado, Krieg, and Aster were gunners in the forward batteries of the *Paladin*."

Rigg nodded. "Skipper, you never want to lose anyone, but it's a tiny butcher's bill for stopping an Evolver. We numbered the casualties on Fenris in the tens of thousands."

"Yeah." She looked up at the Vaughn's descending shuttle, *Duelist*.

"Boss has a ceremony planned for the KIAs," Rigg said, "said for you not to worry about it. He'll make the arrangements, 0900 tomorrow, honor guard and ceremony. They'll be buried on the grounds of the new Confed embassy. Mandela's leased that office building and grounds to the west of the Nekoan legation."

She leaned close. "Dan, should I say something at this ceremony?"

"Yeah," he whispered. "A few words. It'll mean a lot to the crew. They'll be watching on video. I'll help you rough something out later if you like."

"I do and thank you."

Rigg changed the subject. "I'm surprised that Tanaka isn't here to greet Vaughn."

Shasti gave an irritated snort. "She snuck back on the damn *Paladin* before it launched. She wouldn't leave Vaughn. She sometimes acts like they're family."

Rigg grinned. "I wondered when you were going to see it."

"I suppose I'm lucky she hasn't tried to shoot me yet."

"What mother doesn't have some reservation about her boy's intended?"

Shasti gave him a slightly more than playful thump on the back. Rigg grinned at her. "I'll say no more."

She spotted Eris in the crop of well-wishers. The small alien gave her a friendly wave, but her eyes were only for Paolo. When she saw him, she ran up the ramp and embraced the slender, olive-skinned man.

Well, Shasti thought, *I guess I needn't worrying about him getting over me.* She found to her surprise that she was happy for them both. Paolo had been the difference between success and disaster for Shasti, the *Sidhe* and millions of Nekoan colonists. Besides, Eris might actually be able to hold Paolo's fickle attention as she was both a language and a female.

In the days following, the Ribisi ambassador, in his tank-like pressure suit, paid a formal visit to the new Confederate embassy. Encouraged by destruction of the Evolver, he ordered a large factory ship into orbit with the Confed vessels. Ribisi metal-working skills proved as amazing as the Nekoans claimed, and repairs proceeded apace on both vessels despite Perez's grumbling that they had been getting shot to pieces and reassembled non-stop since they arrived in Nekoan space.

As for Mollica, the fight with the Evolver had left the sharp-faced woman a hollow-eyed wreck. She improved a little with rest but declined to come down from the ship for either the party or the funeral ceremony at the grounds of the new embassy. Dr. Mourner took her off duty beyond supervising some of the more basic repairs.

Shasti knew that both Confed starships would be out of battle-readiness for weeks, if not a month, but she was becoming more concerned about relying on Mollica. Beyond that, Shasti had to admit that she faced a sense of disappointment. Mollica had been her pick, originally as a sailing master and then, after Shasti obtained her master's ticket, as First Officer. They had served together for two years, and Shasti had come to rely on the other woman's advice and support. It had not been quite a friendship, but in Shasti's emotionally barren existence, it had provided a constant. There seemed no one to back her up now.

16

Shasti waited until the others retired for the night before calling on Teleera at the legation. Repairs to *Sidhe* had consumed all her time since their return to Kandalor. It would be weeks before the wings were restored enough for a controlled entry. When Shasti wasn't closeted with Chief Engineer Perez, she was dealing with Dobera's near endless list for replacements and resupply. *Sidhe* had shot off almost a third of her magazine stores.

Shasti had not seen the young Nekoan for several days. D'abo hadn't attended the formal state function celebrating the victory. Kadesh took care of relations with the Confed force while D'abo took time off to deal with the loss of Shen. While reluctant to intrude on D'abo's grief, Shasti felt time slipping away and so found herself walking down a carpeted passage on the top floor of the embassy, leading to D'abo's quarters.

The big catgirl answered the door at the buzz, wearing a light, cream-colored robe. She looked up at the human with a curious expression. Shasti overtopped her by four inches, though the pile of rough hair and ears made them look of equal height. Shasti had felt a certain liking for D'abo since they'd met, and she seemed an ideal companion for the adventure Shasti planned.

"May I come in?" Shasti said. "I have an idea I'd like to discuss."

D'abo studied her for a second longer before opening the door and gesturing her in. Shasti followed her into the small anteroom. Both women seated themselves around an oval table decorated with a ship model surrounded by candles. Shasti recognized it as the cruiser *Fearless*.

"I'm sorry for your loss," Shasti said, gesturing at the ship.

D'abo nodded. "I was very fond of Shen. We'd spent some time together when I first arrived. I'd even considered asking him to join me as military attaché, but like me, he was very involved in his career. *Fearless* was his first command, and what female can compete with that?

"Still, there was something special about him. I had hoped it might lead to a term-mating. I knew that…" Her voice trailed away.

They sat quietly for a minute.

"That path," D'abo finished, "is closed to me now. Closed by these hellish machines. At least with the help of your Confederacy, there is some chance of survival, maybe even eventual victory."

"Perhaps," Shasti said. "Mandela has been very honest with you. I have little doubt the Confederacy will help. It's in our interest to fight these things here in your space, but how fast and how effectively help will arrive is open to question."

"I know this as well as you," D'abo said, tucking her legs under her and her tail across them. "For now, our fate is in our own hands. But what more can we do? We hoped the Evolver would attack Kandalor and rouse the power here to our aid, as happened once before with the Conchirri. But we could not lure it in. For five years, using every means we could think of, we've tried to contact whatever mystery rules this world, without result. The Ribisi and the natives have impeded our efforts at every turn. The Ribisans are more frightened of the power here than they are of the Evolvers. I think they're fools."

"I agree." Shasti leaned forward. "I've studied everything you gave me on your efforts here, and on what little the Ribisans learned before that. All that the efforts of both species have established is that any bases outside the capitol area gradually succumb to natural forces. Everywhere but here. What does that suggest to you?"

"The same thing it does to you," D'abo challenged. "Whatever power is here prefers to keep us in one area where we can be easily observed and controlled."

"Which means that we should be close to the source of the power. Yet it has eluded coverage for centuries. How? Perhaps by hiding in plain sight. The dominant feature in the physical and political landscape is Sorokol, the natives' Mountain of Destiny," Shasti said. "It seems a logical place to look for the power. I'm curious that you haven't invested more time in intelligence work in that area."

"Sorokol is important to the locals," D'abo shrugged, "but it has no relevance to the space defenses that we have been able to detect. I told you. We sent some probes. They were deactivated. We judged it useless to continue."

"Yet what better way to conceal a true power than underneath a local religious shrine that it would be impolitic to disturb?" Shasti said. "Your predecessors seem to have been easily discouraged. I've read your initial reports from when you were first assigned here. You were adamant that additional efforts be made: spying, bribery, agents all centered on that area. Then it seemed you lost interest."

D'abo shrugged again. "I am sorry my efforts do not meet with your approval."

Shasti stood. "Please come up to the roof with me."

"Why?"

"I have something important to show you."

D'abo rose. Dressed only in her light golden robe, she followed Shasti out and up the stairwell. The Nekoan waved her hand over the lock for the roof door, which opened at her handprint. They walked onto the railed rooftop. The night air was still warm. Spring had arrived on Kandalor. Above them a cloudless sky glittered with stars. D'abo walked over to gaze at the river with its twinkling of ship-lights.

"You can't even face it," Shasti said.

"Face what?" D'abo said, with a hint of irritation.

Shasti pointed in the opposite distance at the huge mountain. It was a greater darkness than the sky. The only lights that illuminated its vast bulk lay clustered in the holy city at its foot.

"And see what?" D'abo said. Shasti noted the tension in her body.

"What your people have been unable to see. The mountain, Teleera, the mountain. The focus of the native power and religion. Do you know how often your people refer to it? Never. And yet it fills the horizon. Mandela told me a curious story. He asked Kadesh about Sorokol. Kadesh refused to face it, said it put the sun in his eyes."

"What's wrong with that?" D'abo said.

"It was afternoon, the sun was in the west and the mountain lies east."

"Odd," D'abo murmured.

"D'abo," Shasti said.

"Yes."

"Why have you turned your back to the mountain?"

"I haven't," she said.

"You're facing the river."

D'abo jerked upright as if she's been touched by a live wire. "You're right."

Shasti walked over to the Nekoan and gently turned her to again face the mountain. She stood behind D'abo, a hand resting on each of her shoulders. "Look up at it."

A shiver ran through the Nekoan. "It's cold," she said. "Let's go in."

"It's not that cold," Shasti said. "Look at the mountain. Why is it hard? Why did you decide to stop investigating it?"

"Why?" D'abo said faintly. "Why? It seemed so obvious when I first came here. But always there seemed some reason, some obstacle. I kept putting it off. Why? Why?" She shook her mane of rough hair as if a fly were buzzing around her.

"There's a planetary force at work here," Shasti said, "and it is more pervasive and powerful than you ever imagined. Your people have been mind-blocked against considering the mountain. Not in a grand way that would attract attention, but in subtle ways. You have trouble focusing on the mountain. Something else always seems to intrude. You find that it's easier to look in some other direction. You're under a compulsion."

D'abo stood facing the vast dark bulk and shudders racked her frame. "It's true. It must be. It's the same way our installations and expansion have been controlled for centuries. No direct violence. No massive burst of power but rather constant erosion. A constant undermining until we moved into some easier channel. Yes," she said, her voice firming, "it's the same pattern."

"And that tells you what?" Shasti said.

"There is something important on or in the mountain," D'abo said. "Such an elaborate subtle scheme was conducted for a reason." She turned around to face Shasti. "And you, my mysterious alien friend. This compulsion does not affect you and your people?"

"My people?" Shasti said. "No, or at least not yet." She stepped around D'abo to stare up at the vast bulk. "I have a limited psychic sense, sometimes I pick up impressions or images. It's been twinging since I first saw this mountain. I feel as if there is something there, calling me, something that holds the answers to all these riddles. Something that might end the threat of the Evolvers or," she finished, "something that might destroy us for our impudence in disturbing it."

"Interesting," D'abo said, one ear twitching. "Sounds like a job for two somewhat expendable but highly-trained operatives, proceeding on their own discretion and leaving plausible deniability to their superiors."

"Complete deniability," Shasti corrected. "I think my plan is too radical for Mandela. It could provoke problems with the natives and this power, so I need to leave my side with a complete out."

"Very well," D'abo said. "I see your point." She mused on the question. "Our situation becomes more desperate daily. Our so-called alliance with the Ribisans is a sham. Our fleet suffers badly with the Evolvers. Help is years away. We need to do something radical. But we cannot simply land there and poke around. We need local help."

"Is that possible?"

"Fortunately, there is a Kandalorian who owes us his life," D'abo said.

"Mookesh looks a bit old and bulky for an op," Shasti said.

"Oh, it won't be him," D'abo said. "But he has many who owe him. He will arrange for a person on the inside or trade for one. Give me the day to arrange it."

"It's desperate," Shasti said. "This could be a disaster."

"Yes," D'abo said, her sharp teeth very much in evidence, "but it may allow me to personally set tooth and claw in the Evolvers, so I am in. Tell me your plan."

"Well," Shasti said with an evil grin, "I think it's time I introduce you to an old human custom: girls' night out."

The next night, Shasti arranged her schedule so that no one was expecting her, everyone thinking she was with someone else. She reached the roof of the warehouse D'abo had indicated by a back staircase. Once atop the building, she looked about. The roof was dimly lit, and her dark-adapted eyes quickly made up for the lack of ambient light. She opened the heavy, olive-drab duffel bag and drew out and assembled a triple-auto carbine, pistol, and other weapons. Quickly she changed into the tactical vest.

A brisk, warm wind played over the roof as she pulled on her boots, and Shasti found herself humming. The thought of the night's mission made her happy, satisfied in a way she hadn't been in a long while. She felt like she had in the old days when she played a lone hand in the universe.

"There is something badly wrong with me that I like this shit," she said ruefully.

Her sensitive ears picked up the whine of an aircar impeller set low. A small gray and black two-seater popped into view and slid onto the rooftop. The side hatch opened, and Shasti piled into the machine before it could stop, throwing the duffel in the back. She slid into the seat next to D'abo.

The catgirl gave a toothy grin and gunned the engine. The warehouse disappeared into the darkness behind them.

Shasti saw her friend was armed to the teeth and wearing a dark coverall. She'd sprayed her mass of golden hair a dark color, even to the ears. Camo streaked her face.

D'abo looked her over as they climbed to an altitude where the aircar's impeller wouldn't be heard by the mass of tribesman surrounding Bizi in the days following the riot. "Very pro," D'abo said, checking out Shasti's gear. "However, that lovely pale skin of yours will show up—"

Shasti, who had been waiting for the comment, turned her skin flat black. She enjoyed the catgirl's open-mouthed astonishment.

"Amazing," she finally said. "What else can you do?"

"Now that would be telling," Shasti replied.

D'abo ran fingers down Shasti's cheek as if to see if the texture had changed with the color.

"Umm," Shasti said. "How about feeling me up later and flying now."

"Right," D'abo said. "ETA twenty minutes. Assuming, of course, that the power doesn't swat us from the sky."

"Why are you whispering?' Shasti asked.

D'abo gave a brief laugh, then gave herself over to steering. The Nekoan's eyes fastened on the mountain with a look of hatred. Once free of the compulsion, it seemed to have no more effect on D'abo. But Shasti sensed her friend harbored a deep anger at having been manipulated.

I only hope there's no aftereffect, Shasti thought. *I can't afford her folding up on me under some alien influence. Of course, there's no guarantee I'll do any better.*

Sorokol grew steadily in their windscreen, a ghostly height crowned with stars. The mountain's vast bulk lay dark, save for the occasional small campfire from some ascetic, spending the night in its embrace.

Shasti adjusted the control on their scanner, looking down on the nomads. Their camps stretched out beneath the aircar. In the green image of her scanner, she could see thousands of nomads. Their camps were undisciplined tribal rings, well separated, with fabric tents and animals as well as the occasional hovertruck. The camps were guarded, but the arrangements looked haphazard and vulnerable to Shasti's trained eye. From the location of their sentries, it seemed the nomads were as suspicious of each other as they were of the city folk.

D'abo glanced at the scanner. "Let's hope we don't need to walk back."

Fortunately, the mysterious power either didn't have an airborne warning system, or regarded them as too insignificant to be a threat. Their flight to the immense, white-capped peak was undisturbed. D'abo set them down on a rocky outcropping just below the vegetation line. They cut the impeller and popped the hatches, weapons ready and senses stretching into the night beyond. Now was their last chance to escape if their mission had been compromised. Once they left the car, stealth would be their best protection.

They exchanged glances. Shasti nodded, and they raced out of the aircar into cover. Seconds passed slowly, but nothing attacked. D'abo stood, holding her short, ugly submachine gun at her waist. Shasti crouched on the cliff side, looking into the shadowed valley and crags below. Kandalor's two moons had yet to rise, so it was the darkest part of the night. Smoky yellow lights from campfires dotted the plains below, mostly from the more primitive tribesman and nomads. At some points, she could see the steady bright lights of some battery-powered off-world device. Kandalorians did not use yellow-white lights that mimicked sunlight. Instead, they used lenses of emerald or topaz—a sure indication they had evolved under some other star. The effect left Shasti feeling as if she hung in space with stars above and below her.

Her sense of smell brought her dry earth, rock, and faint traces of wood smoke. Her eyes, adapted to the dark in a way no standard human's ever could, picked out the low, scrubby bush typical of deserts. On the rocky soil of the mountain, it was lower and more spread out than near Bizi. Standing over the scrub like sentinels were hundreds of hardy "desert spears," a plant similar to an earthly cactus in both looks and water storage. Such were great cover for a person moving at night. One had to merely freeze in place to be only another vertical shape in the darkness.

Satisfied, she nodded to D'abo. They moved, stalking forward in short moves, then stopping to listen.

It always sounds like one is making enough noise for a marching band, Shasti thought. Earth crunched underfoot, dry twigs and leaves snapped, dislodged rocks slid downhill from them. Nothing on either woman made a noise. Even the buckles on Shasti's carbine were secured with black tape so they couldn't rattle. Their canteens were overfilled so as not to slosh. Shasti knew they couldn't be heard for any distance, but there was always the chance of stumbling into hunters or guards.

She gestured to D'abo, who flicked an ear toward her. "Are there animals on these heights?" she whispered.

D'abo nodded. "We'll likely be thought to be gruns, a small herbivore, if we are heard at all. That will be great unless we run into a nomad hunting for tomorrow's crelick."

Shasti grimaced. "No help for that."

They rounded an upthrust crag of rock decorated with a small bell-shaped plant that emitted a soft, mournful musical note as the night wind blew through it. Shasti reached out and touched D'abo. Below them stood the entranceway she'd chosen. An hour's cautious approach brought them down to the area where their contact, Brelish, should be waiting. Shasti had studied this spot with *Sidhe's* instruments for days. Of the hundreds of entrances to Sorokol, this one was approached only by high-status individuals and with elaborate ceremony.

The entranceway must have started as an avalanche site with a great slab torn off the mountainside. It had been expanded and built both up and in. Now it resembled an immense half-bowl facing the mountainside. The bowl housed an amphitheater and dozens of smaller structures and platforms. Places for worship or gathering, Shasti assumed. Strange globes of a glowing green glass stood atop poles of silver metal around the perimeter. They cast a weak, eerie glow over the deserted gathering place. Many trails led to the site, but all were from lower elevations. Shasti knew they were guarded below, but not from approach from above. It was the logical place to start their infiltration.

"Of course," D'abo had commented when Shasti showed her the photos from *Wildcat 1*, "if we are caught near such a place, they're likely to hang us from a desert spear."

"We will try to avoid deadly force," Shasti had answered, "fewer repercussions if there are fewer bodies."

"A good policy," D'abo had agreed.

Shasti reached out, touched D'abo, and pointed at a figure standing by a desert spear off the polished stone of the entranceway. A young male Kandalorian, he wore the broad-brimmed hat Mookesh told them to expect. Shasti and D'abo circled around him from different sides to make sure he was there alone. The acolyte seemed either indifferent or insensible to their approach.

Finally, Shasti threw a rock to draw his attention. He approached cautiously and froze when she stood up from behind some brush. D'abo rose behind him, and he slowly raised his hands.

"Name," D'abo demanded in Kandalorian.

"Brelish," he said. "The young fool who borrows money he can't repay and indulges in earthly pleasures an acolyte should not."

"Long name," Shasti said.

The Kandalorian did a double take on her.

"What were you told?" Shasti demanded.

"Meet two Star Demons here and take them by unguarded ways into the sanctuary of the Mystery, to the Moon Pool itself."

Shasti walked up to the creature. Kandalorians were an unlovely race, but this one looked active, strong, and young and didn't smell as bad as some. The scent of incense clung to his long carmine robe.

"Your debts must be severe for you to aid us in sacrilege," she probed.

The Kandalorian waved a hand. "I am a monk because I'm a disfavored younger son. It is no plan of mine. As for the mystery, I have never seen any sign of it and think it is like the other gods people make up to explain the unknown. If it is not there, then what harm? If it is there, then I assume it can take care of itself. In any event, it is a less certain doom than if certain images of me engaged in unapproved mating with—"

"Spare me the details," Shasti said. "Let's get moving."

With Brelish leading, the spacers walked under the ornately carved stone of the mountain entrance. More of the green globes hung over their heads, their steady glow giving Shasti and D'abo all the illumination they needed. Murals decorated the native stone of the passage with images of Kandalorians, some locked in combat, some dressed for journeying, others knelt in worshipful prayer. Shasti gave them a bare glance; she was after deeper mysteries. A hundred meters in, there came a dramatic change in the tunnel. It intersected a wide cross hall that dwarfed their tunnel.

"Predecessor work," D'abo exclaimed.

"Tell me more," Shasti said, leaning into the hall to look both ways. The lighting in the huge tunnel was supplied by glowing blue panels twenty-five meters over their heads.

D'abo stroked the smooth material of the walls. "This material is molecularly dense, a metal-latticed polymer. The earliest Predecessors used it extensively in their buildings, particularly underground. It's almost indestructible after it sets. This tunnel must be hundreds of thousands of years old. The landslide uncovered it when this part of the mountain fractured." She stepped out into the hall looking back the way they had come. "Yes, the cut here is ragged, caused by a cave-in. The worst of the edges have been smoothed. I wonder how long that took? But it's beyond Kandalorian technology to enlarge it."

Brelish looked at them impatiently. "Time flees before us. You wanted to see Sorokol's great mystery. If we are to reach the Moon Pool and make it back before dawn, we should move now."

Shasti nodded. She let her skin revert to its normal paleness. Brelish jumped backward, cursing.

"We are full of tricks, we Star Demons," Shasti growled.

Brelish walked off as fast as he could without running. D'abo grinned and shook her head before following the acolyte. Shasti and D'abo kept up easily, their long legs eating up ground. The tunnel sloped down gently, the flooring glassy smooth but curiously not slick. Another feature of Predecessor technology, Shasti guessed, perhaps made tractable on an atomic level. She began to find the blue light disorienting. The passage walls had whorls of decoration carved into them that yielded no recognizable patterns or images but that caught at the eye, inducing a mild vertigo till she looked away.

They walked on and on. Time ceased to have much meaning in the blue tunnel. Occasionally the passage branched, and Brelish consulted Kandalorian markings to indicate the path. They began to pass other, smaller tunnels. From one such opening a pulsing red light bled into the main tunnel. They approached slowly, with Brelish staying as close to the far wall as he could.

Shasti stared up the passage, which gradually bent off to the right, leaving them no line of sight to the light's source. There was a slow, sluggish pattern to the light, like an unhealthy heartbeat.

"What's back there?" Shasti asked, her triple auto up and facing down the passage. The faintest scent of corruption reached her sensitive nose. She looked at D'abo and was familiar enough with her new friend's expressions to read distaste there.

Brelish made complicated warding gestures with his hands. "No one knows. None who have ventured down that way have ever returned. The sensible avoid this place. Let us not linger here."

They moved on with D'abo watching their backtrail as if some terror might emerge from the bloody passage.

Down they went until finally they moved into a broad cavern. In the center of the space, carved out of the very floor, was a huge pool. It held a luminous white fluid that gently lit the cavern. They spread out cautiously.

"The Moon Pool," Brelish whispered. "No one knows what it is or what function it has, but it was obviously important to those who once dwelt here. The High Priest insists it is the eye of God."

The fluid stopped only a few millimeters below the glossy surface of the floor, its still surface lit from beneath. Shasti took one of the small black clips she used to keep her long hair in place and dropped it into the pool.

Brelish gave a choked cry and covered his face. But God did not reach out to strike them down for dropping a clip in his eye. The clip sank slowly in the fluid, as if the liquid was denser than water. As it went deeper, the clip disappeared. Shasti knew that the color of the fluid was not just a lighting effect; it was opaque.

"Tell me everything you know of the Moon Pool," Shasti demanded. Her every instinct told her that the pool was connected to the planetary force.

Brelish's casual insouciance about the force had faded the farther they had gone into the mountain, and Shasti could see the fear in his stance. She had to restate the question to get his attention.

"The Pool...the pool," he said. "It is the Eye of God. There are legends that in times of disaster, Kandalorians, and before us, some of the Predecessors, the Veen, the Borels, or the Unta-yush would come to this place to petition God for help."

"How?" D'abo demanded.

"There were those called Messengers. They went into the pool, some involuntarily, bound as sacrifices. Others walked in. Not all returned, but some came back with magical devices, or in some cases the aid that they sought appeared, a flooding river turned, a storm averted, a volcano stilled, or an invader destroyed."

Shasti considered as D'abo pulled out some instruments.

"I've detected no harmful radiation," D'abo said. "The temperature of the fluid is the same one would expect of a heated bath." She reached down and tested the pool with a glove, then a lock of her hair, cut off with a long thin dagger. Finally she ventured a finger.

Brelish looked at them, his trepidation quelled for the moment. "The High Priest is anointed with the waters of the pool. They are not dangerous, though it is not healthful to drink. One tried, only to be sickened for months."

"What do you think?" D'abo said.

"Hard to say," Shasti replied. "If there is anything in these legends, this must lead somewhere. Give me your dagger. I have an idea."

Shasti pulled out a spool of thin but strong rope and looped it around the dagger, throwing the rest of the line behind her. "Let's see how deep it is."

She tossed the dagger in and watched it sink into the glowing pool, becoming indistinct about three meters down. Suddenly Shasti felt a tremendous pull. Instantly realizing it was too powerful to resist, she released the rope, but the sudden jerk toppled her into the pool. She somersaulted underwater, kicking furiously. As her head broke the surface of the thick oily fluid, Shasti saw D'abo, her foot entangled by the line, fly into the pool with a wild cry. Shasti reached for her, but it was too far. The Nekoan hit the surface with a huge splash, was drawn under in a second and disappeared.

"Teleera!" Shasti cried. She dove down but could not see her friend. Shasti stroked back to the pool's edge and seized both her triple auto and D'abo's dropped weapon. She looked up at Brelish. Her guide stared at her in such terror that Shasti knew he would be useless if she forced him to accompany her.

"Mookesh paid you half," she said. "Wait here for three hours. If I don't return in that time, then I won't be back and you won't get the rest of your payment." He made a gesture she took as agreement and slunk away to an alcove in evident relief.

Shasti turned and dove. It was like diving into the body of a pearl. A milky white glow surrounded her. *This is probably the last stupid thing I will do,* she thought. She thought of the people in her life, the one love, the few friends, and the possibilities that might never be realized. Suddenly the water around her roiled, and Shasti felt herself pulled down.

Her head broke water in the cavern. *What?* she thought. *I was headed down.*

"Shasti," came a glad cry.

She spun around and simultaneously noticed D'abo waving frantically from the side of the pool and that the pool itself was no longer opalescent but rather a deep jade green.

"Are you all right?" Shasti said, swimming for the edge.

"Yes," she said. "And damn glad to see you, though you're a fool for following me."

D'abo helped Shasti out of the pool and gratefully seized her submachine gun. Shasti unlimbered her triple-auto. The weapon was impervious to water, but it was not a good idea to fire the laser feature with fluid in the barrel. Superheated steam could burn the user, so she switched over to bullets.

"What happened?" Shasti demanded.

"When you were pulled in, I stepped forward to grab you," D'abo said, "and right into a loop of the rope. It snapped around my boot and almost pulled my leg off. Next thing I knew I was here on the other side."

"Did you see what pulled you in?" Shasti demanded, her eyes searching the darkness. Unlike the cavern they had come from, this one was far more dimly lit by the Jade Pool. She could see at least one exit from the cavern and thought she detected a faint sheen of blue light in it.

"No," D'abo said, "but I do not think that it was a creature or even a trap. I think that we have passed through some form of gate and that the gate itself pulled us through."

"Why didn't you try to come back?" Shasti asked.

"Because I could not," D'abo said grimly, her eyes glittering in the jade light. "There is a bottom this side. Look." She held up her dagger, complete with the treacherous rope. "It was merely sitting on the bottom. It appears our gate is one way."

Shasti sighted. "Guard here while I double check. I can hold my breath for very long periods. I can even breathe water, though I'd have to be very desperate before I would try it here." She handed her weapons and equipment to D'abo and stripped out of her armor and clothes to make the diving easier. She took only a dagger with her.

As she stepped toward the pool, D'abo took her arm and to Shasti's surprise pressed her lips to Shasti's cheek. "For luck," she said, "and for not leaving me alone and abandoned here."

Flustered and unsure of what to say, Shasti nodded and dove in. Five minutes of searching convinced her that no device or evident trigger lay on the bottom. She came back up to find a worried D'abo stripping out of her tunic.

"I was about to come in after you," she exclaimed in relief. "You were down so long."

Shasti reached the edge and surged out of it. "Sorry. I wanted to be sure that poking around here was unavoidable before we started. Remember the red corridor that no one returns from."

"Yes," D'abo said. "Let's not go down any of those."

Shasti dried herself on her jacket and began climbing into her clothes and armor. Whatever fluid was in the pools slid off them quickly; in only a few minutes both women were dry.

Shasti and D'abo used the lights attached to their weapons to scan the cavern, but it seemed there was only the one immense passage, at the far end. The passage sloped up out of sight.

They looked at each other and nodded. Both dialed down the power of the lights, preferring to rely on their low-light vision. D'abo limped badly as they followed the broad open ramp. She caught Shasti's eye. "Took some anti-inflammatories from my med kit," she said. "It's probably strained, but I should be all right for a few more hours."

The passage cut back and forth, going higher. Shasti noted how their feet stirred no dust. *Something must be maintaining it,* she thought. The ceiling, easily twenty meters away, seemed reinforced with lattices of metal.

After ten minutes, Shasti noticed that the walls had changed to a green crystal and the rampway opened out and up. They entered a large open area of the same crystal. Shasti had never seen such a thing before and wondered if it were natural or created.

The crystal glowed softly with an inner light, like the Jade Pool.

The roof and far end of the cavern disappeared in dim greenness, making Shasti feel as if she stood on the ocean floor. Machinery dotted the space ahead of her, and the floor became sinewy with cables varying from thumb size to thicker than her body. Shasti and D'abo watched their footing as they struggled forward.

Ahead lay a flat area of white stone. Shasti headed for it, glad for easier footing. She could see some peculiar columns backed by a wall just ahead. Shasti reached the white stone flooring and strode forward.

Suddenly the light around her began to change. An orange glow filled the space. A deep thrumming sound began behind her, and some of the cables began to pulse with light. Shasti and D'abo slowly backed away, trying to look in all directions.

"We've tripped something," D'abo said. "Maybe we should hide in the tunnel."

Shasti turned to head for the tunnel then froze. Her situational awareness sense warned her something was near. D'abo slowed and came back to her.

The light strengthened. Now the columns ahead no longer looked like stone and the strange bottoms took on the aspect of hooves. Shasti's eyes reluctantly followed the columns upward.

The titan sat in a chair the size of a building. She had seen the like only once before and then only as a colossal mass of ancient bone. This wasn't bone. Gray elephantine skin covered its body along with yards of metallic cloth. Her eyes continued up against her will. Atop the tower of muscle and bone, three huge black eyes looked gigantically down on her.

It was unquestionably a Prekak and alive.

A sound like a waterfall began to fill her mind. Shasti turned to flee, overwhelmed by blind terror for the first time in her life. She didn't even consider the weapon she held. "Run," she yelled.

Before they could travel more than three panic-stricken steps, Shasti pulled up short to avoid colliding with the little old woman who appeared in front of her. Short, elegant, wearing a dark-blue cardigan sweater, long skirt, and suede boots, the woman wore her silver-gray hair in a long, braided ponytail and studied Shasti from mild blue eyes.

"Don't be afraid, dears," said the woman with a quaint accent. "No one will hurt you."

Shasti stared at the apparition, mind numb with shock. "We've got to run," she managed.

"I'm over two-hundred thousand years old," said the little woman. "I really don't run much anymore."

Shasti looked at her dumbfounded, then jerked back to look at the seated Prekak.

"You don't have to look at me if you find this image easier," said the woman.

Shasti looked back at the old woman. "You're Mrs. Ferguson," she murmured.

"You know this being?" D'abo said, incredulous.

"Robert Fenaday's housekeeper," Shasti began. "No, no, impossible. You've pulled this from my mind."

"Yes, dear," said the old woman. "I did it as gently as I could. I hope I didn't hurt you?"

Shasti backed up a step, her hand cupping her weapon, then remembered the titan seated behind her. She shifted so she could see both the Prekak and the apparition. D'abo looked back and forth in confusion.

The old woman gave them a disappointed look. "I don't much care for weapons, young ones."

The absurdity of brandishing any weapon at a live Prekak struck Shasti. The dead one she and Fenaday fought on Enshar had been more than enough to destroy a world. Shasti straightened, willing her racing heart to slow. The metallic taste of fear, rare and dimly remembered from her childhood as a prisoner of Jalgren Pard, receded. Only her wits could save her now. Her Engineered body began to scrub the chemical effects of fear from her body and her mind functioned again.

How do standard humans manage to handle such intense fear? she wondered.

"Who," she croaked, then wet her dry lips and started again. "Who are you?'

"I am what you think," she said. "You could not pronounce my name, so give me whatever name you would like. What is the name of this older female? I don't want to rummage around in your mind without need."

"Mary Ferguson," Shasti said.

"You seem to have fond memories of her," observed the Prekak.

"She was kind," Shasti returned. "So few are."

"Good, then call me Mary," the Prekak said.

The absurdity of it threatened the stability of Shasti's mind—she fought the hysterical laughter lurking at the back of her throat. If she started, she wasn't sure she'd ever stop.

"Well, Mary, you're not going to kill us?"

"Oh, bosh," Mary said. "Why would I do such a thing?"

"The other one of your kind that I've seen was not so gentle." Memories of the nightmare battles with the creature that almost annihilated one of the species of the Confederacy flashed in her mind. She saw the image of the Prekak's skeleton, lying in its confinement chamber under the slaughtered Enshari capital of Barjan. She watched the giant skull turn toward Robert Fenaday. She remembered the Shellycoats forming out of debris around them and the desperate battle to escape. Finally came the image of her friend, Belwin Duna, who sacrificed himself to detonate the nuclear weapon that ended the Prekak's rampage.

To Shasti's surprise, the old woman's eyes filled with tears and her hand went over her mouth. "Oh, the poor boy. The poor brave boy." The Prekak walked away from her. After a few moments, she regained her composure and spoke over her shoulder to Shasti. "I knew him. He was so handsome and so brave. He faced an enemy that your mind cannot even imagine and it cost him everything. When we confined him in that chamber eons ago, it was in the hope that centuries of meditation might return him to sanity. We had hope then."

Shasti looked at her, uncertain of what to do or say. "It cost many others as well."

"Yes, yes," said Mary. "But you didn't know him before. All you met was the malicious ghost of something that was once brave and wonderful. You never met the being I knew."

"What is going on?" D'abo demanded, limping forward.

"So many questions," Mary said. "The young always have so many questions. Very well, Teleera D'abo, sit a moment so that you do not fall and I will tell you."

D'abo carefully lowered herself to the floor, one leg outstretched. She put her weapon on the ground next to her. Mary waved her hand, and a small stool appeared. She seated herself next to D'abo and gestured for Shasti to sit as well. Slowly Shasti complied, sitting on one of the huge cables, resting the carbine against it as well.

"Much of this your friend, Shasti, knows," Mary said. "Ancient days ago, before your people looked at the night sky with awareness, my kind ruled most of the galaxy, benevolently I would tell you, though others might have disagreed. We fought an enemy, the nature of which I will not show you, for fear of your sanity. A terrible enemy: anti-light, anti-life itself. They came from Outside, we know not where or how, but they were antithetical to all we knew and valued.

"The war between us ended the existence of many species in the galaxy. Indeed it almost ended us before we achieved a great step in the use of psionic weapons. That achievement enabled us to destroy our enemy, though it also destroyed the soul of one of our greatest heroes. About that your friend can tell you another time. She met his shadow in the most unfortunate of events."

Images swirled in Shasti and D'abo's minds. Shasti could feel the catgirl through the telepathic link, though the Prekak held them both distinct. The Prekak showed them worlds of wonder and terror with the giant being locked in mortal combat with an enemy she did not show them, only their ships and fighting machines. Cities surged for miles into the sky, oceans boiled under weapons that made their own armaments look like matches.

Mary gave a deep sigh and turned back to Shasti. "After we left Enshar, we were struck by a plague, a last trap of our enemy. It destroyed most of us. The few that were left had much to occupy us, and when the signal from Enshar failed, we thought our fallen hero dead and gone. And it was so far and we had become so old and tired. We never went back. Another terrible, terrible mistake. Alas, that we made so many."

"You're the force that rules this world," Shasti stated.

"Rule?" said the Prekak. "Hardly. I have neither the desire nor the wisdom to order the lives of millions of children. I keep the peace. I forbid major wars and insist that the more sophisticated and advanced cultures leave the others alone. A combination of a planet-wide psychic suggestion and the work of my acolytes. Other than that, I leave be."

"Your ambitions are modest," Shasti said dryly.

Mary laughed. "For the most part I am already gone from this dimension of space. Only the littlest part of me remains here. A small section of my mind remains to tend the body I have had so long. One gets used to having a body and it dreams its own peaceful dreams here. But most of what I am ranges the dimension above, closer to the Origin. If my full being were here, you would shrivel in its presence like an ant under a magnifying glass."

Shasti shivered.

Mary smiled. "Don't worry, dear," she said, reaching forward, patting Shasti's hand. "You're a very pretty ant."

The hand that touched her held nothing of human warmth in it. Shasti abruptly realized that "Mary" was a manifestation, similar to the Shellycoats she'd fought on Enshar. A creation from whatever base matter was nearby. Only, Mary had vastly greater control than had the ghost that haunted Enshar.

"Do you know anything of the Conchirri and their Makers?" Shasti ventured.

"The word means nothing to me," Mary said. "May I touch your mind, child, and learn?"

Shasti nodded uncertainly. She heard the waterfall roaring sound for a moment.

"Ah, them," Mary said, a stern note in her voice. "They of the black and yellow ships. I sensed them and tried to push them away, but they were mere appetite and anger. They struck this world a thousand years ago. I won't say that they died well, as they stupidly charged in with no hope of winning, but they died just the same." Mary shrugged. "Eventually they stopped coming."

"We fought them to their extermination," Shasti said.

"I doubt that they will be missed," Mary observed. "Of these others in your mind, the Makers, I know nothing. The universe is so vast and holds much. My powers in this dimension, formidable though you deem them, are merely local. Here, I am old and keep to my home these days."

D'abo looked at the fearsome body seated behind them. "Your species is long-lived."

"Yes," Mary replied, "but not so long as you suspect. It has been many tens of thousands of years since we walked in this space. But here, in this place I made for myself, time does not pass. When my mind became too powerful for a body to hold it, and I passed on to higher planes of existence, I made this world a safe place for my old form."

"A hole in time," D'abo said, looking up at Mary. "You have such power?"

Mary smiled down at her and reached a hand over to stroke the Nekoan's fluffy mane. "It is a little thing." She began scratching behind D'abo's ears. For a second D'abo looked outraged, but unsure if she should do something about it. "With distinct advantages, as your friend Shasti noticed walking up here, I never need to dust."

D'abo's eyes were half closed, and a blissful look slid over her face. In a few more seconds she was asleep.

Mary looked over at Shasti. "I wanted a private word with you, dear, and it was a gentle way to keep your curious cat at bay."

Shasti looked at the sleeping D'abo in bemusement. "What did you want to say?"

"You are something different," Mary said, her blue eyes peering sharply at Shasti. "Something unexpected in the universe. Our philosophers used to say that intelligent life is the universe talking to itself. But you, my dear, are a conversation nature did not plan. Space, time, and probability roil about you, disturbed in a fashion I had never imagined. You do not have the senses to detect this, but your existence reorders some things in space-time. Because you are, some other things will never come to be. Others will come to be in a new fashion. I've never seen the like of you."

A frisson of fear struck through Shasti. "What are you talking about?"

"Perhaps," Mary continued, "I merely sense that you have a destiny. You are a nexus and potential for change in this plane of existence. I don't care for change here, youngling. I would take it ill if you disarranged my little home."

"That's not my intention," Shasti said.

"Yes, yes, well, intentions don't always meet expectations. You may go through this existence overturning applecarts that you do not even see."

"What are you going to do to me?" Shasti growled. "I'll fight."

Mary looked down at D'abo, whose rough hair she still stroked. "Yes, no doubt you would, as would your new friend here. She would do battle for you. There is an affinity between you two. Perhaps your souls have touched in some other life…

"No," Mary finished, "I will not harm you. Perhaps I should, but I will not. You have suffered at the hands of my kind. There is a debt owed. I shall make a small payment now. While I hold this planet safe and will allow your kind to land and base here, as I have the others, it is not my desire to be involved in your wars and lives. But from what I have seen in your minds, these Evolvers represent a terrible threat to life in this space. You will need more help if our little friend here," she patted D'abo, "and her kind are to survive.

"Seek out the Skurlocks. They are not yet gone from this plane of existence. In them you will find aid."

"Where?" Shasti asked.

Mary stood, and to Shasti's surprise, she looked weary. "It would take more of me than is here to answer more of your questions. You must seek your own answers."

"Teleera," Mary said softly.

The Nekoan's eyes fluttered open, and her head snapped up. "What? I fell asleep?"

"Follow me," Mary said. The old woman started off back the way that Shasti had come, gliding a few inches off the ground. Shasti had to follow more slowly over the cables. She turned to help D'abo, who shook her head.

"My leg is fine," she whispered. She gave a wide-eyed look at Mary's back.

They returned to the Jade Pool. Mary floated over the center of it.

"Time to go, girls," Mary said. "No need to undress for swimming. I will send you back to the other side quite dry. It's been a nice visit, but I'm old and I need my rest. You should not come back." A note of sternness crept into her voice.

The two nodded carefully.

Mary raised her hands and an opalescent glow surrounded Shasti and D'abo. They lifted into the air and settled into the pool, insulated by whatever field they were in. Suddenly they found themselves rising through the Moon Pool and their feet touched down on the slick surface. The light faded around them.

18

A sharp rap on the door brought Mikhail Vaughn to instant wakefulness. He threw off the light blanket and crossed to the door in two strides. Tanaka stood just outside the door to his fourth-floor quarters in the new Confederate embassy.

"Mmok's here with Dan Rigg," she said softly. "They want to talk to you, won't say why."

Vaughn rubbed a hand over his face. "Show them in."

Tanaka gave him a dubious look but returned in a moment with Mmok and Rigg. Vaughn bade them enter as he turned to the sink in the small quarters and washed the sleep from his eyes. He turned back to face the two and looked a question at the machine-man.

"Didn't figure you for a boxer kind of guy," Mmok said.

Rigg sighed.

"Okay, okay," Mmok said. "Look, Rainhell and Catwoman have taken off for the big mountain. They're after clues to weapons of Kandalor. Shasti thinks there is some being or force there that is controlling events."

"Wonderful," Vaughn said, snatching up clothing and fighting the desire to curse. "So if they make it past the roving bands of nomads, the priests and their guards, they might find themselves up against some deadly planetary force. It's hard to believe she could be so reckless."

"You know our girl," Mmok said. "She doesn't believe there is an ass in the galaxy she can't kick."

"She's worse than my sisters," Rigg grumbled.

"Sisters?" Vaughn asked, as he pulled on his boots. Like all the Engineered, he found the idea of siblings intriguing, for all that standard humans always seemed to be complaining about them.

"Two," Rigg said, "older and headstrong like Rainhell. She kinda reminds me of Susan, the one closest to my age, dark hair, green eyes, always in trouble. I lost track of the boys I've popped in the mouth for getting fresh with her. Course I haven't needed to do that for the skipper, but I've had her back ever since Enshar. You'd think she'd have taken me along on this one."

"You'd have let her go on something this insane?" Vaughn asked.

"Hell no!" Rigg said. "Well, like I could…yeah."

"Thought so." Vaughn grabbed a jacket to cover his sidearm. "She knew she could not get the Nekoans to agree to it and she must have wanted Mandela insulated from any fallout. You would have tried to stop her."

"Makes sense," Mmok said. "She had me fooled too. Said she was heading back to *Sidhe* late. I was plugged into the ship's main computer for diagnostic. It was hours before I realized she wasn't aboard. She's been studying everything she could get on the mountain for days. I broke into her encoded personal files. Wasn't difficult so I suspect that she meant me to be able to in case she didn't come back. She's discovered that the Nekoans are under some psychic compulsion that prevents them from investigating Sorokol Mountain. She broke the compulsion in D'abo, and they set up a covert op. I shuttled down as soon as I realized what was up."

"Did you tell Mandela?" Vaughn demanded.

There was a moment's silence. "No," Mmok said. "I was afraid he'd put the kibosh on backing her up. I left a time message on a computer. If I'm destroyed, he gets the message."

Vaughn looked down at the metal man. "Good," he grunted. "Very good."

"Tanaka," Vaughn called. "We will be slipping out. You must stay here and keep up a pretense that we are with you. Order food for four from the kitchen. Tell them there is an all-night card game going."

The Asian woman nodded. Then looking at both Rigg and Vaughn, she said, "Be damn careful."

"Let's see if the ladies can use a hand," Rigg said, almost hopping from foot to foot. "I've got a mule out back. Couldn't get an aircar without attracting more attention than we want."

"They'll probably have the planetary force bound and gagged by the time we make it," Mmok said, opening the door. "Don't know why we are bothering, really."

"Probably no reason at all," Rigg said, jogging down the hallway.

"Waste of time," Vaughn agreed as Rigg pushed open the stairwell door ahead of him. They took the stairs three at a time.

"Can we pick up the pace, guys?" Mmok said, plunging past them as he jumped into the stairwell. His voice trailed back. "My granny moves faster."

Vaughn and the others slipped out the rear service door of the embassy, past one of Tivka's guards. The trooper, recognizing them, passed them without question. Outside one of *Sidhe's* mules idled with Mmok already standing in the gun ring, holding onto the heavy machine gun. Rask sat in the driver's seat, low-light goggles hanging from his thick neck. "Shake a leg, people, I'm double parked."

Vaughn and Rigg hopped in the vehicle. Fortunately, it was built for eight and could handle the extra weight of the HCR and an Engineered human. Mmok moved to the mule's other side as Rask smoothly powered away from the curb. The mule's atom motor made only a deep hum as they accelerated.

In seconds, they were off the embassy grounds passing onto a broad boulevard. Most of the buildings towering over them were darkened. Only a few other vehicles were on the road and none of the usual daytime animal transport.

"Okay," Rigg said, pulling out a camo stick. "Everybody darken down." He paused, looking at Vaughn. "Hey, can you do that thing the skipper does?"

Vaughn smiled at him. "Change color? I wish. Shasti is unprecedented even among the Engineered. All I can do is bend steel with my bare hands."

"Neat," Rigg said, quickly finishing his camo, "though I've seen her do the same." He handed Vaughn the stick.

"You gonna spray paint me?" Mmok asked. His HCR chassis was made of a dull but light-gray metal. Still, the black jumpsuit he wore covered most of it. The HCR's long hair was essentially colorless but did reflect light.

"You got a hood on that suit?" Rigg asked.

"Yeah."

"That will do. Use some camo stick on your face; it's paler than your chassis."

"Next time I'll spend more time in the tanning salon."

They hit the road out of town and in minutes reached the edge of Bizi, startling a group of creatures that looked like a combination of goat and deer. Their eyes reflected the headlights as they froze, then bounded off the empty road. Kandalorian city guards watched them from their post at the city's edge but evidently saw no need to interfere with Star Demons. They were watching for nomads.

"Night goggles, people," Rask said. He cut the lights and adjusted the motor so its hum lessened as he turned onto a dirt road. The mule's rugged suspension coped well with the rutted cart track.

"Lot of tribesmen out here," Rigg muttered. "Be nice if we didn't have to tangle with any. Mandela won't thank us if we carpet the area with dead locals and start an insurrection on our new forward base."

"Mmok," Vaughn rumbled, "can you reach the *Sidhe's* sensors and scan the area ahead of us for trouble?"

"Already there, Big Man. Passing the course to the mule's comp."

Rask's small screen lit with the faintest of illumination.

"Crap," Rask said. "It looks like a bowl of spaghetti."

"Even with the lights off and the engine muffled, we make enough noise to be heard for a hundred meters," Rigg said. "Can't get too close to the locals, and some of the terrain is impassable."

"We could still get unlucky and run into a stray," Vaughn said.

"In which case it would be handy to have something quiet and less flashy than an HMG to take them out with," Mmok said. "Hey, Assassin. I don't suppose you'd have—"

Vaughn held up his big-bore slug-thrower with its silencer and flash suppressor.

"Nice," Mmok said. "Rainhell said you'd be useful."

Shasti and D'abo looked about for a few minutes but could find no sign of Brelish. Their chronometers indicated that only minutes had passed, but with the Prekak's ability to alter time, it was impossible to be sure. The pair cradled their weapons and headed back up the way they had come, thankful that "Mary" had repaired the Nekoan's leg or the trip would have taken hours more.

They passed the blood-red side corridor with its pulsing, somehow evil light and approached the side corridor leading to the entrance when both Shasti and D'abo pulled up short.

"Smell that?" D'abo whispered.

"Yes," Shasti answered. "Kandalorians, a lot of them. The same incense that Brelish wore. Either our friend has gotten religion or perhaps it has gotten him. Either way, there's a bunch of them waiting for us."

"But too leery of our weapons to come into the tunnels." D'abo grinned.

Shasti hefted her triple auto. "A blast from this would kill everything in the corridor if I used minifrags."

"Do you remember the second passage back?" D'abo said.

"Yes. I noticed that the air smelled fresher when we passed it."

"Yes," D'abo said. "My nose is somewhat better than yours. I scented chlorosols, a pungent desert flower that grows near water. I think it likely that the passage leads to a lower-level exit, near one of the ponds one sees at Sorokol's foot."

"We won't be able to get back to the aircar," Shasti said.

"It won't be safe going back to it anyway. If they have Brelish, they may know that we landed above. Likely there is an ambush at the car.

If they try to open it, they'll trigger the self-destruct. It will blow anyway at sunset if we are not back."

"Very well," Shasti said. "Down it is. But our friends ahead will not wait forever." Shasti pulled two flash grenades and a smoke grenade from her backpack. She set the weapons for proximity detonation and placed them in the dimmest recesses of the hall. Then the women backed away and raced for the second passage. D'abo led. Her sensitive nose was now their best protection.

The side passage made a mad worm's progress through the mountain but always downward. The passage was lit only by blue strip-lights running down the center of the ceiling. They did not dare use the stronger lights on their weapons. If the passage ahead was guarded, their only chance was to suddenly burst on the enemy.

Behind them in the distance, they heard two faint bangs in quick succession.

Shasti grinned wolfishly. "They found our going away presents."

Another five minutes travel and the passage ahead of them lightened. *Must be close to dawn,* Shasti thought.

D'abo pulled up and sniffed, alert and searching. After a moment, she hand-signed to Shasti, pointing up to her nose and holding up two fingers.

Shasti leaned close, her lips almost touching the delicate cat ear. "Hard and loud or trust to luck and try quick and quiet?"

D'abo pointed to the flash grenade on her own belt. Shasti nodded. They approached the entrance to the tunnel. A wooden door had been fitted over it. It was bug-eaten and badly weathered and hung half open. It seemed this entrance was rarely used.

D'abo pulled the tab on the flash-bang and carefully threw it up on and over the open door. Both women closed their eyes.

The flash-bang lived up to its name. The door insulated them from some of the noise and light, but it still set their ears ringing. Both women plunged out, rolling through the door, weapons ready.

Two Kandalorian acolytes had been waiting for them. The one lairing behind the door lay stunned by the concussion grenade. The other staggered around in a circle, blinded. He fired a wild shot that slammed into Shasti's armor. The large, slow slug knocked her sprawling but didn't penetrate. D'abo leapt, slamming her weapon into his head. He dropped to the ground.

Shasti was up in a second, waving off D'abo's concern. "Let's make distance," she coughed out. Her body poured combat chemicals and endorphins into her bloodstream. She suspected a broken rib, but her body's engineered systems were already numbing the area and beginning to heal the simple fracture. Beyond a slight tension in her chest as they ran, she felt nothing. They plunged on, passing a small cabin and some Kandalorian females, nuns perhaps, who shrieked, ran into the cabin, and slammed the door.

After they were clear of the immediate area, D'abo and Shasti moderated their pace. It was going to be a long haul back to Bizi and ahead lay the camps of the nomads. The sky was lightening, and true dawn could not be far off. Both women drank from their canteens, chewed energy bars, and settled into a ground-covering walk. The sky might be light, but below, it remained almost black in Sorokol's shadow. Behind them on the mountainside, they could see many lights, some moving. They had truly stirred up the ants' nest.

The women made good time while the darkness held. Both knew their senses were more acute than those of the Kandalorians, so now was the best time to press forward. But Sorokol's long shadow dissipated too soon. The desert around them began to heat, and they moved more slowly from cover to cover.

"I'm surprised," Shasti whispered as they briefly stopped in a field of scrubby, shoulder-height vegetation. "I thought the whole monastery would be chasing us."

"They would be," D'abo said in a grim tone, "but the land between the city outskirts and the temple has become a no man's territory in the last few days. Only large, armed parties can pass between the city and the mountain. The nomads attack anything less. The priests may fear following us into an ambush or assume the nomads will finish us off."

"We'll have to stay off the roads and the main trails," Shasti said. "We'll get close to Bizi and then get in toward evening."

"We could call for a pickup," D'abo said.

"Last resort," Shasti replied. "I don't want our governments involved in our little expedition. Right now all they have is the word of a disgraced acolyte, if he's alive and talking, and a few glimpses of us in the dark. If they find the aircar, it will be burnt wreckage by nightfall and you chose one that I have seen some of the city-dwellers use."

D'abo smiled. "In fact it's stolen."

"Even better. But if they have to fly out and pick us up, who knows what effect it will have on the local politics? We want our basing rights on this world."

"The creature, what did you call it?"

"Prekak."

"It seemed well-disposed toward you," D'abo said.

"Seemed is the operative word." Shasti grimaced. "I don't plan to count on its benevolence. Concentrate on her warning at the end and remember she wasn't the little old lady. She was the thirty-meter colossus in the chair." Shasti took a slow drink from her canteen. "Let's go before it gets any hotter. We can hole up closer to town."

D'abo nodded and stepped out of the brush onto the trail above the wadi. The sound of the shot and D'abo's fall came at the same moment.

Shasti's triple auto leapt to her shoulder, stuttering out its death song of beams, bullets and minifrags at the line of six luracil-riding nomads who burst from the taller trees to Shasti's right. The leader, riding a white luracil, held a long-barreled rifle. Others waved swords and red-pennoned lances. But the onrushing nomads had not planned on a weapon like Shasti's. The Confed assault-rifle literally swept them from existence in a spray of blood and bone. Nothing else charged from the copse of trees. Either they were all dead, or daunted.

Shasti knelt beside D'abo, one eye for her, the other for the tree line.

D'abo sat on the dusty ground, looking like a child thrown on her butt. "I'm hit," she said thickly, with a tone of faint surprise.

"Where?"

"Right armpit," she said. "Damn. I had my arm up, holding my MG. It must have gone in under my armor." Her breath started to come in gasps. "Cut the fabric away then pull the green and white tab out of my aid kit and pop it over the wound. There's a syrette of painkiller as well. Inject in the neck."

"Keep an eye on the trees," Shasti snapped. She opened the aid kit on D'abo's belt and raised the smaller women's arm. "There's a dent and scuff on your armor," she said, cutting away at the armor straps and fabric with a molecule-bladed aid-knife. "The round was low velocity to start with, probably lost a lot of energy there. It may not have gone in far."

"Great," D'abo gritted. "Pity, the damn bullet is nearly 75mm. The accursed things can take an arm off."

Shasti triggered the bandage tab. Like her own Confed meds, it filled the wound with a thick pad of fluffy material that would harden into a tight bandage. Then she injected the syrette in the Nekoan's neck. Within seconds, D'abo's breathing eased. The wound would have been mortal on a human without immediate medical care, but Shasti did not know Nekoan physiology. "Anything vital there?"

"No," D'abo said. "Thank the gods I wasn't hit low in the stomach where the important stuff is."

Shasti strapped the Nekoan's arm to her side with bandage tape to make sure the wound stayed closed. "Can you fire your weapon one-handed?"

"Yes," she said. "I think I can travel. For a bit anyway. We have to get out of here. The gunfire will bring others."

"Yes, but we won't be outrunning mounted men. We'll head that way toward that area of broken ground by those tall desert spears. They won't be able to charge us there."

Shasti got D'abo up, and the women headed up the high side of a wadi into broken ground. In the distance Shasti heard a shot, but it did not come close. She hastened into the cover of the towering desert spears. The cactus-like plants towered three or more meters into the air and were defended by the branches that gave them their apt names. No luracil would charge into them. D'abo staggered alongside her. A hoarse shout reached Shasti, though she could see no one.

They struggled over two small hills and a dry streambed, spooking a dozen small yellow birds that leapt from a desert-spear. Once, Shasti saw a pursuer leading a brown luracil. He spotted her, but his shot was high, thunking into a desert spear's thick, water-filled body. Shasti calmly raised her rifle and shot him with a single slug. The rider's six-legged mount took off squealing and bucking. The nomad lay face down in the dust. Shasti quickly refilled both their canteens from the leaking desert spear.

As they reached a pile of tumbled stone near the intersection of several trails and a lone road, D'abo pulled up. "Go get help," she managed. "I'll hide out here." Evidently her pain meds were wearing off or were overtaxed.

"No," Shasti said. "There will be hunters among those nomads who will find you in no time." She looked around. The rocks and desert spears made this a good spot for a stand. The land was the highest around. Abruptly, Shasti realized that the mound they stood on was artificial, the semi-buried foundation of some old, very large structure. Her eye spotted the lines of buried walls under sand, gravel, and vegetation.

Two standing stones leaned toward each other a few hundred meters away, almost as if they were a gateway. They were too far to provide useful cover to the Kandalorians. Only two avenues would work for mounted men, and they could cover both. They threaded their way among the desert spears' aptly named leaves and found good cover. Shasti gave D'abo another dose of painkiller while worrying about internal bleeding.

"Looks like we will have to call for a pickup after all," D'abo said, working her into the corner of an old wall.

"Yes." Shasti spotted a score of Kandalorians, dismounted with some acting as animal-holders and others in a skirmish line with long-barreled rifles.

Not good, she thought. *Those aren't ordinary tribesmen. They're somebody's elite troops.*

D'abo shifted, leveling her machine gun.

"Don't," Shasti said. She leveled the triple auto on a rise of dirt and gravel, poking the barrel out through some brush and flipped to single shot. In three seconds, she shot four Kandalorians. Each tumbled to the ground screaming. Two were luracil holders, and the animals bolted, throwing all into confusion.

A wild volley of return fire cut into desert spears and ricocheted off rocks. Shasti shot another nomad who fell clutching his leg as the other ducked into cover.

"Nice," D'abo said, watching the five wounded crawl into cover or be snatched up by other brave nomads, "though I am repenting of my concern about their casualties."

Shasti ducked a spray of rock splinters from a close round and missed her return shot at the bold rescuers. "No mercy intended. But it takes more of their men to tend to the ones I wound. The ones I kill they can ignore till later."

"May I play now?" D'abo wiggled her short-barreled weapon.

"Let them get closer for that. Besides, my weapon is a mass accelerator. If I run out of proper bullets, it will fire out anything you can put in the chamber. Make yourself useful by picking up very small rocks."

Fire slacked but became more accurate. Shasti shot another nomad, this time through the head.

"They're falling back," D'abo said.

"Not for long," Shasti said, pointing to a cloud of dust on their back trail. "Reinforcements."

"Shasti, come in." The radio in her tactical vest came to life with Vaughn's voice.

Her hand snapped up, pressing the send tab.

"Your timing is excellent," she said. "Listen, Vaughn. We need a little rescue mission organized—"

"You mean to get you and Charge' D'abo out of the stand of rocks and desert spears you are hiding in atop that ancient foundation?" he said.

Shasti stared at the radio in disbelief.

"He's good," D'abo said.

"Where are you?" she demanded.

"Over at the standing stones to your left front: Mmok, Rigg, Rask, and I with a mule packing a 10mm HMG. We saw the cloud of dust, heard the shots, and knew it simply had to be the two most reckless women on the planet, waging war with the entire nomad army. We've come to get you out. What's your sitrep?"

D'abo looked over at Shasti. "I swear if you don't sleep with him, I'm going to."

Shasti's hot retort was buried in a blast of submachine gun fire as D'abo fired a burst at three sky-lined riders on a nearby rise. The rounds went short, and they scurried back into cover, their own return fire wildly inaccurate.

"I'm fine," Shasti said. "Teleera is hit. I don't think she can travel far. I don't want you getting pinned in here with us. Have they detected you?"

"No," he said. "And I presume you would like to keep casualties down on the other side. Interesting. I have a TAC download from *Sidhe's* sensors. The nomads are massing on foot well behind your position. Your marksmanship has persuaded them not to charge at you. It will take them quite a while through this broken terrain to get into a position to overrun you. There is a blocking force of about twenty lancers and a few mounted riflemen left in front of you to make sure you don't escape that way.

"Very well then," he said. "This is what we will do."

<hr>

Mmok hopped atop the boulder. "Wooga-wooga," he shouted, jumping up and down and waving. The blasting sound of a ship's siren came out of his mouth speaker. The surprised tribesmen fought for control of their panicked luracils. A few tumbled off their bolting mounts, reduced to chasing after the shying animals. The remainder spurred their mounts at Mmok. Only four had rifles, and these fired as they charged.

The HCR leapt off the rock, running down the narrow wadi, long hair trailing behind him. But the luracils were faster than the machine. Mmok could only run so fast without overheating. As the troop of riflemen and lancers closed, Mmok cut right and raced between two standing stones. The lancers, seeing the Star Demon slowing, howled and leveled their weapons. A few low velocity rounds bounced off the HCR's armored body.

As the Kandalorians raced between the stones, Rigg pulled on the high-tensile rope. A cat's cradle barrier of ropes sprung up and took down the leading rifleman and lancers in a pile of thrashing limbs and hoarse screams.

The trailing lancers pulled up short, only to be hit by Vaughn. The seven-foot tall Engineered cannonballed into the cavalry, booting one Kandalorian clear of his saddle and landing atop the luracil only long enough to leap into another, overturning mount and rider. With a roar of pent-up rage, Vaughn rose. Seizing a Kandalorian, he flung him like a football, clearing two more lancers from their mounts. He leapt up in a spin kick, catapulting another rider off his mount and into a stone pillar. One of the fallen Kandalorians struggled upright and tried to block Vaughn's hammer strike with his rifle, but the Engineered snapped the slender weapon like a match, smashing him face down into the dust. Another nomad lunged in with a broad-bladed knife. Vaughn disdained blocking. He raced forward, hitting the nomad so hard he flew backward, headscarf torn off.

Mmok raced back into the fight, leaping over a downed luracil's thrashing legs and sweeping the last two lancers off their animals. Rigg shot the one man still holding onto a rifle. It was too much for the remaining nomads. They broke and ran, leaving behind a half-dozen of their own, either dead or unconscious. One luracil screamed and thrashed, its leg broken. Vaughn snatched out his silenced slug-thrower and fired one shot, ending the animal's suffering.

Rigg walked out. Pointing his weapon over the retreating Kandalorians, he fired a high burst to encourage their retreat. He'd stood ready to shoot any Kandalorian that broke out of the ambush or if Vaughn had needed assistance. Rigg looked around at the downed Kandalorians. One moaned. The others lay still. "Well, that's the lightest bill we were going to generate on that."

"Pity about the animal," Vaughn growled. His blue eyes glowed with ferocity.

"Yeah," Rigg said. "I hate that too." He gave Vaughn a half-smile. "Feel better?"

Vaughn snorted a laugh.

"Let's book," Mmok said. "While the going is good."

Shasti and D'abo emerged from the stand of desert spears they had taken refuge in. D'abo leaned on the human.

Rask raced up in the mule, slewing around to a halt in a spray of gravel and dust.

"Hop in, ladies. The meter is running," Rask said. Shasti picked up D'abo and gently laid her in the back. Rask spun the wheels as Shasti leapt into the mule, then climbed into the HMG ring. She traversed the barrel, but nothing pursued them.

"The boys lured the cavalry off," Rask shouted as the mule accelerated spraying sand and rock. "Made a hole in the surrounding force. We're heading for it."

They sped for the standing rocks. A few demoralized lancers appeared, fleeing Vaughn's ambush. One had a pistol and fired a few shots at them. A round banged off the bulletproof glass in front of Rask, who cursed fervently. Shasti answered with a burst of MG fire, which cut the desert spear next to the Kandalorian in half. The rider fled.

They passed between the rocks, driving around Kandalorian bodies. The others piled into the mule, which, now overloaded, sagged as they drove on. Mmok threw some flash-bang mines on their back trail to discourage pursuit. With daylight now, there was no chance of hiding the mule, which kicked up a plume of dust.

"We're overloaded for this rough ground," Rask said.

"I'm too overheated to run for long," Mmok said. "Sand in the joints. Drop me here and I'll come when I cool down."

"Screw that," Vaughn said, jumping clear of the mule. "I'm in the mood for a run." He jogged ahead of the mule, making as good time as the machine over the rough ground. He threw Shasti a broad grin. "Join me?"

Shasti leapt off and ran alongside him, still high on chemicals and endorphins.

The engineered humans ran ahead of the struggling mule, glorying in their strength and power. A tribesman crested a hill a hundred meters away, a long-gun in his hands. Shasti snapped up her triple-auto and shot the ugly pack-beast he rode out from under the tribesman. He scrambled up from the fallen animal and ran off. She pegged another round at the nomad's heels, kicking up dust.

Vaughn laughed.

"They're both fucking nuts," Rask said, wrestling with the steering wheel.

Rigg shrugged. "They were literally made for this kind of thing." He held onto D'abo, trying to keep the wounded Nekoan safe from the worst of the jolts. She smiled up at him and rested her head on his shoulder.

"Fucking nuts," Rask said again.

They reached a paved road where the mule could make better time and both Shasti and Vaughn jumped on the running boards. They sped off toward the more civilized environs of Bizi.

19

S o," Mandela said, leaning back in his black leather chair, "the mystery is solved, though we have gained little from its unraveling." He put his feet up on the footstool near his broad, native-wood desk. Confederate flags stood behind him in their somber dark blue and gold. The rest of the large room's decoration had yet to be hung. Boxes still littered the floor.

Shasti shrugged, still moody and upset from the encounter with the ancient entity. She'd come directly from the legation hospital after being assured that D'abo would recover. Now she perched at the window looking over the grounds toward the defensive works of city troops. The morning fight had stirred up the nomads, but beyond a few sniping incidents, the area around the city remained quiet. Reinforcements from the provinces beyond were closing in on the nomads, and a battle loomed.

"I would have liked to have met this Prekak myself," he continued, regarding her over his steepled fingers.

"I doubt your powers of diplomacy would have fared any better."

Mandela shook his head and stood. "You misunderstand me. I would simply have liked to have met a being of such age, such wisdom, so much closer to God."

Shasti looked out at the soft twilight that had fallen over the port and the city beyond. In the distance, she saw a Ribisan globe-ship warming up its drive. The engines glowed a dull, brick-red. She wondered if the Ribisi ambassador was fleeing into orbit for fear of an attack on the capital.

"Ancient, yes," she said finally. "Wise? Perhaps. Their wisdom seems as much born of pain as does our own.

"Closer to God?" She leaned against the wall. "On an infinite slope, does it matter that she's climbed a million miles more than we?"

Mandela gave her a broad and genuinely delighted smile. "An excellent point, Captain, excellent point indeed. It surely matters relatively in terms of power and capability in our universe, but in the face of the Eternal? Who can say? You surprise me, Captain Rainhell. Do you believe in God?"

Shasti gave a bitter laugh. "You forget, I both met and killed my creator. In that regard, I'm more successful than Lucifer."

Mandela's grin grew even broader. "Of course, how could I have not seen it before? Reign-in-hell. You doubtless named yourself. When?"

"After I escaped from Pard the first time. My early education was quite good and included the classics. Milton always appealed to me. Though I had to tinker with the quote a little. I couldn't afford to be that obvious." Shasti threw back her long black hair. "As to God, I do not know. Robert believes. He's very Catholic. He sees himself standing before the scales, all his faults and virtues weighed. I think he fears that day."

Mandela stood and joined her contemplation of the spaceport and the capital beyond. "Any man would. Perhaps it will go better for him than for some. He did many terrible things, but he did them all for love. Love of his wife." He faced her. "Love of you. It's a better motivation than many can claim."

"And what are your motivations?" she asked, not expecting an answer. In the distance, the Ribisi ship slowly lifted off. The muted thunder of its engines barely reached them. The glow from its engines lit the clouds as it arced skyward.

"Oh, I have my loves too," he said, surprising her, "a daughter, the

Confederacy itself. To be and to do. To wield power, for good I hope, but to wield it in any event. I'm afraid that I'm a pyramid builder."

"Expensive monuments to vanity," Shasti said.

"True, and hard on the common man. They say there is a broken heart for every brick of the Great Wall of China. The Okarans say the same of the Temple of Maccasi. But," he raised a finger, "what are the great monuments of either civilization but these same blood-stained endeavors? They are the treasures everyone yearns to see and then never can forget. You see, the universe needs pyramid builders to leave our mark for all eternity to say, *We were here.*"

"Look on my works ye mighty and despair," Shasti mock-whispered.

Mandela laughed again. "Alas, too true. In the end, perhaps it is all just vanity."

Mandela turned his back to the window. "So, we cannot count on help from Kandalor unless this world is attacked by the Evolvers. And likely we will be busy both with arrangements for a treaty and basing here. There will be," he gave her a severe look, "some fallout over your unauthorized adventure with the local authorities."

"Perhaps less than you think," Shasti said, unaffected by his glare. "I wonder if 'Mary' will approve of a pitched battle on her doorstep. While she prefers not to be bothered with our mortal affairs, she likes the quiet. Perhaps the 'desert madman' will have a vision tonight that will see him leaving the area."

"Vision or an attack of sanity, perhaps?" Mandela said. "He lacks the force to carry the city, especially if we stiffen the locals with our own weapons. If he gets caught between the provincial forces and the city guard, he might be wiped out. I'll call to the ships to see if they detect movement. We will see what the sunrise shows.

"Now, Captain, I have calls to make and fences to mend. Kadesh and I are meeting the city powers in an hour. Bring the command crew with you tomorrow for a breakfast meeting. We, or at least some of us, must voyage farther in search of help."

"See you in the morning," Shasti said. "I want to check on D'abo again. She asked me to bring her a few things from her quarters. Then Vaughn and I are having dinner at a restaurant she recommended."

Morning saw most of the command staff gathered around a light breakfast in Mandela's receiving room. The embassy staff had set up a tolerable kitchen, and there were local fruits similar to melons and oranges, as well as some exceptional pastries and crumb cake. Shasti had returned with Rigg, Rask, and Mourner to find Mmok already there. Eris and Paolo, who had become inseparable lately, also came. Vaughn and Tanaka entered last.

A good feeling filled in the room. During the early morning hours, the "desert madman" had moved off to the south, leading his forces back into the deep desert. The city authorities preferred to turn a blind eye to the offworlder's adventures beyond the walls. As for Sorokol, the mountain monastery remained mute. No complaints were made, and it was as if Shasti's intrusion had never occurred. Shasti saw "Mary's" hand in that and wondered again about the Prekak's subtle but pervasive power. It seemed their longshots had all paid off.

Some stood and some sat, chatting casually. After breakfast, Mandela stood at the end of the long table and tapped his juice glass with a spoon. "We have reached a crossroads, and decisions must now be made that will affect the lives of billions. The Confederacy must be warned of the threat in this sector. I will use every scrap of influence I have to get an alliance proposed with the Nekoans.

"Time," he said. "It all comes to time. At the rate Evolver activity is increasing in this area of space, there won't be any Nekoans to ally with unless we can find some power locally to slow them down. The route back to the Confederacy is longer than the route here. Even after combining our hyperdrive maps. It will be years before help arrives in any quantity."

"We need to pursue our explorations farther. But we cannot all go. We have damage and casualties. We must also maintain a presence here."

"Your thinking mirrors my own," Shasti said. "And there is more. We have experienced some disaffection among the crews. It's the usual problems. People are tigers at the start of the mission and now they suffer voyager's remorse. Worst among those is my First Officer, Mollica. Her nerve seems broken."

"I noticed that you didn't bring her. What do you propose?" Mandela asked.

"The time has come to split our forces," Shasti said. "I want to send *Paladin* back to the Confederacy. Mollica will command. She'll take the wounded and the quitters back with her, along with all the data we have found and your report.

"We'll crew *Sidhe* with the best of both ship's complements. We'll open the embassy with you here. There are some folks who don't want to voyage farther but would stay on Kandalor. My landing force commander, Tivka, could join your security.

"That leaves *Sidhe* free and crewed to search this area of space, perhaps to find the Skurlocks, as Mary suggested, or some other help."

"*Paladin's* sailing master," Vaughn rumbled, "is like your XO. He wishes to return home. Some of the Selected would choose that as well. We have lost more lives on *Paladin* than you have on *Sidhe*."

"With your sailing master and your first officer gone," Mandela said, "can you run *Sidhe* effectively?"

Vaughn looked chagrined. "I have a general's knowledge of ships and their employment in planetary strikes. While I can command ships operationally, running one is another matter—that's why I used a sailing master."

"I have another in mind for first officer," Shasti said.

"Yes?" Mandela prompted.

"Teleera D'abo," Shasti said.

A murmur of surprise ran around the room.

Shasti plowed ahead. "She's the logical choice. She's ship-wise, having been raised on vessels in a trade family. She had the rank of reserve captain, has a local master's ticket, and served on a cutter. She knows the races, the history, and the local space."

"Combination of native guide and local ambassador," Mandela mused.

"That would make her Sacagawea to your Lewis and Clark," Mmok said, gesturing at Vaughn and Shasti.

"Do you have any idea what he's talking about?" Vaughn said, leaning back in his chair, with his arms behind his head.

"Rarely," Shasti said.

"Well," Mandela said, smiling at Eris, "it does seem that we are collecting aliens on this trip."

The deer-like alien shifted from leg to leg, seeming uncertain at being addressed and merely nodded her silver-haired head.

"D'abo has proved extremely resourceful," Vaughn said.

"Okay," Mmok said, "catgirls in space. Don't know how you're going to break this to Risky."

"I agree," Mandela said. "I'll remain here with such staff as I select. There is a vast amount that I can accomplish here to facilitate what I anticipate will be the Confederate response. I will take Tivka on. It will be necessary since I am giving you Mmok, Rigg, and Rask. Well, simply recognizing that they're yours now."

Rigg shuffled his feet, looking awkward. "Boss, that's very decent of you, but not necessary. You stood by us—"

Mandela laughed gently. "That's all right, Dan. She'll need you more than I will, and if that ship leaves without you two on board, you'll both mope insufferably until she comes back."

"I don't feel right about leaving you either," Mmok said, his doll-like machine eyes fastened on the spymaster. "Without you, I might have ended up in the recycling bin as spare parts."

"Thank you, Kyle. We've come a long way from when I think you hated me as much as the Conchirri. But to be frank again, she will need you more than I will. And there's something else. I don't know anyone else who has given more in the service of the Confederacy than you. Now, you have a new existence that you need answers for. I think it more likely you will find those answers with Captain Rainhell than with me. I owe you this."

There was a long silence from the metal man. "Thank you, sir."

Mandela nodded.

"D'abo is getting out of the hospital today," Shasti said. "I will make the proposal to her. That done, we'll inform our crews and see who goes with us, who stays here, and who returns to the Confederacy. We'll study the information available on the Skurlocks and see where we can begin the hunt. Meanwhile, all of you are to see to your sections and supplies. We'll be voyaging long, fast, and in harm's way."

"Oh, the usual," Mmok said.

"I want to be able to leave in ten days," Shasti concluded, giving Mmok a sidelong glare.

"Well," Vaughn said. "Assuming D'abo accepts, and knowing our curious cat it will take her only seconds to do so, we've all agreed to voyage farther. Now for the difficult part. Where the hell are we going?"

Vaughn's prediction proved true, to no one's surprise. Teleera D'abo was ecstatic about joining the *Sidhe*. Kadesh, desperate for Confederate help and closer ties, approved it immediately. The Nekoan's relief upon learning of Mandela's plans was patently visible even across the gap of species and cultures. Kadesh raised Mandela's ante by offering a Nekoan detail to join *Paladin's* crew and present their diplomatic credentials in person. Mandela accepted.

The splitting of their force was a more painful affair. To Shasti's intense relief, Dobera, Perez, Mourner, and Nye elected to stay on the star-frigate. Some of the medical staff, with Dr. Fierman, opted for the embassy or *Paladin*. Tivka and his two sergeants chose embassy duty, taking the best of *Sidhe's* landing force with them. None of Rigg's ASATs chose to leave, though he did assign a select few as a personal bodyguard to Mandela. The loss was more than made up for by the addition of all of Vaughn's Engineereds and half of the Selected, including, of course, Tanaka. *Sidhe* ended up with as full a crew as could have been hoped for.

To Shasti's surprise, Paolo volunteered to come. "You might need me to romance another Evolver." He'd grinned.

After she'd told Vaughn that Eris would be coming too as a nurse, the scowl faded from his dark face. "Romita has been useful," he conceded. "One cannot question his mastery of languages or his ability to understand alien thinking."

"And," Shasti added, "as our best chef has abandoned us for the safety of the embassy, we may find him useful in the kitchen. He can cook."

Vaughn raised his eyebrows. "Tanaka will insist on tasting my food from now on."

Work continued on Vaughn's all-important question. "Where the hell are we going?" While the crew worked to prepare both ships for their voyages, Eris, Paolo, and Mmok enlisted D'abo's help to raid every database on the Skurlocks, even spending days in the antechamber to the Ribisan embassy, interrogating the hydrogen breathers.

Sidhe landed at the spaceport eight days later, finally repaired up to atmospheric standards. Shasti flew her down to a Nekoan repair gantry on the most modern part of the field for additional work. The Nekoans offered to repaint the ship in whatever color Shasti wanted, but she stayed with Guards' Red.

Paladin, repaired and recrewed, made record time preparing for her trip back to the Confederacy, motivated both by Mandela's fear that time was not on their side and by the crew's desire to get back to the Confederacy.

The destroyer was soon ready to leave and that left Shasti with one last painful duty. On the day of *Paladin's* leaving, she walked off *Sidhe* to meet a Nekoan groundcar, bearing Mollica to the shuttle up to *Paladin.* She stood by herself, the hot, morning sun already causing the air over the yellowish concrete of the spacefield to shimmer slightly with the promise of worse to come. The sky above was an almost eye-hurting blue, and Shasti's eyes narrowed to keep out the glare.

The car pulled up, Nekoan in origin, it had been repainted Confed dark blue and sported the seven-starred circle of the Confederation of Seven Species.

We'll need new flags soon, she thought.

Mollica got out of the car. Her Nekoan driver stayed in its air-conditioned comfort. Shasti could see the diplomatic pouch Mandela had given her inside the vehicle. It bore Mandela's encoded diplomatic seal and held his complete report, including a request for military and diplomatic reinforcements. *Paladin* was bound for Earth itself.

A lick of hot wind from the desert washed over both women. Shasti's long hair, tied and weighted in its usual fashion, hardly moved. Mollica wore one of *Sidhe's* caps, and it put her eyes in shadow, though tension was evident in her pursed lips and rigid shoulders.

Shasti tried to repress feelings of disappointment and betrayal. Mollica evidently felt the same way. She scarcely met Shasti's eyes as they faced each other on the tarmac.

"All preparations made?" Shasti asked, hunting for something to say.

"Yes. The Nekoan delegation is aboard, and the engineers have cleared us for launch. We've offloaded the last of our spare munitions to the Ribisi tender. The ordnance will be there when you launch."

"Excellent."

"Hope you won't need them," Mollica said.

The silence threatened to lengthen. "Good luck," Shasti said. "Deliver this to Robert for me. Make sure he gets it." She handed over the message crystal that she had spent much of the night recording, telling Robert all—well, almost all—that had happened in her life since she started into uncharted space.

"Thanks, Captain," Mollica hesitated, taking the crystal. "I…I don't…"

"Better get going," Shasti said, wishing an end to the emotions simmering below her calm exterior.

"Yes," Mollica replied, her voice dull and flat. "Good luck to you, Captain. Give the others my best." She turned and walked away to the car. She didn't look back.

Shasti turned away and sighed heavily. It seemed that she was doomed to be disappointed by people. *Is it me,* she wondered? *Robert loved me, but not more than Lisa. Telisan is really his friend and only incidentally mine. I inherited* Sidhe's *crew: Perez, Dobera, Wardell, but they love the ship more than me. Mollica and Tivka were my people, and they are going. I have Rigg and Rask, but again they came through Robert. And Vaughn? Does he love me, really? Or does he love what he thinks we could do together? Who cares about me just for me?*

The padding of feet interrupted her dismal musings. She turned to find a surprising pair coming toward her—D'abo and Risky. The Nekoan wore her usual short cape and unitard. Dr. Mourner had worked with the Nekoans until she had a regenerator setting for D'abo and had her both pain-free and out of her sling.

Despite some people's cracks about cats and dogs, Risky and D'abo had taken to each other with delight. Of course, Shasti thought, the Nekoans were no more cats than the Okarans were bears or the Voit-Veru were kangaroos, but the human mind always wants a simple, recognizable pattern.

Teleera smiled at Shasti and produced a red ball from inside her cape. She gave it an easy toss and Risky sped after it.

"I thought it would be best if I remained out of sight until she left." D'abo gestured at *Sidhe's* giant landing jack behind her. "It seemed only polite."

Risky came running back and with a snap of his head threw the ball to D'abo, who grabbed it out of the air. She leapt back and forth over the dog, holding the ball out as Ricky tried to get it. She chattered in her own language as the dog almost somersaulted. D'abo looked more like a monkey than a cat as she played with the big shepherd. Her tail whipped behind her and her ears were wide and up.

Shasti gave a rueful smile at the sight of her new executive officer playing with her dog in a wholly undignified fashion. D'abo sometimes showed an almost childlike joy in the simple things that seemed incongruous in a deadly operative.

At least, Shasti thought with a tinge of jealously, *she knows how to have fun.*

D'abo flung the ball and again Risky tore after it.

"I'm ready to take up my duties now, if you wish."

"I wish," Shasta said, feeling her spirits lighten. "We have a bunch of disparate elements to melt into a crew before we go hunting for Skurlocks and we are not blessed with time."

2 0

Later in the week, Shasti joined the "Skurlock Hunters" at the Nekoan embassy to find D'abo closeted with Mmok, Eris, and Paolo, pouring over the data the Nekoans had unearthed. The Skurlocks vanished during the great Conchirri War. Records on them were fragmentary and ancient.

As Shasti entered the grand conference room where they'd first met Kadesh, she wondered if such eclectic a group had been engaged in planning an expedition before. Holos, maps, and drinks cluttered nearby tables and a half-dozen screens glowed with info in front of the planners. Overhead, the schooling lights drifted, their silver shimmer challenging the afternoon sun shining through the windows.

The group didn't notice her, their attention centered on a glowing green globe full of multi-colored pinpoints, a nav map.

"How goes the research?" she asked, walking in and helping herself to a cup of cappuccino from Paolo's machine. Perhaps it was his heritage, but he did always seem to have the best coffee.

He gave a bright grin. "I've seen enough material to keep me in academic papers for the rest of my life."

"Useful to us?" she prompted, dropping into a human-made chair.

He gestured at the globe. "Hard to say. Yellow lights are the

Nekoan systems. Blue are Ribisan. Yellow/blue show cohabited systems and there are a lot of those since they use different real estate.

"Here is poor Vikadia." Paolo gestured at a lonely star that glowed a doleful red. Shasti noted how he placed his other hand on Eris's. "Kandalor." He pointed at a nearby pulsing white dot. "Now look at the black dots." He indicated two swathes of black systems that lay between the Nekoan and Ribisi systems and the galactic center.

"We," D'abo interjected, "had very little trade with the Skurlocks. They dealt more with the Ribisi, whose technology was the most advanced of the species of the Concord. Only the hydrogen breathers had tech that the Skurlocks still needed. There was only one system where that trade was conducted." She manipulated a control and one of the black systems developed an orange glow. "Firo, as you can see on the leftmost wing. Firo sits in the middle of the intersection of both species' main systems. It was utterly destroyed, as were the worlds in the nearby systems."

"We have not penetrated far into that area of space," D'abo said, "lacking the ships or time. The Ribisi, who were back in space long before us, have never found any sign of the Skurlocks in the old systems. Or so they claim."

They all faced the cat-like alien.

"You doubt this?" Eris said.

D'abo blew out a breath. "Didn't you wonder why, since they were back in space before us, they did not discover us first? The methane breathers are, as you may have noticed, very cautious. They were loath to contact any alien after the Great War. So it was not until we regained spaceflight, and they were forced to take notice of us, that we met them again. They claim it was sheer chance, but that is not believed among my people. They could have saved us hundreds of years of poverty and rebuilding but for their craven nature."

"So you wonder just how hard they looked for their old friends?" Paolo said.

"Yes," D'abo responded, "between other needs and the bad hyper-space currents from Nekoan space to Old Skurlock Space, we did not have the resources to invest in an expedition to search for them.

Voyages in this direction would take many years round trip from our space.

"However, this area," she gestured toward the right side of the holomap, "has better currents." She manipulated the controls again and another black system developed an orange glow. The outlined world lay far from the rest of Ribisi territory, glowing alone in Skurlock space. "There was a single Ribisi outpost here at Hanghoul. The one useful system in this region that they reached before the Skurlocks occupied all the adjacent systems. The Ribisi held onto Hanghoul as a matter of pride, until a Conchirri/Skurlock fleet action took place nearby. Hanghoul station was then quickly abandoned."

"This," D'abo concluded, "is our best bet to find Skurlocks. We have the old Ribisi coordinates for Hanghoul. The Conchirri hit this area last, after a lot of heavy fighting. We know nothing survived in the left wing of Skurlock territory. We have no information from this section, and we can reach it easiest."

"Care to see a Skurlock?" Paolo said.

Shasti nodded and Paolo manipulated the controls. Another holoimage appeared. Shasti's first impression was of a large, jewel-eyed beetle. According to the scale next to it, the creature was about a meter and half tall. Like an insect, it had six-limbs, four lower and two arms. One of the arms resembled that of a fiddler crab and the other sported a surprisingly human-looking hand.

"This is Skree-ayls, a female in the prime of life," Paolo said. "Apparently she was a major video star and considered quite desirable."

Why am I not surprised he found that? Shasti thought.

"She's a bit bigger than most of the males," Paolo continued. "Despite her appearance, this is not an insect. Skurlocks bear live young, though they do not nurse. There are few females in the species, which is made up of large numbers of unsexed semi-sentient drones. The males are sometimes in relationships with several females."

"Don't get any ideas," Eris said to Paolo.

He smiled noncommittally. "Anyway, if they exist still, this is what they look like."

"Oh, they exist," Shasti said, her voice distant. "I have it on good authority."

Sidhe continued to load and prepare for deep space, though no certain date had been set for her liftoff. The Nekoans installed new survey equipment on her and every spare nook in the starship filled with supplies. Without good starcharts, there was no way to tell how long they would be gone. A few last-minute defections complicated Shasti's preparations. Mandela found a use for all the bailouts in the embassy. Shasti, determined this time not to be saddled with any but the most committed, let them go.

Shasti felt a curious reluctance to leave Kandalor. The immense planet held a thousand mysteries, and she felt they'd only scratched the surface. So when D'abo suggested an expedition to see the Skurlock ruins, Shasti accepted eagerly. They gathered the Skurlock Hunters and drafted Rigg and Rask as drivers. Shasti invited Vaughn, and for Rigg's sake, Tanaka. The fact the two had become an item was a poorly kept secret. She made sure that Eris and Paolo rode in the other truck from her and Vaughn. Her two ex-rivals seemed to be getting on all right, for the moment, but Shasti was still cautious about mixing them.

The spacers drove out the embassy gate early, hoping to beat the worst of the sun. D'abo climbed into Shasti's hovertruck, directing them toward what she called the Skurlock customhouse. Shasti stretched, enjoying the morning, the song of the desert birds, and the early sounds of the city.

They rolled over the huge spacefield heading for the large, strange pile extended for several hundred meters along the field's edge. The buildings were several stories tall, consisting of domes and low, interconnected tunnels with windows gaping in them. Some of the structures were partially collapsed. Towers loomed up looking like ancient rocketships built into the native stone and materials of the lower buildings. Airbridges that no sensible being would have used even when they were new, joined the structures at various levels. Some spanned large gaps while others, partially detached, hung shroud-like on their towers.

"Reminds me of a sandcastle," Rigg said, pointing at the lower levels. "Like a kid made it and stuck the towers in it."

"You're correct, in a way," D'abo said, her eyes narrow in the sunlight. "They were here before we were, but our records tell us that the towers were ships. The Skurlocks landed, built a hive at the base, and then demobilized the ships. I imagine that they were designed for that purpose. The interiors were stripped out long before we arrived."

The hovertrucks settled on their skirts in the shade of the towers, and the spacers climbed out, grateful for the cool breeze near the abandoned jumble of buildings. Though the area was well within the perimeter secured by the city guard, it was still transited by caravans and hopeful treasure hunters. Shasti and the others wore sidearms, with Rigg and Rask carrying carbines. The Morok parked himself on the fender of the hovertruck, taking a swig from his canteen and unwrapping some chewing gum. "Have fun," he called. "I'll make sure no one boosts the rides."

They walked in through the nearest broken wall, unlimbering lights and shining them inside. Tumbled stone littered dusty floors.

Some parts of the roof had dropped, and beams of light shafted down, motes dancing in them. They toured through the empty rooms of the old customs house. The native stone and material sections were in poor condition, save in those main tunnels that linked the old spaceships built into the cluster.

"Seems an odd way to go about building things," Vaughn muttered as he ducked under a doorway and gave a sagging floor a dubious glance.

"They seem to be more like landing barges than true spaceships," D'abo answered. "They never had FTL drive from what we can see. So they were towed here just to make a powered descent. Certainly saved time getting started. *Woomf,*" she said, miming a spaceship landing with her hands. "Instant embassy, just add diplomats."

They spent the next hour touring through one of the spaceship towers with D'abo leading. "The metal of the ships shows no rust," she said, "though there are damaged areas inside and out where some scavenger used a torch or mechanical means to pry things loose."

"Ever find anything interesting?" Vaughn asked as he ducked under a doorway.

"Save for odd bits of metal and plastic lying about," D'abo answered, "the rooms were empty."

The old hatchways and passages, last trod by the chitinous feet of the Skurlocks a millennium ago, were different only in detail from Confed designs, Shasti noted. But the corridors were broader and lower than a human designer would have made them. Hatchways were set closer to the floor to accommodate creatures that had less length of leg to step over things with. In a thousand subtle ways the ship said, alien.

"There's a good observation area near the top of the central hub building," D'abo said.

"Is the flooring safe?" Vaughn asked.

She smiled. "Yes. I led a commando team up there to scout out your vessels when you first landed. It will bear your weight."

The view from the roof was all that D'abo promised, a panorama of the spacefield and the city beyond it. *Sidhe* gleamed out under the rising sun. A few spots of bare metal showed where the latest repairs were not quite finished. A brisk breeze, unavailable at ground level, blew at this height.

"Bet Rask wishes he'd come up here," Tanaka said, stretching out her arms and enjoying the wind.

"Nah," Dan said. "He likes it hot. Says when he gets to Hell it won't be such a shock."

Shasti snorted a laugh and then caught sight of D'abo staring intently up at Sorokol. Ever since the Prekak's spell had been broken, the big catgirl was often found contemplating the mountain. The psychic effect had broken on all of her people, but none seemed as curious about the mountain as she did. A thin wreath of clouds crowned the vast bulk today, and the sun had not yet lit the side facing them.

Shasti went up and touched her new friend's elbow. "That door is closed."

D'abo looked at her. "I suppose you are right."

"We have a saying among humans that when one door closes another opens," Shasti continued.

"Is that why we are here?" D'abo said. "Are you looking for a door?"

The wind sighed mournfully about them. "I don't know," Shasti said. "I don't know why we are here. Just know that I felt I had to come here. I feel…I feel like I am missing something, like I just haven't turned the right corner yet."

"Well then," D'abo said, turning away from the mountain. "Let's see some more of the safe sections."

The feeling of vague dissatisfaction did not leave Shasti over the next hours. The others, even Vaughn, began to lose interest in the structure itself. Some went back to the roof for the view. Paolo and Eris disappeared, and no one looked for them.

Shasti drifted farther from the others as the view or each other distracted them. Something tickled her mind.

She found herself at the intersection below the roof where slender airbridges joined two of the three ship-towers on this side. From the corner of her eye, she saw a pale glimmer. Her hand cupped her sidearm as she walked forward.

About ten meters ahead, she saw the glimmer again. She considered calling Vaughn, but her nose and ears told her there was nothing living down the corridor. It might be only fragment of cloth or a reflection from some shard of crystal or glass.

Nonetheless, Shasti stalked forward, flat-footed, minimizing even the sound of the grit under her boot. The voices of Rigg and Vaughn drifted down to her, reassuring in their nearness in the rooms above. But there was nothing where she had seen the glimmer. She pulled a small flashlight from her breast pocket and shined it down the darkened corridor. Nothing.

Again, the glimmer appeared in the corner of her eye, and this time she drew her pistol as she spun to face it. The room was like every other, almost a honeycombed cell with a vaulted ceiling. Its floor was undisturbed, dust lying as it had for ages. A crack in the ceiling admitted indirect light from a windowed chamber above. She could see nothing but felt a presence.

In the darkness beyond the shaft of daylight, a light definitely flickered. Her eyes could not resolve an image. She aimed her torch, but the glimmer disappeared. When she shut it off, the glimmer returned, like a shimmer of moonlight over a swamp.

"I know you're there," Shasti called. "Come out. I won't hurt you."

As if her voice had dispelled it, the glimmer faded.

Shasti tried another tack, reaching out with her nascent PSI sense, as she had when Vaughn first trailed her through Morokat. It felt strange to defy her acute senses' assurance that there was nothing in the room.

Come out, she sent. *I won't hurt you.*

One instant she was facing nothing more than a dimly seen glimmer, the next she saw the wavering, ghostly image of a Skurlock. Smaller than the one Paolo had shown her, somehow she sensed it was diminished, weak and feeble in an almost dwarfish fashion. Where this knowledge came from, Shasti had no idea.

Shasti's ears and nose continued to war with her mind and eyes, insisting that nothing was there. *A holo?* she wondered. But there was no machinery in sight.

"Who are you?" she demanded, her pistol pointed at a spot on the floor between them. "What do you want?"

The wan image of the Skurlock started, as if only now detecting her. She studied it as the creature slowly turned, apparently searching. This was no ghost, she thought, unless Skurlock ghosts wore tool belts and carried portable coms. Yet the whole image, tools and all, was dull, filmy white.

Help, a voice chittered faintly in her mind.

"Help who? Where?" Shasti asked, her voice harsh.

As if blown about by the sound of her voice or by her discordant emotion, the image wavered like a candle flame nearly snuffed out.

Shasti throttled down her impatience and again reached out with her mind. *Where?*

It seemed that the voice that came back to her was fading into the distance. *Come to where light and time end. Come soon. We fade.*

And then Shasti found herself alone in the small, vaulted room with only dust motes for company.

A soft footfall sounded in her ear. She didn't react, instantly recognizing it as Vaughn's tread.

"Were you speaking to someone?" he said as he walked up behind her. "I thought I heard your voice."

Shasti stared, at a loss as to how to explain her strange vision. *Could I be going mad?* she wondered.

No, she thought firmly. *I am myself and I am whole. Something is reaching for me.*

"Bring the others here, please," she said finally.

Vaughn returned quickly with the rest of the group, all but Rask, who remained on guard below. Shasti quickly relayed the strange visitation. To her relief, everyone took her seriously.

"You're not a woman given to idle fancies," Paolo said. "And I remember how you sensed me behind that closed door when we met."

"Engineered PSI senses are real," Vaughn said. "I share this with Shasti, though her abilities far outstrip mine. I have never heard of them functioning over a distance, but no one knows what Shasti is capable of. Her genetics are unparalleled among the Engineered."

"Still," Eris said, "a medical exam is in order to rule out some organic cause."

D'abo walked into the center of the room, her ears up and her tail twitching. "Odd. One feels that this visitation is not of those who dwelt here. From what you say, it was a demand that we journey and soon."

"You're thinking what I am," Shasti accused.

"Yes," D'abo replied. "This vision may come to you through Mary from under the mountain."

"Or there is another possibility," Vaughn mused. "That contact with this Prekak may have opened some door in your mind. You may have powers now that you did not before."

Shasti's lips drew into a narrow line as she considered. "I know only one thing," she said finally. "That we need to voyage and we need to do it now. Things are moving and so must we."

"It seems then," D'abo said, "that you found what you came here for."

———

Shasti resolutely refused to allow parades or ceremonies down at the *Sidhe,* pleading the need for security and last-minute preparations. Truth was that the starship was already in top shape. They had test-flighted all repairs on several short hops in the system. The flights helped shake the combined crew into one force, familiarizing everyone with *Sidhe's* Conchirri peculiarities as well as the new Nekoan surveying equipment.

On the last trip *Sidhe* rendezvoused with the Ribisi tender that had repaired her after the Evolver battle and took on all the spare munitions *Paladin* had left. The star-frigate was as fully armed and provisioned as she had ever been, which was as well; *Sidhe* was going far beyond any possible help, with neither the sled nor *Paladin* for company. Since she had her vision in the ruins, Shasti had ruthlessly driven preparations for the voyage, somehow sure that time was now critical.

On the morning of the launch, Shasti looked up at the lowering sky of Kandalor's first fall storm. Gray rags of cloud scudded across the sky. The wind blew in short, sharp gusts, driving ripples over the shallow puddles that dotted the spacefield.

Behind her, *Sidhe* towered ten stories into the sky. The gantries and scaffolds were all rolled back, and the ship sat on her landing jacks, operating on internal power. The star-frigate seemed to mirror Shasti's impatience to be gone. Most of the crew had already boarded the ship, laboring in her bowels to prepare for liftoff. Their goodbyes were said last night at the embassy function or in bedrooms and barrooms around the spaceport. But Mandela had asked her to meet him on the field just before take-off. D'abo relieved Shasti from her prelaunch checklist long enough for her to come out to see the spymaster.

So now she stood waiting on the hard footing of the field as his embassy aircar landed and rolled toward her on its ground wheels.

The large blue car pulled up and Mandela, clad in the same beige rain-coat he wore when they met on Morokat nearly a year ago, stepped out. He gave a broad smile as he stood up and closed the car's gull door.

"You wanted to see me?" Shasti said, raising an eyebrow.

"Yes," he said. "Walk with me a little, Captain."

Shasti fell into step with the stout black man, and he strolled quite leisurely. His eyes swept the horizon, and she followed his gaze, noting the activity. Improvements were being made to the field in anticipation of a larger Confederate presence. *Optimistic perhaps,* she thought. Still, it was dotted with the orange-and cream-colored vessels of the Nekoans as they brought in supplies, diplomats, and equipment. Even an increased Ribisan presence could be seen. Several bathyscaph-like starships of their ominous, dark-green metal shone wetly under the clouds.

"You must be pleased," Shasti said. "You find yourself at the center of a massive influx of power, with your hands on all the controls."

"Quite," he said. "I've found the enemy I suspected was out here. I have found allies for us and, as you say, I'm in a position to exercise my poor skills for the good of the Confederacy."

Shasti snorted a laugh, and he smiled sidelong at her. But there was a hint of sadness in his face.

"What did you want to say to me?" she challenged, disturbed by the introspective look.

"I wanted to wish you a safe voyage, Captain. Your mission is critical. If you don't buy us time, we may not have sufficient of it to get our feet under us. The Nekoans' survival may depend on your finding us more help."

"I remember the speeches," she said dryly.

"I'm sure. But there was something else I wanted to say. Now, when it is just the two of us and we can speak frankly."

She looked a question at him.

"I've followed your career from various distances for most of your life," he said. "For far longer than you know. This time, you'll be completely out of my sight and hearing. I find myself anxious about your safety."

Now Shasti did laugh. "Are you going to miss me?"

"Yes," he said, looking up at her. "I will miss your intelligence, your unpredictability. So few people surprise me, Shasti. You have done so constantly. So yes, I will miss you."

"You're getting soft, old man," she said ruefully, shaking her head.

"Perhaps," he said. "Getting soft and a little old. Not all at once, but time chips away at you, a little bit each day. You don't notice it most of the time. Then all of a sudden you find yourself a little surprised by how much time has gone by, by the gray hair and the thicker waistline, a certain slowing of memory and wit."

Shasti stopped. Mandela turned to face her.

"And it may be that I am a little weary of playing the 'Great Game' but the Game goes on, as it always has and always will. Someday another player will pull back the Confederacy's chair and sit in my place and play the Confederacy's hand. It will fall to me to have something to say about who sits in that chair."

"What are you saying?" Shasti asked. The wind gusted, raising her black hair around her like a storm cloud.

"That I want you to come back alive. That I agree with Vaughn, you *are* meant for great things. I have never seen another human being with your scope and reach. Shasti, someday you will sit high in the Confederacy and will guide the fate of millions."

"Oh, no," she said, softly. "No, no and no again. I know you mean this as a compliment and I am sensible of that. But I can only barely guide my life, much less anyone else's."

Mandela shook his head. "You'll find as you get a little older and gain some wisdom to go with your other natural gifts that the needs of others have a gravitational force of their own. As does power itself. If you do not wield it, you will see it be wielded badly by lesser beings. You may see worlds fall and cultures decline. One person cannot run the universe, but they can make a difference. Think about making that difference, Shasti."

Shasti stared at Mandela, a medley of emotions running through her: surprise, outright shock, and a curious reflexive mix of fear that anyone could lay a claim on her and, finally, pride that Mandela saw these things in her.

"I don't know what to say," Shasti said. "I never imagined that we would be having a conversation like this."

"Everything changes," Mandela said. Overhead, a stubby air transport rumbled by heading for a Nekoan ship. "For now," he continued. "Simply think about it. The universe is vast and holds an incredible potential, as do you."

"Well," Shasti smiled. "I guess I'll have to make it a point not to die young and miss all this."

Mandela gave his usual broad grin, and Shasti sensed the walls going up. "Please do, Captain Rainhell. It would distress me greatly."

Before he could turn to go, Shasti put out her hand. "You too, old man. Try not to get killed while I'm away."

Mandela looked surprised but took her hand and shook it. Then he placed his other hand over hers.

"Good fortune, Shasti. Be safe." He did not look at her but gently let go of her hand and walked back to his car. Shasti stayed rooted to the spot until his aircar headed off. She turned slowly in a circle as if locking in the sights, sounds, and smells of the moment in her mind. Then she headed back to the winged dagger-shape of her ship.

An hour later with a roar of engines and impellers, *Sidhe* lifted from the field. Kandalor's rare rain enveloped the starship and her winds pressed against the great hull. The starship accelerated, and lift from the wings took some of the weight. *Sidhe* burst through the sound barrier, quickly picking up Mach numbers and altitude. The clouds were left behind, and the sky began to turn gray-blue, then the sharp blue of high altitude before fading to black.

R ibisi tender, in orbit where planned," D'abo announced. "The booster sled is with them." She sat back in the specially designed chair newly installed at the executive officer's station. It was the only seat that could comfortably accommodate her tail.

"Good," Shasti said. "Mr. Nye, dock us with the sled."

The helmsman lined the ship up for with the boxy arrangement of girders holding four giant solid fuel boosters. The Nekoans had prevailed on the Ribisi for some of the thrusters they used for lifting loads out of their gas giants. Swarms of Nekoan and Ribisans raced over the sled making connections. An hour later, D'abo turned to Shasti. "All systems synched and locked. Ready for thrust."

Shasti keyed the alarm on her chair. "Light them up, Mr. Nye."

The four expendable rockets roared to life, boosting the star-frigate with over eighty gravities of thrust, mercifully canceled by the ship's AG field. In an hour, the boosters burned out and explosive bolts blew the framework free of the warship's hull. Shasti was determined to jealously guard her fuel as they headed into the unknown. They headed outward to the system's edge from where they could engage the stardrive.

Days of drill followed. People were shunted from assignments and sections as Shasti tweaked her diverse crew roster. *Paladin's* old crew needed to learn the peculiarities of *Sidhe*, built by aliens and only partially reworked to Confed standard. The drill schedule kept Dr. Mourner busy with a constant stream of bumps, cuts, and bruises as people learned how to navigate their new home in pitch darkness and even in zero gravity.

D'abo turned out to be as good a first officer as Shasti could have hoped. She quickly mastered *Sidhe's* schematics and interior with a speed that left Dobera and Perez scratching their heads and looking for new things to teach her.

As D'abo expressed it to Shasti, Confederation technology was not that different than Nekoan, just "more and better." Her new exec's informal command style puzzled Shasti; it seemed equal mixes of flirtation and cheerleading. D'abo was "first among equals" and as yet no one had sought to test the bounds of her forbearance. On her previous voyages, Shasti had delegated personnel matters on *Sidhe* to Mollica. Only the most severe breaches came to Shasti's attention, and she knew she was more feared than loved. D'abo, on the other hand, seemed closer to the mostly human crew than Mollica ever had and unimaginably more so than Shasti herself.

"You," D'abo told her at the end of one watch, "are a remote, monarchic presence to the crew. You speak seldom and expect instant obedience. I give people an ear," twitching one as if to prove her point, "into which to pour troubles and frustrations. I need to know everything going on inside the ship among our disparate crew. As an outsider, I don't belong to any group, so I am equally accessible to all."

The discussion had left Shasti feeling even more isolated than usual. While she treasured D'abo's company, it was distressing to realize that her entirely alien first officer seemed to relate better to humans than she could.

Good thing this isn't a democracy, Shasti thought. *I'd lose to my first officer.*

Well, she concluded, *at least there's one vote I can count on.* Since they had cleared atmosphere, she had seen a great deal of Vaughn, spending more and more time with him. Originally, it had been under the cover of their mutual duties but later simply for the pleasure of his company. Morning coffee in the wardroom became a ritual as they planned how to integrate his people into the *Sidhe's* complement and that led to dinners at the captain's table. They were hovering on the edge of the next step in their dance.

In just a little while longer, she had promised herself, *just a little while when I am more sure...*

On the morning before jump, Shasti headed in to the wardroom hoping to find Vaughn waiting there for her as usual. She nodded to Dobera, who was leaving, a cold drink clutched in his clawed hand.

"Skipper," he said, taking the extra-long straw out of his snout.

She nodded.

Shasti was not disappointed. Vaughn sat in a quiet alcove in the room contemplating the holoscape on the far wall. It was the cliffs of the island of Elmesh, with its thousand-foot-tall walls of white stone facing a wine-dark sea. Hard, bright stars lay reflected in the water, but were fading out as the orange sun climbed over the horizon. It was a scene the mind could fall into forever, though not always popular with even hardened spacers because of the dizzying perspective. Shasti and Vaughn both loved Elmesh, particularly the sunrise. Since he had found the scene in the database, it greeted her each day.

"Good morning," he said. In the background, the sound of ocean and breeze picked up as the rising sun stirred the sea.

"Morning." She sat next to him, noticing that he had already brought her a huge cup of her favorite chai. She smiled and picked it up with an approving nod.

"Someday I must see Elmesh with my own eyes," Shasti said.

"You like heights," he observed.

"Yes," Shasti said, feeling an unaccustomed shyness. "I like the sense of freedom such places give me."

"Freedom," he mused, "which is so very, very important to you."

"No one," she said, "loves freedom more than one who has had it forcibly taken away."

He nodded slowly, as if aware of how significant it was for her to even acknowledge her brutal past in conversation. They sat in companionable silence watching the ocean ripple in the morning light. Shasti hoped nothing would interrupt them.

"Preparations going well?" she asked.

"Exceptionally," he replied. "D'abo has us so far ahead of schedule that we are cooling our heels until jump. It will be a quiet watch."

Maybe less than you think, Shasti mused. She looked at him, ruggedly handsome, powerful, centered, and felt her heart speed up. Something about the moment told her that a time had come. Tomorrow was their jump into the unknown. Perhaps tonight it was time for her to make a jump of her own.

"What do you say," Shasti asked, not looking at him, "to dinner in my cabin tonight? Just us. At eight?"

"I would say, anything for my captain."

Shasti settled back in the chair next to him and sipped her chai. "Good answer."

Vaughn appeared at her door at the stroke of eight, making her wonder if he had been around the corridor bend with his eyes fixed on his watch. Shasti had arranged for dinner to be delivered well before, on a warming tray, so they would not be interrupted. She'd also left strict instruction with D'abo that she was not to be disturbed for anything less than a nova and asked the Nekoan to keep Risky overnight. D'abo's ears and tail had twitched at the request, and Shasti knew that curiosity was killing the cat, but D'abo asked nothing.

On the other hand, Shasti thought, *she does seem to read me like a book.*

When she opened the door, Vaughn surprised her with a bouquet. For a second, she thought it was of real flowers then realized it was of exotic papers, some in metallic colors.

She cradled the small bouquet. "What is this? It's beautiful."

"Something I learned from Misa when I was a child. It is called origami."

"Exquisite," she said. Something tickled her nose. "Why, there's even a scent."

"A spot of perfume," he smiled. "They wouldn't be flowers without scent."

"Come in," she said, leading him back to the table in her cabin. Usually covered with work, tonight it was dressed in linen and the ship's silver. Shasti carefully placed the origami bouquet as a centerpiece, and they settled around her table.

"Dinner is some of the chef's best," Shasti said. "Beef, of a sort, from Kandalor along with fresh vegetables and a Syrah from Mandela's stores."

"Excellent," he smiled. "Does he know that you raided his stores?"

"Dobera is still *my* quartermaster," she said. "And unless he wants to be made into a purse and shoes, he'll keep my secrets."

The meal was excellent, but it occupied very little of her attention. For once words spilled naturally out of her mouth and the conversation between them flowed like the Syrah. Vaughn spoke, carefully she knew, of his childhood on Olympia, not the killings, the training as a Denshi assassin. They both knew of these things and spoke around them. Vaughn told her of hikes in the uplands when spring flooded the barren highlands with color, of fishing in the sun-drenched sea off Marathon. Until he'd taken to the stars to look for her, he'd never left his homeworld. Vaughn was eager to hear of different worlds.

Shasti told him tales of her voyages, trying to minimize references to Robert's name. Vaughn knew all about her and Robert, and it was time for that to simply be past.

"And what of you?" she asked. "You have the unfair advantage of knowing about my love life. Tell me about the women in your past."

He sipped the wine before answering. "Less to tell than you'd think. Oh, there were women in abundance. But it was always hard to tell if they were trying to use me for their own purposes in Denshi, or even if my enemies had aimed them at me. I took what was offered and gave back little, I suppose. There was one girl at university." He hesitated.

"Go on," Shasti prompted.

"You'll think it foolish."

"I swear on my life," Shasti said, "that I will not."

He shifted then began. "Editya was her name. She was a dancer, such a delicate graceful creature. She seemed so far removed from my world. You see, she was Selected, not Engineered. A real human, with a family. You know she had five brothers and sisters. Five. Imagine that."

"I can't," Shasti said. "Any more than you can."

"She was the first woman, the first person other than Misa that I ever cared about."

"What happened?" Shasti asked.

"What always happens on Olympia," he said, bitterness darkening his voice. "Some enemy, whether of mine or of….well, of Denshi, chose to move against me. I never knew who. It was not a sanctioned strike. Someone preferred to make it look like an ordinary crime gone wrong. Shots from a speeding vehicle. One struck Editya."

"Was she…"

"No. Thank God. But it struck her in the leg. The damage was severe. After she recovered, things were not the same. She was afraid to be near me after that. So I left. I put it about that she was damaged goods now and I had no further interest. It was the only protection I could offer Editya or her family, pretending to lose interest in her."

She reached a hand across the table. "Vaughn, I am so sorry."

He shrugged. "Old pains. I am interested in the now." His eyes locked on hers.

They both stood as if on an unspoken signal and came together. Shasti's arms wound around his broad back. Shasti bent her head back to receive Vaughn's kiss, something she rarely had to do, being so much taller than most men. She hadn't had to do this since—

It flashed through her blood like freezing water, killing the growing heat in her body instantly. Since Pard, since Jalgren Pard, her creator, who had tried to master her in ways no man should. Her body remembered this posture, remembered humiliation and pain.

Vaughn felt the change immediately. No great trick, she'd literally frozen in his arms. She sensed the struggle in him, the desire, the wish to press ahead, brushing aside her doubts. But instead, he stepped back, his breathing deep and ragged.

She stood there, her arms open, but her heart slammed closed through no volition of her own. She knew a numb shock covered her face.

"Easy, easy," he said in a soft voice, "there is nothing to fear here."

Shasti found her voice. "I'm sorry."

"Do not apologize, he said. "I know something ails you from the past. I fear that I even know what it must be. It only pains me more than I can say that somehow I remind you of it."

She managed to move her head, slowly shaking it. "Not your fault."

"Thank you," he said.

"My problem."

"I would make all your problems mine," he whispered, "if you but let me."

Shasti stood frozen. "I…I…"

"Shall I say good night?" he asked, his heavy face gone dark and sad.

Like a mechanical puppet, she nodded.

"Good night, Shasti. There is always tomorrow." He turned to go.

"Sorry," she whispered to his back. "Sorry."

He paused and nodded to her, then vanished through the door to her cabin.

After it whooshed closed, she walked forward on legs that did not feel like they belonged to her and leaned her head against the bulkhead.

I thought I was past this. When I made love with Robert, it was beautiful, free and easy. My body was like a musical instrument. Why do I feel this way now?

It came to her in a cold flash of self-knowledge. Fenaday was gentle, but beyond that, he was a standard human. At any point she could have asserted her strength and taken control. She could risk him. She'd never had to be that vulnerable.

Vaughn was another matter: Engineered, powerful, almost as big as Pard. She was the superior design, more powerful, pound for pound. But he massed a third more than she. In that dark, doubtful part of her soul, she knew there was no guarantee that she could control him.

I'd have to be vulnerable, she thought. So the dam in her soul that had once held back her desires had returned.

A growl of frustration burst from her, and her lips peeled back from her teeth. Shasti's fists drummed out a tattoo of pent-up rage and pain on the bulkhead. Tears filled her eyes, but she refused to let them come, preferring her anger.

Her cabin door chimed. She ignored it. She knew it was not Vaughn.

It chimed again.

"Go away," she screamed.

After a few seconds, it rang again.

The Conchirri had better be boarding us, an Evolver fleet attacking, the reactor melting or I will kill someone. She slapped the panel, and the door slid open.

D'abo stood there, facing into Shasti's flat, murderous stare. The two women looked at each other across the silent seconds.

Finally D'abo broke the dangerous silence. "Less sensitive ears than mine might not have heard anything."

"Not a good time," Shasti whispered, eyes blazing.

"No. Not a good time to be alone with pain that afflicts you so."

"Get out of here or I will take you by tail and ears and pitch your ass out the airlock."

D'abo instead took a step closer. "You and I were born under different suns to different kinds of people—"

"I wasn't born," Shasti spat. "I was made. I'm a *thing*!" The last came out as a scream that shocked them both.

The pair looked around the corridor. If any crew were in the area, they wisely made themselves scarce.

"You are not a thing to me," D'abo said. "You're a friend. And even though our time together has been short, you are very important to me. I don't know why. I just know that it is true. I'm afraid for you. There's a darkness inside you. I'm afraid that if you continue to try and face this darkness alone, it will overwhelm you."

A single tear tracked down Shasti's face. She felt like she was spinning through space, dissolving, lost. Anger washed out of her, leaving only a deep weariness. Shasti backed into her cabin. D'abo followed. The door closed, locking out the universe.

Shasti almost fell into her desk chair. D'abo perched on the plastic and metal desk next to her. For a few minutes, neither moved nor spoke. Then, slowly and gradually, Shasti turned toward D'abo, leaning her face against her. She felt the Nekoan's arms go round her, felt her hair being stroked.

"I was made," Shasti whispered against the other woman's chest. "I was made for an old, powerful, and cruel man. He grew me for a sex toy. He didn't wait long, and it was... it was…disgusting when he began to use me."

D'abo's hands tightened in Shasti's hair. She felt the point of D'abo's chin on her head as the other female pulled her closer.

"He used me. Used me in ways no one should touch another. I fought free of him. Then I darkened my soul further by all the killing I did to remain free. Finally, I killed Pard with the help of a man I loved and lost. And yet Pard is still inside of me."

"Vaughn," D'abo whispered, "is not this terrible man. I do not know your kind well, but I know males."

"I know," Shasti whispered, more weary tears tracking down her face. She put her arms around D'abo's slender waist. "But when he touches me, sometimes I feel the other one: huge, dark, and terrible. How I want to be free of him. For a while I thought that I was."

"Do you love Vaughn?" D'abo asked in a strained whisper.

"I don't know," Shasti said. "There is so much there, but I cannot touch it. He may be the right man, but this is not the right time. Maybe it never will be."

"Shasti," D'abo said.

"Yes."

"You don't need to release me, but I can't breathe."

Shasti eased her grip, but D'abo did not let go of her.

"I'm sorry," Shasti said, patting one of the Nekoan's arms. She looked up at D'abo's big violet eyes.

D'abo smiled. "You've saved my life. Now you are risking yours again to save my kind. You and I… we are somehow connected."

Shasti stood slowly, and D'abo gently released her. "Yes, we are. I don't know how or why, but I have felt it from the beginning. I doubt that too many captains get to cry on their first officer's chest. Not very professional."

D'abo smiled and waved the comment away, leaning back on the desk. "Do you feel better?"

"Yes," Shasti said, slowly pacing the floor. "Not so overwhelmed. Not so alone." She wiped a hand over her face, amazed at herself. "Please forgive this ridiculous weakness."

"I see no weakness in you, my big friend. Only someone who had carried too much too far and alone."

Shasti shook her head in bitter self-examination. "I'm twenty-nine, but my life has been so narrow, so unnatural, with no mother, father, or siblings. Even friendship was beyond me for so long. I'm stunted. More than a decade behind where a normal person would be. Robert told me that he finally understood me the day he realized that emotionally I was sixteen.

"This voyage has held so many firsts for me," Shasti said. "Including," she hesitated, "the first time I ever turned for comfort to anyone I wasn't sleeping with."

D'abo's ears twitched back and forth. "You mean the others got to sleep with you and all I get is a lousy hug?"

A laugh rippled through Shasti, and she picked up a pillow from the nearby sofa, winging it at the Nekoan, who playfully batted it up into the air.

Shasti shook her head. "Were you just passing by?" she asked, grateful to retreat to neutral subjects.

"Yes. But I do want to discuss the situation with the Number 4 auxiliary power reactor. I don't like the small power spikes. I'd like to take it offline before we jump tomorrow…"

The next morning, Shasti headed to the bridge in dread. She had to face the man she had rejected and the alien she'd turned to like a hurt child.

God, she thought, *so much for my command presence. Thank heaven I can count on them both to keep my secrets or I'd be too ashamed to be seen in public.*

The doors clicked open. Shasti took a deep but shaky breath then walked out onto the spade-shaped bridge of her command. Both Vaughn and D'abo stood there. It took everything Shasti had to walk forward and face them.

"Morning, Captain," D'abo said, crisp as a naval cadet. "Situation nominal. Ship is stable at .7334C and on course. All crew and stations accounted for."

"Aux 4 secured?" Shasti asked just to have some reply.

"Yes, ma'am," D'abo continued, her eyes level and clear with no hint that she had held her crying skipper in her arms only hours before. "Ship is prepared for jump."

"Very well," she said.

D'abo turned back to her station, just another day at the office.

Shasti knew she had to turn and face Vaughn. Knew she had to meet his eyes. Slowly she managed to force her body to obey her and turn.

He gave her the barest hint of a gentle smile. "All damage control parties are on standby. Not that I think they will be needed. I'm sure there are no more pieces of gravel with our name on it."

"You can never tell." Shasti's mouth was so dry she almost choked on the words.

My god, she thought to herself. *That's fear. I wasn't made to feel fear like this.*

"Always prepared," he said softly, "that's me. Well, better get back to my station."

As he passed close by her, Shasti reached out a hand and stilled him. "Are you all right?" she whispered. There were a million more things she wanted to say to him, and none seemed confinable in mere words.

He looked her in the eye. "I have learned patience. All's well. Coffee later?"

"Yes," she said, relief flooding through her. "On the other side of jump?"

"I'll be there. I will always be there."

"Jump space in forty minutes," Nye called from the helm.

Shasti let go of Vaughn's arm and made her way to the command chair, feeling her world settle back into its accustomed shape. She had her ship. Maybe life was confusing now, but there were things she understood and things she was good at, time to concentrate on that.

"Initiate countdown to jump," she said. "Start the checklist. All stations report jump status."

22

idhe reappeared in the universe, her slender hull bathed in the light of the emerald-green star, Hanghoul. Her atomic drives flared to life as she reoriented and drove toward the gas giant that the ancient charts promised. People shook off the effects of jump and hurriedly activated their instruments. Their charts were at least a thousand years out of date, and anything could be waiting for them.

Shasti stood on the bridge, watching the green star glow on the screen. Her command staff filled the bridge, brushing elbows with the day-watch crew. From the science station, the planetologist, Tanges, relayed the information sent back from one of the Nekoan-made probes. She wiped a hand over her face. The jump possessed an odd quality; the colors that swam in her eyes during exit had been different—more blue and purple. Even the air held a sweet scent she had not encountered before.

"I wonder how long we were gone," D'abo said, fluffing her mane of golden hair in a gesture Shasti associated with nerves.

Nye and the navigator bent over their instruments, checking a number of quasars to establish, as much as possible, their absence from space-time. "Best estimate is that we have been out of the universe for 37.5 standard solars," Nye finally said, "a little better than expected."

"Calculate an orbit with atmosphere braking on the gas giant factored in," Shasti said.

Tanges started working with his board, coordinating with Nav and Helm to find their destination. "Got it," he said. "Exactly where expected, so our current approach vector is good. Image coming up on screen."

A bright blue ball of a world flicked onto the main screen. At first it looked uniform but then differing hues of blue could be seen in bands on it.

Dan Rigg stretched and yawned. "It's nice to be visiting the outer edge of a system for once. No days of travel in normal space."

"Indeed," D'abo said. "We are not overly blessed with time to line up for orbital braking. Three hours to orbit. Right, Helm?"

"Three hours, four minutes, and two seconds," Nye returned.

"Initial scan results," Tanges said, his thin face intent on his instruments. "Planetary orbit for Hanghoul V is 4,004,000,000 km from Hanghoul primary, with a diameter of 48,532 km, equatorial. Mass, 1.0247e26 kg. Sidereal period… I'm estimating 140 years with a rotation of 17.3 hours. Gravity is 1.3 of standard. Mean temperature -220 C. Number of moons, so far seven. Escape velocity 76700 km/h."

"That's a pretty good match for Neptune," Rigg said.

"Even looks like it," Rask said. "Remember when we were assigned there?"

"What god-awful duty that was," Rigg said.

"Yep," Rask agreed. "That was during the dog-house days, right after the Voit-Veru incident."

Rigg shrugged. "It could have been worse."

"Yeah, we could have been assigned to the 24th," Rask said. "Then we'd have to wear that damn patch with the unit motto."

"How's that?" Shasti asked absently.

"Don't ask, Skipper," Rigg said with a pained look.

She looked at the big man. "Well, now you have me curious."

Rigg glared at Rask. "Okay, big mouth, you brought it up."

Rask grinned. "The 24th stopped an unexpected Conchirri assault in the home system early in the war. Unfortunately, it was in the outer system, seventh planet. Ever since then their motto has been, 'We saved Uranus.'"

A groan circled the bridge. Shasti turned to Rigg.

"I told you so," he said.

"Captain," Tanges interrupted. "I am getting an occlusion on one scanner. No energy reading as yet. Just visual, but if it's a space station, it's a big one. Altering the probe's orbit for a better look."

A minute later, the image swam into focus on the main screen. Other screens filled with the image in radar, thermography, and microwave.

"Creepy-looking place," Paolo said. At his side, as usual, stood Eris, a pensive expression on her small, gray-skinned face. The alien had thrown herself into mastering the physiology of the aliens she lived with. Mourner felt it was part of Eris's learning to cope with her new life. Perhaps she found it easier being in a ship in space. Maybe it allowed her to delude herself that there was a homeworld behind her teeming with life. Certainly she had come far from the desperate refugee they had unearthed in a fort.

She's an alien, Shasti reminded herself. *Quit trying to liken her to humans, not that I understand even standard humans that well.* For now, it was enough that the Vikadian was functioning as crew.

"The station's immense," D'abo said, peering over Tange's shoulder, "over ten kilometers long and made of the black-green metal the Ribisi favor. It has the overbuilt look of their engineering."

Shasti's eyes narrowed as she looked at the foreboding mass. The station rotating slowly in front of her had none of the pleasing symmetry of the disc-shaped Confed stations, which were covered in highly reflective paint and metals to bounce off energy weapons. This looked more like a collection of children's blocks around a central core.

"Odd," Carlos Perez said. The engineer's face looked out from a small screen to Shasti's left. He was far from the bridge, down in the main reactor room. "Look at that central core area. If those aren't engines, I'll trade in my degree. What the hell did they need those for? They'd generate a huge amount of thrust."

"Enough," Vaughn said in his deep rumbling voice, "to drop a station into a hydrogen giant's atmosphere and push it back out?"

Perez gnawed at the end of his mustache as he stared off to the side and manipulated some controls. "I don't know. That would take a lot of thrust. Maybe."

D'abo looked at Vaughn. "Very good, big man. And in keeping with Ribisi temperament. If they can't run, they want to be able to hide."

"Then why didn't they?" Paolo said, gesturing at the screen.

"That one is easy," Perez chimed in. "It can only have been a temporary measure. Even in the upper atmosphere of a gas giant, heat and friction would quickly degrade any orbit you assumed. If they'd hid in atmosphere, the station would have crashed ages ago."

"Still no sign of power," Tanges added. "But the hull is immensely thick. I'm not getting any reliable readings on the interior."

"Were you expecting something?" Eris asked.

"No," Shasti replied. "But we didn't expect you either. In the confusion of the mass evacuation, anything could have happened. Some Skurlocks could have opted to stay behind. Some might have been abandoned or overlooked."

Shasti frowned at the looming station. "Looks like we'll have to send a party aboard. I don't want to risk docking until we know it's safe." She turned to D'abo. "After braking, launch the fighters for cover and move *Sidhe* to within five kilometers of the station. Send a probe on a close pass of the station to trigger any booby traps, then have the fighters make passes too.

"We'll take two shuttles over. Mmok, I want all the crab robots. Vaughn, Rigg, assemble two full squads of landing force troops. Paolo, I may need your language skills. Eris, you can join us as a medic."

"Permission to join the party?" D'abo said, looking eagerly at the station.

"No," Shasti said. "I'd like to take you, if only because a Skurlock would probably recognize a Nekoan, but I need you here on the ship."

D'abo's ears and tail drooped in disappointment. "Yes, of course."

It took eight hours and three passes for *Sidhe* to lose her tremendous speed on Hanghoul V's atmosphere. As she slowed to proper orbital speed, Nye lined her up for an oblique approach to the orbiting station. The two *Spacefire* fighters preceded her, watching for any sign of attack. When nothing threatened, Shasti secured the ship down to yellow alert and assembled her landing party.

Shasti led the Confederate forces in the *Pooka* with the *Duelist* flying top cover. They headed for an area that looked like a staging platform for small ships, gradually drifting down on the titanic station.

"There." Shasti pointed toward the center of the stage, a broad, flat area several times larger than their shuttle. *Pooka* settled slowly to the surface, her magnetic grapples drawing her down the last few feet with a soft jar. After a few tense seconds, Shasti nodded to the others, who suited up. After everyone was sealed, Shasti signaled the pilot, who depressurized the shuttles. People spilled out the back and side hatches. The crab robots, which had ridden over attached to the outside of both shuttles, unlatched. Those carried by the gray-and-green-hulled *Duelist* drifted down in a form of peculiar multi-legged steel rain. Vaughn and Rigg's troops sought cover behind the mechanical monsters for lack of anything better.

Shasti looked about. The stage sat on the dark side of the station; its immense hull lay between them and the blue gas giant. She felt as if she stood on a great, black plain, surrounded by distant, strange, square mountains limned in the reflective blue of the gas giant. It gave her the oddest feeling of standing at the beginning, or perhaps the end, of time with her few companions as the only life. "As on a darkling plain," she murmured.

"What?" Vaughn rumbled in her ear.

"Nothing," she said, "a fragment of an old poem."

"Yes," he said with a seeming note of sadness, "it is a place for darksome poetry. Night holds here forever."

She smiled up at him. "Planning to write some?"

"As if I don't have enough problems without trying to be a writer," he grumbled.

Shasti laughed silently, then keyed her mike. "Bring up the shuttle lights gradually. I don't want to startle anything into nastiness, but let's see the real estate."

Lights from the two shuttles built up an oasis of visibility in the vast dark bulk, but it made the darkness beyond all the more foreboding.

Mmok trod into view. His HCR body needed no space suit, but he wore a vest that would stand the rigors of space. "Where to, boss?" came his voice over the speaker.

Shasti pointed to a pillbox-like structure a hundred yards away. "Check that out and see if it's safe to approach. If it's not a fortification; it may be a personnel airlock. I don't want to open a station hatch until we know what is on the other side."

Mmok nodded and communed with a crab robot that bounced over in the low gravity. "Clear," he said seconds later. "It looks like an airlock."

"Dan," she broadcast, "keep everyone on the alert. Send Paolo and Eris over to meet me at that airlock." With Mmok and Vaughn following, she moved toward the lock, taking care not to let her magnetic boots break traction. She spotted Eris by her tiny suit with the Red Cross on the armband. *As if it would mean anything out here,* she thought.

The lock towered over them, easily twice Vaughn's height, set within an octagonal doorway. On the left side was a meter-wide assemblage of what looked like varicolored glass cubes, each about three-inches square.

"What do you make of that?" Shasti asked.

Mmok shrugged. "The station was designed as a meeting point for at least three or four different species, one of which was a hydrogen breather. I suspect that it is some sort of control mechanism that all known species could use."

"There are some symbols," Eris added.

"Can you read it?" Shasti demanded of Paolo.

"There's nothing to read," Paolo said. "It's more likely some sort of interface, like a keyboard." He shook his head in frustration. "Ribisi isn't even really a spoken language. They communicate with lights, smells, and on a radio frequency. The Skurlock were the first ones to come up with a Ribisan translator. The Nekoans eventually improved it, but that took two hundred years. This station was built long before any of that happened. If there is an AI still active in the station, I doubt we will be able to talk to it."

In the middle of the screen, a white cube suddenly emitted a soft glow.

They all stood very still.

Two cubes emitted a blue glow.

Nothing happened.

"I wonder," Paolo said. Before anyone could stop him, he touched three yellow cubes.

The lock replied with four reds.

Paolo grinned at them through his helmet. "Numbers and colors," he said, then keyed five brown.

"And possibly degrees of heat in decreasing order," Vaughn added.

The airlock opened. "Sort of an intelligence test," Paolo crowed, obviously proud of himself.

"Odd thing on a space station," Shasti said. "It's not like spear-throwing natives were going to be trying the airlock."

"Yeah," Rigg said. "That had a jury-rigged feel to it. As if it's being used for something other than what it was intended for."

"Like contact with unknown aliens," Vaughn growled. "It would show you that they appreciate heat and light the same way you do. Meaning that you were likely from a certain type of world, with a certain type of sensory apparatus."

"Meaning," Shasti said with a glare at Paolo, "that we just told whatever is attached to this airlock that we hail from a small, rocky world lit by a yellow sun as opposed to a gas giant, where we would never see yellow sunlight. You just told whatever this was that we're not Skurlocks."

Paolo gulped. "Sorry, Captain."

"In any event," Eris said, with a hint of defensiveness, "we've been invited in."

"Said the spider to the fly," Mmok sing-songed.

"Well," Vaughn said, "we did come here to find Skurlocks, or at least clues."

Much to Shasti's annoyance, both Rigg and Vaughn opposed her leading them in, insisting nearly to the point of mutiny that more expendable members take point. Finally Mmok and Rask passed through the lock.

"We know the core reactor still has juice," Mmok called. "There's an AG field going here."

"How bad?" Shasti demanded. "Is Rask all right?"

"I'm fine, boss," Rask answered. "It's about a standard G, maybe a little more. What's the concern?"

"Ribisans live on gas giants between 1 and 2.5 standard gravs," Shasti said. "Bad for the back if you're not expecting it."

Finding no threat on the other side, the rest of the crew entered. The lock was big enough to hold all of them and a crab robot. The inner door opened to show a yawning black space beyond a railed platform. The area beyond it was filled with machinery and hydraulic lifts.

"That's familiar at least," Mmok said. "It's a stage, all right. We should be able to lower the shuttles inside if the machinery is working." Mmok moved over to another panel of plastic cubes. As he approached it, the cubes lit. The lights formed patterns, which repeated every few seconds. "Oh, I get it," he said and manipulated the controls.

Vibration rumbled through their feet, and an excited gabble filled their earphones.

Shasti hit the command override. "All quiet," she ordered. "The stage is simply being lowered into the airlock. Remain calm."

She turned to the others. "The next person who hits a button without clearing it with me is going to see if my entire foot fits up their backside."

The hydraulic lifts worked, lowering the stage with the shuttles and the rest of their force into the station. Mmok waved at the irritated troops on it as it came into sight. The stage continued to sink below the control platform before stopping. Overhead, massive interlocked doors closed off the stars.

"I'm detecting pressure and gas venting into our space," Mmok said.

"Everyone follow me," Shasti said. They raced down a spiral staircase that was made more of bars than stairs, requiring careful footing. Shasti wondered what Ribisi feet looked like, or if they even had them. "Mmok, check pressure and content. Ribisi atmosphere could be pretty heavy for our suits."

The machine man, speeding ahead of them, answered over his shoulder. "It's gas giant stuff—hydrogen, helium, a few trace elements of methane. Pressure is coming up on three Earth standard. Ribisi homeworld is just under four standards."

"Everyone adjust suits to compensate for 4X pressure," Vaughn called over the command mike.

"Uncomfortable," Eris said, "but not dangerous."

"It's all the nasty breathing you meaties do," Mmok said. "Exchanging all that gas. Never use it myself."

"Oh, put a sock in it," Rask said.

"Don't wear any," Mmok returned.

The stage holding their ships now lay on the bay floor, which remained lit only by their ship lights. On the far side of the ships, they could see a series of hatches and entrances of different sizes. The troops on the stage were covering all possible approaches.

Mmok and Paolo turned to look at Shasti like expectant children.

"Yes," she said. "Go push buttons. Carefully."

It took her crack team of button pushers only a few minutes to open the inner airlocks. Meanwhile, Shasti arranged her teams to both penetrate the interior of the station and secure their shuttles.

Mmok waved to them as a door rolled back, and the teams stepped through into a bizarre, circular space, such as none of them had ever seen inside a station. Each level seemed composed of a different type of brightly colored plastic. They stood on a level of glossy orange. Over them, a chrome-yellow level was pocked with various entrances and tunnels. Farther above, the colors deepened to crimson. The effect was that of a galleria. As if someone had piled three layers of multi-colored glass and then run pipes and holes through at random while it was still molten.

"Kinda looks like a Salvador Dali painting," Rigg said.

"Never heard of him," Shasti said, "but if he painted anything like this, he must have drank a lot."

"Light seems to be coming directly out of the walls," Vaughn said. "I don't see any fixtures."

The half-melted, random look of the galleria made it hard to recognize anything, but the upper levels looked like they might be stores or shops. At the ground level, the walls were continuously interrupted with openings as if this were a transit hub.

"Rangers out," Rigg ordered over the tac net. "Area security."

The ASAT rangers spread through the area, peering into the hallways beyond the galleria, which were much more dimly lit. Crab robots moved forward to face each of the bigger entrances while Denshi troops scanned high and low for threats.

"Is that furniture?" Paolo asked. He pointed to some large tray-like objects that sat on the floor, each about five meters long, four wide, and one deep. What looked like broad, very deep seats extruded from the floor of the trays. In the center of each tray was a large, round hump, flat as a tabletop.

"Café?" Shasti hazarded.

"Doesn't look like any food service area nearby," Mmok said.

Shasti, Paolo, and Mmok walked onto one of the tray platforms.

"More cubes." Mmok pointed. Possibly mindful of Shasti's earlier rebuke, he did not go over to them.

Shasti bent down over the cubes. These were far smaller than the ones at the airlock.

Of course, she thought, *these aren't meant to be handled with a space glove.* They formed a large blocky pattern in green that looked vaguely familiar. One area was a different color, a pleasant medium blue.

"Wonder what happens if you press that?" Paolo said. Shasti gave him a look, and he held up both hands. "Keeping them to myself."

Curiosity gnawed at Shasti's resolve. They were here to find Skurlocks, as Rigg said. "Probably just dials out for a cappuccino," she said. "Well, nothing else has been harmful." She pressed the blue button.

And was immediately thrown on her rear as the tray vaulted into the air. From the smooth edges of its side, rails popped up, and the tray, now revealed as a sled, accelerated smoothly and rapidly over a crab robot and into one of the yellow translucent halls. Shouts and cries reached Shasti, who struggled to her feet only to be knocked down as Paolo tumbled into her, thrown backward by the sudden acceleration.

Mmok hung onto the railing as the sled whooshed down the halls faster and faster.

"Sure," he said, "it's a big deal when I push a few harmless buttons..."

Shasti and Paolo untangled themselves and climbed into the seats, which for all of their hard plastic appearance, conformed to their bodies.

"Where are we going?" Paolo shouted.

"How the hell would I know?" Mmok snapped back.

"I do," Shasti said. At the last instant before the sleds raced off, she realized why the shape on the scanner looked familiar. It was an abstract in blocky lights of the station itself. "I must have punched a destination," she shouted over the roar of the whipping wind, which buffeted her helmet.

"I hope it's in a good neighborhood," Mmok said. His white hair flagged out behind him and he looked like the family dog enjoying a ground car ride. "Whee, this is better than a roller coaster!"

Levels, tunnels, and bridges over deep chasms flashed by in a whirl of red, orange, and yellow as the sled sped on.

"Should we stop it?" Paolo asked in a calmer voice.

Shasti debated. "No. Pushing another button in mid-flight might have disastrous effects. The destination button that lit up after we got in should be for a valid destination. Maybe the station AI wants us to see something."

"Shasti," Paolo said. "Lie back next to me and relax."

She looked at him. "You're kidding."

"No, no," he said. "I'm reclining in the seat. Look. No buffeting. Either they weren't as tall as us or they rode this way."

Shasti took his advice and lay back in the seat, her chin almost on her chest. The buffeting ceased as the sled somehow redirected air from its supine passengers.

Shasti reached for her com. "Stormcloud to Cossack," she said, using Vaughn's code name.

"No good," Mmok said. "I already tried all freaks. It can't be the metal or distance, so I assume it's something to do with the propulsion unit of the sled."

They roared on through the vast station. Shasti began to notice peculiarities in their surroundings. Not just that the levels were different, some being residential and other obviously commercial or industrial. Nor was it the differing colors, as some levels were cobalt blue, topaz, or sea-green. Large sections of station interior looked like they'd been taken apart.

"Did you see that damaged section?" Shasti asked Mmok as they flew over a factory complex.

"Yeah. It looked more like demolition than fighting," Mmok said. "There have been a bunch of spots like that."

An immense iris of blue steel closed the tunnel ahead of them. Before Shasti could even consider jumping or punching more buttons, it dilated open. The sled slowed as they passed through, then the iris shut as quickly behind them. Shasti and Paolo could feel the atmosphere around them being sucked out as their suits clung less tightly.

"There's a sign," Paolo said, jumping to his feet. He gestured at a panel next to the iris, covered in what looked like tracks from a berserk chicken. "That's Skurlocki." He whipped up his videocam with its built-in translator. *"Entering Nitrogen-Oxygen Sector. Warning: Low Pressure."*

Ahead was another iris, this one painted gray, and it swung open to reveal a cavernous space lit only by a few small blue-white lights. The sled lunged into the darkness and came down without a jar on a landing stage in the echoing space.

"Last stop," Mmok said. "All out."

Shasti and Mmok leapt from the sled, taking cover, weapons ready. A second later, Paolo joined them, videocam away and sidearm out.

"No shooting unless I fire," Shasti ordered, peering into the darkness. Paolo nodded. She was pleased to see he looked more curious than afraid.

They had landed in a section partially filled with sleds, though some were of a larger and clearly commercial type with large cargo boxes. The area around them showed none of the semi-melted look of the rest of the Ribisi section, looking more like the interior of the *Sidhe* than anything else. As their eyes adapted to the low light, Shasti could see that they were facing a triple layer of banked stores and offices with railed walkways in front extending for most of a kilometer in both directions. Far above them were panels of some material through which they could see stars. Other panels appeared to be lights, but none of them were operating.

"Looks like they turned off everything but the emergency lights when they bugged out," Shasti said. "Good lights to have been running for five hundred years."

"Remember that station AI," Mmok cautioned. "Something is still working here, maybe making repairs or redesign. It's even maintained atmosphere. The air is good. You can open your helmets. Pressure is within normal limits for humans."

Shasti risked the light from her triple auto. It slashed through the darkness, revealing details of the storefronts. While there were no bodies, she saw desiccated trees and plants in containers dotting tables in what had clearly been bars and restaurants.

"Big open space for a station," Mmok said.

"They had a lot of confidence in their engineering," Paolo said.

"We'd better call the others," Shasti said, reaching for her com.

The iris behind them suddenly opened with a loud whoosh, startling them back into cover. Two sleds emerged, full of armed ASATS and Denshi. They grounded next to their sled.

"Shasti," Vaughn shouted, leaping clear of the sled before it touched down, with Rigg, Rask, and Tanaka in hot pursuit. "Are you all right?"

Shasti rose from behind her sled as more troops leapt out. "We're fine."

"What happened?" Rigg demanded.

"*Somebody* was pushing buttons," Mmok said.

"Speaking of buttons," Shasti said, glaring at him, "button yours." She turned back to Vaughn. "When we got to the sled, the screen illuminated with what turned out to be a destination. There's an AI at work here. I think it wanted to bring us to this spot."

"Which is?" Vaughn looked around.

"The oxygen breathers section," Shasti replied. "This is a trade concourse."

The iris boomed open again and another sled popped out. This one bore crab robots. At the same time, two of the sleds nearby stirred. ASATS jumped away, cursing as the sleds headed back to the hydrogen section.

"Well," Mmok said, "looks like we will be able to stage the whole force up here. I'll order the rest of the crabs to join us. I've got communications with the shuttles now. It was only the tunnel EM field that was blocking us."

Shasti shook her head. "Leave a third of the force with the shuttles. Tell the shuttles to stay where they are, but have the fighters find a staging area closer to us. I want to move everything closer."

"Rangers out," Rigg called again. "Look out for traps. Something wanted us here. We ain't sure why."

The crab robots deployed their red, low-light lanterns and created a wide pool of blood-red light. Troopers moved out behind the machines, save for the rangers, who slipped out beyond the robots in pairs, visible only when they used the lights attached to their weapons.

"Mmok," Shasti ordered, "take Paolo and see if you can find another AI interface somewhere. Something more complicated than a sled panel. And—"

"Yeah, I know, don't punch any buttons." He stalked off into the darkness.

Shasti and the others walked up to a storefront. It was unlit, and shelves of goods were arrayed about, some on the floors as if strewn there in the disorder of the last evacuation. She shone a light about. "Still no bodies; makes for a nice change."

"The station wasn't under attack when they evacuated," Vaughn said. "Yet we saw damaged sections as the sleds flew through."

A quick perusal of the area showed more shops and warehouses, and spaces that might have been restaurants and halls. In all were signs of hurried evacuation. Souvenir hunting broke out among the spacers, and pockets filled with small, unusual statues, cups of crystal or exotic metal and other such treasures. Shasti debated putting an end to the looting, but Rigg, in a rare display of temper, beat her to it.

"Get your goddamn eyes off the trinkets and into the shadows," he bellowed. People shamefacedly got back to work.

Mmok returned. "No luck on an interface, but I found something else you should see."

Rigg and Rask stayed to keep everyone on task. Vaughn and Shasti followed Mmok down the concourse. They found Eris and Paolo standing over what, at first, Shasti thought was an abstract sculpture. But a second look disabused her of the notion that this was anything artistic. The decking around the tangle of melted metal was blistered, gouged, and darkened by fire.

Shasti looked at Mmok.

The machine man shrugged. "Some of it looks like a fairly standard form of maintenance robot. There's a broom/sweeper attachment underneath that gray boxy section there. There's a lot of tubing around. Not sure what this other stuff is. I'm not sure if this was one or two machines."

One section of the mass looked like a golden melon, or more like the football some of the ASATs threw around during their games around the ship back on Kandalor.

"I wonder what the hell this was about," Vaughn said.

The fighters called in, distracting Shasti from further consideration of the melted tangle. They had found a nearby landing area, so close that when Shasti looked up she could see the delta-winged *Spacefire* hanging above them. She ordered the shuttles moved up. Mmok and Paolo saw to their safe landing, using another platform to bring the shuttles inside. They found no active links to the station AI, and now even the sleds remained stubbornly inactive.

Rangers reported signs of fighting up and down the trade concourse, with weapon fire scoring bulkheads and signs of explosions. Mmok sent robots back into the hydrogen section. They found even more damage than they had seen from the sleds.

"Not sure what's going on, boss," he reported to Shasti, "but it looks like some nonessential sections might have been cannibalized for raw material. Though what was done with the material, I don't know."

With her force regathered and the immediate area secure, Shasti considered their next move. "Thoughts?" she asked.

"If this station is anything like one of ours," Paolo said, "there should be a trade control area, with customs agents, and both live and computerized translation services. There must be connections and interfaces to the AI there. Trade was the whole point of the station."

Mmok's head swiveled almost all the way around. "If I had to take a wild-assed guess at it, I'd bet on that tower there." He pointed to a multi-level area that looked like an office building jutting from the station's interior bulkhead.

Shasti nodded. "It does have the look of a customs house." It occurred to her that in her crew of former privateers, assassins, spies, and professional military, that she was the closest thing they had to a respectable merchant. *At least I've actually run cargo,* she thought smugly, *even if it was usually contraband.*

Their boots rang on the metal plates of the deck, raising disquieting echoes. Shasti went more soft-footed, hating to give away her position just from force of habit, until they reached a carpeted section just outside the customs house. They entered through a large round door decorated in red and gold.

"Reminds me of a Chinese restaurant," Paolo said.

But inside it was clearly a trade office. Consoles, computer banks, and desks filled the space. Unlike the concourse outside, the office was covered in dust and the air had a stale smell to it. Shasti backed out quickly. "Check the air," she ordered Mmok.

The machine man walked in. After a few seconds, he gave the all-clear. "I can't vouch for the smell, but there's nothing harmful in the air. Maybe somebody left their lunch behind during the evacuation."

They walked around the lobby area and reached the silent computers and machines. Mmok examined them. "Intact," he said.

"We know there is power in the station still, so I suppose they were all turned off. Shall I try turning one on, Skipper?"

"Do it."

Mmok pulled a power jack from a panel in his chest and hooked himself up via a port in the side of the machine. "No dice," he said. "Either the power isn't enough or some security routine is inhibiting them. Should have worked."

They looked around for any sign of active machinery but found none, nor could Mmok's best efforts rouse any response from the station's AI though he swore that the main console had to be the connection. "Either it's hiding from us or it doesn't talk to this part of the station anymore."

"I'm liking this less and less," Shasti said.

"Shasti," Vaughn called. "Look at this." She joined him at the far end opposite the entrance. He was staring at some slagged machinery in front of a meter-wide hole that had been melted through the metal bulkhead.

"Dan." Shasti triggered her throat mike. "We've found more evidence of fighting here. Put everyone back on light and noise discipline and pull back the rangers and bots. Let's be inconspicuous for now."

"Copy, Stormcloud."

Shasti noted the lights outside the office windows quickly disappeared. Only the crab robot torches remained lit, and even their red glow was turned down.

"Skipper," Mmok said. "Why don't I get a couple of portable generators off the shuttles? Maybe that would give this junk enough juice to restart."

Shasti nodded and Mmok headed out.

Alone for the first time since they landed, Shasti looked about the trade office and through the open door to the station beyond. The oxygen-breathers section was a small percentage of the station, maybe only five percent, and even that was on the outer edge of one wing of it. Beyond the interior wall she faced were hundreds of square kilometers of methane-filled corridors and chambers holding God knew what.

A feeling akin to desperation flitted through Shasti. She had brought her crew across the unknown light years to this place on a guess and a visitation in the Skurlock ruins.

God, she thought, *the risks I am exposing my people to.*

She braced her feet shoulder length apart and raised her hands as if reaching toward the unknown. She closed her eyes and bowed her head, reaching out with her little understood PSI sense.

Are you there? she sent, holding in her mind's eye the pale image of the Skurlock from the ruins. *Are you there? Is this the right place to look for you? Am I on the right track? Help me. Reach back to me.*

Time dragged and Shasti concentrated, feeling the power of her mind as a searching beacon. *Are you there?*

Something cold and alien suddenly skittered across her brain. Shasti gasped and shuddered at the shock of it. Then it was gone as if it had never been, making her wonder if she had even felt it.

Her eyes flew open, and she looked for any pallid glimmer, but there was nothing. She drew deep shaky breaths trying to reach out again. Nothing.

"Damn," she swore.

"Something wrong?" Vaughn asked.

Shasti had to suppress a start for once in her life; she'd been concentrating so hard that she lost track of who was near her. "Nothing," she said. "I was trying to raise something here. For a second I thought I felt something then…"

"Bubble, bubble toil and trouble," he said.

"So," she said, "I remind you of witches."

"Very sexy, beautiful ones," he replied.

She smiled. "Nice. Paolo better watch out; you're becoming quite articulate."

"Now if you are going to get nasty…" Vaughn said, an eyebrow arched.

She returned to the interior, accompanied by Vaughn. They found another set of ornate red doors, marked with a series of four interlocking circles. Vaughn pushed them open as Shasti covered. Beyond was another room filled with machines and desks. Over them all hung a large board, its function familiar and obvious.

"Trading room," Paolo said, having walked up behind them.

They walked in under the silent boards. This area showed even more signs of disorder with odd-shaped chairs knocked over. Shasti even found a dark-green cloth jacket lying across one chair. Its odd, asymmetric shape clearly allowed it to fit over a Skurlock's large fiddler crab-like right arm. It crumbled at her touch.

Shasti looked up at the silent boards, imagining the room buzzing with the activity of several races trading goods and services. The image made the silent room all the more oppressive.

Paolo also seemed to sense it. His usual ebullient curiosity was dampened. "Shall we get back to the others? There seems to be nothing here."

Shasti smiled at him. "Haunted by the ghosts of traders past?"

He gave a short laugh. "Guess so. Maybe it's just that on this voyage we've seen so many places empty of the life that they should hold."

"Too true," Vaughn said.

They headed for the round door of the building when a clattering sound brought them all up short.

"Mmok's robots?" Paolo whispered.

Shasti motioned for silence as she and Vaughn stalked forward. They flanked the slightly open door. Shasti peered through into the darkness beyond. A metallic, clicking sound came from farther inside the station. She started to lean out when it came into view. For a second, her eyes had a hard time resolving what it was. Then it moved again.

Shasti stared with revulsion at the machine. It looked like a cat's cradle of bending flexible poles around a golden oval of metal the size of a human head. Small hatches covered the smooth ball, probably hiding weapons and sensors.

Vaughn caught her eye, and she gestured for him to look at the window behind him. She saw him take a small mirror from his pocket and, like a good assassin, look out without risking being seen. She again motioned for silence from Paolo.

They watched it move effortlessly across the deck, turning end for end past some long-abandoned shops on the spaceport concourse. Its cradle shape adjusted for every surface, and it quickly climbed over a stopped electric cart. The drone came to a ladder and elongated itself to wedge its way up the hatchway. But the machine must have misjudged the coefficient of friction of the walls. It slid down to the floor with an abrupt bang. Paolo jumped. Shasti prayed wordlessly that no one outside would be startled into shooting.

The machine gathered itself up and appeared to consider the accessway; after a few seconds, it went off in another direction and vanished up the passage. The little display of fallibility and frustration cheered Shasti.

Vaughn crossed the space between them in a stride. "If there's one, there's more."

"Come on," Shasti said, "back to the others."

But it was already too late. The first shots and cries rang out as they reached for the door.

23

Shasti ran out of the trade office with the others on her heels. She glanced both ways across the broad plaza they'd have to cross to get back to the main force.

"Report," Shasti shouted over her com, but the speaker gave her only a harsh buzzing.

"Jamming," Vaughn growled.

To their right and up a corridor, Shasti saw the flashing of weapon fire but could not see who was engaged.

"This way," a voice called. Shasti looked left. Misa Tanaka, Eris, and an engineered trooper sheltered behind a crab robot. They stood at bay by a pile of abandoned cargo and carts, facing another alcove lit by intermittent flickering.

"Go." Vaughn thrust Paolo ahead of him as he and Shasti jogged forward covering each other. They had almost reached the Asian woman when Dan Rigg and Rask came pelting out of another corridor, red beams lancing past them. Both rolled and the crab robot fired its 30mm back down the corridor. Shasti hoped desperately that none of the rounds would breach the hull and admit hard vacuum or deadly methane. Tanaka raced forward toward Dan, firing a burst from the hip. A thin red beam flashed out of the corridor and struck her across the chest. Tanaka spun with a cry and fell in the open, well short of Rigg.

"No!" Vaughn shouted.

Rigg and Rask scrambled up, heading for Tanaka. A volley of beams and particles sparkled on the floor near them, driving Rask back. Rigg threw himself forward and covered Tanaka with his armored body. The crab robot charged, drawing fire and shuddering under the impacts. The Engineered trooper nearby flew backward as a ricochet hit him, spraying his blood on the gray hull of the crab. Eris, deprived of cover, dropped behind the downed Engineered, then started dragging the downed man, nearly twice her size, toward the entrance of a small store.

Fire exploded all around them. Paolo emptied his pistol over his shoulder at their unseen pursuers and cut into a side hall. Vaughn plowed ahead toward Tanaka but was pinned down behind the cargo boxes. Shasti ran toward his position just as he rose up to run for Tanaka. A red beam touched him, and the big man was flung backward over a cart, landing with a crash.

Oh God, Shasti thought. *No.*

From the inner corridors a veritable flood of machines similar to the one Shasti saw earlier, poured out. The crab robot slagged many and absorbed their fire and attention as Shasti, firing short bursts, slid to the deck next to Vaughn. He was already struggling up, a furious expression on his face. An energy bolt had cut a smoking trough in his armor, but he snapped his rifle around and started firing again.

Next to them the crab robot sparked, shuddered, and collapsed.

"We can't hold here with three men," Shasti said.

"Tanaka!" Vaughn bellowed.

"Hang on, Dan," Rask shouted. The ape-like Morok swung over a parked sled and into cover just ahead of a volley of shots and beams.

The Evolver machines came on like army ants, then exploded in a maelstrom of shattered steel and flame. Shasti whooped with joy as she spotted a wave of crab robots behind the charging figure of a white-haired HCR, coming from the direction of the spacedock. Mmok's triple-auto blazed, creating disaster among the Evolvers.

"Dan!" Mmok's artificial voice boomed. "Stay down. We're

coming." Rigg lay unmoving, either playing dead or actually dead. Shasti could not tell.

Vaughn gathered his feet under him, eyes on Tanaka.

"No," Shasti yelled seizing his shoulder. Only her Engineered strength and desperation allowed her to stop the huge man. "Look."

Mmok and the other Confed robots had frozen in place and their weapons fell silent. Two of the crab robots fell over as she looked, their locked postures unstable. Mmok, too, was locked in position.

"What?" Vaughn growled. "What treachery is this?"

The crab robots stood immobile as more Evolver drones filled the space. The alien machines had ceased fire for the moment, possibly intent on prisoners. In the distance, Shasti saw a far larger, more complicated unit rolling forward in its cat's cradle of metal bars.

"Must be a controller," Rask called out to them from his position behind the sled.

Shasti rose up for a shot at it, and a beam licked over her head, its hot breath singing her hair. She ducked. Vaughn also popped up, only to receive the same treatment.

"Yeah, they're after prisoners," she said.

"They will not take me," Vaughn swore. "Wait till they get close. I will take their fire. You run."

"The hell you say," Shasti blazed.

"Woman, don't argue with me!"

"I'll shoot," Shasti yelled. "You run."

His blue eyes bore into her green ones. "I won't lose both women I love today. You run."

She smiled at him, confounding his anger. "You don't get rid of me this easily."

"Shasti...please."

"We fight together," she said with finality.

"And I'll hang out too," Rask called. "In case you were curious."

"You were already counted in," Shasti shot back.

"It's been fun, Skipper."

"We're not dead yet," she shouted.

Vaughn gave her a sad smile and shook his head. "So much we missed."

Shasti snuck another peek, and perhaps because she did not aim a weapon, she did not draw fire. Vaughn joined her.

The controller, seeming more spider-like than its smaller companions, made its way around and over the smashed ranks of its lesser brothers. It passed the prone figures of Rigg and Tanaka. Smaller machines surrounded the downed pair, making Shasti hopeful that they were still alive. The Evolvers reached the line of Confed crab robots and the still form of Mmok, frozen in the act of firing his triple-auto.

Shasti shot a glance to Vaughn. If the hit the big man had taken before affected him at all, it could not be seen. He glared at the onrushing machines.

"If we start firing again with them caught out there…" Rask called.

"I know," Shasti said, looking desperately for any way out of the trap.

The controller moved cautiously forward, then ducked behind a disabled crab robot. In the same instant, several things happened. All the cat-cradle drones went into spasms as if being electrocuted. The spider controller reared back, and Mmok blurred into life leaping onto the crab robot and blasting the Evolver controller with a long burst from his big triple auto. The spidery machine shredded and flew apart, as did part of the deck below it.

The Evolver drones collapsed from their strange seizure and lay still. Shasti, Vaughn, and Rask stood, cautiously advancing toward Mmok, Rigg, and Tanaka. Rigg ignored everyone to start working on Tanaka.

Mmok danced about like a berserk scarecrow. The long, pale hair his body used for antenna whipped about it. "Yee-haw," he shouted. "Woo-woo-woo." The HCR hopped from foot to foot.

"He's blown a circuit," Rask shouted, his triple-auto wavering uncertainly.

Shasti and the others stood dumbfounded, staring at each other. Not even Shasti and Vaughn together dared to try seizing the deadly machine body.

"He's doing a war dance." Rask suddenly laughed. "He's gone Sioux on us."

Shasti stared at him without comprehension, but Mmok stopped his bizarre behavior and turned to face them all. He clicked his metal heels together with a sound like a pistol shot and bowed.

"Are you all right?" Shasti asked, stepping from behind the crates.

"Right as rain," Mmok said.

"What the hell happened?" she demanded. Eris and another medic appeared and elbowed past her, headed for Tanaka with Vaughn hot on her heels. Around her the crab robots whirred to life again and closed in on the quiescent Evolvers to begin tearing them to pieces with their pincers and claws.

"Just what you suspected," Mmok returned. "Our little friends here," he gestured at the growing pile of scrapped Evolver drones, "launched a cybernetic attack on us. A good one, too, came in through a code I'd never expected could be used that way. Shut us down. Hell, they were halfway to turning us on you.

"But there," he paused to tap himself on the chest, "is where they didn't reckon on me. Me. The human element. I ain't just a sparking box of circuits and relays. I'm people, dammit. I've got free will. I used it to reset some of my circuits, freed my body, and blasted their controller. At the same time, since they so nicely let me into their little net, I sent a full hard shutdown command to all units on this station."

He pointed to where the crabs were worrying the last of the Evolvers like terriers on rats. "Don't want to risk them having some sort of auto reset so we're going to destroy them now."

"What was the war dance about?" Rask demanded.

"Finally found a reason to hang onto my humanity," Mmok said. "My HCR body is superior to my old one in every way; I was beginning to wonder if there was any point to trying to retain my human identity. Now I know. It makes me unpredictable. It makes me unique."

Shasti nodded and placed a hand on the HCR's shoulder, giving it a gentle squeeze. Then she turned to where Rigg and Vaughn were hovering over an unconscious Tanaka. Vaughn's bear-like hand cradled Tanaka's head as Rigg helped Eris cut open the Olympian's body armor and clothes. The Evolver weapon had burned a quarter of her chest and shoulder. Red and torn skin across her front looked painful and deep. Mercifully, she was still unconscious. Eris quickly covered Tanaka's chest with wound foam.

"We have to get her back to the ship," Eris said.

"Be best if you all went," Mmok said. "I picked out from the controller's AI that there is a big booby trap in the reactor core. I need to clear that, and the crabs need to find and cut up any additional Evolvers."

"Okay. Let's get going," Shasti ordered. She keyed her mike. "General retreat to the shuttles. Report to me first. I don't want to leave anyone behind."

Mmok and his machines scattered, save for two that moved into position to guard Shasti's party.

She looked at Rask. "Gather the teams and set up a secure corridor for pulling out the wounded to the shuttles. Get me a sitrep and a report on casualties."

The Morok raced off, barking orders into his com. Another trooper staggered into view from a side corridor, holding a crushed hand. Eris ran over to the man, who fell to his knees. Two more appeared, including an Engineered from Vaughn's group.

Rigg and Vaughn both leaned down to pick up Tanaka. They stared at each other.

"I've got her," Rigg said.

"With respect," Vaughn said, "I'm far stronger and can be more careful."

"Pretty strong myself," Rigg said.

"You've known her for six months," Vaughn said quietly. "She's guarded my life for seventeen years."

Rigg's lips thinned, but he nodded. "Very carefully, big man. Very carefully."

Vaughn lifted Tanaka as if he were gathering an armload of crystal, and Rigg gently settled Tanaka's head on Vaughn's shoulder.

"Stay beside me," Vaughn said. "Watch her feet and head." The two sped off.

More of the team began to appear now that the all-clear had been sounded. Paolo appeared with the young ASAT, Sandy, over his shoulders in a fireman's carry.

"Help," he shouted. "She's run through the midsection."

"Over here," Eris called. Paolo ran the small ASAT over to Eris, who immediately tore open Sandy's armor and clothes. But Paolo had done a decent job of bandaging the holes. Eris gave her anti-shock meds and hung a bottle of replenishing fluids for her. Quickly, she drafted an Engineered trooper, who easily lifted Sandy. They disappeared in the direction of the shuttles.

Rask returned, his face grim. "Four dead, Kordov, Ramirez, McDonough, and Anders. Sandy is missing—"

"No, she's alive. Eris is evacing her."

"Great. Then that's eight wounded."

"Back to the shuttles," she said. "We'll recover the dead later. We won't leave without them."

Shasti and Rask acted as rearguard as the Confed party fell back on their shuttles, then she dispersed her troops to guard the landing stage, hoping that nothing would impede the giant doors overhead from opening if they needed to flee. Everyone outside the shuttles resealed their space suits.

They accounted for everyone and prepped the shuttles for launch, leaving the two crabs to guard their retreat. Shasti had all the wounded loaded on *Pooka* so *Duelist* could loiter near the station if they had to launch. D'abo brought *Sidhe* in closer to expedite the pickup and cover them from any attack that might come across the surface of the station.

"Are you ready to withdraw?" D'abo asked, her face appearing in a small screen in Shasti's helmet. Her ears were up and practically vibrating.

"We're waiting on, Mmok," Shasti returned. Her eyes searched the landing pad outside the shuttle. Over her head, the long barrel of the top turret swung out to cover the entrance to the spacedock.

As if on cue, Mmok cut in on the circuit. "Canuck to Stormcloud."

Shasti clicked on her com. "Stormcloud, go."

"No need to evac, boss. The booby trap was pretty simple. It's disabled. I got a fix on all the Evolver drones from their controller before I whacked it. My crabs are finishing them off now. It's safe to stay."

"Okay," Shasti said, blowing out a breath. It seemed they would not have to flee after all. "We'll hold up here. I am sending *Pooka* back with the wounded."

"This is Vaughn," a voice cut in.

"Go."

"I will remain with you. Rigg wishes to return with Tanaka. I have said yes."

"Of course. Hop over here so we can decompress and get them on their way."

In seconds, Vaughn raced over from the *Duelist*. They signaled the accordion doors, which rolled back, allowing the *Pooka* to head for safety of *Sidhe* and her sickbay.

As soon as atmosphere was reestablished, all the able-bodied piled out of the *Duelist* to join Shasti and the ASATS in the bay Mmok sauntered casually into the cavernous bay, his weapon over his shoulder at a jaunty angle. He gave every sign of being well-pleased with himself. Shasti and the others moved to greet the returning HCR, who accepted the handshakes, backslaps, and congratulations as his due. He motioned Shasti aside after the crowd dispersed under Rask's snapped orders to get back to work.

"I got the bodies collected," he said quietly, "back where Crab Six got slagged fighting the controller."

The elation of victory ran out of Shasti like spilled champagne. "More parents and loved ones to get the letters saying that their children, their lovers, are gone. Is what we do worth this?"

"You asking me?" he said.

"Why not?" she answered. "You're people too. If you weren't, the Evolvers would have overrun us and God knows what would have followed."

The machine face was incapable of expression, but somehow the black doll's eyes looked thoughtful. "That's always the question. Isn't it? How many lives is an expedition, a battle, a mountain, or skyscraper worth? What's the value of a human life? We tell ourselves that we are all unique. There will never be another one of the four that we lost today, but there are a hundred million people that you could switch interchangeably with any one of them or us. And no matter what we do, whether it is after a run of ten years or of two hundred, we die. So is it more of a tragedy when we check out young and full of promise or old and worn out with cares, woe, and loss?"

"Got any answers, Tinman?" she said.

"No more than you," he said. "I have a question though. Don't answer if it bothers you and I swear I don't mean to hurt your feelings."

"Ask."

"Do you write the letters?"

Shasti felt her cheeks burn with an unaccustomed shame.

"Hey, boss, forget I opened my stupid speaker—"

"No," she said. "It's okay. Rigg's written them for me before. No more. I'll write these."

Mmok looked her over. "Fenaday would be proud of you right now."

"Thanks," she said and put a hand on his shoulder.

"I'll get the medics and the body bags and take care of it," Mmok said and headed off.

Shasti stood silent and alone until Vaughn joined her. "Are you all right?" he asked.

"Yes," she said. "A little more each day I think."

He gave her a puzzled look, but she knew that she could not tell him the answers when the questions had not yet come to him.

"Meant what I said," Vaughn said.

"Yes, I know," she whispered, unwilling to confront the words.

Vaughn's face closed up, but his disappointment was palpable.

Shasti cursed herself. *Always I hold back. Always. Will I ever find some man better than this one? What am I holding back for?*

"Walk with me, if you will," she said, fighting a choking sensation. "I don't know my own mind just now and I want neither to be alone nor to have other company."

He nodded silently and followed her.

24

D’abo reappeared on *Pooka's* screen hours later, after the shuttle brought up replacements. She reported on the wounded. "All the seriously wounded are in sickbay," she said. "Minor injuries are resting comfortably in their quarters. Mourner says they are all in stable condition. Tanaka is already complaining about being confined and asking about Vaughn."

"Tell her I am well," Vaughn said, "very minor burns. I shall return to the ship and see her soon."

"What is happening at your end?" D’abo asked.

"Mmok and Paolo are investigating the databanks of the controller," Shasti returned. "Some parts aren't totally slagged. They hope to gain some intel. From what we have learned, the station AI has been waging a low-intensity battle with the Evolvers since they landed, converting its limited supply of drones and workbots into combat models. They managed to keep the Evolvers confined to the oxygenated parts of the station, seems they don't perform as well in the methane-pressurized sections. The Evolvers, for their part, didn't prosecute the fight except when the station AI interfered with their operations."

"And of course the station saw a chance to get a leg up on the Evolvers when we landed," Vaughn said.

"Yes," D'abo said. "It can't be a coincidence that you were dumped almost literally on the front line of the battle for the station."

"Agreed," Shasti said.

"Wait a second," Vaughn said. "If these units were here to interrupt reinforcements and warn the Evolvers of a counterattack, wouldn't there be some sort of ship here? At least a courier drone? Even if they blew up the station, they could not hope to get all of an attacking force. The intelligence must be worth more than the damage they could cause. They had to have a way or reporting back to the main Evolver fleet."

"Good tactical thinking." D'abo smiled. "He's right. There must be a ship or drone hidden aboard somewhere."

Shasti switched over to Mmok's channel and filled him in.

"Makes sense," he said. "We're talking something interstellar and way bigger than a fighter. Still, it's a big station."

"Fetch boy, fetch."

"Arf," he said.

Mmok proved to be a very effective foxhound and located the Evolver vessel two kilometers away in a badly damaged section of the station. Shasti and her team, with D'abo joining them, walked through a depressurized area of hull. The fried and disassembled piles of machines showed how bitterly the stations mix of servos and workbots had contested the landing, but clearly Evolvers had carried that long-ago day and their spacecraft lay amidst the severed beams and sliced hull of the station. The vessel was a pleasant golden color and over two hundred meters long, a small ship rather than any form of fighter.

"Well," Rigg said over his helmet com, "if there was any doubt that the Evolvers and the Conchirri came from the same source, this would seem to answer it."

"Yep," Mmok said. "That's a Conchirri *Crissel* scout-raider. We called them dartships. I got to see one of them slam into the cruiser *Warspite* over 61Cygni2. Paint job is different. Conchirri used black and yellow; the Evolvers seem to love gold. I wonder if this came first.

There's a more refined look to this, like the ones we saw were cruder copies."

"I've also thought so," Paolo said. "There are old elements in the Conchirri tongue that did not seem to fit with the Conchirri temperament. It's as if they were pulled from some older and more rational speech and corrupted over time."

A beep sounded in their ears. "Okay," Mmok said. "That's the all-clear from crab Eleven, no booby traps. Let me go in first and double-check."

Mmok disappeared into the open hatchway. After a minute, his white-haired head popped out the hatch.

"Still can't get over the fact that he doesn't need a suit," Rask grumbled as they walked over to the ship. "Every time I see that hair, I think somebody's head is going to explode."

"Yes," D'abo said, "very unfair. When I think of how much conditioner I have to use on my hair..."

The men laughed. Shasti smiled to herself, one of the very minor advantages of being Engineered, perfect hair.

The dartship hatch stood far enough off the deck that they had to pile some boxes to reach it. To their surprise, the vessel held a large central compartment filled with seating and bunks. Mmok stood in the middle of it, illuminating the space with built-in lights from his HCR chassis.

"Why is it designed for biologicals?" Paolo asked, looking at the seats and bunks.

"Prisoners," Rigg said, "or knowing the Evolvers—converts. Either way, they had to be able to transport them."

"This ship gives me an idea," Shasti said. "*Sidhe* is of a class they didn't have in the Confed navy. She acted as a tender for a flight of smaller vessels. We have heavy-duty grapples and tiedowns below the main hull for salvage or towing. We could take this ship along with us. If we need to do any snooping near Evolvers, it could come in handy."

Paolo gave it a dubious look. "A five-hundred-year-old ship?"

Mmok shook his head in a holdover gesture from his previous humanity. "This isn't like the starfort. The Evolvers have been maintaining it continuously. Hell, they had nothing else to do. Remember their mission, to alert the main body in case of a force returning here. They had to be ready to go at a moment's notice. It's in top shape and ready to fly."

Paolo gave him a puzzled look. "I thought these," he gestured at the small starship, "had been abandoned here. Lost and forgotten."

"You're thinking like the rapidly decomposing bag of protoplasm that you are," Mmok quipped. "Machines don't fear time and they don't fear boredom. These were here because there was no huge need for this tiny force to be elsewhere and this station is a high-value asset. Somebody was going to find it sometime. Machines plan for the long term."

Rask looked at Rigg. "*Machina uber alles?*"

"Not so." Mmok wagged a digit. "If it wasn't for the little bit of brain plasma left over from Mom's original model, we would all be space dust. It's just," he said placing a prideful hand on his mechanical chest, "that I have the best of both worlds."

Perez and his shipwrights soon confirmed Mmok's opinion that the dartship was in perfect maintenance. They spent the next few days installing Confed controls and tearing out enough Evolver machinery to fit a flight chair from the *Spacefire's* spares. They also removed any remote-control units that the Evolvers had used to fly the ship.

Shasti brought *Sidhe* in for a docking at the edge of the oxygen-breathers section where they first fought the Evolvers. It facilitated the shipwright's work on the dartship and allowed them to easily resupply *Sidhe* with raw materials found on the station, notably oxygen. It also allowed D'abo to come aboard before curiosity did her in.

Mmok worked round the clock on datamining the shattered controller and the smaller computer brain in the dartship. "The memory core," he reported to Shasti, "has not been updated in a long, long time. I am having trouble figuring out the time increments since they are based on some unknown planet's rotation, a hangover from when the Evolvers were under the direct control of the Makers." He looked over at Paolo.

"My best guess," Paolo said, "based on the information we have and what we found in the memory core is that, over five hundred years ago, this Evolver boarding party landed on the station shortly after the evacuation. But that's a patchwork filled in with a lot of guesses."

"But," Mmok raised a digit, "five hundred years ago, a massive force of Evolvers was being gathered to deal with something I translate as, the Skurlock Redoubt, a last stand where the Skurlocks were causing the Evolvers real hurt. The unit here was left to deal with and report on reinforcements and to delay or destroy those forces with the booby trap in the main reactor."

"We've had a narrow escape," D'abo said, her ears flattening.

"So do we go on from here?" Vaughn said.

"Give me a few minutes alone," Shasti said. She looked away toward the giant plast-steel view port. To one side a sliver of Hanghoul glowed blue, but the rest of the port was filled with darkness and the hard, unwinking stars. The others walked away, leaving her in silence. Well, not quite a silence; there was always a background ambient to a ship or station: blowers coming on and off, relays clicking open and closed, metal contracting and expanding as the sun warmed the station. All this, she tuned out. She closed her eyes and raised her hands again to help her focus on seeing without sight. Shasti faced the stars and opened her mind.

The black skittery thing that had raced across her mind was gone, confirming her suspicion that the mind she'd felt before belonged to the Evolver controller. A distant muttering filled her mind like a conversation in another room that could barely be heard. She realized this must be the station's AI. Shasti was afraid that Ribisi AI might blanket the signal she was looking for, but the muttering retreated. She realized that the AI, born from the mind of a methane-breathing creature, was simply too far off her wavelength for her mind to hold it in.

Hardly surprising, she thought, *the brain that conceived that AI was not flesh and blood but bits of crystal and silicon in a blood supply of icy liquid hydrogen. The Evolvers were born from the mind of the Makers, who had also spawned the Conchirri, and must have been similar to the races of the Confederacy to want to harvest their genetic materials.*

Freed of the AI's distraction, she concentrated, reaching out farther and farther, refusing to be daunted by the impossible, insane distances involved.

A glimmer caught her eye, and Shasti focused on it. As if switched on, she saw the Skurlock again. Only a few feet away, a small creature, pallid and flickering like candlelight, faced her. Her impression was of a bug crossed with a crab, made even more bizarre by the toolbelt and clothes it wore.

"Who?" she demanded.

Fushol, a voice made of clacks and hisses said in her mind.

"Where?"

She sensed confusion in Fushol as if the question had no meaning for it. *The hidden star* was all that came back. *Are you real?*

"Yes," Shasti said. "We are real and looking for you."

Come soon. We fail.

"Help me find you," she said.

But she felt a wave of fatigue and Fushol visibly staggered. *Too far, too tired. Come soon. The hidden star...search for the hidden star.*

And Fushol was gone.

Fighting a wave of exhaustion, Shasti returned to the others. "Paolo, Mmok, dig into those databases look for a reference to something called the hidden star. We leave as soon as you find it. Time is not our friend."

But despite their best efforts over the next two days, the site of the Skurlock Redoubt could not be located in the Evolver's databanks.

On the third day after the fight, they gathered in the trade station. The Confed spacers had pulled back to the landing stage area and secured it with their remaining robots, barrier wire, and all the troops from *Sidhe.* While the Evolvers were destroyed, Shasti was leery of the station AI. Since Mmok was adept at hacking into computer systems, she knew the AI was aware of them but resisted their contact efforts. The machine had recognized them as useful for its ends and thrust them into combat with the Evolvers. She suspected that it was content with the situation for now but that any long-term occupation by them would meet resistance.

"Any luck with the datamining?" Shasti asked. She'd brought a cup of coffee in with her as she entered the temporary HQ.

"Not quite yet," Paolo answered from a desk. Shasti looked beyond him at the prone figure of Eris lying asleep in a cot nearby.

Paolo caught her look. "She's been very depressed. The fight brought it back to the fore, especially that Engineered soldier getting shot right next to her. I've been trying to spend as much time with her as I can."

"Good for you," Shasti said, fighting a feeling of surprise.

As if divining her thoughts, Paolo smiled ruefully. "Surprised?"

"A little," Shasti returned. "You?"

"A little." He laughed.

"Why don't we take it into the next room," Shasti gestured, "so we don't wake her."

The door to the next room bore a sign saying, "Under New Management."

Paolo grimaced. "Mmok's sense of humor, he's a devoted graffiti-ologist."

"Yes," Shasti said, "he's defaced objects from here back to Old Earth."

They found Mmok and Vaughn paying court to D'abo, who wore her usual faintly scandalous half cape/swimsuit outfit. They stood around a table covered with paper charts and readouts.

"Any luck?" Shasti asked again.

"No," Mmok said, "though your arrival is timely. Paolo, we are looking at a translated Skurlock term in a communiqué that the Evolvers intercepted and stored. It was a Ribisi message about a series of disastrous battles. They were pinning their hopes on a new Skurlock super weapon."

"Any indication of where the super weapon was or what it was?" he asked, scratching his head.

"Only one," Mmok said. He touched a screen, and a series of characters that meant nothing to Shasti scrolled across it. "That's the term, Paolo. What do you make of it?"

"It's a long term," he said, brow furrowed in concentration. "It refers to a place where time ends, where the stars become strange."

D'abo's tail lashed about. "That could be anywhere: a nebula, or a ringed star."

"Where time ends," Shasti said. "Remember when I told you about my vision. The creature Fushol said something like that. 'Where time ends…' Anything else?" Shasti demanded.

Paolo rubbed his face. "Those last three characters could be interpreted as the 'special star.' But there is a modifier on it that I do not recognize, and I am not sure that's exactly the right translation. It looks like the word for subterranean."

"The Subterranean Star," Vaughn said. "It sounds like a bad Tri-V title."

"All we have are a place where time ends, where the stars look strange, and a reference to something subterranean. Something buried," Shasti summed up.

"Yes," Paolo said, "but some of that may be a metaphor or a simile. We shouldn't let our thinking get too literal. Remember how figurative our own native tongues are."

"A good point," D'abo acknowledged. "Subterranean bothers me as a reference to stars. Could it be something else?"

"Easily." Paolo shrugged. "The literal translation is, 'hidden from view below.'"

"Hidden?" D'abo said, one ear twitching.

"Stars are hidden in nebula, clouds of gas," Vaughn offered.

"Yes, but the effect of time is no different there," D'abo said.

"A star hidden in a nebula," Shasti said. A hidden star. Something was tickling her memory. How could a star be hidden?

"Of course," Shasti said, snapping her fingers. Everyone turned to her expectantly. Shasti leaned back against the wall, crossing her arms in triumph, a broad smile across her face.

"Well, well?" Paolo said nearly hopping from foot to foot.

"You can hide a star in a nebula," Shasti said almost lazily, "but it does not alter time, nor do the stars end, or look particularly strange near it. There is one place where stars end, where they look strange, where time is altered, and the star below is hidden from view." She looked expectantly at D'abo.

The catgirl did not disappoint. She leapt to her feet. "Yes," she shouted, "a hidden star, a singularity. A star is hidden in a black hole."

"Indeed." Vaughn smiled. "The original star is hidden below the event horizon. Time slows as you near that horizon. The stars around would be drawn into lines of red-shifted light. Any star drawn into the singularity is drawn into the accretion disk and torn apart."

"So we need to locate a black hole in the Skurlock records. There we should find the Skurlock's Redoubt," Mmok said.

"Back to the databases," Paolo said. "With this, we have a good chance."

"There's got to be info in the Evolver memory core on local navigation," Mmok said. "There must be something on singularities." The machine man and philologist headed out shoulder to shoulder, tossing ideas back and forth.

In hours, they had the answer. Paolo and Mmok burst back in the middle of lunch. "We've got it," they chorused.

Shasti, who'd been sitting with D'abo, put down the bowl of soup she held. "Tell me."

"Paolo was able to isolate all references to hidden stars, which, as you suspected, was the Skurlock expression for singularities," Mmok said.

"I'm embarrassed I didn't see it before," Paolo said. "I had forgotten that it was the same expression in an old Terran language called French. Mmok cross-referenced my information with what was in the Evolver's combat records. We came up with a good match, a singularity forty-three lights from here in Old Skurlock space. The Evolver records for the boarding party left here are five hundred years out of date, but when they were sent here, the Evolvers had just started fighting in that area and had taken heavier losses there than anywhere else in the whole campaign."

"Sounds like a new super-weapon to me," Mmok said triumphantly.

"There's a lot of supposition in that," Paolo said, with a warning glance at Mmok.

Shasti gave a rueful laugh. "We have been running on visions, hunches, and wild-ass guesses since we got to this sector of space. We might as well be consistent."

D'abo stood. "I'll work with Nav to turn this into a course, but forty-three light years is a long jump in an unsupplied sector. I think in universal time that will put us out of normal time space for at least six months. It terrifies me to think what will happen in home space while I am gone."

Mmok shrugged, a gesture still incongruous with his mechanical body. "No point in returning without more help. Our one ship can't make that much difference even if she is way more powerful than yours."

"True," she sighed.

"Talk to Dobera as well," Shasti said. "See if he thinks there is anything more we can scavenge on the station. This may be the last filling station for a long while."

"Oh, on that," Mmok said. "We are seeing more and more of the station AI's altered workbots. Now that they are free of fighting the Evolver boarding party, they have been tooling around and repairing the methane parts of the station. No overt hostility yet, but they are showing up more in the O2 sections now. There was a standoff between two of my crab robots and ten modified cleaners. After about twenty minutes, they moved off. The crabs could have torn them to shreds with little risk, so I'm guessing that it's the station AI's way of making it clear that our long-term occupation is unwelcome."

Shasti frowned. "Maintain full security and make sure no one goes beyond our area. Let's accelerate preparations to get off the station. I don't want to risk any more people. Unless Dobera has some desperate need, I want to pull off the station by 0900 tomorrow. We can complete our course work out in space."

"Yes," D'abo said. "We must finish the funeral arrangements for our four dead."

"That, too, we will do in space," Shasti said. Though she dreaded having to conduct a service, she was determined no longer to hide behind Rigg in such matters. Part of becoming fully human was to embrace both the pain and the pleasure of a standard human's life. She'd completed the letters in a long sleepless night, though she asked Rigg to read them over. She'd thought of Vaughn, but though his life had been more normal than hers, his insight into standard humans was little better.

"Meanwhile, Mmok," she finished, "see if you can make it clear to the AI that we are leaving. Also make it clear that it would be unfortunate if it tried to shove us off before we are ready to go. If I lose another life on this station, I'll put a nuke into it by way of goodbye."

"Understood," he said.

Whether through Mmok's machinations or the AI's good sense, they were unmolested as they withdrew to *Sidhe* the next morning. D'abo had hard docked the ship with boarding tubes. The shuttles were already aboard, and the fighters circled protectively. The Confed spacers, weighed down, despite Rask's best efforts, with souvenirs and goods looted from the station, withdrew aboard. Then in came the screen of troops, having removed the barrier wire and obstacles. Finally, Mmok and his robots appeared at the entrances to the space-dock where *Sidhe* lay.

Shasti and D'abo stood at the main dock, with Vaughn, Rigg, and Rask, all toting heavy assault rifles. They watched as Mmok's crabs, many still burned and dented, came out of the side passages. With them, wearing Confed battle-dress, came Mmok, looking over his shoulder, literally, as the HCR body allowed him to entirely swivel his head. The machines tapped their way onto *Sidhe's* deck.

"Look," Mmok said, gesturing with the hand that did not hold his heavy particle weapon.

In the distance, a motley band of machines came out of the same passages that the crab-robots vacated. They came slowly, as if trying to signal a peaceful intent. Some were obviously workbots, sweepers, cleaners, and other such auxiliaries; others had a more militant look to them and carried tubes or implements obviously for banging and rendering other machines into scrap.

"Looks like the mob of villagers from an old movie," Mmok said. "All they need are some pitchforks and torches."

"Hostile?" Shasti said. Vaughn and the others were in cover behind a returned crab robot or at the side of the five-meter-wide hatchway.

"No," Mmok said. "They just followed us back as if to say, 'Nice to see you, we'll take it from here.'"

"They can have it," Vaughn growled.

"Ma'am," Rask called. "Can I respectfully request you get your ass behind something?"

Shasti joined Vaughn behind a crab robot, leaning on it, her arms under her chin as she watched the AI's machines stop a distance away. Shasti turned to D'abo. "Seal for space and prepare to move off. I'll take care of this hatch."

The lithe catgirl gave the machines a dubious look and headed for the bridge. The rest stood alert and watched as the other entrances closed and umbilicals separated.

One tall unit that looked something like a heavily modified restaurant auto-server caught Shasti's eye. It held a large display screen on its chest. As she looked, the screen glowed a pleasant green color.

"The color of growing things," Shasti said, "the safe color for a critter that evolved under a yellow sun."

"A thank you?" Vaughn said, bemused.

Mmok shrugged. "Mebbe."

Shasti rose from cover and waved once. The machine stood still for a few seconds then slowly blinked its green screen.

"Goodbye for now," Shasti said. "Okay, Rask. Seal the door. Let's get going."

Sidhe kicked free of the station and its curious mob of machines. Her course took her in a dive past the Hanghoul's blue mass for two reasons: the free acceleration of her gravity and the less happy duty that awaited Shasti.

The shuttle deck was full of *Sidhe's* complement. Everyone who did not have an immediate duty lined the bay. There was no talking as Shasti and her command staff walked in to face the four spacetight shells holding the remains of their four dead. Shasti did not know any of them well. They were names on a roster, faces that she had seen, but held no emotional resonance for her. But they had friends aboard. Several of the wounded were openly choked up; one was crying. All the wounded, even Fernol, the severely injured Engineered soldier rescued by Eris, stood there. The small alien was present, as usual in Paolo's company, but her face looked haggard and her eyes more haunted than usual. Paolo didn't look up as they entered. He was watching Eris and his face held a worried expression.

If he doesn't watch out, he will find himself seriously in love, Shasti thought.

Shasti stopped before the lectern someone had set up on a dais. In her hands was a small book. Three years ago, Robert had pressed it in her hands on the day he signed over the ship. "I'll pray you never need it," he'd said, "but I fear that will not be the case."

She'd remembered that conversation the night before, while writing the letters to the families of the deceased. She'd paused to sit with Risky and pet the dog, something that always comforted her, when the memory surfaced unbidden. A few minutes search through her cabin turned up the small, well-worn book. To her utter surprise, when she riffled its pages, she found a letter in it from Robert.

Shasti opened the envelope quickly and carefully, as if it were both urgent and precious. In it, she found these words.

Hello, my love. I hope I can still call you that.

Though I have had my heart's desire returned to me through your efforts, never think that the love that I had for you will ever dim. It must just find another expression.

I am so proud of you, Shasti. For how far you have come through such fire and torment. Now you are out in the galaxy, and what you will make of it, no one can know.

Perhaps you have found this letter because the day I feared has come and you have lost people. Now you must stand in the place that I did and speak to the survivors and say something that sums up the lives lost, that somehow justifies that appalling sacrifice.

Do you remember that horrible night on Enshar? The night we lost so many to the Shellycoats? The night of our own terrible fight? In the morning our crew lined up around that hole where so many bodies were placed and looked to me. Never before or since in my life have I felt so utterly inadequate, so unable to make sense of it all. I wanted to scream at everyone that it didn't make sense. To tell them that their captain had no more idea of where God's love goes in the moments before violent death than did they. But of course I could not do that to them. Somehow the words of this passage filled the empty space in my mind and soul. Maybe you will find other words, but these served me that day. May they serve you too.

Love,

Robert.

She'd knelt beside the big German Shepherd, buried her face in his fur, and cried for ten minutes. Risky sat with her, his chin on her shoulder, whining occasionally but not moving.

Now, she stood ramrod straight before her own crew, in a dress uniform of black and green and, remembering another terrible day, opened the book and read. "Man that is born of woman has but a short time to live…"

25

This is the worst jump in I've ever felt, Shasti thought, fighting the barrage of discordant scents and colors that greeted her on *Sidhe's* emergence. She clung to her command chair and waited for her vision to clear. Moans and retching sounds let her know she was not alone in her misery. A quick dose of biofeedback restored enough of her sense of order for images to begin to make sense to her outraged eyes.

On the bridge screen ahead of her lay the accretion disk of the black hole they had come so far to find. It glowed softly like a child's pinwheel. The distances were so great that the material seemed to be moving very slowly, though nearer the event horizon, the dust and gas raced around the singularity at tens of thousands of kilometers per second.

Shasti tore her eyes from the screen to focus on her crew. Nye, the helmsman, looked back at her with a weak grin. Tanges vomited into a jump bag, then slumped on his board. Others lay in their seats, groaning.

Shasti felt a warm weight fall against her shoulder and grabbed D'abo before the catgirl could fall to the deck. She was shaking with emergence shock, and Shasti pulled her close.

"Ooohhhhh," D'abo moaned. "What a terrible scent. The colors are clawing at my eyes."

"Close them and concentrate on breathing," Shasti said. Feeling stronger, she slid out of her seat and helped D'abo into it, wincing a little. D'abo hung onto her like a frightened child, her claws reflexively sliding in and out of their sheaths.

"Sorry," D'abo said, visibly bracing up. "I'll be all right in a few seconds."

"Status," Shasti called. Then she flicked open the com line. "Medics to the bridge. It's been a rough jump."

Wardell answered first. The old gunner had been through thousands of jumps, but even he looked green this time. His assistant sprawled on the panel next to him, barely conscious. "No targets detected close aboard."

"Scan," Hafel added shakily, "is clear in mid to long range so far. Heavy interference is reducing scan range at least ten percent and effectiveness twenty percent."

One of the engineers opened a panel, releasing a small cleaning robot, which rolled out and began buzzing about the deck, cleaning up. The engineer handed fiber towels out for cleaning the instruments of those who'd missed using the jump bag.

The doors whooshed open. Eris and another medic walked out with two orderlies. Shasti did a double take on Eris, who she had not seen in the days since they left Hanghoul station. The Vikadian's skeletal thinness shocked Shasti, but Eris moved briskly enough. She gave a shot to Tanges, which brought the planetologist back to consciousness; the orderly helped him to the refresher off the bridge to clean up.

Eris quickly passed out drinks of restorative fluids, and people began to function again. The doors whooshed open and Mmok walked in with Vaughn. Mmok took a look about. "Glad I can't smell anything."

"You should be," Vaughn said, waving a hand in front of his nose.

Eris appeared at Shasti's elbow. She gratefully took the drink and quickly downed the bland fluid. D'abo did the same, but Eris was not satisfied and gave the tall catgirl an anti-nauseant pill.

"Are you all right?" Shasti asked the small alien, still disturbed by the Vikadian's gaunt appearance.

"The jump had little effect on me," she said in a monotone. "I was lucky from all the reports. Some of the wounded are particularly ill."

"Tanaka?" Vaughn demanded.

Eris hesitated. "Yes. Daniel is with her. It's not life-threatening, just very unpleasant."

Vaughn's eyes snapped up to Shasti's. She nodded. The big man quickly left the bridge.

Shasti opened the intercom circuit. "We have arrived at the black star system. Those of you who feel up to it should take a look out the viewports to starboard. It's spectacular. While there is no immediate threat, we will stand at yellow alert. We don't know what we are to find: another station, a planet, maybe a fleet of ships. So stay alert.

"All damage control teams assist maintenance crews in clean up. Anyone who was sick can change clothes. Let's get cleaned up, people."

D'abo stood shakily and looked about. "I'll make an inspection tour and report back."

"You up to it?" Shasti asked.

"Better every second," D'abo answered with an embarrassed air.

Eris and her staff headed for the turbo.

Shasti took D'abo's arm. "I don't like how Eris looks. I think she's been avoiding Mourner. Have the doc check her out. I don't want a suicide on my hands."

D'abo nodded and caught up to Eris before the doors closed.

Tanges came up the gangway at the rear in a fresh uniform. "Reporting back, ma'am."

She nodded. "Get with Scan and Nav. We're here, but no wiser yet. There has to be something out here."

"Yes, Captain."

For lack of a better course, Shasti headed *Sidhe* in toward the black hole. Tanges and Scan studied the various sensor and probe reports. Paolo stood by in case they contacted something.

"I'm confused, Captain," Tanges said, hours later. He straightened up from his bridge instruments and massaged his lower back. "I know that there's a lot we still don't know about singularities, but this one is odd. I simply cannot account for the variations in gravity in this section of space."

"Nor can I," Hafel added. "Gravity forces are fluctuating enough to give a physicist a nervous breakdown. It's been giving Helm a bit of fit too. He has to add a constant ten percent differential for course. It's like there's some mass out there that we don't see. It doesn't vary but it shouldn't be there. Helm says it's like having an invisible retrorocket on the ship. The distortion on long-distance sensors is getting worse too."

"Any sign of planets or stations?" Paolo asked, looking at the scan displays over their heads.

"No," Tanges said, "but you wouldn't expect any near a black hole. The very process of creating a singularity usually eliminates any planetary bodies first. At most you'd find fragments in the accretion disk."

D'abo came up behind Shasti. "A rogue planet?" she asked.

Tanges shrugged. "Planetary captures are rare but possible. An inward-moving body going into this system wouldn't achieve a stable orbit. It would be drawn in."

"So no planets and no space stations to orbit them," Shasti mused.

"You might have been right," D'abo said. "We may be looking for a fleet of ships."

The panel near Hafel chimed and a red light appeared. She quickly turned to it, relaying the contact to all boards. "Ship contact," she said. "Amplifying."

An image appeared simultaneously on a dozen screens over the spade-shaped bridge. It was merely a silhouette, a gray image outlined by the computer in white.

"Oh my God," Wardell exclaimed. "That's a silhouette I never thought to see again."

"Specify," Shasti snapped.

"Yes," said Wardell, his voice firming. "That's a Conchirri heavy cruiser of the *Fultok* Class. I see a few oddities in the superstructure, but it's Conchirri."

Shasti rounded on Nye. "Maximum burn on engines, come right 90 degrees. All ahead emergency."

"Ninety turn. All ahead emergency, aye," he replied, hands flying over the boards. The artificial gravity systems didn't quite eliminate the entire sudden load. People grabbed for handholds as the AG system struggled with the surplus.

"Sound General Quarters," Shasti ordered. The alarm began to shrill.

"Can we outrun them?" D'abo asked.

"*Fultoks* are fleet escorts," Shasti said. "We have the same top speed, but they mass so much more that we will out accelerate them and open the distance. If we get out far enough, we may be able to break contact."

"Problem is," said Vaughn, who had returned to the bridge unnoticed, "that it carries a better sensor rig than we do and more fuel onboard. We will accelerate faster, but he can do that longer. Eventually he will close on us." If the fact that a major enemy warship was only light minutes behind them bothered him at all, it didn't show.

"Can you pick up a visual on it?" Shasti demanded, thinking of the golden dartship nestled below *Sidhe's* hull. "It may give us a clue as to whether it's crewed by Conchirri or Evolvers."

"Won't matter to us if it's crewed by Conchirri or Evolvers if it catches up to us," Mmok said. "He'll outgun us five to one."

"Maybe another form of camouflage will work," D'abo said. "The holo trick worked on the Evolver we fought in Kandalor system."

"Not so simple," Mmok answered, with a hint of disdain. "They saw us before we had time to prepare. If our scanner image changes now, they'll know it's a fake. We don't have whatever IFF is current for the bad guys. Besides, a certain person's boyfriend painted the ship a brilliant crimson. Not exactly Conchirri standard."

"It still might work," D'abo insisted. "Think. That ship doesn't have our IFF either. They might think we are from a long-lost branch of the Conchirri. And we have the only known Conchirri speaker in all known space aboard."

Paolo shook his head. "I'll try, but we don't even know if that ship has Conchirri aboard, Evolver drones, or some other species that they made over. We might fool a drone again, but I'll never fool a native speaker into thinking my speech came from the voicebox of a two-meter lizard."

"Captain," said Nye, "navigation sensors are picking up gravity disturbances. I'm putting them on screen." Images coalesced in grids of blue and green and formed a shape obvious to anyone who had ever flown space. "Uncharted singularity ahead," Nye added.

"What?" D'abo said. "But we are tens of millions of miles short of the accretion disk. How can there be another black hole out here? Why doesn't it have an accretion disk of its own?"

"Who knows?" Shasti snapped. "Maybe it formed recently. But it gives us another chance. Mr. Nye, how are you at maneuvering in a big gravity well?"

"Gives me the dry heaves, Captain," Nye replied, "in addition to violating the manufacturer's warranty."

"No problem there," Mmok chimed in, "the manufacturer's rep is just twenty light minutes behind us."

Shasti looked at him.

"Hey," said Mmok, "I'm very sensitive to warranty issues these days."

"Hmph," Shasti said. "Mr. Nye, like it or not, we will be handier in a gravity well than a heavy cruiser. Best plot to take us in toward that new singularity. It will be your job to see we don't get too close."

Shasti found Vaughn at her elbow.

"The cruiser may not be so handy," he said softly, "but they have more powerful engines. They will allow them to go closer to the singularity."

Shasti shrugged. "Only marginally, against an event horizon's pull, all ship drives are inadequate. Besides, what choice do we have?"

"Bad news, Captain," Wardell called. "Plot shows the enemy cruiser turning. With light speed delay, that means he did it ten minutes ago. My guess is he went to full burn as soon as he detected us. I'll correct for best estimate of his relative position."

"Be nice if it was easy for once," Shasti murmured.

"Has it ever been?" Vaughn asked.

She shook her head.

"Captain," called Susan Bernard, "we have a composite visual on the Conchirri vessel. Computer is filling in the last data off the microwave and radar systems now."

"Let's see what's chasing us," Shasti said.

The main screen flickered as the view switched back to the *Fultok*. Its sinister shape, bulbous and spiky, like some over-muscled arachnid, began to fill in with colors and details. The designation, *Fultok*, appeared on the screen, and data on the type scrolled out next to the name detailing a terrifyingly large weapon array.

"Must have been a special on gold paint in Evolverville," Mmok drawled, "though they did alternate with some bands of black, very pretty."

"Confirmed," Wardell said, his lips pressed thin. "Those aren't standard Conchirri colors."

"There's a lot of distortion from the singularity...singularities," D'abo said. "If we roll a pattern of proximity mines, max dispersion, he may hit one. At the least, if he detects it, he'll alter course and we can open the range."

"Good thinking," Shasti said. She turned to her gunnery team.

"What the hell?" Wardell and Hafel said simultaneously.

"Captain, look," Nye cried, his eyes gone wide.

Shasti whirled back to face the big screen.

The enemy cruiser crumpled before their eyes. Its gold hull twisted and deformed like a beer can being crushed. A flare of light escaped but only for a second, seemingly sucked back into the diminishing mass of the cruiser. Then it was gone, as if it never existed.

"Ca-captain," Hafel stammered. "He's gone. Completely gone. I'm not getting any return of signal on any system. No wreckage, no vented atmosphere, he's totally gone."

"Helm, get us out of here," Shasti ordered. "Random vector away."

"Captain," he responded after a few seconds. "No can do. I've got engines on full. We're being pulled."

"Into the singularity?" D'abo asked.

"No, sir," he responded. "Just dead ahead."

"Divert all sensors on that track," Shasti ordered. "How long until the original signal returns at that distance?"

"Over an hour, Captain," Hafel responded, "assuming something's there."

"Oh, something is there," D'abo said. "Something is most definitely there."

The chronometer on the bulkhead took a maddening time to reach the hour. As the last seconds slid by, everyone turned back to the screen. Suddenly something was indeed there, and the bridge was filled with a stunned silence. As if a curtain had been drawn, a star appeared in front of them: a yellow orange star, only two astronomical units away.

"The Hidden Star," Shasti breathed in shock, "literally, a hidden star."

"How?" D'abo said. "How?"

They looked at the planetologist, but he simply stared open-mouthed at the screen.

A jet of material from the Hidden Star tailed out in the direction of the black hole, thinning to invisible after several astronomical units. It glowed with such violence it should have been visible over light years, even to the naked eye.

Tanges finally found his voice. "I'd wondered where all the material for the accretion disk came from. It's a binary star, or was before one part of it imploded into a black hole. It explains the gravity fluctuations. There was a whole star system here and we couldn't see it."

"But how is it that the star is hidden?" D'abo exclaimed.

Shasti was not sure of the source of her certainty, but she somehow knew. "I think we have found the Skurlock Redoubt. I think that somehow the Skurlock have found a way to manipulate and project the gravity fields of a singularity."

D'abo's huge eyes grew even larger with shock.

"Oh, my God," Mmok said. "Oh, my God. I can see some of the math. Not enough to know how. Not enough to be sure, but if you could project a gravity field, you could do all this. Bend light rays on a cosmic scale, tow starships—"

"And crumple them like paper," Vaughn added dryly. "If this is true, then it is no wonder that neither the Conchirri nor the Evolvers could carry this system."

They did not need Tanges' services to find the planet they were being pulled toward. It lay one astronomical unit away from the G-5 star, and *Sidhe* was drawn to it as if shot from a bow.

"We are being pulled into a geosynchronous orbit over the planet's equator," Nye reported. The usually imperturbable Vietnamese was showing the strain of having something dragging *Sidhe*. His hands hovered over the instruments like a frustrated pianist longing to begin a piece.

"No return on any of our messages," Hafel added. "I don't know if they are hearing us or not. Continuing to broadcast in Ribisi, Nekoan, and Skurlockian."

"Weapons," Shasti called. "Stand ready but passive locks only. I don't want to frighten the ship-crushers."

"Yes, ma'am," Wardell returned.

Vaughn and D'abo stood near Shasti as they watched the world grow in their screens. It was more earthlike than any other world they had yet seen, though the polar icecaps seemed far larger.

"Looks like a blue and white marble I had as a child," Vaughn said, "my favorite shooter."

Shasti gave him a curious glance, finding it hard to imagine the huge man playing as a child, shooting marbles. She wondered for a second if Tanaka had watched him doing it.

"Looks cold," D'abo said, her mane roughing up as if an icy wind were already blowing on her.

Shasti gave her a first officer an amused look. As usual, D'abo wore the minimum amount of clothing decency required.

"It's not so bad," Tanges said. "The orbit we were given puts us over a temperate zone. From what I can see of the planet, we have arrived in high summer."

Shasti waited for Mmok to make some reference to the evidently frozen hell that was his native Canada, but the HCR had not spoken since the stunning revelation of the hidden star. Either he was still busy trying to figure out the math or simply in awe.

"So long as we leave before winter," D'abo grumbled, her tail lashing as she stared at the blue world.

If we leave, Shasti thought.

"Shasti," Vaughn said. "Why not try to reach out to this Fushol? If this is the place, then he should know we are friends."

"Worth a try," D'abo said.

Shasti nodded and without standing from her command chair reached up with her hands and lowered her head, fighting off a feeling of looking ridiculous.

Snap. The connection was instantaneous and powerful. She gasped at the sharpness of it.

A wave of joyfulness reached her. *You are here,* Fushol sent. *Why have you not responded before this? We feared the Evolver ship had done some evil to you before it came into our range.*

We are unharmed, Shasti returned in confusion. *And we have been broadcasting in all the languages we know hoping to hear from you.*

Mechanical means? Fushol returned. *You use machines for this?*

Yes, Shasti sent.

Yet you mind speak to me?

I am unusual among my people in having this ability, and in truth, I have little understanding of it. We do not speak to each other this way normally but use modulated sound in person or in projection.

We do this as well, Fushol said, *though the ability to mindspeak is common among us. I am the strongest, designated the Farseeker. It has been my mission to reach out to the heavens to summon help. In truth, I never believed it would happen. Never thought I would touch anything but the cold mechanical enmity of the Evolver fleet that blockades our system.*

We come in friendship, Shasti sent. *Representing many species who have opposed the Conchirri and will oppose the Evolvers. We wish to meet you.*

Easily arranged, Fushol returned.

The universe around Shasti turned a deep violet and then seemed to invert. She heard a sharp cry that faded quickly as if into the distance. Shasti felt her body float upward and dissolve.

26

With a rush of indrawn breath, Shasti found herself standing in a vast, dimly lit amphitheater. She swayed with the shock of it. Dream? Illusion? Projection?

Something seized her arm, and her fist snapped up. But it was only D'abo. Her first officer looked at her, ears up, tail rigid, and the rough of her hair raised.

"What? What happened?" D'abo demanded. "Where are we?"

The pinpricks of her friend's claws through the sleeve of her coverall convinced Shasti this was not an illusion.

Do not be afraid. I am Fushol.

Both females spun to face the creature that addressed them. It stood three meters away, looking up at them with compound eyes. Fushol appeared as Shasti had seen him on Kandalor and Hanghoul Station. Only this time, it was not a will o' the wisp apt to vanish. The creature stood over a meter tall, giving the impression of a huge beetle, upright on four rear legs and with two arms. One arm ended in an overdeveloped pincer. The other looked like a human hand covered in a chitinous yellow. The reflective chitin was not an exoskeleton but merely a surface over bone and flesh. The face held

356

compound eyes and a humanish mouth filled with rows of disturbingly sharp teeth.

The alien wore a robe and a cape of white material trimmed in red over the tool belt Shasti had seen before. Its skin reflected jewel tones of gold, brass, and a deep purple. A sense of benevolence and peace rolled from the creature. Shasti realized it was projecting to calm them.

Shasti looked about. The echoing chamber could have held many thousands, but only hundreds filled it. Still the metallic, almost astringent smell of the aliens filled the air and made Shasti fight a sneeze. D'abo's nose wrinkled, and Shasti knew the Nekoan was struggling with the smell as well. Shasti remembered the near phobia Robert Fenaday had for insects. *Guess it's a good thing he isn't here now,* she thought.

Ah, what grave stupidity by me, Fushol said. *I brought you here in response to your wish but foolishly did not prepare you. I have alarmed you and doubtless your vessel.* It turned and shot out a stream of buzzing and clacking sounds in its own language. *We are modulating one of our machines so you may voice transmit to your ship. It is an old machine we use little, but it should work. Give us a few minutes.*

Meanwhile, I beg you both to forgive me. I am so overwhelmed by your presence that it has made me stupid. When you said you wished to meet, like a child on holiday unable to hold back from opening presents, I ordered our teleports to bring you. We could only bring two over an orbital distance. So I took you and the person standing closest. Fushol gestured with his larger pincer toward a mass of similar creatures clothed in a dull gray, which sat utterly still, filling ten rows of the immense amphitheater.

Fushol made a bowing gesture. *Again, I must apologize for my stupidity. I would return you instantly, but it will be several hours before the teleports can again reach such a distance.*

"Well, we are here," Shasti said, as D'abo let go of her arm. "And while we wait for your engineers to contact our ship, an endeavor in which I urge all haste as our comrades doubtless fear for our safety, we should talk."

Fushol seemed agitated, its claw and hand-pincers clacking rhythmically. *Is there another aboard with your gift who we might reach out to while the techs prepare our machine? Do you have some portable mechanical means of communicating?*

"Not on us," D'abo said sharply, reproof evident in her voice. "We did not expect to leave our ship."

"Wait," Shasti said. "Are you delving into my mind or D'abo's?"

No, Fushol assured her. *I receive what you project and indeed to me it feels as if you are shouting, pushing your thoughts at me. Your mind is too alien to penetrate far without your active help. The tailed female is opaque to me. I feel her presence and her gender. She hears my projected thoughts, but I cannot sense hers.*

"Fortunate, Fushol," D'abo growled, tail-lashing.

"Quiet," Shasti whispered, "and remember you're a diplomat too."

"We have another who has some of the same talent," Shasti said as she shaped a mental picture of Vaughn, huge, dark, his eyes glowing with interest or ferocity at need. "Can you reach him?"

Fushol's head bent, and he seemed to jump. *Yes,* he sent. *His mind is powerful but violent, disciplined, but almost unaware of its talent. I am sending to him. He is suspicious and thinks of weapons and attack.*

Shasti believed Fushol's protestations of innocent misunderstanding. A devious enemy would have concealed teleportation until they were sure it might not be in their interest to transport bombs or troops aboard *Sidhe. If I know Vaughn,* she thought, *he's arming every crewman and posting guards in all spaces.*

"Tell him Stormcloud and Lynx are fine. Tell him to do nothing until he hears from me. He will accept this message," Shasti said. The code-names were the best assurance Shasti could send that the message was genuine.

It is done, Fushol replied, weariness evident in his mental tone. *He is calmed by your words.*

While we await the work of the technicians, Fushol continued, *let me introduce you to our leader, Istal the 23rd, Chief Scientist-General.* Again, he gestured, but this time in a series of circular motions that hinted of ceremony, to a group of Skurlock clad mostly in red and blue raiment. One, wearing only black, appearing older or perhaps crippled, limped closer to her, mounting a small dais that faced the spacers.

Greetings, Captain Rainhell. Its mental voice possessed a scratchy quality. It also spoke aloud, but the chitinous whirring meant nothing to her. *Do not fear. Fushol has satisfied us that you are not of our enemies, albeit we have never seen your kind or kinds before. We mean you no harm and indeed your coming may bring a new hope to what little is left of our species.*

"So you are also enemies of the Conchirri and the Makers?" D'abo asked.

There was a slight delay as Fushol picked meaning from Shasti's brain and sent it to the Scientist-General.

For a hundred cycles of our sun after we encountered the Makers, we had been safe from their attack. Our psychic powers gave us an edge over superior alien ships. Skurlock mind-masters confused the Makers and their AIs, causing them to fire on their own or crash.

Then came something new: the Makers had created the Conchirri, creatures with minds of ungovernable ferocity, forged with a hatred of all things alien and a genetic imperative to migrate through the stars. The Makers bred and armed millions of them and expended them in similar numbers. They were not so easily confused as the Makers, as they focused on killing at an instinctive level.

Our defense began to fall under the terror of the Conchirri. Our colonies were overrun and eaten. Finally came the assault on the homeworld and again something new. The Makers themselves took the field in huge, new golden ships. Using the Evolver technology, they suborned our people to where we could not recognize them. Thus, our homeworld fell. Fortunately, they were not able to use our psychic power after the change. Perhaps the Makers' DNA was too strong and they were unable to refine what they took from us.

Shortly after they destroyed our homeworld, conflict broke out among Conchirri and the Makers. The Makers withdrew. The Conchirri remained, wiping out our last footholds until only this station remained.

Our greatest scientists came here to develop a weapon in sheer desperation, a weapon using the gravimetric power of a singularity to power it. Such a thing could only be tested near a star with no life, and this black hole proved ideal. We made the gravity lens, succeeding and failing in part. The lens works, but only the titanic forces of the event horizon of a black hole can power the weapon. We could not move it to our own sun or protect our homeworld.

The Conchirri came to us, flocking like a pestilence. It gave us a last bittersweet victory as we fed them to the gravity lens. Ah, the slaughter we wrought among them. The gravity weapon ate the distress calls of those killed so they could not warn the followers. In the end, even their ungovernable ferocity was daunted and they turned aside.

Since then, we few have maintained the weapon as a sacred trust. While the Makers never returned, their machines, the Evolvers did, hundreds of years later. The Evolvers have blockaded our system, waiting with the tenacity of the machine for some weakness. We live only for the hope of using the weapon on them, their Makers, or the Conchirri.

"And have you?" Shasti asked, dazed by the tale.

Not for fifty cycles and more, said the alien, rich overtones of grief in its mental voice, *until you brought one of their ships within range to be destroyed. It is fortunate that Fushol was able to reach out and touch your minds. Else we would have used the weapon on you. How came you by a ship of our enemies?*

"The Conchirri pressed on after destroying your world," Shasti said. "On our voyage we have discovered that they annihilated two other species before they reached our space. About fifteen hundred years after they struck you, the Conchirri attacked the Confederacy of Seven Species. This time they bit off more than they could chew, and we fought them to their extinction."

Waves of joy and savage satisfaction beat into Shasti's mind, catching her off guard.

You bring the greatest of news, Istal cried in her mind. *Oh, great day that I have lived to see it. Tell us, tell us all. Tell us how they suffered; tell us how they met the ultimate darkness in despair.*

Shasti related a brief history of how the Conchirri had unexpectedly struck the Confederacy in their ferocious millions, almost exterminating the Okarans and how the human-led Confederacy annihilated them in return.

Fushol interrupted Shasti as she told them of the first attack by the Evolver ship on Confederate space. *We have reached your ship. Our translating technology has sufficed to establish contact but little more. Simply speak aloud. They will hear.*

"Stormcloud to Canuck and Cossack," Shasti called.

"Stormcloud," Vaughn's deep voice rumbled through the chamber. "Are you all right?"

"Affirmative, as is D'abo. Fushol misinterpreted my request for a meeting as immediate and of course we had no idea that they could teleport."

"Request that he not do so again," Vaughn growled. "Shall I send a landing force?"

"Prepare a single shuttle with an honor guard under Rigg and Rask," Shasti said, "to pick us up. Get Paolo working with their people on integrating our translators. Some of them can mindspeak but only to certain of us."

"He will be delighted, another alien language, complete with live speakers. I will have to chain him to the bridge or he'll sneak onto the shuttle."

"He'll get his chance," Shasti said. "You've set defense condition four?" It didn't pay to trust too much to Fushol's explanations.

"In all spaces," he replied, sounding miffed that she felt she needed to ask.

"Excellent," Shasti said. "We will carry on here and check in every four hours until the shuttle lands."

"Affirmative."

Fushol came forward. *The counsel wishes to meet. In the meantime, I am to give you a tour of our settlement. Your trip has brought great fortune. I feel that we have met at the turning of the tide. The Evolvers have claimed this area of space and laid waste to all that the Conchirri did not already destroy. But with your mighty Confederacy and the surviving races of this sector, we may yet reclaim our stars.*

Come with me. I shall show the weapon we will put at the disposal of our allies. Fushol turned and headed up the stairs of the amphitheater.

Shasti followed, as did D'abo after a moment's hesitation. In a minute, they found themselves out in the bright sunshine of a cool day. The orange-yellow star rode high in the sky and shed a gentle light over the Skurlock settlement. Very ordinary-looking, three and five-story rectangular buildings of yellow and white stone, stretched away below them. After the close and tainted air of the amphitheater, the air outside smelled like a fine wine. Almost too much so, and Shasti wondered if the oxygen content might be higher than she was used to.

They'd stood on a mountainside over a valley where a goodly-sized population lived. Cars and aircars dotted the sky and roads in a scene of surprising domesticity. Yet Shasti noted that this was more of a large town or small city than the capital she expected. She remembered how empty the amphitheater had been.

This is Kreenauk, Fushol said, waving a pincer. *The last stand of the Skurlock, at least so far as we know. Come this way. I will show a beautiful view.*

Fushol led them to a small aircar. A Skurlock driver stood by the vehicle. Curiously, he showed no interest in Shasti or D'abo, as if tall aliens were a daily occurrence. They managed to wedge themselves in the too-small seats.

Something of Shasti's reaction must have made its way to Fushol.

Pay no attention, Fushol sent. *It is merely a drone. Much of our species is only semi-sentient and fills basic functions. Curiosity is not part of their make-up.*

The flight was short and nearly straight up the looming mountain. They landed on a weather station atop the peak. A stiff wind greeted them as they walked around the railed platform to face the other side of the mountain. The mountaintop seemed honeycombed with bunkers and science stations.

As they walked up from the landing pad, the ocean came into view, an infinity of gently rolling green waves, with no shore or vessels in sight. Fushol guided them to a railed overlook facing the ocean. They walked over packed dirt, which raised a faint dust, and a blue lichen, which felt springy underfoot. After so many weeks in space, it felt odd to be on anything other than an utterly flat deckplate. Shasti looked down to where the sea surged against the gray and white cliffs two hundred meters below. Small, hardy trees that reminded Shasti of a bonsai clung to those cliffs. The wind tried to disturb her hair, but by chance she had weighted and braided before the jump.

Shasti looked about, able to see both the ocean and the valley behind her. The Skurlock base sat by the sea, built into the reverse of mountainside, protected from storms and tsunamis. The Skurlock had built down from the massive cliff to sea level, and stone wharves lined with small fishing vessels jutted out into the sea.

Be lovely to paint this scene, Shasti thought, *if I can get the universe to stop trying to kill me long enough to set up an easel.*

"Are there other cities?" D'abo asked. She raised her face to the wind as if hunting for a scent. The wind ruffled through her leonine hair and caused her ears to twitch.

No, Fushol mind sent. *There is something in this world that is not healthful for my species. Our numbers decline, generation by generation, despite our best efforts. And in those that are born, there are mutations and defects. Some, like the drones we tap for telekinetic power, are useful. Many are not. Even those who are born whole and proper are lesser in stature than our ancestors. We have lost so much of the knowledge of our species, and we are slowly dying out. Our forebears were better engineers than life scientists and physicians, and this lack may spell our doom.*

"Radiation from the black hole tearing up your sun would be bad enough," Shasti mused. "God knows what other effects the black hole has. There are no inhabited worlds near them in our space, and it is dangerous to starjump so close. Our own emergence was not pleasant, and we were quite far out."

Indeed, Fushol replied.

D'abo gestured at the mountaintop installation. "Is this the weapon?"

No, Fushol returned, with a hint of amusement in his mental tone. *But we may gain entrance here. This installation services the weapon, as does most of our settlement.* He turned and stumped into the building behind them. Shasti and D'abo followed.

More Skurlock worked inside, and these were not drones. They skittered about and clacked furiously in their own language, seeming both excited and a little afraid of Shasti and D'abo.

Please understand, Fushol said. *While we are joyous at your arrival and hope that it means we can at last fully avenge ourselves on our adversaries, we have been besieged for many lifetimes. I shall conduct you to the weapon and you may see the non-classified region. It will be some time before we are able to share all that we still know with you.*

"Of course," Shasti said. "I'm a little surprised that you're taking us to see it."

Though as helpless as we are orbiting their world, they have little to fear from us, she thought.

Do not think us naïve, Fushol replied, *or totally dissolute. We sense that you and those who travel with you are favorably disposed to us. There are others who will not be. Our records tell us that our relations with the alien Ribisi were not always cordial.*

Suddenly he turned to Shasti. *Have you seen a Ribisan? We have no surviving records of what they look like.*

"Yes," Shasti said.

Concentrate, he said, *remember and perhaps I can see them.* The alien's tone crackled with excitement.

"D'abo is more familiar with them than I."

Yes, but while I can hear D'abo's mental voice, I can see nothing in her mind. She lacks your psychic ability.

Shasti concentrated, remembering the images of the Ribisi ambassador in his armored suit at the ceremony for *Sidhe's* launch.

Almost, Fushol said, with a tinge of disappointment. *Almost I see an image of a large, armored creature, like one of us but with a clear bowl on, well, I guess it is a head. Ah, it is gone.*

Fushol swayed. *I must be less reckless with my energy. Your minds are so different.*

But to finish what I was saying. We here are a dying race. If we are to survive, we will need help. We have only one thing to offer, an inviolable staging area for ships and forces. Under our protection you can strike. Under yours we may yet survive, may find others of our species huddled in the ruins of our old worlds.

They followed Fushol to what turned out to be an elevator. Doors whooshed closed, and a skittery voice made some demand. Fushol answered, and the machine dropped with more speed than Shasti was happy with.

They exited into a titanic underground tunnel, which gently sloped away from them. Ahead was what looked like a subway car. He sent the other Skurlocks nearby back into the second car, leaving the first one just for them. The cars rose with a sigh characteristic of a MagLev line, and they headed out into the tunnel.

"The air smells of the sea," D'abo said.

Your senses are acute, Fushol said. *We are heading out under the sea to where our mighty ancestors made the gravity lens.* Fushol gave a mental sigh. *It also means that there is again seepage into the tunnels. Drones and others labor ceaselessly to maintain these tunnels, but even with the best machinery that we still have, we can barely keep ahead of the work.*

The tunnels ran out under the ocean, massive things hundreds of meters wide and filled with cables and conduits. Shasti and D'abo looked in fascination at the other shuttle cars taking Skurlock out to the weapons station that controlled the gravity lens.

"Why all the ninety-degree turns?" D'abo wondered.

The weapon is dangerous at all times and more so if we must fire it in volleys, Fushol said. *Should disaster strike—*

"Of course," Shasti added, "if there is an explosion, the cutbacks would lessen the effect."

Yes, Fushol said. *But even the cutbacks would avail us little against the forces involved. At each turn our ancestors installed blast doors of adamantine metal, ten meters thick. Collectively, they might save the valley shelters.*

"That's why you built on the reverse slope of a mountain on a cliff coastline and in a valley," D'abo said. "Excellent blast protection."

A few minutes ride took them to another platform. As they exited, Shasti noted that while the station was both clean and neat, it was badly in need of painting and even the permacrete they walked on showed cracks. A single drone worked nearby, repairing a lighted sign.

Fushol led them to a window. Below them, stretching out for kilometers under ceiling-mounted lights and overhead trams, were hundreds of transformers and power units. Each machine was topped with a white globe that pulsed softly. They walked out to an overhead tram. Once outside, the noise of transformers humming, relays opening and closing, and power machinery running made speech impossible. The air was sharp with ozone and metallic smells of lubricants and hot machinery.

D'abo's hair rose from the static electricity in the air. Fushol looked at her curiously but did not comment.

They clambered aboard the small tram gratefully, once again having a car to themselves. The low roof of the car forced Shasti and D'abo to sit on the floor.

The tram doors shut out the roar, and they grabbed the seats as the tram smoothly accelerated.

These spaces were cut with shaped-charge fusion bombs, Fushol sent. *Then scrubbed of radiation by a method we have lost. We are many kilometers down, impervious to the most powerful spaceborne weapons, protected by both rock and ocean above us.*

The tram approached a huge, utilitarian block that dominated the center of the acres of power transformers. Doors cycled open, admitting them into an air-conditioned and mercifully quiet space. Armed Skurlocks guarding the station regarded them nervously, despite Fushol's presence. They passed the guards into an immense room that looked like the combat information center of a flagship. Overhead floated holos of the Hidden Star with its binary companion, the singularity, and its accretion disk, spinning like a pinwheel. Skurlocks, wearing the same white robes as Fushol, manned banks and banks of computers and consoles.

Several Skurlocks came over and Fushol spoke with them. They returned to their duties, though with what Shasti felt were dubious glances at the aliens in their command center. Fushol's chitinous feet tapped on the material of the floor as he returned to them.

Shasti turned to Fushol. "The uniforms." She pointed. "Are you one of the gunners for the weapon?"

Fushol bent in a gesture like a stiff bow. *Yes, and I was the least among the gunners as you call them. You see the position of Farseeker had become somewhat ceremonial, even disrespected. It was a duty thrust on the least of the gunnery class. And then I contacted you and everything changed for me.*

Istal and the elders are overwhelmed by the change brought by your appearance. For over five hundred years, we have had no contact with the outside. They do not know how to proceed. So I, who have loved the stories of aliens all my life, who have read and reread and speculated over all that is known, am empowered as ambassador, guide, and guard for you.

D'abo looked down at Fushol with more friendliness than she had displayed before. "It seems we have this in common."

That is good, Fushol sent.

"How does it work?" Shasti said, expecting to be refused an answer. But to her surprise, Fushol turned to her and, waving his larger claw, began to explain.

One can tell you what it does, he added, pacing back and forth with a skittering motion that reminded her of Mmok's crab robots. *Though as to the original science of how such a thing was discovered and done... Well, we have lost those secrets to death and decay over the ages. We are not the engineers our ancestors were.*

The Great Lens, he gestured with his major claw toward the kilometers of machinery, *uses the magnetic field of this world. Much of the machinery you see here stretches down to the planet's core. By warping the field of this world, our ancestors somehow stretched the event horizon of black holes. It allows us to bend light rays around our star system, hiding us from our enemies. It also creates a tunnel in space between the black hole and any object.*

"Like an Evolver Cruiser," Shasti said dryly.

Just so, Fushol answered. *The Ancient ones learned this technology, but as with every other static defense, one must lure the enemy to it. We could not use it or the technology to save our homeworld or colonies. Only here were the conditions right. When first we became operational, we did great execution among the Conchirri. Oh, but they were days of glory as we skeeted their ships from the sky and fed them to the singularity!*

Eventually they grew wary and moved off. Our few ships were either destroyed by the blockade or simply never returned. The Conchirri lost interest in us and went on to bloody feasts elsewhere, until the blessed day that your kind annihilated them.

"Yes," D'abo said. "Blessed day."

We were left alone until the great golden ships came. We tried to communicate with them but could only feel machine minds. Fortunately, we could tease though those and discover their intent and then began the present siege. Almost they broke us by weight of numbers, causing the great lens to over-

heat. But we threw in our telekinetics and planted fusion bombs amongst their fleet and this stayed them.

"The weapon fires through 360 degrees?" Shasti hazarded.

Yes, or they would simply use the planet's bulk to shield themselves. Think of what you see here, not as the weapon, for truly that is the singularity itself. Think of it merely as a sighting device and primer.

Shasti let her eyes drift over the immense cavern, filled with lights and cables and the hum of power. It was many times the size of the largest Confed base she had seen, far larger than even the starfort where they had unearthed Eris. The power and scope of the project that allowed the Skurlock to twist and extend a black hole made the hair on the back of her neck stand up.

"Such power," D'abo mused.

It concerns you, Fushol sent.

"It should concern any sentient," D'abo snapped. "Already we do battle with weapons that contain the power of the sun. And these have been deadly enough. Now we look into a future where even the stars can be turned on worlds. Yes, it terrifies me."

Fear it a little less, Officer D'abo. If the great weapon could have been moved, our ancestors would have moved it and scoured space of our enemies. The tragedy of the weapon is it only works in proximity to a huge singularity. The small ones that are generated in a ship's drive are not supermassive enough to be projected. It is a terrible power, but think of it as a mythic monster chained to one rock and only free to strike those who disturb its lair.

We no longer have the knowledge to recreate the weapon and dare not disassemble anything for study, for fear of attack. So the knowledge that you fear will not travel from star to star.

And in the end, what choice have we? Powerful enemies surround us, and if we do not develop the weapons to destroy them, they will destroy us.

"That's always the answer," D'abo said, with a tinge of bitterness. "It's either us or them. And so sentient life whips itself through greater and greater weapons and onward to destruction."

"As Fushol said," Shasti said with a shrug, "what choice do we have?"

D'abo said nothing further, and Shasti knew her friend was far from convinced. But the Nekoans and all the other species of this sector faced extinction at the hands of the Evolvers. The Skurlocks couldn't counter that threat alone, but the idea of having two indestructible bases in the depth of enemy space was doubtless going to cheer Mandela. The Prekak held Kandalor, and the Skurlocks held the Hidden Star. They might catch the Evolvers between those two fires.

You bare your teeth, Fushol sent with an overtone of fear. *Have I offended you?*

"No," Shasti said. "I was merely thinking pleasant thoughts of the destruction of our enemies. In my species, the display of teeth is indicative of a happy state of mind."

Fushol looked at D'abo.

"I know," D'abo said, "it didn't make a damn bit of sense to us either when we met them. I kept thinking she wanted to eat me."

Amusement rippled through Fushol's mind.

You have seen enough for today. I will soon be recalled to brief the Council of Elders. Shall I arrange with our teleports to send you back to your ship? I am sure that enough of them are rested and available to send you—

"No," Shasti said. "No. Thank you. Our shuttle should be arriving soon. We would prefer to travel back in a more conventional way."

As you wish, Fushol sent. *Our people are in touch with your shuttle and are guiding it in.* Shasti thought she detected another emanation of amusement from the alien. *There is a landing stage nearby under a range of rather pleasant hills. Our people use them for recreation. I will escort you there. Your vessel will meet you there.*

"Excellent. We will work with you to arrange for a landing of our ships soon."

Ships? Fushol sent.

"We carry a captured Evolver scout slung under our ship," Shasti said. "It will have to detach and land separately."

I shall look forward to hearing the full tale of such a capture, Fushol sent. *And if you are willing to share the knowledge, our engineers would treasure the opportunity to examine such a ship.*

"I'm sure we can accommodate your wish," Shasti said.

Then let us finish our tour and I will conduct you to the landing, Fushol sent. He turned, ceremonial cape flaring out, and scuttled back toward the trams. Shasti and D'abo followed.

An hour later, the MagLev returned them through the tunnels to the mainland to another great underground space. *These are the hangers and repair shops that once held Skurlock vessels. All those are gone, destroyed in the fighting around this world or lost in expeditions back into Skurlock space,* Fushol sent.

The cavernous hangers were empty and dark, filled with hundreds of years of refuse, debris, and dust, save for one. A crew of Skurlocks directed the activity of both drones and robots as they worked furiously under harsh temporary lights.

We prepare it for your vessels, Fushol sent. *You are invited to land your vessel in friendship,* Fushol said. *The Scientist-General asks that you come down near the shelter areas of the reverse slope of the mountains. We can accommodate your ships in these ancient subsurface docks.*

Once you are safely down, the Council will begin deliberation on the new alliance and on a deputation to return with you to your worlds.

"Thank Istal for us," Shasti said. "We will return to our ships and land them here. We did not bring diplomatic personnel with us, but I am empowered to begin these discussions. We must find a way to break out of the blockade and bring word to our people. Then we can hope to bring aid back to you."

Excellent. Our engineers have been working with your people. Our translators are now synched. Imperfectly for now, but enough to steer your shuttle for a landing. By the time you land, our translators will work for any of your people and mine.

Fushol seemed for a moment to listen to a voice neither of them could hear. *Let us take the elevator to the surface. Your shuttle is approaching.*

The elevator smelled of disuse and its doors opened slowly, but it worked well enough to take them to the surface. They emerged from a pillbox structure onto a landing field that had obviously only today been scraped free of the vegetation that had overgrown the permacrete and tarmac. Indeed, the heavy machinery was parked under the trees. Skurlocks headed for other elevators nearby. Pole-mounted lights had hastily been erected, and Shasti could see aircars full of Skurlocks, their engines idling. Security, she guessed.

Shasti was surprised to see that it was near evening. The sun was going down to the west over the vast interior of the continent the settlement faced. Nearby stood a range of gentle hills, landscaping, and benches showed that it was used for a park. Auroras shimmered over their heads, indicative of the sleeting radiation and EMG disturbances from the binary stars. The air was sharp with a biting cold.

Shasti turned to find D'abo shivering, with her arms around herself. Of course, Shasti realized, her first officer was still dressed in her cut-down version of a crew suit. Shasti had unconsciously simply raised her body temperature. The Nekoan, with bare legs and arms, had no such ability. Even her tail circled around her hips.

Fushol, who had wrapped his own cloak about him, sensed D'abo's distress or picked it up from Shasti, who he could read better. A Skurlock exited the neared aircar and hurried over with a heavy black cape. He handed it to Fushol before speeding back to the warm confines of the aircar.

Fushol handed it up to D'abo, who gratefully wrapped herself in it. It, at least, covered her upper body.

Overhead, a bright star grew steadily larger, and the familiar whine of *Duelist's* engine reached Shasti's ears. She smiled. Vaughn had sent the more heavily armed assault shuttle rather than the peaceable *Dakotas*. He always covered his bets.

The gray-green shuttle, with all running lights on, hovered above the landing field. Shasti waved them down and the shuttle landed smoothly in the field's center. Hatches opened and in perfect formation Rigg and Rask led a squad of troopers down the ramps. Shasti noted that they were all in full battle armor.

"When will our landing place be ready?" Shasti asked.

We shall call, Fushol sent. *But I fear it will be a day at least. Still, that is not all bad. It gives my elders some time to come to grips with the new reality.*

"Not a problem," Shasti said. "It will be a while before we reach the orbit of our ship. We too would like some time for consideration."

We will look forward to your return, Captain Rainhell and Officer D'abo, Fushol returned. *This day of your arrival will forever be a day of joy among our people.*

Shasti and D'abo walked slowly to the shuttle to face a relieved-looking Daniel Rigg.

"Hello, Dan," Shasti said.

"Good to see you, Skipper," Rigg said, handing her a belt with a pistol and a handcom on it. Rask had a similar one for D'abo, but the Nekoan waited neither for pleasantries or the weapons, fleeing into the warmth of the shuttle.

"Well," Rask muttered with a grin, "she would be running around in next to nothing all the time."

"Let's get back to the ship," Shasti said. "Tomorrow will be a big day."

27

idhe's shuttle took several hours to climb back to the orbiting starship where Shasti faced her command staff in the wardroom.

"They are incredibly grateful to the Confederacy for destroying the Conchirri. They want to share their best with us." Shasti finished relaying all that had passed on the planet below. "With the Evolver blockade, there is little chance of our slipping back out of the Hidden Star's envelope. We are invited to land until we find some way to escape back to Nekoan space."

"Great," said Mmok. "Party at their place. Slime for everybody."

"So do we go down?" D'abo asked.

"Yes," Shasti said. "We need to replenish and repair. With their gravity lens weapon protecting us, we don't have to worry about being attacked on the ground. Our Skurlock friends can synthesize fuel for us, and we can recharge air, water, and foodstuffs. Dobera says we're getting marginal on some supplies, and we have no idea how long we will be out here. Always rest your legs before running for your life."

"Sound logic," D'abo said, flexing the muscles of her lean thigh to the evident distraction of the nearby male crew.

"We'll have to decouple the dartship for an atmospheric landing."

"Shall I fly her in?" D'abo asked.

"No," Shasti said. "We rigged it up with fighter controls."

"I've flown fighters before," D'abo said.

"Yes, but we put in a human fighter seat," Shasti said.

"Oh," D'abo said, swishing her tail around and into her arms. "So, no place for my..."

"None," Shasti said. "I'll take the dartship in. She's far larger than any of our shuttles or fighter. I don't want one of the fighter jocks to take her. I've flown more small vessels than anyone else aboard and I want you to have Nye on the helm for the approach. As for the alterwatch helmsmen, one's ill and one's inexperienced in planetary landings."

Shasti rose. "We'll establish standard security on landing, despite our hosts' avowed good intentions."

"You'll have to dispossess Paolo," D'abo said. "He's been working nonstop on the computer drive in the dartship. Says he's found a Rosetta, whatever that means."

"He can ride down in the dartship," Shasti said. "We'll start down at 1530 hours as agreed. Bridge is yours, Teleera."

"Yes, Captain."

As Shasti started for the back of the bridge, the doors cycled and Vaughn walked in.

Shasti nodded at Vaughn, suffering the usual mix of exhilaration and constraint she felt around him.

The big man kept his face neutral, but his eyes lit up on seeing her. "Good afternoon, Captain. Glad to see you haven't been teleported away again."

"Interesting experience," she said with a smile, "but one I'm not eager to repeat. What if one of them sneezed while I was in mid-teleport?"

He looked past her at the activity by the helm. "We are landing?"

"Yes, I want us down before planet nightfall."

"Excellent," he said softly, "then we shall be able to avail ourselves of the fabulous nightlife of the Hidden Star: the music, the food, the lights."

Shasti couldn't hold back a laugh. "Optimist. There will likely be little more than gruel, alien music that sounds like the waste disposal malfunction, and emergency lighting in bunkers from centuries ago. I have only the slimmest of hopes for the bathroom facilities."

"Ah," he said, with a dismissive wave of the hand. "One travels to encounter the strange."

"Remember that when you're trying to figure out what the local commode looks like," she said as she placed a hand on his shoulder. "I'm taking the dartship down. See you on the ground."

"Hmmm." He frowned. "You'll be locked in a relatively small ship with Paolo. Perhaps I should come along as a bodyguard."

Shasti made a sound of mock exasperation and rolled her eyes, then gave him a light thump on the chest. "I am, if you recall, quite capable of defending myself. Besides, he's only interested in Eris these days."

"One suspects his interests," Vaughn rumbled, "to be very flexible. Still, you are very formidable…"

"Very." She smiled and walked past him. The closing doors cut off his admiring glance at her.

The turbovator deposited her two levels below, and she took gangways down to the boarding tube that ran alongside the main grapple to the dartship. Both guards snapped to attention as she passed them. Dobera looked up from the controls set in the small flight cabin as she came in. The lizard-man handed her a manifest showing the dartship to be adequately stocked with necessities, then he headed up the boarding tube.

One of Perez's engineers appeared to hand Shasti a pre-flight checklist. "Engineering checks out, ma'am. Left the pilot stuff for you."

"Very well," she said. The engineer saluted and headed up the boarding tube. Shasti double-checked the airlock before signaling for the tube to be detached and retracted. A few steps down took her to the passenger/prisoner compartment where she found Paolo sitting in the midst of the portable computers and usual piles of paper that marked him as hard at work. He cast an appreciative eye over her as she came down the small spiral stairway from the pilot deck.

Shasti barely noticed. Flirtation from Paolo was like background noise.

"We are going down shortly," she said.

"May I keep working? I finally feel like I am getting somewhere with these encoded records."

"I figured you would. Don't complain about the bumpy ride."

"I have every confidence in my lovely and talented captain."

Shasti smiled and just shook her head, walked back to the pilot compartment, then slid into the flight chair Perez had installed to continue the checklist. The Confed controls grafted into the alien tech worked perfectly, but it still took twenty minutes to finish the pre-flight.

It may have fighter controls, she thought, *while looking at the readings, but this thing is going to handle more like a lighter or barge in atmosphere. Good thing I didn't have one of the fighter jocks fly it. They'd pull the wings off.*

Her mind flipped back to the image of her old friend Telisan, the Denlenn ace, as he whipped a *Wildcat* fighter into a landing on Enshar that made Fenaday duck for cover. *I just made the last payment on that thing!* he'd complained. The memory of both her old friend and old lover warmed her for a second. *I hope they're all right,* she thought.

"Stormcloud to Lynx," Shasti called.

"Lynx here," D'abo replied from *Sidhe's* bridge forty meters above.

"Ready to decouple dartship," Shasti said.

"At your discretion, Captain."

Shasti flicked the intercom with her thumb. "Paolo, buckle up. We're cutting loose."

"Yes, Captain."

She switched back to D'abo. "Okay, Lynx. Decouple now." The physical and magnetic grapples of the star-frigate withdrew. The dartship floated free. She goosed a thruster, and the dartship drifted away from the star-frigate. When they reached three kilometers' separation, Shasti began to line up for entry. *Sidhe* had orbital preference, and Shasti wanted the starship to head down first. She watched as the blood-red frigate maneuvered for entry and started down.

"Captain Rainhell to Ground Base," Shasti called, "commencing entry."

"This is Ground Base. Fushol speaking. You are welcome, Captain. Your main vessel is already on path to ground and breaking our upper atmosphere. Please start your clock for entry in 400 seconds."

"Affirmative, Ground Base."

Suddenly an excited gabble burst from the speaker. Shasti could not understand the Skurlock language, but distress was obvious. "Rainhell to Ground Base, did not copy that last transmission."

"Captain," Fushol called, "a large force of Evolver ships is approaching the planet. It is a major attack such as we have not seen in hundreds of years. Oh, what an opportunity!" A savage joy communicated itself with such certainty that Shasti was sure it had come directly into her mind from the tiny Skurlock. "The Great Lens is being readied. We shall make a full harvest of them. Please abort your entry and prepare to steer to a safer orbit."

"This is *Sidhe*," D'abo's voice came through heavy static. "Negative on abort. *Sidhe* is committed to her entry window."

"This is Rainhell," Shasti said. "I can abort. Give me a vector for a safe orbit."

"Affirmative, Dartship. Please steer course 140 and climb at 2000 meters per second for 100 seconds. *Sidhe*, if you can increase your rate of decent by 1000 meters per second, it will greatly simplify our firing solutions."

Shasti manipulated her controls using gimbals and thrusters to kick the nose upward before applying thrust. "Ground Base. They clearly waited for us to start down. Are they hoping we'll block your fire?"

"It must be so," Fushol's voice came back. "But they delude themselves. The Great Lens does not work so. Your ships are inconvenient, allowing them to get closer than before but nothing more. The Evolvers are doomed."

"Makes you wonder why they would do it," Paolo said from behind Shasti's shoulder.

She glanced up at him. "Grab that take-hold on the bulkhead. Belt in, in case I have to maneuver." Shasti rolled the dartship on its side and looked out the clear-plast canopy. Below she could see a line of white smoke and flame as *Sidhe* broke atmosphere. The turbulence made it impossible for her to talk to her ship and would for minutes more.

"Gravity lens firing," the Skurlock announced over the speakers. Even across species the Skurlock's glee at the chance to lay waste to the Evolvers came across, payback for the slaughter of their home-world and exile to this outpost above a dead star.

Shasti could see nothing. The gravity lens was as invisible as it had been when it crumpled the cruiser.

"Wonderful," cried Fushol. "Ten ships destroyed, now eleven."

Shasti shifted the hands-on stick and throttle control to right the dartship. Nothing happened.

"Cycling weapon," Fushol announced. "Seven more ships destroyed. The survivors are scattering and reverse course. Ah, but it will not help. We shall destroy many more."

Shasti frantically wrenched the HOTAS. The dartship responded, but not to her. The engines roared and its nose elevated, turning away from the planet.

Shasti's brain lit up. She knew the reason for the Evolver's sacrifice. She turned a grim face toward Paolo as she activated the com. "Rainhell to Ground Base, I know why the Evolvers are attacking now. The planet is not the target. They were trying to get close enough to activate some hidden control in the dartship. We'd thought we ripped out everything they had in her, but they have some way of controlling this vessel that we don't understand. Our ship is heading for the Evolver blockade."

"Captain," Fushol replied, "this is disaster. What can we do for you? Can you raise your starship?"

"Negative. *Sidhe* is in reentry blackout and will be for several more minutes at least. In any event, she won't have an orbital reentry window. It would take hours to calculate a new one."

Shasti hopped out of her seat and headed for the hatch at the back of their small bridge, but as she feared, the hatch would not open.

"Ground Base," Shasti said, a feeling of deep fatigue coming over her. "We are trapped on the flight deck. No way to get at the engines and disable them. We will be in enemy hands long before *Sidhe* can be relaunched."

"What can we do?" Fushol asked again. "We cannot tow you back. The Lens is not capable of crushing and towing at the same time. If we seek to tow you, we shall be vulnerable."

"Yes," Shasti said. "Doubtless if you lock on to tow us, the enemy ships will double back and attack. What about the teleports?"

"Alas, they are not gathered and prepared. It will take some minutes to prepare them; by then you will be beyond our range."

Shasti looked at Paolo, who unbelted himself from the takehold. His face was set, lips thinned. "I've been a prisoner of aliens once. Never again."

She nodded. "I feel the same." She keyed the mike. In a way, she was grateful that *Sidhe* was blacked out. She had no idea what to say to Vaughn or to D'abo if she'd had the chance. *Maybe it's better this way,* she thought. *The sharp knife cuts cleanest.*

"Ground Base," Shasti said, "fire on our ship and destroy it. We have no taste for becoming prisoners of pitiless machines. Say to those who ask, those who we love and who loved us, that they should remember us as free and defiant."

"Star-captain, Star-captain," Fushol said in an obvious distress. "We cannot do this. Your people might not believe us. They cannot see what is happening and might turn their weapons on us."

Shasti's lips pressed together. "I understand, Ground Base. We have the means to do this ourselves. Farewell." From under her jacket, in the small of her back, she pulled out a small pistol.

"Farewell, Star-Captain Rainhell," Fushol said. "We will avenge you."

"Do that," she said and clicked off.

She turned to Paolo, holding the small pistol in her palm. "Do you want to do it yourself?"

"No." He smiled sadly. "I'm afraid my hand might not be steady enough. I will ask it of you as a final favor."

"It won't hurt," she promised.

"How about a last kiss before we depart this life?" Paolo said.

Shasti thought of Vaughn for a second. *What harm,* she thought, *he'll never know, and it seems a fitting way to end one's life.*

They came together in a kiss, slow, sensuous, and full. Paolo started to say something, and she silenced him with a finger across his lips. He smiled broadly and turned away. Mischievous till the end...

Shasti stepped back and raised the pistol. A feeling of shame burst on her. The weapon seemed so heavy, her movements slow, as if she were in molasses. *When did I become so weak?* she thought fiercely. She raised the weapon to point at the back of Paolo's head, striving for the cleanest shot. He slid in and out of focus. In a last moment of despair as the blackness closed in, she realized that she'd been outwitted once again. The Evolvers must have done something to the atmosphere on the dartship. Shasti and her pistol tumbled to the deck next to the unconscious Paolo.

28

W hat?" Vaughn roared, surging to his feet, his blue eyes burning with the desire to kill.

Sidhe's screen was fractured into several views: Shasti's golden ship accelerating out of view, their landing zone ahead, and Fushol, his limbs twisting in misery.

"We have destroyed all the Evolver ships we can reach, but most of the fleet lies outside our reach. Her ship continues toward them," Fushol said. "We cannot raise her, and she is already beyond the range of our teleports even if we could gather them."

Vaughn's volcanic gaze locked on Mmok. "You said we'd pulled out every control device the Evolvers had."

The machine man hung his head, shaking it back and forth as if in pain. "We did, we did. They must have some other technology we don't know of. Something on a subatomic level in ship's metal perhaps. Damn, damn, damn."

Vaughn spun to the navigator. "How quickly can you take us back up?"

He and the helmsman conversed frantically, hands literally dancing over their instruments. "We have most of our impulsion still.

We need a zoom climb on 34 by 267. It's going to burn fantastic amounts of fuel, but it's the only way to get up there fast enough to do anything."

"Do it!"

D'abo leapt to the communications. "Action stations, all hands. Prepare for atmospheric maneuvering. We're taking her back up. Captain Rainhell's ship is heading for the Evolver fleet. Man your battle stations. Engineering, stand by on atmospheric jets. Ready Main Drive. Take hold, take hold, take hold."

Sidhe nosed over into a dive, hurtling down in an effort to get enough inertia for her engines to drive her out of atmosphere.

"Shasti," Vaughn swore. "We're coming for you."

Sensations fell in on Shasti as she regained awareness. Lights stabbed at the back of her eyes. Bitter, tangy metallic smells filled the cool and very dry air. A savage headache had taken up residence at the base of her skull. She devoted a few seconds to biofeedback, adjusting her body's chemistry. The pain disappeared.

She found herself strapped on a table in a large, dark room, lit by blinking telltales and sharp white lights that cast impenetrable shadows. Machines of unknown purpose and unpleasant aspect surrounded the table she lay on. She threw herself at the restraints to no avail. They bit coldly on her wrists and throat and showed no sign of giving.

A voice sounded over her head. Deep, bass, and incomprehensible, for all she assumed the spaces in it indicated words. Somehow she was sure no living voice had made the sound. Footsteps sounded to her left. Shasti's head snapped about as a figure walked into a pool of light to the right between two banks of machines. Shasti stared for a few seconds before she recognized him.

"Oh, Paolo," she said, "you poor thing."

The linguist was altered and distorted with layers of muscle and slabs of bony plate under the one-piece coverall he now wore. The face was the worst; his eyes looked out from an immobile, almost lipless, countenance, with a pronounced brow ridge. All his fine, wavy hair had fallen out.

"No need to pity me for my enlightenment," Paolo said. His voice was deeper, with an odd metallic clack, but was still his. "When I think of how close I came to throwing away my life just on the verge of finding out what my purpose in life was. Before acquiring my newfound strength and health. They woke me first to make the change and invite you to join us. The Evolver is fascinated with your genetic code, Shasti. It needed to practice on me. Apparently, you are very, very special.

"We were fools to fear this, Shasti. The Makers have the greatest of gifts awaiting us all. Free for the taking to all with any vision. The Makers offer us protection."

"They don't *offer* us anything, Paolo," Shasti raged. "They take, they force, they rape your mind. Paolo, remember when we met back on Morokat? Remember Rigg telling us how the Evolver that crashed in the Confederacy had altered the populace into its slaves?"

"You don't understand," he said with evident sadness. "How could you in your unenlightened state? Can a chimpanzee make an educated decision about becoming a Homo sapiens? Wouldn't it be criminal to deny people the chance for greater intelligence, strength, and long life, even if it was forcibly given?"

"Paolo, you know this is wrong. You know that your humanity was what you prized most: rich red wine, fine food, soft music, a woman's lips on your own. Paolo, set me free. It's not too late."

Paolo seemed to be struggling with himself. A whimper escaped his lips. "Shasti," he said. He struggled forward, a step, another. The voice boomed over their heads, startling them both. The humanity faded from his agonized eyes.

"No," he said in a dull voice. "All that frivolity, all that vanity is behind me now. I have a mission and a purpose in the great plan of the Makers. We shall serve together in that mission, Shasti."

"I will serve no one and nothing save of my own will," she said, her lips peeling back from her teeth.

Machines moved close and began to whir and hum over her.

She braced herself.

"Do not fight it," Paolo said. "There is no escape. It causes pain and only delays the inevitable."

The machines played over her.

"Why are you talking to me?" Shasti asked, trying to distract him. "If you can just change me, why try to talk me into it?"

"Why, indeed?" answered the thing that had been Paolo. Its hard, cold eyes, so different from Paolo's laughing ones, studied her. "Perhaps it is merely the hangover of old memories. No matter. Soon you too will be one of us. You will gain the advantage of a superior genetic code."

"So superior that it went extinct?" she shot back.

"Extinct?" Paolo said. "Hardly. The Makers have died, but so long as the Evolvers function, the Makers' code goes on. We rise again."

"Slave," Shasti spat. "Hapless automaton."

"You will feel differently after the change." His claw-tipped hands played over the instruments.

The voice boomed over them again.

"Fuck you," she shouted.

"The machine does not address you," Paolo said. "It only tells me that our ship...your ship still seeks to penetrate the blockade. Your ship relaunched and pursued the dartship. Quite a remarkable job of escape and evasion. It has led us on a splendid chase over the last solar day. D'abo keeps trying to lure our other vessels in range of the gravity lens while trying to reach this ship. I am not sure how they know you are aboard this one, but so it seems.

"But they came out too far this time and are being boxed in. They will not again reach the safety of the Lens' protection.

"As for the Skurlocks, we now know that their line is failing. We need only wait a little longer, decades, perhaps a mere century, and the Skurlocks will be so degenerate they will be unable to defend their world. Then they and the great weapon will also be ours."

The voice sounded again. Shasti thought she detected an imperious tone in it and noticed how Paolo jerked and twitched in response. "Yes," he said. "No more delay. We shall begin. Now."

The chamber began to glow, and Shasti felt as if a thousand tiny fingers were playing over her body. She threw herself against the restraints, but they held.

"No," she shouted. "No. I will not change. I am Shasti Rainhell. I belong to me!"

Shasti's perception exploded. She felt as if she was looking down on her own body. Watching it, as the radiation of the Makers began to take apart her genetic code.

Or as it tried to. Shasti's body fought back on a molecular level. Things latent in her genetic code, unique in all the human species, began to awaken. The Makers' code sought open places in her DNA to invade and remake her, but the beams found DNA that was far more resistant to their effect. Pain washed over Shasti.

"No," she screamed. "I won't be remade."

The pain grew worse, and it felt as if Shasti's mind was being ripped apart. Colors exploded in Shasti's brain, and the pain faded. She looked at Paolo, and to her astonishment, realized she could see into his mind. Not with the dim sense of situational awareness, but with complete clarity. And she knew he was afraid. The Evolver's machine mind was talking to him.

Noncompliant, the Evolver said. *The organism resists conversion.*

It is worse, Paolo responded. *Her potential, both physical and mental, is increasing, yet her genetic code is remaining intact. It is as if she is cannibalizing the best of the Makers' code.*

Query: Is the genetic code of this human typical for the species?

Before Paolo could reply, Shasti desperately reached into his mind.

Initiating containment program, she forced into his brain. Paolo's hands, under her control, initiated a barrier that protected her from the Evolver. Ruthlessly, she parsed his mind, draining the knowledge of the Makers. She found and threw protective barriers over his original personality, mentally chained in a disused corner of his mind.

Maybe I can save him, she thought. She snapped an order at the machinery on the table and the restraints burst off her.

But the mechanical mind beyond his became suspicious. The AI began to probe around the barrier.

In desperation, Shasti's mind ranged out looking for help to ward off the AI. *Vaughn?* she thought. *D'abo? Anyone!*

An answer came. Sharp, impossibly clear over the distance.

"Mary," Shasti breathed in shock.

On board *Sidhe,* Vaughn stood next to D'abo's command chair and wiped a thin rill of blood from his mouth. The last near miss had shaken the ship with a ferocious vortex of expanding gas, and he wondered how many rads they had all picked up. *Not,* he thought, *that it will matter for much longer.*

Rigg grabbed his shoulder. "Are you all right, man?"

He nodded. "D'abo, return fire."

Next to him, D'abo glared up at the main screen, lit by beams and blasts. Her teeth were visible. No more the coquettish kitten, she was the lioness on the hunt. "Helm, emergency turn to port V+30. Fire anti-shipping missile at target Delta, full main battery salvo on target Theta."

Sidhe shuddered as some small munition struck her.

"*Spacefires* have exhausted all ordnance save lasers. No hits," Hafel reported.

"Have them fall back on us for anti-missile defense," Vaughn ordered. He turned to Wardell. The gunner was frantically working his damaged panel. Mmok stood next to Wardell, plugged into the panel and actually serving as *Sidhe's* fire control. "Where is target prime?" Vaughn demanded.

Mmok's head swiveled. "It's still at the back of the pack. They're just trying to herd us using these light ships. I think they want to capture us. We haven't even engaged the main Evolver line, and we ain't going to reach it at this rate."

On the main screen Vaughn saw lines of the golden, ovoid ships, each one many times a match for the star-frigate. The hopelessness of it rose in his throat like bile. He scanned the bridge, seeing the red warning lights, the acrid smoke, and the faces of Tanaka, Rigg, Rask, Eris, and the others. A flash of white light from a beam lit the bridge in merciless starkness, and he knew that he had led them all to their deaths. Recklessly taking command after the dartship was taken, he'd set *Sidhe* in frantic pursuit. He'd used his limited PSI sense, driving himself to the breaking point and possibly even burning it out. But not before finding a hint of Shasti's presence on the ship that always took position out of reach.

D'abo looked at him as if reading his mind. "I gainsaid you in nothing," she said, "and had you not led, I would have. No one is to blame. But the game is ending. Checkmate, as your people say."

"Yes," Tanaka said. She stood by the bridge takehold, belted in as she had only one good arm. "We did what we needed to do. But, Mikhail, don't let us be taken. Better a quick and clean out."

Rigg walked over to her and took her good hand. "Yeah," he added. "What she said."

"No enemy shall set foot on our ship," Vaughn promised, his eyes glowing with ferocity. "We shall fire till our weapons are exhausted. Then we shall ram. They will not have us."

"But I must apologize to you all," he said. "I let my heart rule my brain, something my creators would never have credited."

"Don't recall any debate about going after the skipper," Mmok said.

"It's been a trip," Rigg said.

"And a half," Tanaka added.

"Wouldn't have missed it," Rask said.

"I am glad I met you all," D'abo said. "I only wish we could have recovered Shasti and Paolo so they could at least die with their friends."

"Main gun recycled," Wardell called.

"Let's get some more before we check out," Mmok said.

"Old news to you," Rask snorted. "You've already been dead."

The image used by the mighty Prekak in dealing with Shasti appeared before her. The small, gray-haired woman with mild blue eyes adjusted her shawl sweater.

Hello dear, she sent. *Well, well aren't you full of surprises? Never in a million years, and I've lived a good bit of that, would I have imagined you could reach this plane. And to summon me across such a distance, it seems the universe can still surprise me. How delightful.*

Help me, Shasti pleaded. *I may be no more than a bug to you but please, help me.*

Why so I shall, young one. You are rapidly becoming my favorite pretty bug. I don't believe I am going to put up with these little mechanical toys forgetting their place. It's time for a little house cleaning.

Suddenly the image of Mary disappeared, and she saw the Prekak as it saw itself, a mighty tower of bone and muscle, and beyond that, a might of mental power that could warp time and space.

Follow me, Mary said, in a voice no longer gentle or quaint. They stormed across the barriers the AI sent. Shasti perceived the barrier as a huge blue bubble over a world of mechanisms and flashing lights, which was the AI's conception of itself.

Mary strode across the virtual world of the AI, tearing up its crust with vortices of force and volcanoes and earthquakes of raw, seething data. Its defenses struck back, trying to assimilate the Prekak, as data, as a genetic code. The AI's weapons, datapackets that Shasti perceived as a monstrous combination of shark and hawk, were batted from the sky of the AI world by the towering Prekak.

The AI switched targets and struck at Shasti, causing Mary to devote some of her energy to protecting her. The datahawks gained ground. Mary began to falter.

Black fury exploded in Shasti's mind. *No one bends me to their will,* she hissed. *Never again.*

Shasti's arms rose from her side and violet energy poured out of her fingertips. She skeeted datahawks from the space around them, freeing Mary to renew the attack.

Well done, Mary said, surprise in her tone. *My pretty little bug has a sting.*

The AI's world began to shatter. Blackness yawned in it, sucking down data and memory. Shasti and Mary drew upward into the sky.

Shasti watched in fascinated horror as the world below her tore itself to pieces. Was it death itself she was seeing?

Of a sort, Mary sent. *Death as an AI perceives it. I am within their subsystems. The main AI is done, but the lesser systems operate still. I lack the power to destroy them all at this range.*

Can you issue commands to them? Shasti thought frantically.

Yes, I have made them cease fire on your ship, but I cannot overcome their defenses to order them to self-destruct or fire on each other.

You don't need to, Shasti sent. *Command all vessels other than this one to head for the planet. The Skurlocks have waited hundreds of years for their revenge. Today is their day.*

Yes, Mary said. *They are turning. We have won. And you made the difference. I'm feeling my years today, and I could not have protected us both and fought on. Well done, my dear. Oh my, I think I must rest for a little.*

Shasti felt Mary recede. Not entirely, but a distance asserted itself as the exhausted Prekak became unfocused. Shasti found herself floating in an indigo sea without form or substance. Her mind ranged across space and time, plunging and stooping like a falcon. *This must be how God feels,* she thought.

In an instant she touched the mind of her first love, Robert Fenaday. Then she saw him, as if she were hovering over him in the ornate study of the Fenaday mansion on New Eire. She could hear the crackle of the fireplace but not feel its heat. He sat by the fire, a paperbook in hand, reading.

She touched his troubled mind, feeling the scars of all he had done to find his wife, Lisa, and all that he atoned for daily. She felt the deep and abiding emotion he had for her and the ambivalence it generated in the simple soul of a man who loved his wife. Shasti knew that she was never far from his thoughts and even as she was there, he was thinking and worrying about her. And she understood.

In her mind's eye, she stooped over Robert and gently brushed her lips across his brow. *I will never forget you,* she thought, *never, ever. You will always hold a part of my heart, always and only yours, my first love.*

You cannot stay here, Mary sent from a great distance. Her mental voice still fatigued and halting. *You are a million years away from reaching this level. If you stay, you will destroy yourself.*

Shasti knew the rightness of it in an instant.

Farewell, dear Robert, Shasti said. As she drifted up and away from Robert, he seemed to recede to a great distance and disappear.

Shasti suddenly felt a great coldness, a force that was concentrating on Robert Fenaday. With her fading power, she cast about. The universe had faded to a cool blue emptiness, but in it she heard a voice.

First we kill Fenaday, then the Confederacy falls and we sweep the stars themselves into our hands.

Shasti focused her mind in the direction of the deadly thought. For the barest of seconds, she brushed another mind. Impressions flooded her, eyes of startling blue, hair the color of blood, skin as pale and flawless as her own and a mind, feminine and deadly and somehow... wrong. Then it was gone and Shasti tumbled down from godhood to mere humanity, confined again within her own skull. She felt the Prekak's mind and the link between them attenuating.

Thank you, Shasti sent.

Goodbye, pretty little bug, the Prekak sent back. *We won't meet again. Not on this plane of existence anyway.*

Wait, Shasti called. *Who was that?*

But the Prekak was gone.

Across untold billions of miles, Robert Fenaday sat bolt upright in his chair, looking around the firelit hall. Had he been dozing?

"Shasti," he whispered. "No, of course not." Yet somehow he was filled with the conviction that wherever she was, she was somehow safe. More than safe, whole and content. With that knowledge came a feeling of peace that had so often eluded him. *She's all right,* he thought. *She's all right.*

"Wait a minute," Wardell cried. "All enemy vessels have ceased fire."

"What?" D'abo said. She looked up at the screen. On it, hundreds of ships of various sizes, including dozens of the giant, golden ships, filled nearby space. "They've all gone ballistic. What's happened? No, wait. They are turning toward the planet. Hafel, alert the Skurlocks."

"Wait one," Mmok snapped. "Target Theta is not maneuvering, firing, or heading for the planet. It looks like she is breaking up."

"Steer for it," D'abo said. She turned to Vaughn. "Get a boarding party together. Find her."

But the last fell on empty air. Vaughn, Rigg, and Rask were racing for the turbo. Mmok turned to D'abo. "Skipper, nobody is shooting—"

"Go," D'abo said.

Mmok tore free of the panel and took off after the others.

Sidhe closed on the giant golden oval many times the size of the one she'd fought near Kandalor. It shuddered and rolled, great rents opening in the smooth golden skin.

Fushol and his team stood to the Great Lens as it harvested death such as its original designers could only have dreamed of. At each pass, more of the Evolver fleet was fed to the singularity.

Fushol's assistant raced up to him. "The containment field is failing. The old repairs are not as strong as we hoped."

"We cannot stop firing," Fushol said, his compound eyes gleaming with hate and more, the need to honor all those who had served the Great Lens and had died, hopeless and unfulfilled before this day.

"No," his assistant said. Behind him an arc of blue ripped out from one of the great capacitors, and the crew working it shrieked and died. With no hesitation, the standby crew raced into the machine, to the stations of their dead brethren. In the distance, another arc flared.

"But we shall not all perish today. The race of Skurlock will live on in hope. Have all noncombatants flee toward the northern shelters. We gunners will remain. We will not break faith with the slaughtered dead, or with the generations that have served before us."

"It shall be done," his assistant said and raced off.

The light hit Fushol first, then came the numbing sound. Fragments of the main control panel cut down the team near him.

Fushol pulled himself off the ground, ichor leaking from a

mangled digit. He looked at the terrified faces near him. "Don't be afraid, younglings," he said. "Today is our day. We die but those who will now dwell free will remember us. Come die with me and save our people."

Their young faces hardened in grim resolve, and they followed him into the smoking machine, heading for the auxiliary-one panel. Above them the Great Lens roared out retribution. Fushol smiled at the sound.

Shasti pulled herself together. She was still on the Evolver ship, and it seemed to be coming apart at the seams. Dull explosions sounded in the distance, and the deckplates below shifted and vibrated. Paolo lay on the deck nearby, returned to his human form. The genetic changes wrought by the Evolvers had faded, though his hair was still gone. God knew what it was doing to his insides. She half-crawled, half scrambled over to the fallen man. A quick touch at his throat revealed a thready pulse.

"Good," she said. "I'm not losing an ex today." She hauled him to his feet, his eyes opened but he had trouble focusing on her. Still, he stayed upright and responded to her tugging him into forward motion.

Shasti and Paolo staggered through the shuddering, flaring insanity that had become the interior of the Evolver flagship. Fortunately, there were gangways and passages bipeds could use. The machine ship had been designed to carry and care for Evolver converts. Otherwise, it would have been impossible to escape from the conversion center.

Paolo's knees buckled. Shasti knelt beside him and shook him to focus his attention. "Paolo," she demanded. "Paolo."

He looked up at her glassy-eyed. "Save yourself," he mumbled.

She shook him again. "Paolo, do you remember where our dartship is?"

"What?" he said, struggling to focus.

"The dartship we were captured in. It's our only chance. Think about what you knew when you were one of them."

His brow creased as he fought to concentrate. "Specimens removed to nearby converter," he said in a monotone. "Directly up three levels."

It made sense. Prisoners were processed nearby as soon as they got off the transport. The Evolvers were nothing if not efficient. Shasti looked about frantically. She couldn't trust any elevator or turbo; it might stop functioning at any second and entomb them.

The flickering light actually saved them; its strobing called her attention to a metal ladder that led up. "Can you climb?" Shasti asked.

Paolo looked back at her without comprehension, his eyes rolled up in his head. Shasti looked at the ladder, then down at the unconscious man, and wondered whether to leave him.

Whatever would I say to Robert? she thought and hauled the smaller man onto her shoulders. Dull, distant explosions sounded in her ears as she started up the hard, narrow ladder. Even her Engineered strength was severely taxed as she struggled upward. She clung to the ladder, her universe narrowing to the next rung that bit at her hands. Level passed level and she found herself heaving Paolo onto the decks of a giant hanger. Wind whipped at her hair, which could only mean a rupture to space somewhere.

The hanger extended for kilometers in all directions, but only a few ships lay within, variants of Conchirri warships far larger than the dartship. She spotted three dartships lying in the middle distance, their slender hulls lit by flickering overhead lights. Shasti hauled Paolo up and ran for them. The wind was dying. If they did not find their ship soon, they would be, too. Already her lungs strained for oxygen. Again, her Engineered physique came to the rescue. Her lungs were far more efficient at scavenging and storing oxygen than a standard human's.

Shasti reached the trio of dartships and stared up through red-tinged vision. She had only seconds more and had to select the right ship while she had strength left. The vessels took up hundreds of meters of dock space.

The ships were exactly alike, gold metal, lethal darts.

Her desperate eyes fell on a strange discoloration on the first ship, near the airlock. Her eyes focused on the image and a flash of light showed the painted words, *Under New Management*, next to the image of a human hand, thumbs up.

"Mmok, you wonderful bastard," Shasti said, as she made a halting run for the ship. "You never could resist scrawling graffiti on everything."

She raced up the scaffolding that held the ship and plunged inside. The Engineers had marked the controls for the airlock inside. She hit them with relief, then dropped Paolo in a bunk and strapped him down.

A lurch threw her off her feet. She scrambled up, racing for the small bridge. Fortunately, the Evolvers hadn't pulled out the fighter seat or the grafted-on Confed controls. Shasti had no time for a checklist. They either had fuel or they were dead. Systems powered up and the dartship tore free of the links and moorings and floated free. Shasti glanced at the ceiling above and checked her rise, then flicked on the ship's lights. Beyond her canopy, the hanger lights guttered out and bits of metal flew about the deck. Shasti saw a large hatchway a half-kilometer away. She hit the thruster and headed for it. Her instruments showed her hard vacuum outside as the last of the air outside vented. Her right hand danced over the safety interlocks to free up the dartship's small particle accelerator.

The weapon proved unnecessary. The hatchway, triggered by the dartship's approach in vacuum, yawned open. Shasti opened the thrusters full and dove for the safety of open space. The dartship leapt into free space, and Shasti slipped back into her seat, exhaustion dragging at her senses.

It took *Duelist* hours and strained Vaughn's failing PSI sense to where he had to fight a blinding headache, but they found the dartship. The golden vessel was running ballistically, no engines firing and only bare power registering. Vaughn's headache retreated the instant he sensed Shasti's nearness.

Duelist rolled and matched airlocks with the dartship. Her boarding tube snaked out, attached, and made a hard seal. Armored troopers readied their weapons. Vaughn strode past them and practically ripped the airlock open.

Shasti stood on the other side with a wicked, triumphant grin on her face, Paolo under one arm. Wild cheers broke out in the crowded space. Rask, Rigg, Mmok, and the others surged forward to touch Shasti's arm, pat her back. Mmok gently relieved her of Paolo's weight and passed him to a frantic Eris, who checked his vital signs and sagged in relief.

Only Vaughn held back, his eyes drinking in the sight of Shasti, alive. The others, as if sensing the moment, fell back to either side, forming a living corridor. Silence fell. In two long strides, Vaughn crossed the space and caught Shasti up, kissing her full on the mouth as she wrapped her arms around him. Cheers broke out again.

Duelist made record time back to *Sidhe*, which fell back on the planet. The frigate was battered, but flyable. Her magazines lay empty, many systems were damaged, and her crew was exhausted. The dartship nestled below her was actually in better shape than *Sidhe*. The Evolvers had provisioned their recovered scoutship before Shasti stole it back.

Secretly, Shasti had the dartship prepared for a solo voyage, assigning it a crew and mission. She had come to a decision.

The space they flew through was emptier than usual, swept free even of atoms by the last firing of the Great Lens. Shasti learned with sadness of Fushol's death. He'd stayed with the Lens as it fired its final salvos, wiping out the last of the Evolver's fleet before it could free itself of the Prekak's last command. Many of the Skurlocks died in the fantastic explosion of the controlling mechanism. It left a crater five miles wide in the ocean floor. The weapon itself had melted its way down toward the planet's core.

Only the shelters and outlying outposts came through. The mountain and cliffs stopped the tsunamis from the dreadful blast, as the planners of the settlement had hoped.

Paolo lay in sickbay, recovering slowly and still confused over the false memories from his brief tenure as a servant of the Makers. Shasti turned aside his frantic apologies and simply accepted his thanks, leaving him in the care of Eris, who rarely left his side. Even Vaughn found time to visit the philologist in his convalescence.

The trip back to the planet was a short one with *Sidhe* already up to her full battle speed, leaving Shasti and Vaughn with little time for each other. But she had already made plans for something special after planetfall. *Sidhe* would land in hours in a beautiful valley north of the shelters. She would make time then. There were things that needed to be said, decisions that had to be revealed.

29

Shasti came up behind him on the hillside of the Skurlock park, beneath the strange, alien stars. He would know she was coming. Nothing could sneak up on Mikhail Vaughn. No one would disturb them; she'd ordered Mmok to see to that. She stepped lightly on the mossy foliage. It yielded to her step and sprang back behind her, leaving a gentle perfume in the air.

Vaughn waited at the top as she had asked, his face toward the sky as if trying to read something in the stars. He turned when she was a few strides away. "A beautiful night," he said. "I didn't think I would be here to see it."

The comment was so like something that Robert Fenaday said to her on their first night on doomed Enshar that it took her aback.

No, she said to herself. *Back into the box of precious memories you go, Robert. You're not here tonight.*

Aloud she said, "You did well."

"Did I?" he asked almost idly. "I was just a hare for the hounds to chase. The Evolvers merely played with us, hoping to capture us."

"You outlived those hounds," she said. "We succeeded."

"Yes, the Evolvers are destroyed, at least locally, and the Skurlock revenged. Mandela will be restored to power. You have the *Sidhe*. Romita has Eris and nursing him back to has given her a purpose. It seems everyone has succeeded in their missions but me. I have not accomplished what I came for."

Shasti raised a hand to his face, her pulse racing at the touch of his skin. "Say rather that you have not yet succeeded."

He turned slowly to face her. She didn't move away, only looked expectantly at him.

Vaughn's arms circled her and drew her close. His lips met hers as her hands played over the muscles of his broad back. Shasti could feel the strength in him, gathering like a storm. He drew her off the ground in his embrace, something no other man she'd chosen to be with could have done.

Sudden heat rushed into her, and they pulled off their clothes. Shasti, so much stronger than a normal human, had her match in Vaughn. She did not have to hold back and lost herself in animal passion. They came together in an act of savage, mutual satisfaction, then began again, as if their bodies demanded a release from the strictures of minds and wants. There was only a physicality that drove off all thought, giving them over to their need to be together.

They lay together on the soft dry moss, spent for the moment. His hands were tangled in her hair, his breath hot on her breasts. Shasti reveled in the afterglow of it, completely satisfied for the first time since she'd left Robert Fenaday. Paolo might have the technique; he practiced love as a hobby. Robert had given her both love and passion. Vaughn supplied passion in the body of a young god.

Could he love and care as well, she wondered? *Even if he can, have I grown enough to learn to be someone else's person? Do I want to?*

He looked down at her as if trying to divine her thoughts. "It seems that I have much to learn about women. This is not how I expected this meeting to end."

"That a complaint?" she teased.

"No," he said, his lips finding hers. They made love again, this time more slowly, savoring the moment.

Afterward Shasti sat up, looking at the plain below their hill, to where her ship lay. With her enhanced sight, the night held no terrors for her, particularly now.

Vaughn lay on his back, hands behind his head, looking at her.

"I wanted you to have something of me to take back to Olympia," she said. "A memory, and a hope. I won't ask you to wait, that's not fair. I don't know when I'll be ready, if ever. The things that Pard did to me cut holes in my soul. Some may never be filled, and life on Olympia with an Engineered may be the wrong medicine for me."

"There are other worlds," he said.

"Perhaps," she said. "I have a lot growing and becoming left to do. I don't know what I am to be. I don't know what my place is going to be in the universe. I have to find this out and for now at least, I have to do it on my own."

"I will wait," he added.

A little stir of panic moved in her heart. It was a tie, an obligation, and unwanted. Yet it also called forth another feeling, an inchoate longing and a hope that he would.

"It may be a long wait," she warned.

He smiled easily. "We Engineered live a long time if we aren't killed. You have now given me all the reason I need to avoid death."

Shasti looked at him. She loved the easy confidence, the power, and the courage. *Am I making a mistake,* she wondered? *Is it possible that we are destined?* Doubt and confusion warred in her, drowning anything she might say.

He reached up and drew her down to rest her head on his chest. The crisp hair tickled her nose, but she pressed her face against him. "No more thinking for tonight," he said. "You've given me enough for now. I won't push. Rest your eyes. I'll watch over you." He pulled a jacket over her.

A small smile crossed Shasti's face. Worries and cares drifted away into the future. For now, she was safe.

Hours later, they rose and dressed. With the dartship repaired, crewed, and reprovisioned she was sending Vaughn and Tanaka to Mandela with word of the awful battle. From there Vaughn would head for Olympia. The Evolvers were shattered as a force. And there was the chance to save what was left of the Skurlock. Shasti wondered if it was not a good thing that their great weapon had melted its way down to the core of the world. No one alive knew its secrets and perhaps all would be safer for that.

They came down the hill in a companionable silence and passed the screen of crab robots Mmok had left out to guard their privacy. The machine man was nowhere in sight.

"Just as well," Vaughn said. "I feel he is no bigger on goodbyes than I am. Say what is needed to Rigg, Rask, and the others. Scratch D'abo behind the ears for me, once she stops leaping about the bridge over going to the Confederacy. I have no heart for talking to others just now."

"I know," Shasti said. "This is a time just for you and me. The others will understand."

Shasti stopped beside the sleek golden ship. "I'm afraid it's a used spaceship, but it has low miles, and I only flew it on weekends."

"As consolation prizes go," he said, "it's not bad. I even like the color."

She reached for him, and their lips met for a long, aching moment. She stepped back finally, breath ragged, looking up at him.

"Dear Shasti, you're like this hidden star above us," he said, his fierce, blue eyes locked on her jade-green ones. "You have been long in the dark, unseen, but that time is over now. I think that in the future you will be like a great comet, lighting up space. Come find me and light my world." He reached forward and stroked her face, then as if he feared he could not make himself go if he hesitated, Vaughn turned and strode up the ramp into his ship.

Shasti turned and walked away slowly, her eyes too full to see well. Behind her, she heard the roar of engines. Tanaka and the small crew had the ship ready to move and she was grateful for that. *Maybe it's true that the sharp knife cuts cleanest*, she thought, *but it is still a cut.*

She saw a figure standing on a hill and walked toward it. Dan Rigg looked up at the golden dartship as it rose, taking Misa Tanaka with it. His face was remote, but his eyes were locked on the ship. Shasti stood next to him as they watched the dartship disappear into the sky.

After the minutes stretched out and they could no longer even pretend to see the glimmer of gold, he turned to her.

"We're bound for New Eire," Shasti said. "There's trouble at home. I'll fill you in as we go."

The End

ALSO BY EDWARD MCKEOWN

The Maauro Chronicles

My Outcast State

Against That Time

The Lost

All The Difference

When Fighting Monsters

The Shasti and Fenaday Chronicles

Was Once A Hero

Fearful Symmetry

Points of Departure

Hidden Stars

Sha'Daa Series

Tales of the Apocalypse

Toys

Inked

Pawns

Last Call

Facets

The Lair of the Lesbian Love Goddess Files

On the Case

Other Works

Knight in Charlotte